A CASE OF
INDIAN MARVELS

Also by David Davidar

The House of Blue Mangoes (2002)
The Solitude of Emperors (2007)
Ithaca (2011)
A Clutch of Indian Masterpieces (ed.) (2014)

A CASE OF INDIAN MARVELS

DAZZLING STORIES
FROM THE COUNTRY'S
FINEST NEW WRITERS

EDITED BY
DAVID DAVIDAR

ALEPH

ALEPH BOOK COMPANY
An independent publishing firm
promoted by *Rupa Publications India*

First published in India in 2022
by Aleph Book Company
7/16 Ansari Road, Daryaganj
New Delhi 110 002

This edition copyright © Aleph Book Company 2022.

Copyright in individual stories vests in the respective authors/translators/proprietors.

Introduction copyright © David Davidar 2022.

The Acknowledgements on p. 378–81 constitute an extension of the copyright page.

All rights reserved.

This is a work of fiction. Names, characters, places, and incidents are either the product of the authors' imagination or are used fictitiously and any resemblance to any actual persons, living or dead, events or locales is entirely coincidental.

No part of this publication may be reproduced, transmitted, or stored in a retrieval system, in any form or by any means, without permission in writing from Aleph Book Company.

ISBN: 978-93-91047-64-1

1 3 5 7 9 10 8 6 4 2

Printed in India

This book is sold subject to the condition that it shall not, by way of trade or otherwise, be lent, resold, hired out, or otherwise circulated without the publisher's prior consent in any form of binding or cover other than that in which it is published.

To
The three colossi
who shaped my career:
Rajmohan Gandhi
Dom Moraes
Peter Mayer

CONTENTS

A Case of Indian Marvels   DAVID DAVIDAR   ix

1. The Alligator of Aligarh   A. M. GAUTAM   1
2. Making   AISHWARYA SUBRAMANIAN   9
3. The Devouring Sea   AMAL   15
   Translated from the Malayalam by A. J. Thomas
4. The Current Climate   ARAVIND JAYAN   24
5. The Power to Forgive   AVINUO KIRE   32
6. A Story That Lived   BHAVANI   41
7. Eggs Keep Falling from the Fourth Floor   BHAVIKA GOVIL   51
8. Air   DILSHER DHILLON   56
9. The Teeth on the Bus Go Round and Round
   DINESH DEVARAJAN   61
10. The Adivasi Will Not Dance   HANSDA SOWVENDRA SHEKHAR   72
11. Swimmer Among the Stars   KANISHK THAROOR   84
12. Public Record   KARAN MADHOK   95
13. The Great Indian Tee and Snakes   KRITIKA PANDEY   110
14. The Accounts Officer's Wife   LAKSHMIKANTH K. AYYAGARI   120
15. Lorry Raja   MADHURI VIJAY   130
16. How to Host Your Europeans   MEENA KANDASAMY   158
17. Mrs Nischol   MEERA GANAPATHI   161
18. radha, krishna   NEEL PATEL   172
19. The Annual Pig Parade of Kharagpore   NICHOLAS RIXON   188
20. The Girl Who Haunted Death   NIKITA DESHPANDE   199
21. The Twenty-sixth Giant   PRAYAAG AKBAR   211
22. Spider-Girl   PRITIKA RAO   217

23. Twenty-first Tiffin   RAAM MORI   222
    Translated from the Gujarati by Rita Kothari
24. It Ends with a Kiss   RIDDHI DASTIDAR   230
25. Greetings from a Violent Homeland   RITUMONJORI KALITA   242
26. Gobyaer   SADAF WANI   248
27. Fate   SAMHITA ARNI   253
28. After Half-Time   SHAMIK GHOSH   261
    Translated from the Bengali by Subha Prasad Sanyal
29. Journey   SHANTHI K. APPANNA   268
    Translated from the Kannada by Srinath Perur
30. The Smear Papers   SHAWN FERNANDES   280
31. Gul   SHREYA ILA ANASUYA   284
32. My Grandmother Talks About Shit   SRIVIDYA TADEPALLI   297
33. The Issue   TANUJ SOLANKI   302
34. The Octopus: A Fable   TUSHAR JAIN   307
35. My Time at Boyonika   UDAY KANUNGO   313
36. Shabnam   UROOJ   326
37. The Demon Sage's Daughter   VARSHA DINESH   339
38. Crippled World   VEMPALLE SHAREEF   359
    Translated from the Telugu by N. S. Murty and R. S. Krishna Moorthy
39. Sunday, Bloody Sunday   VINEETHA MOKKIL   364
40. The Crossing   VRINDA BALIGA   372

Acknowledgements   378
Notes on the Contributors   382

A CASE OF INDIAN MARVELS
DAVID DAVIDAR

I

Many years ago, on a blustery day in autumn, I took the train from London to Cambridge to meet a man who had taken the Western literary world by storm. I was just starting out in publishing at the time, and I was keen to ask Bill Buford, then the editor of *Granta*, about the essential quality he looked for in the stories he chose to feature in his magazine. We'd arranged to meet in a pub in one of the narrow streets just off the city centre. Huddled into my coat against the cold, I set off from the station through drifts of fallen leaves on the pavements stirring restlessly in the bladed wind. No sooner had I sat down in the pub, pint in hand, than the door swung open and Buford blew in, a stocky, bearded man in a fisherman's jersey and blue jeans. An American student at King's College, he had stayed on in Cambridge after he took his degree to successfully resurrect and reshape a defunct literary magazine, *Granta*. Within a short time, his inspired stewardship of the journal had turned it into one of the world's best showcases of contemporary literature. The years have blurred away much of what we talked about, but the essence of what he said lodged in my head: what was necessary to elevate any story or long-form narrative to greatness, in his eyes, was that it needed to be adventurous, original, and, above all, have the narrative drive to keep the reader pinned to the page.

I never met Buford again, but I was reminded of our drink together recently when his name cropped up in a book by one of the peerless short story writers of our time, George Saunders. Entitled *A Swim in a Pond in the Rain* (after a Chekhov story), it's about a few of the Russian immortals and their creations. In the introduction, Saunders attempts a definition of what constitutes a flawless piece of short fiction. He writes: 'Years ago, on the phone with Bill Buford, then fiction editor of the *New Yorker* (to which magazine Buford had moved after his stint at *Granta*), enduring a series of painful edits, feeling a little insecure, I went fishing for a compliment: "But what do you like about the story?" I whined. There was a long pause at the other end. And Bill said this: "Well, I read a line. And I like it... enough to read the next." And that was it: his entire short story aesthetic and presumably that of the magazine. And it's perfect. A story is a linear-temporal phenomenon. It proceeds, and charms us (or doesn't), a line at a time. We have to keep being pulled into a story in order for it to do anything for us.' Ruskin Bond, one of the contemporary mages of short fiction, emphasizes the point about the very best stories needing to glide effortlessly along in order to carry the reader with them: '(Stories) should flow like a stream of water—preferably a mountain stream. You will, of course, encounter boulders but you will learn to go over them or around them, so that your flow is unimpeded.' The insights of Buford, Saunders, and Bond intersect to reveal the ingredients essential to all memorable short fiction: line after superb line creating a narrative so compelling that the reader wants to keep reading. This is something all the stories that feature in *A Case of Indian Marvels* possess.

II

Both practitioners and academics have tried for hundreds of years to codify the short story, but there is no one definition that can be taken as definitive. I remember an aside from R. K. Narayan, another adept of short fiction, on the difficulties of defining the genre. Apparently, he once attended a lecture on creative writing in which the instructor said: 'A short story must be short and have a story.' We laughed about this hapless take on the form but perhaps we laughed too soon. Here's why. Joyce Carol Oates, the American novelist and short story writer, wrote: 'Formal definitions of the short story are commonplace, yet there is none quite democratic enough to accommodate an art that includes so much variety and an art that so readily lends itself to experimentation and idiosyncratic voices. Perhaps length alone should be the sole criterion?' (I see the man that Narayan and I were mocking rising above our laughter, an I-told-you-so expression on his face!) Oates adds: 'Whenever critics try to impose other, more subjective strictures on the genre...too much is excluded.... My personal definition of the form is that it represents a concentration of imagination, and not an expansion; it is no more than 10,000 words; and, no matter its mysteries or experimental properties, it achieves closure—meaning that, when it ends, the attentive reader understands why.' As a working definition of the genre that's pretty good, but let Anton Chekhov, who is regarded as the father of the modern short story, have the last word on the subject: 'Remember that writers whom we call great or just good, and who make us drunk, have one very important feature: they are going somewhere and calling you with them....'

III

The short story, a relatively recent literary genre, began to flourish in several parts of the world at about the same time—the nineteenth century. The United States had renowned practitioners of the form, like Nathaniel Hawthorne, Mark Twain, and Edgar Allan Poe; France's Guy de Maupassant and Alphonse Daudet produced masterpieces; in Germany, Thomas Mann was redefining the shape of fiction even as the Brothers Grimm remade fairy tales into contemporary marvels; and, in England, the likes of Thomas Hardy, H. G. Wells, and Arthur Conan Doyle crafted, in addition to literary stories, some of the earliest crime and science fiction. Short fiction in the West was heavily plot-driven until the coming of Chekhov who revolutionized the form by largely doing away with plot, focusing on the internal and external lives of his characters, and making his fiction true to life.

As the nineteenth century stole into the twentieth century, the short story blossomed all over the world, fertilized by vaulting literacy, the proliferation of literary magazines, and the packaging and marketing of authors as superstars, especially in the West.

In our country, the modern short story made an appearance almost simultaneously in several languages, beginning with Bengali. According to writer and translator Ranga Rao, Purnachandra Chattopadhyay published the country's first short story, 'Madhumati', in 1870. While the early Indian efforts at short fiction were pale imitations of British writers, hardly surprising considering the country was still in the grip of colonial rule, these derivative stories were soon replaced by work that was often very political in nature—this shouldn't occasion surprise as well given that the country was striving to win its freedom, while simultaneously trying to get rid of a variety of social evils. Overtly political or didactic fiction is seldom very good, and a fair bit of the short fiction of the period is merely of academic interest. But this period also saw the emergence of giants, among them Rabindranath Tagore who was soon hailed as one of Bengal's finest short story writers; in Hindi, Munshi Premchand (who was influenced by Chekhov) had an equally stellar reputation as a result of the many short stories of genius he wrote—several were published in *Hans*, the literary magazine he edited; and, in Odia, the writer Fakir Mohan Senapati crafted stories that are still read today.

In the first half of the twentieth century, most of the major literatures in the land threw up remarkable short story writers—Saadat Hasan Manto in Urdu, Kalki in Tamil, Gurzada Appa Rao in Telugu, R. K. Narayan, Ruskin Bond, Khushwant Singh, and Raja Rao in English, Thakazhi Sivasankara Pillai and Vaikom Muhammad Basheer in Malayalam, to name just a few of the numerous distinguished practitioners of the literary form.

Some decades after Independence in 1947, a new generation of writers redefined the genre. These writers were unencumbered by colonial baggage and the need to pander to the West or anyone else, and this helped them make the form new and exciting by drawing on multiple traditions that few other literatures could access. Readers in this country, as well as around the world, lapped up dazzling books by writers who had been nourished by India's deep and wide literary traditions dating back thousands of years, as well as influenced by other literatures they had been schooled in or immersed themselves in. In addition to the various classical and international canons they were drawing their inspiration from, the confident new novelists and short story writers also had access (albeit limited because of the paucity of good translations) to dozens of regional literatures—the 2011 census recognized 1,635 'mother tongues' in India; of these, thirty were spoken by more than a million native speakers, and at least fifteen had literatures that were ancient and complex. This nuanced literary heritage was described by critic, translator, and poet A. K. Ramanujan in this way: '(Our literary roots and traditions are) indissolubly plural and often conflicting but…organized through at least two principles (a) context-sensitivity and (b) reflexivity of various sorts, both of which constantly generate new forms out of old ones.' Shaped by this rich literary tradition, in addition to everything else I have enumerated, the cream of Indian fiction produced from about the 1980s to the early 2000s was, in a word, marvellous.

At this juncture, mention must be made of a problem with Indian literature that has existed for a long time and shows no signs of disappearing any time soon—the disproportionate amount of attention and resources devoted to the work of writers and writing in the English language in India. I am one with those who believe this is unfair and discriminatory, but practically speaking, it will take time and a great deal of effort before we can expect to see any radical transformation of the situation. Things are somewhat better now, thanks to the publishing of an increased number of literary works in translation by excellent translators, translated work being eligible for a few prestigious awards, translations receiving review attention, and so on, but much remains to be done. Suffice it to say here, that as a reader, editor, and anthologist, I feel frustrated by the lack of quality translations that will help writers from all of India's languages find wider audiences and look forward to the day when readers will have the opportunity to sample the wide-ranging riches of our literary tradition as a whole. One of the manifestations of this issue is that anthologies that purport to represent Indian fiction largely comprise the work of writers in English, and this anthology is no different. I would have been delighted if I'd been able to access enough work of writers from all the other major Indian languages in which literature is created—but that proved impossible. We have some fine stories in translation but the stories in the anthology are preponderantly written in English. This does not take anything away from the quality of the stories because the sole criterion I had for including any story was its literary excellence—by that yardstick all these stories are masterly.

Any account of modern Indian literature must make mention of what has been described as the 'golden age of Indian writing in English'. The publication of Salman Rushdie's *Midnight's Children* in 1981 opened the sluice gates to a torrent of outstanding fiction that lasted about twenty years. This was the period that saw the publication of scores of seminal works, among them *The Great Indian Novel* by Shashi Tharoor, *A Suitable Boy* by Vikram Seth, *The God of Small Things* by Arundhati Roy, *A Fine*

Balance by Rohinton Mistry, *The Inheritance of Loss* by Kiran Desai, and *The White Tiger* by Aravind Adiga to name a few of the works of fiction that would make their mark on India and the world. In an effort to capture the work of the golden generation, and the generations that preceded them, I published an anthology entitled *A Clutch of Indian Masterpieces*. Closing my introduction to that collection I wrote: 'In the future, as the Indian writing tradition matures and grows in confidence, we will see an ever-decreasing tendency to seek "approval" from cultural arbiters other than our own peer groups—in other words, we will gradually grow out of the dreadful syndrome known as "cultural cringe" that so many former colonies have to deal with. All this would seem to project a bright future for Indian literature in the twenty-first century....' A couple of years ago, the time seemed right to capture the work of writers who had come of age in the twenty-first century or thereabouts and belonged to the millennial generation (born between 1981 and 1996 in most accepted definitions) and Generation Z (born between the late 1990s and early 2010s). That's the conceit and basic premise of *A Case of Indian Marvels*—it seeks to showcase the very best work of the very best writers belonging to these two cohorts; these writers are presently aged forty and under (with 2020 as the cut-off year).

IV

Sublime Goan feni is triple distilled. The stories in this collection which are, if anything, even more intoxicating, have been filtered through an even greater number of sieves, as a result of which their power, complexity, and bouquet are exquisite. Their quality first came to the notice of editors of literary magazines and supplements—print or online—who published them in their journals. A fair number of them were then included in various anthologies. Aleph's editors (many of them belonging to the millennial generation or Generation Z) then trained a third lens on them in order to prepare a longlist that was presented to me. I whittled this longlist down to the final forty that made the cut. So, the stories in this anthology have been adjudged brilliant time after time—it's what makes them extra special.

When I began work on this book, I was surprised by the lack of anthologies that focused exclusively on the work of writers belonging to the millennial generation or Generation Z or both. When I was discussing this omission with one of our literary pundits, she said this could possibly be because many of them were still very young with their best work yet to come; several, she pointed out, didn't even have a single published book to their credit. It's a fact that only half these writers—Kanishk Tharoor, Madhuri Vijay, Meena Kandasamy, Hansda Sowvendra Shekhar, Prayaag Akbar, Amal, Avinuo Kire, Neel Patel, Raam Mori, Samhita Arni, Aravind Jayan, Nikita Deshpande, Shamik Ghosh, Shanthi K. Appanna, Tanuj Solanki, Tushar Jain, Vempalle Shareef, Karan Madhok, Meera Ganapathi, Vineetha Mokkil, and Vrinda Baliga have published books. However, most of the others have books in the making so that's no reason to doubt their eligibility for inclusion. While there was something to be said about the critic's comment that the finest work of these writers possibly lay ahead of them, there was little or no merit in her musing that they were too young to produce work of lasting greatness. Lest we forget, superlative short fiction by writers of the calibre of Premchand, Nikolai Gogol, Ernest Hemingway, Gabriel García Márquez, Nadine Gordimer, and Peter Carey (to randomly choose maestros of fiction from every continent barring Antarctica) was published before they turned forty, and some of them, like Chekhov and Manto, didn't live much beyond the age of forty!

Having got these quibbles out of the way, let's turn to another question. Could these writers match the achievements of those who had gone before them, especially the golden generation, their immediate predecessors? Here, it needs to be stated, unambiguously, that literature and literary achievement are not the equivalent of a horse race or a high-jump competition and that the prize doesn't go to those who gallop the fastest or clear the tallest height. Rather, multiple prizes are awarded for artistry, originality, literary genius, and powerful storytelling, and by these criteria all the stories in this selection deserve the highest honours.

What are these stories about? Many of them reflect the dismal times the country and the world are passing through, including 'The Current Climate' by Aravind Jayan, 'The Adivasi Will Not Dance' by Hansda Sowvendra Shekhar, 'The Great Indian Tee and Snakes' by Kritika Pandey, 'How to Host Your Europeans' by Meena Kandasamy, 'The Twenty-sixth Giant' by Prayaag Akbar, 'Greetings from a Violent Homeland' by Ritumonjori Kalita, 'Gobyaer' by Sadaf Wani, 'The Smear Papers' by Shawn Fernandes, 'Sunday, Bloody Sunday' by Vineetha Mokkil, and 'The Crossing' by Vrinda Baliga. The Indian literary tradition has been heavily influenced by mythology and history, and these generations are giving it a new and alluring spin as evidenced by 'Making' by Aishwarya Subramanian, 'Fate' by Samhita Arni, 'The Girl Who Haunted Death' by Nikita Deshpande, 'Gul' by Shreya Ila Anasuya, 'Shabnam' by Urooj, and 'The Demon Sage's Daughter' by Varsha Dinesh. Black humour underpins 'The Alligator of Aligarh' by A. M. Gautam and 'The Annual Pig Parade of Kharagpore' by Nicholas Rixon. Forbidden love and the courtship and sexual rituals of the twenty-first century animate 'The Accounts Officer's Wife' by Lakshmikanth K. Ayyagari, 'Mrs Nischol' by Meera Ganapathi, 'radha, krishna' by Neel Patel, 'Spider-Girl' by Pritika Rao, 'The Twenty-first Tiffin' by Raam Mori, 'The Issue' by Tanuj Solanki, and 'The Journey' by Shanthi K. Appanna. Fabulism, satire, and futuristic scenarios undergird 'Air' by Dilsher Dhillon, 'Swimmer Among the Stars' by Kanishk Tharoor, 'It Ends with a Kiss' by Riddhi Dastidar, 'The Octopus: A Fable' by Tushar Jain, and 'Crippled World' by Vempalle Shareef. Penetrating insights into Indian society—whether in big cities, small towns, or villages—are brought blaringly alive in 'The Power to Forgive' by Avinuo Kire, 'A Story That Lived' by bhavani, 'Eggs Keep Falling from the Fourth Floor' by Bhavika Govil, 'The Teeth on the Bus Go Round and Round' by Dinesh Devarajan, 'Public Record' by Karan Madhok, 'Lorry Raja' by Madhuri Vijay, 'After Half-Time' by Shamik Ghosh, 'My Grandmother Talks About Shit' by Srividya Tadepalli, and 'My Time at Boyonika' by Uday Kanungo.

I wanted the stories included in this anthology to reflect the country's ethos and every one of them does that exceptionally well—this bodes well for the future of Indian literary fiction.

V

'Black milk of morning we drink you evenings / we drink you at noon and mornings we drink you at night / we drink and we drink....' wrote the German–Romanian poet, Paul Celan, in his celebrated poem, 'Death Fugue', that lamented the destruction visited upon the world by Nazi Germany, fascist Italy, and the Great War in Europe. While in this country we may not yet have plumbed the depths that led to Celan's lament, India in the twenty-first century can hardly be characterized as sunny and hopeful. The slow drip of sectarian hatred into the open veins of our society, and the all-out assault on liberal values and creative expression by an assortment of uneducated, illiberal thugs, often egged on by those at the top, will permanently reshape the country—and not for the better.

How will our writers transmute these dangerous and depressing times into art? As noted, some of the stories that feature in this anthology already memorably record the period we are passing through and it's inevitable that the writing of the future, no matter how obliquely, will be shaped by what the country's writers have witnessed. The tragedies of our age may not appear immediately in fiction, for it often takes time for traumatic events to be recorded in the annals of literature, but it will happen, of this I have no doubt. Our writers, the writers represented here, and others like them, and yet others who will follow them, will record this time in new, unsettling, and truthful ways—it's what will ensure the murk that enshrouds India today will not be forgotten. Dark times often make for unforgettable literature—it's probably the only thing of any value that comes out of them. As Saadat Hasan Manto once wrote: 'Hard times made me a good short story writer.'

1

THE ALLIGATOR OF ALIGARH

A. M. GAUTAM

Kalua listened to his belly groan with hunger. He mopped at the beads of sweat on his forehead with a gamcha and peeked over his wife's shoulder into a pot in which she was cooking some nameless concoction the colour of mucus, with a few pieces of onion here and there trying to drown themselves. The sight of it was enough to dull his appetite a little. To make things worse, there wasn't nearly enough of it to sneak some off to Safeda. His friend would just have to go hungry again.

He looked at Gudiya, his little sister, reading a scrap of a newspaper in a corner, and felt guilty about thinking of Safeda when he was failing to provide enough even for his family. Only last month, Gudiya had fallen sick and the doctor had advised Kalua to include meat in her diet at least once a week to make up for protein deficiency.

Despite this guilt, however, Safeda was also important to Kalua. Like many other people in the world, Kalua had found his best friend at his workplace. Only, the workplace happened to be a gutter, and the best friend happened to be an alligator.

Kalua didn't know how Safeda came to be there, only that the creature was hurt and starving when they first met. Kalua fed it his own lunch and applied cool mud to its bruises. Because of the whitish grey colour of its skin, which Kalua thought unusual, he named the alligator Safeda. The absence of sunlight in the creature's life might have had something to do with its unusual pigmentation. Or maybe it was just an anomaly. Whatever the cause, the contrast between the alligator's pale hide and his own had amused Kalua to no end.

A few days later, Kalua heard someone in the nearby market talking about a man arrested for smuggling exotic reptiles to Indian connoisseurs. The police were forced to release him from custody soon afterwards; apparently he had flushed his specimens down the toilet to remove all incriminating evidence. Kalua knew now where a part of that evidence had ended up, but not intending to get mixed up with the police, he kept his suspicions to himself.

That was twelve years ago.

Kalua had not been married then and Gudiya hadn't even been born. In those days, he used to go into the sewers only when his father's cough was exceptionally bad. He hated every second of it and swore daily to himself that he would become anything but a jamadaar.

That, of course, was before the world had explained the inescapability of his caste to him, and before his parents had died of tuberculosis, leaving him to bring up his baby sister all alone.

'Ae, Gudiya, what are you doing reading in this bad evening light? You'll ruin your eyes,' he called out to the girl whom he had managed to keep away from the sewers, and had even sent to school.

Up until now, at least.

Gudiya was now almost ten years old, but looked like she was only six or seven. This wasn't unusual in their neighbourhood, though—malnutrition made the kids all look younger than they actually were, and the adults older.

Gudiya looked at him and threw aside the newspaper scrap she was reading. 'Went to the butcher in the afternoon, but he had already gutted and skinned everything. He asked me to come only when my cut had healed completely.'

After school, Gudiya often went to help the neighbourhood butcher in his shop, and he tossed her a few coins for her labour every now and then. Two days ago, she had cut her hand while slicing a piece of meat. It was an ugly gash, and Kalua had tied a clean piece of cloth around it, hoping that it would not get infected. The butcher, Kalua knew, had sent Gudiya away not out of concern for her but because he did not want to risk her blood making the meat impure for his customers.

'It's okay, beta, don't worry about it. This is just a temporary situation. Things will go back to normal soon,' Kalua told her with a conviction he did not possess himself. His wife joined them and put the cooking pot between them, holding it carefully with rags in her hands. She rotated it a few times, as though trying to pull off some magic trick that would turn that mixture of water, flour, and salt into real food. There were only two spoons in the pot.

'Aren't you eating, Bhabhi?' Gudiya asked.

'I'll eat later. You two eat now, and please make sure you wipe the pot clean.'

But, there was nothing to be had later, Kalua knew that well enough. Tomorrow it would be a week since either of them had gone to work. This muck in the pot, this was the last of their rations.

He got up so quickly that his head swam a little and his stomach growled in protest.

'I am sorry, I remembered just now—Varshneyji had asked me to visit his house today. He wants me to help unload some stuff from his terrace. I'll just go there and come back in a while, okay?'

'But your dinner?' his wife asked, not meeting his eyes.

'You two finish it off. I'll have some chai–nashta with Varshneyji.'

Kalua did not wait for her response, but at the door he paused for just a moment to look at her moving slowly to sit beside Gudiya. After he emerged from the hut, he took a few steps to the right so that they wouldn't see him standing there. Then, he let out a long, heavy sigh, the sort that can crush those who hear it and must, therefore, only be released once you are at a safe distance from the people you love.

His wife must have seen through his lie. She knew full well that he wouldn't even be allowed to sit on the curb outside a baniya's house, let alone be invited inside and asked to handle his possessions. Not in a million years—a pamphlet of Swachh Bharat Abhiyan fluttered near his feet and Kalua spat at it in disgust—not after a thousand more Swachh Bharat Abhiyans had come and gone could that happen in their world.

The only place Kalua, or anyone from his caste, could go to in the house of someone from an upper caste, like Varshneyji, was the latrine. Straight in, straight out, and a few coins dropped on their palms at the door without a word exchanged. Kalua and his kin were like elves. Shit-scooping, latrine-scraping elves. Invisible and inaudible to everyone.

Still, even while wading through all the literal and figurative shit in their lives, they had kept going, one way or another. Until a fortnight ago, when a saffron-robed rally had snaked its way through the jamadaar basti where they lived, holding up bright posters that most of the residents couldn't read.

Fat government men with sweat-shined faces, saccharine smiles, and noses scrunched up against the smell of Kalua and his people. They declared proudly through their loudspeakers that no one would be required to lower themselves into a sewer any more. If anybody asked them to do so, the government would penalize that person.

They were told that the credit for all this went to their chief minister and the prime minister, both of whom cared deeply for all Hindus, including Dalits like Kalua and his neighbours.

Once they had finished making their speeches, the fat men got in their vehicles and waved to Kalua and the other shanty dwellers; they were careful not to shake hands with them or touch them in any way. Amidst much fanfare, with satisfied smiles, they departed the same way they had arrived and breathed freely once more in the clean air outside the slum.

It was only a couple of hours later that Kalua, his wife, and their friends realized that the government men had forgotten to mention what jobs they would be doing now that their present employment had been declared illegal.

And so it was that the slum had begun to crawl towards starvation. They had held up until now by dipping into their meagre savings. A few of them had managed to get odd jobs here and there, but no one really wanted to employ a jamadaar in their shop or house, or anywhere that there would be a chance of being touched by them.

Kalua wondered where he could go to pass the time while his family had their dinner and decided upon the only place that felt a little like home. A horrible home, true, but still a home, with the comfort of an old friend.

Maybe he would also be able to catch a few rats down there and feed them to Safeda.

༄

'Do you think Bhaiya will be able to get some work today?' Gudiya asked her bhabhi, back in the house.

'Yes, yes, of course, he'll find some work. Don't you worry about it.'

But Gudiya did worry about it.

She worried that her brother had not been able to feed his pet for the past two weeks and it was making him even sadder than usual. Gudiya had never met this pet, but she knew its name was Safeda; it had slipped out of Kalua once, though he had not noticed it.

Gudiya liked to imagine that Safeda was a fluffy white dog like the pet one of her classmates had. Only, her bhaiya kept his pet in a sewer instead of at home. This didn't seem strange to her ten-year-old mind because she knew that Bhabhi would never have allowed Bhaiya to keep the dog in the house, not when they never had enough food or money for the three of them.

Like most kids in the neighbourhood, Gudiya knew that the last couple of weeks had been especially bad for everyone. It was evident in the way that people she had known all her life to wake up at dawn and go to work now spent their days sitting despondently in front of their shacks, waiting for something to happen. The desperate wait reminded Gudiya of the days when she was a toddler and would keep looking out anxiously for the ice-cream man, who never came to their gully. The worst of it was the change that had come over her bhaiya. No matter how bad things had got in the past, he would always have a joke tucked away somewhere in his head, ready to be summoned and released to laughter all around when things began to look too grim. He was a doer who liked to make things happen, rather than wait passively for situations to resolve themselves for better or for worse. Like, when Gudiya had waited, and waited, and waited, for the ice-cream man day after day, one day Bhaiya had just brought back three orange-flavoured ice creams from God knew where. These past few days, however, he hardly talked to her at all.

Some days, while taking a bath, Gudiya would move her fingers slowly underwater in the bucket and watch them for minutes on end. That's how her brother looked these days. Like a man living underwater in his head; walking around in a bubble of empty space where no one could really reach him. Except for his pet, maybe. It might cheer him up if Gudiya brought it to the house and surprised him. Anyway, she was sure that it would cheer her up!

So, after her bhabhi had put her to bed, and gone to sleep herself, Gudiya put on the robe that Kalua wore when he went into the sewers. He had made it by stitching together discarded polythene bags. It was too large for her, of course, and fluttered behind her like a superhero's cape. In the weak light leaking into the hut from a street light, the multicoloured robe of polythene bags shimmered like an undisciplined rainbow. She then put on Kalua's yellow safety helmet and his brown leather boots.

Quietly, Gudiya stole out of the hut and closed the door behind her.

She walked up to the open manhole down which she had seen her bhaiya disappear many times. Then, with a look at the moon overhead, she lowered herself down into the darkness, down the iron rungs of the sewer.

∽

This manhole into which Gudiya had lowered herself was connected to other manholes in the city through large pipes constituting Aligarh's sewage network. As Gudiya descended further down the hole, she could hear the water splashing at the bottom and her guts contracted a little with the inherent fear of invisible damp things.

The stench of sewage was overwhelming and made her feel a little faint.

To steel herself, she looked up at the circle of the night sky through the open manhole, but it looked so far away suddenly that she thought it better to concentrate on her descent.

Finally, after a few moments, or minutes, or millennia, her boots found mushy ground.

A small part of her mind wondered how a dog could live in a place where the water came up to her ankles. But before she could give it a thought, there was a sound of water splashing nearby.

It sounded like she wasn't alone. Someone else was also taking a night walk here. Or maybe it was just the sound of her heart tumbling out of her mouth and falling into the sewer.

Gudiya moved forward, putting one foot in front of the other, like a little soldier in large boots. Her polythene robe made an almost-but-not-quite-silent slithering sound behind her.

A few more steps and the darkness would be absolute. Gudiya pressed a little wire in the helmet and the bulb–battery combination that Kalua had taped together came to life. The feeble light threw long shadows on the sewer's walls and Gudiya saw that the pipe turned sharply to the left a little way off in the distance.

Again, she heard the sound of water splashing. Despite an instinctive urge to run back, she kept walking in the direction of the sound. And then, as she stood at the bend in the pipe she saw in front of her a man tossing something into the water at his feet.

No, not into the water. Tossing something to a creature on the ground.

A creature that definitely was not the fluffy white dog that she imagined Pinky's pet looked like. Sharp white teeth glinted in an evil grin at her.

A pair of dull green eyes with black slits for pupils measured the flesh on her bones. In the wavering light of Gudiya's helmet-bulb, she thought she saw a ripple of excitement pass through the monster's dirty rubbery-white body.

The man standing beside it, startled by the light, turned to face Gudiya. It was her bhaiya, of course, and how shocked he looked! Dead rats dangled by their tails in his hand like the balls of the neighbourhood butcher, who had shown them to Gudiya last week and had given her twenty rupees just for touching them.

She looked from her brother to the monster at his feet and opened her mouth to scream but found the sound missing. She closed her fists so tightly at her sides that the cloth Kalua had tied as a bandage came off and two tiny drops of blood dropped down from the open cut into the water. The starving alligator, half-blind, but no less a predator for it, caught the whiff of fresh blood and lunged towards it.

∞

Kalua's mind tried to make sense of the situation and failed irrevocably. His thoughts came to him only as snatches of the self-evident truth. Must do something. Quickly. His friend, whose primary trait in the last twelve years had been laziness, was now paddling furiously towards his sister, who stood rooted to the spot.

A large piece of stone, dislodged long ago from the sewer's wall, was lying near where Safeda's tail was thrashing around in the water, and Kalua picked it up.

'Gudiya! GUDIYA! Run. NOW!'

But Gudiya's eyes were locked on Safeda, as though hypnotized, and she looked like she could not even hear Kalua.

Kalua moved towards Safeda, stumbling in the water and almost falling down. He righted himself and was near the alligator's head in a couple of strides. Safeda turned to look at him and, for a moment, Kalua thought he could see a trace of human intelligence in the green eyes, a hesitation in moving towards Gudiya.

But hunger is hunger.

It turned again towards Gudiya and with a flick of its tail almost hit Kalua, as if warning him not to meddle with its dinner.

Kalua raised the stone high above his head, stepped forward, and brought down its jagged corner into Safeda's left eye. He wanted only to buy enough time to send Gudiya away, but it was as if the violence had unleashed something inside him which he did not know existed.

Before Safeda could turn towards him, he straddled the creature and brought the stone down once again with all his strength. And then again, and again, until there was no movement left in the body and the light had gone out of Safeda's eyes. It felt a little like the final cleaning away of the shit that other people had flushed his way. Regular work, nothing odd. A frightened little giggle escaped Kalua's mouth at this thought.

He did not know what made him stop finally. Maybe it happened when Gudiya managed to find her voice again.

'Bhaiya, please. Enough.'

Her face looked so small, so fragile, in the half-light-half-shadow of the bulb in her helmet. It reminded him, strangely enough, of how little Safeda had been when he had found it starving in the sewer.

'Come, let's go.'

Kalua got off Safeda's lifeless body and took Gudiya by her hand.

He took one last look at his friend before turning away. An eyeball, dislodged from its socket, dangled from the destroyed face by a thin string of flesh. Even as he watched, the eyeball fell into the sewer water...Plop!

Kalua bent down for Gudiya to climb on to his back and like that they walked to the manhole's ladder. Slowly, Kalua climbed out.

∾

In her cot, tucked in by her brother, the monster in the sewer seemed little more than one of her regular nightmares to Gudiya.

With half-closed eyes she watched Kalua put on the polythene robe she had taken off—he had thrown his own on the street, blood-stained and grimy as it was—and picked something up from the kitchen shelf before going out again.

Fear crept back into her heart. 'Where are you going, Bhaiya? Come to sleep, please?'

As he put the thing that he had picked up from the shelf into his pocket, Gudiya saw that it was the knife she took with her when she went to work at the butcher's shop.

'Don't you worry, I'll be back up in no time at all,' he said with a tired little smile. Then, with a little hesitation, he added, 'And maybe tomorrow, we will have meat again for lunch. It'll be good for you, the doctor said.'

2

MAKING

AISHWARYA SUBRAMANIAN

Months from now a god will casually touch a squirrel. A deceptively human gesture of thanks, his touch will burn through it and alter its very squirrelhood; searing the marks of his fingers on to the backs of all squirrels forever.

Mythili has been touched by a god. He has given her no ornaments, but has traced lines around her neck that glow like chains of gold, anklets for her feet, a line of light that sweeps up into her hair. He has drawn bracelets around her wrists (his hands gripping them tightly, thumb and forefinger just about meeting at the point where she can feel her pulse). These are the marks he has made deliberately but everywhere he has touched her she is radiant. His lightest touches have dappled her skin with brightness. Wherever she stands she will always look as she does now in this forest under these trees patterned with leaf and sun.

Yet it is she who looks at him. Her husband's long eyes are shaped like lotus petals. His skin is so much finer than her own that the blue tracery of his veins shows through. He is leaning against the wall of the shelter he coaxed the trees to form in this glade where it is always breezy and mild. When he hums to himself, tiny flowers spring up out of the earth in response. He smells of earth and herbs and the very trees yearn towards him, bending their heads closer to the ground to be as near him as possible. Mythili recognizes that feeling better than anybody.

They are being watched. Brother and sister hide in the bushes. When they leave, the grass where they stood is brown and dead.

∽

Meenakshi in her workshop crafts a body fit for a god. Limbs long and smooth, skin petal-soft. The feet are long and narrow, the hands small but with long nails. The hair is copper (they must stay true to their roots) and as it captures the light of the forges it glows. She cannot help but wonder what it will look like when the man in the forest has laid his light-giving hands upon it. Underneath the hair a perfect face—straight nose, wide mouth, lovely, fish-shaped eyes that slant. She lines the eyes with coal dust.

'It won't work,' her brother Vishravan sounds almost sorry.

She plays with the hair (her hair) and runs a finger down the lovely profile that will soon be hers.

'It will.'

His own workshop is as far away from hers as possible. Meenakshi can do a thousand things that he cannot. She can imitate the waxy texture of the surface of a leaf. She can make small birds that fly, look, and sound exactly like the real thing. Only Meenakshi could make herself a body fit for a god. If he asked her to, she could fill the city's gardens with trees and flowers and birds, make of it the place he dreamt of when he begged for ten years for a kingdom of his own. He does not ask.

Vishravan thinks too often about the frenzied sea turned white and the huge, pliant, living rope so strange under his hands. He has brooded for so long on that ancient story of a contract that was broken that sometimes he believes he was there himself. He knows how proud the Daityas were at being approached, how strange it was to be around these beings with whom they were now equals. The twinge of triumph at being needed, even if only to make up the numbers. And then, when it came time to divide the fruits of that great labour, finding out that the decision had been made without them. He doesn't remember how the gods looked at him, but he remembers that they lied.

They were promised nectar and given poison. It seeped into them and leached away what powers they had. They crept into the dark corners of the world (often forests, out of some perverse need for revenge) and nursed their wounds. Where they lived nothing would grow. Daityas turn the grass brown when they stand for too long in one place, and animals flee from them as if their breath is toxic. But they can still make things.

Meenakshi's greatest creations are the ones that look the most real. Vishravan will have no truck with the real. He will let her have her workshop but everything on the surface of the city he prayed for must look *made*.

He watches as Meenakshi leaves her workshop and brings back the broken body. Even now it is so lifelike that he can barely look at it. There is a gaping hole where the nose was; one ear still dangles on a tag of flesh and her skin is melted and corroded as if someone had thrown acid at her. His sister is shaken and hurt and also furious. As he comforts her he plays with her beautiful hair and notices how the light falls upon it. The god in the forest must have touched it. He prefers not to think about this.

∞

Mythili's husband sits under a tree. When he returned from his hunting he wore smears of demon blood and an expression of distaste. Asked where he had been, all he would say was 'protecting you' before cleaning himself in the river and sitting down to meditate.

The low, rumbling note that comes from his throat is the oldest thing in the universe. Every living thing in the forest feels it stirring within them when they hear it. What must it be like to be at variance with that sound, as is the creature he has defended her against today? What must it be like to be forever, fundamentally discordant?

The thing the demon has built in his forge bears little resemblance to an actual deer. It is unashamedly fabricated (as if anyone could be taken in by a gold deer)—all polished gears and gleaming metals. But its gait is rather lovely and the bowing of its neck as graceful as that of any real animal. It is very beautiful.

'Capture it for me.'

Mythili has never ordered her husband to do anything before. She is prepared to argue her case (it is the most beautiful thing she's ever seen) but he is already off chasing it through the trees.

∞

Her captor seems strangely uninterested in her. He is a huge man dressed entirely in bronze armour. She cannot see his face. She thinks that he must be blisteringly hot in there. He speaks to her just twice on the journey south, both apologies. Once for the kidnapping, and once for the 'barrenness' of his city. They arrive at night and all she can see of his home are the lights in the houses and the gleam of the domes.

Her servants (she has had none since her marriage) are automata, and her home is pink marble. She spends most of her time in the garden outside. There is no grass in Vishravan's city, but the ground is paved with coloured stones. There are trees of dead wood and dull iron, and the leaves and flowers (she will learn that they were made for her by her captor's wife) are tinted glass. The strange deer-like thing she saw in the forest is also here, though she doesn't ask how.

Of necessity she spends a lot of time in the palace. Everyone is wary of her, all but Vishravan's wife, Mandodari. From her she learns that her captor has many brothers (she never sees them while she's there and all that registers is that one is particularly pious and one particularly sleepy), and that the quiet, middle-aged lady who sits next to him on a throne is his sister, a widow and a clever craftswoman. She senses that Meenakshi avoids her on purpose, but even her new mentor doesn't know why.

She learns that this palace (a wonder in crystal and coloured stone) was made by her protector's father. In years to come he will make other celebrated palaces but this one, for his daughter, is his masterpiece.

So thoroughly has she been taken under Mandodari's wing that she is safer in this city than anywhere else in the world. They even hear a story about how her new protector dramatically stepped in to save her from rape by a besotted kidnapper.

In Vishravan's city, the physically strong are called upon to build. They make bridges and monuments and roads from strong blocks of grey and pink stone. The king himself works alongside them, carrying massive quantities of rock effortlessly. His sister is there too, as strong as he. Mythili has grown up among farmer kings and the first sight of the vast engineering works of Vishravan's city fills her with awe. The great turbines are constantly in motion on the shore. Water and steam power the city, and massive machines powered by systems of toothed wheels. She will learn that Vishravan has war machines as well.

Those who do not build apply their skills elsewhere. Mandodari is teaching Mythili how to weave cloth from the thin metallic wires that she herself draws from her forge. They are so thin as to be as soft and pliant as thread. Mythili learns to make elaborate pictures in the resulting cloth, and hangs her home with tapestries that gleam where the light touches them and make tiny chink-chink noises when the wind shifts them against the walls. As she becomes more proficient she weaves a cloth for herself in the rich copper of Meenakshi's beautiful hair.

She does not like the forges themselves. But the one time she enters Mandodari's workshop she does make something—a thick ring of pure gold. She presses her fingers into it to decorate it; the metal is still hot and it blisters her fingers but she is pleased with the result. Even when she learns (Mandodari laughs at her) that pure gold is so soft that she could have let it cool. She has had no ornaments since her marriage either.

She will give the gold ring to the first of her husband's ambassadors along with a message: 'Can he not rescue me himself?' By himself, for her, a personal act. Not some sort of cosmic war.

Word comes that her husband's army has reached the mainland shore.

Ridiculous to imagine that it is outraged pride that propelled the long chase southward. He is hardly a jealous local king. Yet, for some reason she has never quite understood, he must act out these petty human performances, as if he could not merely think different circumstances into existence. So he performs rage, and standing on the edge of a sea he could part with the mere flick of a hand, sends mortal creatures to do his work instead. A vanar is crushed to death when he strays into the path of a boulder that is being rolled into the sea. He reaches out a hand to stroke a passing squirrel whose only contribution to this huge enterprise is a handful of pebbles.

Everybody knows the war is coming.

It is while her husband and his motley army are throwing stones into the sea that Mandodari leads her into the forges for a second time. Around them everyone who can be spared from their regular duties has been drafted into making more weapons of iron and bronze; Mandodari is the only one to use gold. Mythili watches as her friend crafts first a necklace and then a thick belt of linked panels of gold.

'To remember us by,' she says, and Mythili realizes that she knows how this is going to end. This is the worst moment of all.

The belt is a story. She sees the birth of Vishravan in one panel, and she sees him praying for ten years for his city. And she learns what everyone in the city knows, no matter how hard Vishravan tries to escape it. And she learns that when he crouched in the bushes with his sister, he wasn't looking at her.

When the city catches fire, molten bronze flows through the cracks in the paving into the forges below. She does not know if her friend has escaped. On the day that she is to be tested Mythili arms herself in metals as an act of defiance. She wears the copper cloth that she wove for herself as a sari, and covers her head. She wears Mandodari's necklace and belt and covers her arms in bangles.

When she moves forward, the heat blisters her skin. She can feel molten copper and gold running down her arms and legs. The ground has begun to rumble even before she steps into the fire.

3

THE DEVOURING SEA

AMAL

Translated from the Malayalam by A. J. Thomas

Taking a long drag at his cigarette, Andrews cast it aside and looked impatiently into the darkness for signs of Ambrose's van. It was quarter past two in the morning. From where he sat on a rock, he could see his motorized boat, *Thomaasleehaa* or *St Thomas*, rocking gently on the small waves of the harbour. He eyed the boat with a kind of loving fondness. Andrews had purchased it from his former employer, Rappai Muthalaali, a wealthy man. The boat had been named *Saagarakanyaka* or *The Maiden of the Sea*, when he had acquired it; Andrews had converted 'her' into a 'him' by christening the vessel *Thomaasleehaa*. He had first begun to covet the boat when he had been driving it for Rappai. Over the years, he had grown so enamoured of the vessel that he was desperate to possess it despite having no money; he had taken loans from numerous friends and the Service Cooperative Bank and pleaded with Rappai to sell it to him. His employer had balked at the idea of a minion becoming the owner of a boat and rising in status to equal his own, but in the end he'd had no option but to sell, because in the long years Andrews had worked for him, he had been privy to many of the dark and unsavoury deeds Rappai had committed so he couldn't afford to alienate him. Still, being the low-life that he was, Rappai tried to discourage Andrews from buying the boat by quoting an astronomical price for it. But Andrews wouldn't be denied. He had developed such an intimate bond with the vessel that he raised the money that was required and virtually flung it at Rappai, thinking as he did so, 'You are really mean, you wretched black money dealer, I am glad I am not like you.'

After the boat became his, and he had changed its name and gender, Andrews revelled in the joy of taking it out to sea, making it walk on water. But the occasional storm he encountered on his voyages were nothing compared to the storm of debt he had to overcome after he had purchased the boat. Its gigantic waves threatened to swallow the *Thomaasleehaa*. He had borrowed so much money to buy the vessel that the income generated from fishing alone could not repay what he owed to all his creditors. That was when the drunkard Lazar told him how he could make extra money, a lot of it, by transporting waste and garbage from various establishments in the town in his boat and illegally dumping it in the deep. It was a low-risk operation, and the money was welcome, but he felt guilty at the thought of polluting his beloved mother, the sea, even though he wasn't doing anything particularly unholy or illegal such as smuggling or human trafficking. When he voiced his discomfort, Lazar had laughed and said: 'There's nothing to worry about. Think of it as something you are doing for the betterment of this locality and its people. What you are doing is a virtuous act, elder!' And so it was that every second night, at a time when the sea and the light of the moon were fast asleep in each other's arms, Andrews's boat with its foul-smelling cargo would crawl across the sea without disturbing its sleep. He would get two hundred rupees per load. There were only six customers when he began, but their numbers had increased to ten, twelve, and now, fourteen.

There was still no sign of Ambrose or his tadpole-like van. Andrews picked up a bottle of liquor that he had planned to drink earlier that night, before he had been distracted by other things, and began swigging from it. A while later, he lay back on the sand and looked up at the face of the sky on which the stars were stuck like bindis and began counting them. He began to nod off. Just then Ambrose's ungainly looking vehicle came crawling along the sand, its headlights blinking on and off. Stopping next to where Andrews lay sprawled out on the sand, Ambrose got out of the vehicle and began shaking the boatman awake. Waking up with a start, Andrews yelled: 'Why are you so late? Who the hell do you think I am? If you think that I signed on for this so I could spend the night sleeping on the beach drenched in dew, then you had better look for other boats to do this job.'

'Not my fault, Syrang. When I was ready to move from the market with the cargo, I found two vehicles full of policemen blocking the way. We had to wait for them to move on before we could roll.' Andrews looked into the van; he could see it piled high with the reeking sacks of waste that he would have to get rid of. Ambrose wasn't finished. He said, 'And that wasn't all. When we took a shortcut around the Church of Our Lady of Lourdes we found even more police there.' Ambrose was so excited by the story he was telling that he was bobbing up and down like a Chaakyaar Koothu performer, his arms and legs flying about.

Ambrose continued melodramatically: 'O my Syrang! In the middle of all this mayhem, that Lazar fellow who was supposed to be helping me downed two full bottles! Just as we finished loading the consignment that swine passed out. He lay on the ground as if he were dead; I left him behind the church.'

'O, my Jesus! What happened then?'

'What happened? The police had been lying in wait for some car thieves who had been coming down from Delhi to lift luxury cars. Somehow, I managed to give them the slip and drove into Peethaambaran's garage and lay low there. Only after the police had cleared off could I take a detour around the cemetery. And that's why I got delayed, struggling and taking a lot of trouble on the way, O my Syrang!'

Andrews could see what Ambrose was leading up to; the fellow was going to bleed him of more than the agreed payment.

'For you this is a hugely profitable business, Syrang!' Ambrose said slyly. 'It looks like you might even have to take one more trip out to sea as the Honeymoon Residency hotel-people are interested in getting rid of the loads of waste that pile up in their storage every day. They don't mind paying more.' Ambrose was jumping around in his excitement like children do when they have won a game they have been playing, 'Just say the word! We can turn millionaires in no time through this business with so many hoteliers around here!'

Andrews who was already in a bad mood because of the delay and the nerves that overcame him whenever he had to go out to sea on those illegal expeditions had been getting more and more angry and bothered as Ambrose had continued to babble on. Now he flew into a rage and knocked the delivery man down.

'Do you want to get me locked up, you son of a bitch? Haven't I told you a hundred times to do all this quietly, keep your mouth shut, and here you are, going around town, making a big noise about our operation.

Once the cops get wind of this, that's the end. They catch you just for transporting garbage around town, imagine what they'll do if they found it on my boat to be taken out to sea to be dumped! Why don't you gulp everything down yourself, you avaricious pig…!'

As Andrews continued to abuse him, Ambrose staggered back to his feet, wiping the sand from his face, and yelled back: 'Don't play the saint, you hypocrite! You are the greedy bastard, doing roaring business with this filth.'

Andrews launched himself at Ambrose and the two men began grappling with each other. Just then the front door of the van opened and an apparition leapt out. Startled, Andrews broke free of Ambrose and retreated from this new threat. Ambrose burst out laughing and said: 'O Syrang! This is our Claudia!'

Embarrassed now, Andrews tried to cover up his discomfiture and laughed. 'O, is it you, Claudi…? I thought it was some cop!'

'Ha! Why are you panicking like little kids? Don't you know that for me, Claudi, cops are nothing? Don't you also know that our Inspector Ananthan Sir has four restaurants in the city? "Chicken Corners", no less. I will make him fall at your feet and beg you to take away a load of the chicken waste and help him out. Do you want me to do it?'

Andrews looked at her in astonishment. Claudia was the widow of Laban, the oarsman. Laban had been an alcoholic, always floating on a sea of liquor. Whenever he was drunk, which was pretty much all the time, he would grow mad at Claudia and begin abusing and beating her. He needed little or no provocation to get mad at her. He would drag her out of the miserable hut they lived in and beat her until she collapsed. During one particularly brutal beating, he started hitting her with an oar. One of her cheeks was torn open before she made her escape, weeping. That was the day the story changed.

Claudia's approach to Laban changed faster than the time it took for her torn-open and sewn-up cheek to heal. One day, the neighbours heard Laban wailing; they ignored his cries, it was something they had heard often. But, on this occasion, he was in real agony for Claudia had smashed his kneecap with an oar when he had tried to beat her up. When the vicar of the parish had tried to intervene, he was unceremoniously turfed out of the house by the furious Claudia. Enraged beyond belief, Laban had limped out of the hut, found an aruval, a machete, from somewhere, and returned to the hut, determined to hack his wife to death. But, stone drunk as he was, he was no match for his wife who bashed his head in with the oar that she hadn't let go off once that night. A fisherman returning from a night's fishing spotted Laban, dead and bloated like a sardine, floating on the waves and brought him ashore.

Following her arrest and time in prison, Claudia disappeared from the fishing village for about six years. When she returned, she dropped anchor at the seafront, surviving by doing odd jobs. Her cousin, Lazar the drunkard, who had first suggested that Andrews get involved with the illegal dumping of waste, introduced her to the boat owner and asked him to give her a job. She was taken on and had helped out on a couple of trips. And now here she was again, dressed in a checked lungi and full-sleeved shirt, her disfigured cheek visible in the dim light of the kerosene lamp. A large towel was wrapped around her head. Looking at the ropy muscles of her forearms that had smashed Laban's skull in, Andrews could only feel awe.

'O Syrang, Lazar will raise his head only by tomorrow evening. So, I brought Claudi along. Boss, I will not send you to the deep sea all alone, so much is this Ambrose's love for you.' He snickered, brushing away some of the sand that was still stuck to his face. Andrews waited for him to demand more money, but Ambrose didn't say anything else and got to work, unloading the malodorous sacks from his van. The three of them began to feed them into the belly of the *Thomaasleehaa*, filling it up. The remaining sacks went on the deck. Ambrose and Andrews took a break but Claudia continued to work, taking the towel off her head and winding it tight over her nose and mouth to shut out the foul smell and taking great care not to let the putrid, sticky sacks touch her body. Finally, after dragging the last sack to the deck of the boat, the three of them dropped to the sand, panting with the effort of moving the fetid, noxious cargo. A foul-smelling fluid had leaked out from the sacks and the deck was covered with it.

'It's three in the morning, fellows,' Claudia said and Andrews sat up quickly, it was time to get moving. Ambrose did not move. Remaining prone on the sand, he said: 'Launch the ship, O captain! Let me slumber awhile, in the time you take to go and return.' Too exhausted to get up, he rolled over and over until he fetched up by one of the wheels of his van. He fell asleep.

Andrews and Claudia walked across to the boat. He could see her eyes shining in the moonlight. He thought about the day her cousin Lazar had told him that Claudia wanted to be employed as a deckhand on his boat.

For a handsome wage, of course. There was no way he could say no because he regarded Lazar as his saviour—without him he would not be making all this extra money and would have been sucked under by a whirlpool of debt. And that was how Claudia became a deckhand on Andrews's boat. And so here they were again, going out to the deep, clandestinely, while Lazar lay passed out behind the Church of Our Lady Lourdes.

There wasn't much for Claudia to do once the boat was loaded. All she had to do was cling to the boat's gunwale in rough seas so she wasn't washed overboard. When they reached the spot where the sacks were to be dumped, her job was to keep a lookout for fishing boats and dump the sacks one by one into the black water while Andrews steered the boat. As they approached the dumping spot, Andrews noticed Claudia had taken the towel she had wrapped around her nose and mouth and re-tied it around her head. As the boat puttered along on the gently heaving sea, Andrews was amazed to see a smile lift her disfigured cheek. This was the first sign of any emotion she had shown during the entire journey except once when she had vomited, an expression of extreme haughtiness on her face. Noting him looking at her, she said, pointing to some ghostly phosporescence on the waves, 'Don't know whether that's there because some white man's ship has just passed through here. If that's the case, we will be shot today.' Seeing that Andrews wasn't amused by her joke, which rose out of a recent incident in which some local fishermen had been shot dead by a couple of Italian navy men, she glared at him and said grumpily: 'Why are you so afraid? It's not as if we are smuggling gold biscuits!'

'Still....'

'What, still...?'

'That fellow Ambrose has told many people that we are doing this. Apparently, the Honeymoon Residency hotel people are prepared to give a full boatload....'

'Oh, that's great! You've struck it rich....'

'Forget it, Claudi! I am not going to do this job any more. Mother sea feeds me. The sea is my be-all and end-all. Should I do something like this to her? Is it right?'

He remembered Lazar mocking him when he had said something similar to him. He dismissed his contrite thoughts outright, 'The problem is that you know nothing of this world, O Syrang!' Lazar continued. 'Not just here; it happens everywhere in the world. Do you think that people around the world eat their waste? White people are not like us. They are intelligent. They are the ones who eat the greatest number of chickens, goats, sheep, and pigs. Do they take all the waste that's generated by their consumption to the moon, and not to the sea? And the fish in the sea love to eat up this waste! Isn't that right, O Syrang? What kind of a fisherman are you? Look! Don't you see that the sea is sooooo vast! We dump twelve sacks, the white men dump two thousand! Does the sea mind? No, not at all! Isn't the sea strong! Double strong!! You know, the sea is like fire. It will eat up almost anything...!'

Claudia looked at him curiosly. 'Do you know what I was thinking the first time I travelled in the boat for such a long distance, sitting among these stinking sacks?' Without knowing how to respond to her, Andrews looked away from her to the hideous, oozing sacks piled high on the deck.

'I was thinking about jumping into the sea along with the sacks as I was throwing them overboard.'

Seeing that torn-up cheek trembling with emotion, the good-natured Andrews felt very sorry for her. But he found himself unable to think of a single thing to say to her. Fixing him with her gaze, Claudia continued: 'Just a single whack with the oar! I smashed his skull with a single blow. Weird are the ways in which humans act if you really think about it.... I remember thinking: what is the difference between the filth-filled sacks to be thrown into the sea and me? So, when those sacks went overboard, shouldn't I too have followed them?'

Andrews didn't know what to say. Irrationally, he started feeling afraid. He looked at her muscled arm, thought about it wielding an oar. Unwinding the towel from her head, and wiping her face with it, Claudia continued: 'There's only you and I here, all alone on these waters. Have you thought about what could happen now, Andrews?'

He felt his throat turning dry. What the hell was she going on about?

'Tell me....' she lisped coyly like a child.

He still couldn't bring himself to say anything. It was as though his tongue was crucified to his mouth.

'When you sit like this without uttering a word, terror-stricken, suspicious, looking at me as if I am another stinking sackful of filth, I think about many things so that I won't die of boredom. In one way, it was this shit-scared expression of yours that made me fantasize about those things. Do you want to hear about them?'

He nodded. Even in his fearful state, he didn't forget to take a sidelong glance at the sea to ascertain whether they had reached the spot from where they could start dumping the waste.

Claudia continued: 'In the first fantasy the boat was caught in a tsunami. The storm was gigantic. The gargantuan waves hauled our boat up and hurled it down to the bottom of the sea. You and *Thomaasleehaa* sank like lead. But I noticed one of the sacks of garbage floating on the stormy sea. Without paying attention to the stench, I clung to it and was saved. I rode out the storm and somehow reached the shore. As they say in the scriptures, the sack worked like the stone the mason discarded, which eventually became the cornerstone of a mansion. On my first trip along with you and this filthy load, that was what I fantasized about....'

Has she gone completely crazy? Andrews thought. What did she think she was doing? But there was nothing to say, so he sat listening, the boat rocking on the surface of the deep, deep sea.

'On the next trip, you did not even look at me once. I turned into something more worthless than these filth-filled sacks that day. During my fantasy on that occasion, I wreaked vengeance on you in full measure. There came another cataclysmic tsunami. At that time, you were saved, clinging on to one of those sacks we brought to throw into the sea. But you were tossed hither and thither on the waves, clutching that stinking sack for days on end, without an iota of an idea as to where you were heading. You were feeling hellish agony from hunger and thirst. Sharks surrounded you, scaring the hell out of you, but they didn't attack you. Finally, driven mad by hunger, you bit open the sack, devoured the rotting entrails and skin, licking, chewing, chomping, guzzling up the putrid contents....'

Within Andrew's eyes, shipwrecks occurred and chaos ruled the waves. Claudia was laughing close-mouthed. 'At the same time, I swam and swam, and reached the shores of another land. The inhabitants were good-natured, but naive, tribespeople. Thinking that I was a deity of the sea, they honoured and worshipped me, offered me delicacies, and anointed me their princess....'

He began to summon to his mind Rappai Muthalaali, Lazar, Laban, Ambrose...and began to lash them with whips. His expression said it all, though he didn't utter a word. 'Are you done with your craziness? It's not for nothing that Laban beat you with an oar.... He should have split open not just your cheek....'

He switched off the engine and got up and began to walk towards her. From the experience of her several trips with him, Claudia realized that they had reached the spot at which they could begin dumping the cargo overboard. As he swayed across the heaving deck of the *Thomaasleehaa*, towards the heaps of stinking, oozing sacks, Claudia, a menacing frown on her face, stayed put, showing no sign of rising or beginning to dump the sacks, remaining like another one of them. She muttered to herself: 'You stinking Syrang! Years before you had even dreamed of slinking away at midnight into the sea in your motorboat with these sacks, this Claudi had come all alone in a rowboat out to the deep sea...in that sack was Laban whose skull she had spilt open with one blow.' Then, she twined the fingers of both hands together, and using them as a pillow, lay down supine on the sacks, and grimaced at Andrews who was standing over her musing to himself, 'Only I know what Rappai Muthalaali used to do to such women, bringing them out to the deep sea in this boat, while I was with him as his employee.'

Neither of them said a word to each other. The *Thomaasleehaa* rolled and skittered on the vastness of the sea. On its heaving deck, the silence of the dark blue sky had fallen between Claudia and Andrews.

4

THE CURRENT CLIMATE

ARAVIND JAYAN

The new branch manager, Mr Chandru, noticed the idol as soon as he entered the bank. It stood on a white pedestal in the centre of the foyer, was about two feet tall, and depicted Shiva, Parvati, and Ganesha sitting together. It looked heavy—and might have been made out of brass—though he couldn't be sure. Mr Chandru introduced himself to the staff and learned their names. On his second day at work he asked to have the idol moved into the storeroom.

The bank branch was a shoebox with around twenty-five staff. Apart from one Muslim loan officer named Asif, and two Christian tellers, they were all Hindu like him. Anyway, it wasn't the denomination of the staff that mattered to Mr Chandru. What mattered was that they were a national establishment, and the nation was secular. Religious artefacts had no place being displayed so prominently in the bank.

Mr Chandru's order was received with some reluctance. He'd expected this, given the general climate and he'd looked forward to explaining himself. During his college days—a long time ago now—he had been involved in some local politics. In his final year, he had even published not one but two revolutionary poems in a magazine run by the student body. Such experiences had little to do with banking, but as they'd said at one of his management seminars, when you take charge of an office, you're in charge not only of the staff but also of the culture.

Amit Agarwal, the assistant manager, was the first to react. He'd listened to Mr Chandru's explanation and nodded with a sullen expression. Having to explain in Hindi, Mr Chandru, a South Indian, felt he had been less eloquent than he'd hoped.

'But you're a Hindu, sir?' Agarwal said.

'Yes, but that's beside the point.'

'It's just that the idol gives us a feeling of protection. Nothing political, sir.'

'I'd like to have it removed, nonetheless. That's all.'

After some hesitation, Agarwal left his cabin. Later, almost as an afterthought, he popped his head around the door to extend a dinner invitation to Mr Chandru for the following night.

Mr Chandru was not only new to the branch but also to the town where he'd been posted. The bank had provided him with a one-storey, two-bedroom house that wasn't too far from work. The house was small, but it came with a dining table, a double bed, a stove, a velvet sofa, a fridge, a television, and a small alcove on the wall that was supposed to be used to set up a puja unit. The dusty floor was tiled in a mosaic pattern and the windows were dirty. In fact, everything needed a thorough cleaning. Mr Chandru had planned to do just that, but by the time he got back from work, the temperature had dropped to a single digit. The sky had turned grey, and a sharp wind had picked up.

Unused to this sort of cold, Mr Chandru felt tired and lazy. He boiled some rice in a cooker, made dal, and ate it by the small red heater he'd borrowed from his office. Afterwards, he washed up and sat wrapped in a blanket, watching the news and thinking about the day's events. Something about the cold and the bland food made him uncomfortable. It was homesickness, he decided—that's all.

When the power went, Mr Chandru pulled the blanket even closer around himself and wished the stray dogs outside would stop howling. If he felt spooked, it was only for a moment. Soon his wife and his son would join him. Things would start to fall into place, and he would feel better about everything.

The idol was still there when Mr Chandru reached work the next day. Now the whole thing had become a matter of insubordination or at least laziness. Either way, it wasn't good. Most of the staff members had already arrived. Those who were walking in wished him a good morning.

Mr Chandru went around looking for a peon, then failing to find anyone, he decided to move the idol himself. This would not only make the peons feel bad but would also establish that he was a hands-on manager who wasn't afraid to sweat a little, if need be.

The idol was heavier than he had anticipated. Having picked it up, though, there was no way he could put it back down without looking foolish. Even though he felt several eyes on him, no one stepped forward to help. Perhaps they were unsure of his exact intentions or didn't want to seem overfamiliar.

Wobbly on his feet, and thinking he probably looked comical, Mr Chandru carried the idol some twenty-five feet, pushed open the storeroom door with his shoulders, and placed it on a metal table that was covered with dust. Among the broken computers and racks of dumped files, he found a piece of white cloth, shook it twice, and covered the idol with it. That done, he closed the door with an officious air and went to his cabin, sneezing so hard he felt some of his hair come loose. That morning, as Mr Chandru was doing his rounds, he wondered if Asif didn't look somewhat happier. He even sensed some admiration in the man's smile.

When Asst Manager Agarwal came to his cabin later that day, Mr Chandru said, 'By the way, I moved the idol to the storeroom myself.'

In between licking his finger and turning a page of the file he was checking, Agarwal looked up and nodded. 'Okay, sir.'

That was all he said, though something in his tone didn't feel quite right—so much so that in the evening, Mr Chandru wondered if the dinner invitation that had been extended to him the day before was still valid. It wasn't that he pined for friendship; just that he hated the thought of going back and eating yesterday's food.

Thankfully, at precisely six, Agarwal came in and asked him if he was done with work. Mr Chandru packed stuff away in his briefcase, got in his old Maruti car—freshly shipped—and followed the other man's bike. Agarwal's house was farther from the bank than the house Mr Chandru had been allotted, and when they arrived, he saw that it was noticeably smaller too.

Agarwal's wife was a thin woman who looked much more dignified than the man she had married. She wore a plain housecoat—clearly not dressed to receive a guest, especially her husband's boss.

'So good to have you here,' she said.

'Thank you for having me,' Mr Chandru said.

Dinner was served as soon as they entered the house. Nothing fancy: white rice, chickpeas, a few tough rotis, aloo jeera, and spiced curd. Agarwal's wife was quiet throughout the meal and, at one point, apologized for not cooking non-veg.

'We are not used to that kind of food here,' she said.

Maybe he was reading too much into it, but the statement felt like a barb.

'I hardly eat any non-vegetarian food myself,' Mr Chandru said. This was a lie, though he didn't know why he had bothered to say so considering that he didn't care about sparing the woman's feelings.

After dinner, there was no dessert and no apology for this omission. Maybe it wasn't customary. What did he know?

In all, by the time Mr Chandru was done, he was tired and a little bit offended.

'Do you know the way back, sir?' Agarwal asked him.

'I can manage, yes.'

The town was small, and most of the roads were an unpaved mess. Several of the shop signs were written only in Hindi, and there were hardly any vehicles on the road. Most shops had been shuttered already. The streetlights were few and far between. Every now and then, he would pass a pool of construction workers huddled around a tyre fire. Broken bottles, garbage bags and, at one junction, a burned bus lay on the side of the road. The windshield of his car began to fog up, and he had to wipe it clean every so often so he could see where he was going.

No sooner had Mr Chandru reached home than he latched his door. He looked out of the peephole at the compound. For some reason, he had the feeling that he was being followed. It was nonsense, but still, a feeling was a feeling. He switched on the heater and squatted in front of it, wiping his wet nose. He had marked the date of his wife's arrival on the calendar pinned to the living room wall. He looked at it for reassurance and thought, almost there.

Later, Mr Chandru noticed through his front window several figures carrying flashlights and walking about on the road outside his house. They were only there for a few minutes.

When the idol reappeared in the office foyer the following day, Mr Chandru stood in front of it, baffled. He summoned the peon who was supposed to remove it in the first place, before he had done so himself.

'Why is this back here?' Mr Chandru hissed.

The peon scratched his head and mumbled that he had no idea.

Then his finger shot up. 'It's the other fellow!' he said. 'The other peon, sir. He was on leave till now. He must have thought we put it aside for cleaning. But I'll take care of it, sir. I'll remove it. Maybe I should find another place for it besides the storeroom?'

'Not in the foyer, and not on display.' With that, Mr Chandru went into his cabin and closed the door.

He was unaware of the confabulations that went on in the background, but when he returned from lunch that afternoon, Mr Chandru was told that a priest from the local temple was waiting in his office.

'Why is he here?'

'No idea, sir,' the peon said.

Mr Chandru grew nervous but told himself that perhaps the man was there to ask about a loan or introduce himself to the new manager.

The priest did not get up when Mr Chandru walked in. Instead, he gestured towards the foyer.

'It's not a good idea to have something like this gathering dust in the building,' he said. 'In fact, it's a bad omen. If it's okay with you, I'll have the idol placed in the temple. I'm sure we can find a spot for it.'

Mr Chandru tried to project the same manner of seriousness that the priest was putting on.

'If you think that works, you have my blessing,' he said.

'Then we'll send someone next week to get the idol.'

'Great.'

After the priest left, Mr Chandru wondered if his use of the word 'blessing' had been too mocking, even though he hadn't intended it to be.

He found himself thinking about this all evening. Maybe once his wife arrived, they could visit the temple together and be properly introduced to the priest.

∞

That night, there was another power cut in his lane. Mr Chandru would not have noticed had the dead heater not made it impossible for him to stay asleep. He had a scratchy throat, so he decided to make himself a glass of hot tea. As soon as he opened the bedroom door, he heard the dogs. And closer than the dogs, he heard voices. He parted the curtains and saw people holding flashlights. They were standing in front of his house, deep in conversation. He waited for them to pass, then tried to reassure himself that, in all likelihood, these were no more than labourers unloading goods late at night to avoid union trouble.

Mr Chandru couldn't sleep well the entire week. His ears kept tuning into whatever was going on outside. Everything bothered him: the creatures scuttling across the terrace, the tumble and drag of dry leaves that had begun to accumulate in his compound. Even when there was no sound out there, his brain would conjure it up.

The following Monday, Mr Chandru stepped on dog shit. It was on his porch, right outside his door. He lifted his foot and frowned at the floor. The main gate had abnormally wide slats. It was entirely possible, extremely plausible even, that a dog could have wandered in and done the deed on his doorstep. Still, Mr Chandru stood there, staring at his soiled shoe for a long time. He took it off, inspected the underside, and retched as the smell met his nose. Then he took a short walk around the compound, looking for signs of human activity in the mud: footprints, a pan masala wrapper, anything....

By the time he had washed up and left for work, he was late. A few employees tittered, probably making fun of the big speech he'd given about punctuality just last week.

Mr Chandru checked the date on his watch. Three days till his family got here. It made him nervous.

⁌

'Excuse me, sir,' the peon said, pressing his face against the glass wall of his cabin. 'The men from the temple called. They want to know if they can come get the idol today.'

Mr Chandru was in a meeting with a local seth, a jewel merchant who owned a two-storey building in the centre of town—one of the few that showed a recent coat of paint. The interruption annoyed Mr Chandru. What annoyed him even more was the fact he'd been put on the spot.

'Tell them to check with me later,' Mr Chandru said quickly.

'Okay, sir.'

When the peon left, the seth said, 'I was wondering where the idol went. It used to be the first thing you saw walking in. Are you getting it cleaned?'

Mr Chandru said it was in the storeroom for the day, then started discussing a new credit scheme.

∽

Mr Chandru's wife and son were arriving on the last train into town. He drove up to the two-platform station and waited for them in the cold. It was past eleven at night, and as he had come to expect, the train was late. From the car, Mr Chandru grabbed a shawl, wrapped it around himself, and began pacing the length of the platform. The only other person there was a homeless man sleeping against a large sack of cement. Mr Chandru avoided looking in his direction.

Occasionally, sharp sounds of clashing metal came from further down the tracks. It startled Mr Chandru each time he heard it. His breath came out as heavy puffs of mist.

Finally, just as he was thinking about calling up the bigger station a few kilometres north to find out why there had been a delay, the train crept up to the platform and came to a stop. The only passengers who got off were his wife and, asleep on her shoulder, their six-year-old son. Mr Chandru took their bags and hurried them into the car. Even when they got inside, they were too cold to talk. Mr Chandru asked if the journey was okay, then without listening to the muttered answer, started the car. The engine revved but after that went silent.

'What's the matter?' his wife asked.

'Must be the cold,' Mr Chandru said, trying to keep his voice calm. 'Everything was fine when I got here.'

Could someone have snipped a wire or loosened a screw?

Mr Chandru turned the key in the ignition again—so hard, he feared it might break off. The car spluttered and went silent.

'I told you, we should have bought a new car a long time ago,' his wife said, trying to sound playful.

Mr Chandru didn't respond. In his rearview mirror, he noticed two men approaching. By now the fog had picked up, and it felt like they were in a slowly sinking boat.

'Lock your door,' Mr Chandru said.

'What?'

'Lock your door.'

In the back seat, his son woke up and rubbed his eyes.

The men approached Mr Chandru's side of the car.

The fatter of the two asked, 'Brother, is everything okay?'

'Yes,' Mr Chandru said. 'All good.'

'Engine trouble?'

'No no; I'm sure it'll start in a second.'

'We'll give you a push if you want.'

'That's okay. It's all good.'

The other man asked, 'You have fuel in the tank?'

'Yes.'

'You sure?'

'Yes. Full tank.'

'Then all you need is a push. You'll have to come out and help, though. My hand is sprained.'

'It really is all right,' Mr Chandru said. 'We'll manage.'

Then he turned the key one more time. Suddenly, the engine came to life. Mumbling a quick thank you, he accelerated out of the station yard faster than was safe on such bumpy roads.

That night too, Mr Chandru heard people outside his front gate. With his wife and son asleep, he came out to the living room to check the windows. Again, there were those flashlights and soft-footed scurrying. He watched the figures through his curtains, then once they were gone, lay down on the couch, unable to fall asleep.

The next day, Mr Chandru called the peon to his cabin and asked him to return the idol to the pedestal in the foyer.

The peon stood there for a few seconds, his mouth half-open.

'Just move it from the storeroom to the foyer,' he said, slowly, as though the peon were an idiot. 'Then leave it there till someone from the temple picks it up. Understood?'

'Yes, sir. I'll do so right away.'

Later that evening, when the temple called, Mr Chandru declined to talk to them. They called the following day, and then again, later in the week. Both times, he pretended to be busy. Finally, they stopped calling altogether.

5

THE POWER TO FORGIVE

AVINUO KIRE

On bended knees, she riffled through pages of old documents and other papers, some of which would remain forever necessary and others which had long fulfilled their purpose. She had never been a particularly organized person. Marksheets, old Christmas and birthday cards, and various outdated church programmes were all jammed inside a single brown cardboard file with the words 'Government of Nagaland' on the cover. A piece of paper made a crackling sound of protest as she crumpled it into a ball and threw it towards the waste bin.

She was getting married soon. Sorting out her meagre belongings was the first phase of preparation for the new life she would soon embark upon. He had proposed a few nights ago and she had shyly accepted, as they both knew she would. She was twenty-eight and still retained youth's fresh-faced sweetness. He, on the other hand, was an unattractive man already well into his mid-forties, but she had no complaints. If anything, she was grateful that he had asked to marry her at all. She had long resigned herself to the likelihood that marriage was not to be part of her destiny. Therefore, it did not matter to her that he was unemployed or that he could seldom hold his liquor. He had asked her to be his and that excused all his weaknesses. A feeling of affection overcame her as she recalled his uncharacteristic solemnity while discussing plans for their impending nuptials. 'I shall ask my elder brother and grand-aunt to ask for your hand in marriage. You can tell your parents to expect a visit from my relatives this Saturday,' he had promised. To be treated so sensitively, as if she were as pure and untouched as any other sheltered young woman, moved her, endeared him to her. In the past she had been suspicious when other men had treated her similarly. 'Don't you know?' she would want to ask them.

Shaking free from her habit of ruminating endlessly, she gathered the papers together and tapped them against the floor to align them. As she did so, a newspaper clipping slipped from the pile and fell to the floor. **FATHER FORGIVES MAN WHO RAPED DAUGHTER**, read the headline in bold capital letters. 'In a supreme act of Christian forgiveness....' But she did not have to read the words, did not need to, she had felt their weight even before the clipping hit the smooth mud floor. She had been acutely aware of the clipping while sorting out her papers, and had been very careful to ignore it. Yet there it was, forcing her to confront once again a single devastating memory that clung to her entire past like an overpowering rotten smell, effectively erasing all else. It seemed to her that memory was partial to pain and loss. A torrent of emotions—the old familiar wave of anger, shame, and betrayal, a mind-numbing tornado of resentment that always left her with disastrous headaches—all these threatened to destroy her happy mood.

She picked up the tattered newspaper clipping with distaste and tucked it beneath the mattress on the bed. She no longer wanted to preserve it in her file. At the same time, she could not bring herself to destroy it. A thought struck her as she resisted her immediate impulse to consign the clipping to the waste bin. Perhaps it was quite natural for a person to form an attachment to anything—one simply had to live with it long enough.

∞

It had happened sixteen years ago, when she was only twelve. Her rapist had been her paternal uncle. To this day, though other details had become vague with the passing of time, she distinctly remembered the nauseating smell of him—a mixture of sweat and a faint eggy sourness—and the wave of hot, heavy panting. She was alone in the house and her uncle had left hurriedly after committing the crime. He had murmured something to her before leaving but she could not remember what it was. A curious and kindly neighbour had come into their neat three-roomed bamboo house and found her curled up in a corner, dazed and crying. Upon the woman's concerned questioning, she had told her what had happened.

The little Naga village rose in righteous rage when the incident came to light. The story was reported in the local newspapers and various organizations voiced their strong condemnation of the incident. Never had her little village received so much attention. She remembered her mother comforting her in the hospital while some police personnel recorded her statement. She also remembered a group of women from some women's rights organization who had come to visit her all the way from Kohima, the capital town. Her mother had described the horrific incident in dramatic detail to the visiting delegation, as though she had been a witness to everything. All this had happened a long time ago. There had been life before the incident and life after it as well. So it frustrated her that the incident alone often seemed to sum up the story of her existence.

Over the years, she had learned to accept what had happened to her. There were moments she even forgot—happy times while gathering water, or washing clothes beside the village river with other girls, when she imagined she was as carefree as any one of them. But such light-heartedness was always short-lived. 'People will think you have no shame!' her mother was always quick to remind her. Mother never failed to lament the stigma that had become attached to their family because of her; at the same time, she never encouraged anyone, her least of all, to put the incident behind them. She realized that Mother had changed irrevocably after the incident, maintaining a detached relationship with her own daughter, fearful that any intimacy would lead to unpleasant, hurtful emotional exchanges between them. Although nothing was ever said, she sometimes felt that her mother blamed her for what had happened. She sensed judgement in her mother's furtive glances, her pursed lips, her grimaces, her narrowed eyes. She thought no one understood the meaning of the silences between them better than her mother; in time, she too had learned that language well.

She would endlessly brood over the events that had unfolded that fateful day—should she have been more alert, more wary, fought harder? But above all, her most agonizing thought was whether life would have been simpler if she had kept that one day of her life a secret. She often wondered whether things would have been different had her mother discovered her first. Somehow, she believed she would have got over the violation of her body; found a way to bear her shame if it had all remained private. It only became intolerable when society 'shared' the shame.

She had been belatedly informed of her father's decision to forgive her uncle. It was a few weeks after the uproar had died down that her father came to her room and sat down beside her at the edge of her bed. He had said many things about forgiveness, justice, and family honour. He said so much in such a grave voice. But nothing had prepared her for what he announced at the end. He stood up slowly as he spoke, indicating to her that his speech was winding up. With an air of parental authority, her father had concluded:

'I have decided to forgive your uncle. But you need never worry about him; you will never see or hear from that man again.'

At his words, a strange and alien emotion stirred deep within her; feelings much too complicated for a child of twelve to grasp. Frustrated at being unable to express what she felt, she burst into helpless tears. Her father, a good but undemonstrative man, looked at her uneasily and said in a heavy voice, 'One day you will realize that this is the right thing to do. Hatred will only destroy us.' He said something about her uncle being in jail and also being excommunicated from their village. But, at that moment, nothing mattered more than her feeling of anger and resentment towards her own father as well as the unfamiliar emotion she had been unable to interpret. She did not realize then that the alien emotion she felt was betrayal. 'As if *he* had been the victim,' she would wonder aloud to herself many times in the years to come.

That night, she had an especially vivid nightmare. In her dream, her uncle's giant face seemed pressed to her and she could not escape. She tried to scream, but her voice died as the face of the enemy slowly morphed into her beloved father's worn features.

∽

Sixteen years had passed since. Once a happy and cheerful child, she had now become withdrawn and reserved after the incident. She was still a dutiful daughter to her parents but it ended there. Her relationships with other people could be described as cordial at best. Though always polite, she was unable to forge close friendships. She had heard that her rapist uncle was now a free man. He had served seven years behind bars. Seven years in exchange for devastating her life. He had actually gone on to marry, have children, and was now living with his family in Dimapur district. She wondered bitterly who had married him. She often broke out in a cold sweat whenever she encountered anyone who resembled her uncle. Her biggest fear was the thought of meeting her uncle now, after all these years. This constant anxiety resulted in recurring nightmares. She knew it was illogical but she actually felt ashamed, even of what he might think of her—as if she had played a role in her own disgrace.

Except for the youngest, all her other siblings—three sisters and two brothers—had married and relocated elsewhere. She was not particularly close to any of them. The one person in the world she truly held dear was her youngest brother, Pele. He was the only one who saw her as she was; without sympathy or judgement, without the shadow of what had happened to her hanging over her head. It seemed incredible to her, that her sixteen-year-old brother actually looked up to her as any sibling would to an older sister in normal circumstances, and she loved him all the more for it.

And now, here she was, finally getting married and about to move out of the house she thought she was destined to live out her life in. A wry smile touched her face as she realized that she was not much different from other women after all. Shifting required a sizeable amount of baggage, although in her case, the bulk of it remained unseen. It had become a part of her; she could not leave it behind.

'Your father will need a new suit,' her mother remarked. She looked at her mother, contentedly picking stones out of the rice while helping her make plans for the wedding. It had been a long time since she had seen her mother look so serene. She realized with sadness that she was not the only one who had changed. Her mother, once a warm and somewhat boisterous woman, had become timid and developed a pessimism about life; she was so unlike the fearless woman she had once been. Her mother, she decided, had developed three dominant personality traits—she was fierce towards her husband, long-suffering towards her children, and timorous towards society in general. A long time ago, she had witnessed her parents quarrelling after a visit to her paternal grandmother. Eavesdropping through bamboo walls, she gathered that her grandmother had blamed her mother for what had happened to her. 'You stood there without defending me while your mother accused me of being a bad mother! How dare she blame me for our daughter's...?' Her mother broke down before she could finish what she was saying. Her father had replied, 'You are overreacting! She does not blame you, how could she? All she said was that mothers should be careful not to leave young daughters unattended!' Her younger self had not wished to listen any more. She had put her hands over her ears and faked sleep until it finally came.

Mother poured the cleaned rice into an empty barrel, humming a soft lullaby while doing so. Her mother did not gossip. Perhaps she used to, but not any more: there was too much at stake. 'We each have our cross to bear,' was her mother's ambiguous response to everything and anything unsavoury she heard about anyone. She sometimes pitied her mother's naivety in hoping that by not judging others, she would escape being judged herself.

Her silent reverie was broken by her mother's quizzical glance.

'Girl! Where is your mind, did you hear what I just said? Your father will need a proper suit to walk you down the aisle.'

She braced herself; she had been prepared for this conversation.

'Yes, of course. Actually, I am planning to ask Pele to walk me down the aisle,' she replied tentatively.

'Nonsense! Your father should have that honour.'

'No, I want Pele to give me away, it's my wedding after all,' she said firmly.

Her mother gave her a pained look but did not argue. She simply said, 'Think about it, your father will be very hurt.'

She felt a savage satisfaction at Mother's words.

Her brother's reaction was predictable. 'Dear sister! Of course, I would be honoured, but don't you think it should be Father?'

'I'd rather you did it,' she insisted.

'It's your wedding,' he said.

She did not feel the same satisfaction at his reaction.

Traditional wisdom discouraged long engagements—delays gave rise to second thoughts and gossip. And so, a date was fixed quickly and before long the wedding preparations began in earnest. The villagers arrived in droves to help; different groups for different work. The menfolk came together to construct a makeshift bamboo pavilion for the reception, and later helped to butcher two cows and a pig for the wedding feast. The women arrived to decorate the reception area and helped with the cooking and cleaning. The villagers felt good about being kind and generous to her; she was their tragic child. As for the bride-to-be, for all her cynicism, she experienced a renewed faith in human goodness. She found it overwhelming that all the fuss and hectic preparations were for her benefit. Also, the strained relationship she'd had with her mother all these years had silently begun to heal of its own accord; the two women had never been as close as they were now. It was as if the prospect of her becoming a bride had finally released her mother from her unhappiness.

The brief period of her engagement was the happiest time in her life, so much so that she felt a sense of loss as the wedding date drew closer. The only thing that marred her happiness was the niggling unease that persisted whenever she thought of her father. He had calmly accepted that her brother would be walking her down the aisle but she knew he was disappointed. She knew that he was a good father, and in other circumstances she would have adored him. However aloof, he was an honest, hardworking man and provided for his family the best way he could. However, an invisible barrier had come up between father and daughter the night her father informed her of his decision. It was the last time they discussed what had happened. She had been angry and had resolutely avoided speaking to him the first few months, and he had let her be. After she entered adolescence, she became too ashamed to ever broach the painful topic. In vain she waited for him to take the initiative; considering her father's retiring nature now, she knew it had been foolish to expect that of him. So then, words that should have been spoken were bottled up instead, feeding the resentment within her. Denying her father his right to give her away was her manner of punishing him for taking away her right to forgive a crime committed against her. However, when she saw how calmly he had accepted her decision, she wondered whether he was all that affected by it. Had she managed to hurt him as deeply as he had her? It tormented her, this unfinished business. Finally, she resolved that she would tell him how she felt, how he had let her down. She would let it all out, only then would she find the peace that had constantly eluded her.

She found an opportunity to have it out with him the evening before her wedding. She had been sent home early to rest and prepare for her big day. Her mother, brother, and the rest of her married siblings who had arrived for the wedding with their respective families were still at the reception venue, making some final arrangements. She knew her father was alone at home. She carefully rehearsed her speech, the precise words she would say, and how she would begin. When she reached the house, she was so flustered and jittery that she lingered outside on the doorstep, willing her heart to slow down and stop beating so violently. She took a deep breath to steady her frazzled nerves. As she did so, a raw guttural sound from inside the house startled her. She quietly pushed opened the door and stepped inside. She heard unintelligible sounds broken by tormented sobs coming from inside her parents' bedroom. Her heart hammering against her chest, she looked inside the room. What she saw devastated her. Her father sat weeping awkwardly on a chair, his head in his hands, his prematurely greying hair in disarray; on the bed next to the chair was his new suit for her wedding and a rumpled copy of the church solemnization programme. She had never in her life seen her father show any strong emotion, let alone cry. It embarrassed and distressed her all at once. She was not sure what to do.

Her father was unaware of her presence, and so she quietly stepped back and retreated to her room. Feeling numb, she sat on her bed and tried to collect herself. She looked around the bare room, stripped of all its belongings but for three pieces of luggage neatly stacked beside her bed. All the worldly evidence of her twenty-eight years was packed inside those three pieces of luggage: a worn-out VIP suitcase, which had once belonged to her father, and two colourful bags. One she had owned for some time, and the other was a wedding gift from her parents. She made a mental checklist of the things she wanted to take to her new life. Her soon-to-be husband had revealed a surprisingly kind and thoughtful nature during their time together. Despite his shortcomings, she knew that he could make her happy if she allowed him to. Her thoughts turned towards the tragic figure a couple of rooms away. Instinct told her that she was the cause of his profound grief. She closed her eyes and her body trembled. She knew then what she must do. For the first time, she felt like doing what should have been done a long time ago. Her right hand reached under the mattress and pulled out the newspaper clipping, cosseted and kept for too long. For the first time, she felt no dread of the words staring back at her. She had allowed herself to play the victim for too long. It was now time to let go. She walked to the kitchen and threw the incriminating paper into the fireplace. She did not bother to look as the flames consumed it in seconds.

With every brisk, purposeful step she took, the carefully constructed wall around her heart began to break; each brick loosened and crumbled, one by one. Emboldened, and with a confidence she had never felt before, she pushed open the final door. Her stricken father looked up, and on seeing her, stood up clumsily. He faced her, all his defences down, a grown man unashamed about the tears and snot streaking his cheeks. It did not matter who closed the distance; they embraced and he kissed her forehead. That unadorned, loving act dispersed with the need for words or anything else.

Tomorrow would bring new challenges with it. Yet, somehow, she knew she was going to be all right. She even thought about the fear that had dogged her—the prospect of accidently running into her uncle. This possibility no longer filled her with dread. In fact, she hoped that she would meet him one day. She would hold her head high and look him in the eye so he would know that he had not 'ruined' her, that his evil had not tainted her. She revelled in the liberating absence of the bitterness that had long plagued her. For the first time since forever, she felt free.

6

A STORY THAT LIVED

BHAVANI

The old peepul tree stood to one side of the only busy intersection in that village 160 kilometres from Chennai. A large dilapidated temple to the side of that tree spoke of its peaceful past to anyone who cared to examine the cracks in the garish paint that now covered it. Between the tree and temple lay a wide courtyard paved with loose cement slabs. The area appeared to have been recently swept and was not littered with rubbish as was usually the case with temple courtyards in the country.

A woman stood in the middle of the courtyard with a toddler by her side. Her hair was tied back in a ponytail, but stray strands escaped and flew in the gentle breeze. People walked around them, continuing their daily routine; the woman, unmoving, her eyes soft with wonder, appeared to be an island surrounded by churning waves. The toddler looked at his mother's face and asked, 'Ma, where are we?'

∞

It was 4 a.m. and I was sitting on the toilet. Sleep had evaporated. I found myself awake, on the bed, urgently needing to pee. The leaflet had said it was best to test the first urine of the day. So there I was, waiting, after having peed on a stick. I was three days late. I was never late; my uterus could make even a clock envious. I looked at myself in the mirror, my hair wild around my face, my eyes big and puffed up…how did I feel?

The little lines on the stick turned pink. Was there supposed to be one pink line or two? I looked at the instructions on the kit. I had more urine in the sampler, so I did another test to be doubly sure.

That evening, we announced the news to my parents over the speaker phone. 'We have something to tell you. Do you want to guess first?'

'Good news?'

'Yeah.'

'Then there is only one thing on my mind, nothing else…. I keep praying for it. I don't know what else to say,' my mother stated.

Like all parents, ours too, were keen on a grandchild. It had never been an outright demand; rather, subtle requests and questions would be inserted into conversations about whether we were planning to have children or not. It would be the first one on both sides: I was an only child and my husband's brother was still unmarried.

'Maybe….'

The rest of the phone call was a riot of screams, shouts, unending thank yous, 'I am so excited', 'need to meet you', et cetera, ending with, 'We are coming to Bombay right now!'

∞

Almost every evening Aru, Suma, Abi, Lila, and I would sit in a circle on the cool mosaic floor. Paati, our grandmother, would sit in front of us, her left hand holding a wide steel plate while her right would shape mounds of rice mixed with ghee, powdered jeera, and pepper, which she would plant in the centre of our palms. The balls of rice would feel large, circular, and warm on my hand, and in my mouth the ghee would rob the jeera and pepper of its fire. Sometimes, she would make balls of curd rice packed tight with pickle pressed inside. The pickle was usually home-made, tender mango pickle kept in a cupboard in jars, stirred only with a wooden spoon. I remember how the piquant sourness would make me squeeze my eyes shut but wanting more…although there was no way to say 'Enough!' or fuss about eating. Paati decided when each of us was done. The older ones got more, the younger ones got less. As she placed the mound of rice on my outstretched palm, I would break away a bit from one side, then another, gnawing at the mound, finishing the last bite only when it was my turn again.

All the while, my eyes fixed on her face, my ears trained on her voice, and my attention never wavering even for a minute. Food went in, mosquitoes got swatted, legs crossed and uncrossed when they went numb, the diamond on her nose shone—an early star at dusk—her eyes were wide and bright, and her hands kept moving automatically, like our mouths. Paati continued in Tamil, 'A fox, with black and grey and brown fur lives in the huge forest just around the corner of this street.'

A whisper: 'The corner of this street?'

'Yes. He lives with his mother and father, both big and huge! If you should ever meet them outside, just turn and walk away. Do not make eye contact. Okay?

'But this guy, he is a baby fox. He has this large white stretch of fur that runs down his back, so he is called Lightning. Like all babies, he is adventurous and gets mixed up in all sorts of funny situations. Sometimes, the brave can also be foolish, right? But then we've all been there!'

∽

We lived in different cities across India and every summer we met in hot Chennai, bound together by our common grandparents, and there we stayed under the shade of Paati's umbrella. Our parents would drop us off, stay for a few days, and then go back home to work, to a life without children—a vacation. And we remained behind for at least a month, often longer. Paati, an enthusiastic caretaker, cook, entertainer, and warm hugger rolled into one, never complained.

∽

I sat by the window after throwing up all my breakfast. My stomach felt like it would never want food again. Would this nausea ever end?

'I know mine continued for the first trimester, and then it went away.' Amma tried to cheer me up when I spoke to her on the phone. 'You'll be fine.'

'I was thinking about Paati today. All those stories she told us.'

'Yes, she told you so many stories.'

'Did she suffer from nausea while carrying any of you?'

I could hear Amma hesitating on the phone and could see her shrug as she said, 'Hmmm...I don't really know. Can't remember talking about it. She might have. It was a long time back, you know...you forget these things.'

'Do you remember any of the stories she told us?'

'She must have told me those stories too when I was little...but I don't remember now. I know that her mother and grandmother who lived in the village told her all these stories. I know that she loved to add little things to each story so you always thought you were hearing a new one....'

'This monkey was really smart. His brain was huge and so tightly packed that it felt like the brain of two monkeys in one body. And he said....'

Six of us lay in a row with Paati in the middle. The cool grass mats felt hard on our backs, our bodies tired from the heat and an entire day of play, yet craving a bedtime story. The whirring fan, on the fastest speed it could manage, was the background score to Paati's tale, which took us into a jungle filled with monkeys and scary animals. The only light came from the mosquito-repellent machines plugged in the two corners of the room.

By the time she was halfway through, some of us were already asleep. I lay on my stomach, chin resting on the palms of my hand, huddled close, looking into the whites of her eyes as she took me further into that dark jungle. When she finished, I took a deep breath, and asked:

'Paati, who told you these stories?'

'Oh, my mother, and her mother, and her mother. All my aunts and uncles would tell us stories too. There was no electricity in our village and every evening someone would tell a story. It was usually in the open space in front of the temple. The floor was smoothened with cowdung, a peepul tree stood tall, spreading its branches above us, and the rustling leaves seemed to take on the character of every story. We would crowd around, close to the storyteller, eager to not miss even a word.'

'In those days,' Paati continued, 'stories weren't just for children. Everyone enjoyed a good tale or two and the night would go on and on.' I could picture that scene: the dark village, the night sky clearly lit by stars and the moon, men sitting in their loosely tied lungis, women with their pallus tight around them to keep warm, the children, their eyes wide and bright, sitting closest to the man or the woman telling them a story. I could hear the leaves of the peepul rustling. On that warm night in Chennai, I felt a shiver run down my spine.

'But, Paati, some of these stories happened in Madras! Your mother didn't live here.'

'Oh, I changed it a bit, the story can't be the same forever. Everyone should hear something different, and all of you know Madras, you don't know my village. You've never been there! Stories are living things, they breathe, they absorb little things from around them. You see a beautiful flower and the story tells you it wants the flower to be in it, so you add that flower....'

'Really?' I whispered.

'Yes, if you are a good storyteller, then stories talk to you.'

'Ohhh….'

'If you were to let a story stay as is, and create this big, strict rule that no one can ever change anything about it ever, then it gets boring. The story gets dull. It is the same thing again and again and again. No one wants to listen to that story. And what happens if you don't listen to a story?'

'It dies?' I whispered.

'Yes, the story fades away and slowly dies…it's as if it never existed in the first place. Stories live in people, and if people don't hear them, then…you don't want stories to die, do you?'

I shook my head, my curly hair bobbing up and down. I wanted stories to live forever and ever, especially the ones Paati told me.

∞

'Are you eating right? I hope you aren't starving or doing any of your fancy diets. It isn't good during pregnancy. You need to eat for two people now!'

My mother was worried that I would obsess about my body. I tried to tell her that with the nausea I couldn't eat anyway. No food was tasty. Every morning, I struggled to find something that even a tiny part of me wanted to eat. Most often, I threw it up fifteen minutes later. I moved to a diet of muesli and milk, the only two things I could tolerate.

'I'm fine, Amma.' To change the topic, I asked her, 'Do you know some of the stories Paati told you?'

'Don't remember them…my memory is really bad. She told them to you much more recently—you must recall them better?'

Memory is a fickle thing, never there when you attempt to revisit something precious. It flits in like a temperamental breeze and goes away when it chooses to. I often found myself wondering if I would ever be able to access an entire piece of my past.

'Those stories were something else, Amma! They grew in her brain. Like seedlings planted in fertile soil. They were adventurous, fun, and ever-changing. They were unpredictable.'

I bought myself a Kindle after much debate and loaded the digital library. I devoured the content, attempting to conquer my churning stomach by travelling across the seas. I read authors from Iran, faraway Canada, and close—yet distant—Myanmar. I read stories constantly, searching for glimpses of Paati's originality, for the timelessness in her stories, and their immediacy.

For Paati added elements from the everyday. If you told her something you did that day, it would appear in a story that night, sometimes in an uncomplimentary fashion. We cousins grew cautious, singing tales of only our bravest and smartest deeds.

Paati called the stories family stories, heirlooms she wanted to pass on. She didn't believe in lockers stuffed with gold that were divided amongst the surviving family, but wanted to gift her children stories. Perhaps she hoped they would soak them up like a dry sponge and then give them their own spin.

∞

'No more, Paati,' Aru said. He was thirteen, and had the trace of a moustache on his upper lip. He no longer enjoyed sitting in a circle with younger cousins and listening to stories.

'Why?' she asked, her face small but curious.

'Shiva Mama got us a new video game. We want to play with that this summer. Master it before the summer gets over. Besides, stories are for babies, Paati.'

She looked at him, nodded, and then looked into the distance, 'And the rest of you? Want a story?'

I wanted to say I would sit by her, and that she could tell me stories, all kinds of stories about all kinds of creatures, and that I still wanted to hear them. But I didn't. We were all silent. She pulled her pallu tight over her chest, gave us a small, tight smile, and went away.

Aru was the coolest cousin, he was the first one to enter those mysterious teenage years and he was erudite, at least in our books, about the world beyond the games of our childhood. We followed him around like lost puppies that entire summer. Most of the time was spent lounging in front of the television set, screaming and shouting when we were close to winning the video game and arguing about who got to play next. Food was forgotten, meal times were now random, and we took turns, each eating when the controls were not in their hand. Every now and then, a fight would break out. It would get mean—bitter—and tears would come gushing down a few cheeks. Then Paati would appear, hug the crying kid, wipe away those tears with her soft pallu, and tell us to take a break. We never took that break. Playtime merged with evening and then slipped into night.

That was also the summer she took to baking cakes. These were made in steel tumblers that she 'baked' in her Butterfly pressure cooker. We would get a new kind of cake every few days, sometimes with jam on top or in the centre, sometimes topped with home-made chocolate sauce; once there was even Horlicks in it! Her creative experiments didn't always result in the tastiest cake but I remember gobbling them up and always wanting more.

One night, as the sun set on us, we lay on the grass mats, our heads resting on soft pillows, each pillow demarcating our space on the mat. My older cousins were playing games on their devices. I wasn't ready to sleep just yet so I asked Paati how stories were told in her village. She spoke about the ritual of storytelling in her village. There were always a few good storytellers at any given time in her village. There was once a contest to see who could keep the audience regaled for the longest time. Different people walked up to the space in front of the temple and told their stories, and by a show of hands the villagers decided who went to the next round. There was much cheering and booing on that cold night. Someone lit a few fires. I could picture Paati in the audience, huddled with others around one of the fires, warming her hands and toes, while a single voice took them far, far away. That night, Ramu was judged the best.

'Was he a famous storyteller, Paati?'

He was her favourite, famous in the village for his ability to transport them to worlds no one had ever seen or would in their lifetime. That night, he told them a story based far away, in North India. It was set in the cold Himalayas, which remained covered in snow for most of the year—such a distant reality from their safe, warm village in Tamil Nadu!

'He narrated his story in just a few words but I could feel the cold punch of snow as he described it. I felt like I was touching snow, crumbling it in my fingers, walking on it, sinking into it. And those shimmering snow peaks, with the moon rising over them…it was real, right in front of my eyes. I have never been to the Himalayas, but even today, deep down, it feels like I have.'

'Had he been there?'

'To the Himalayas? Ramu?' Paati shook her head, her eyes far away. 'He hadn't even been out of our village, but he was a magician of the truest kind. He could conjure up worlds based on what he heard from people, pictures he saw, and movies he watched. Everything was a clue, an input, a small inflection in a story. He could make anything spring to life.'

The silence deepened as I thought of Ramu, standing in front of the entire village and taking them to a snow-capped peak, making them touch snow in a way that even he hadn't.

'Stories don't need to be lived to be told, they just need to be told.'

⁂

The next summer, Aru and Suma didn't come back; there were classes and other things back home in Delhi. We were down to three. Summer was filled with mangoes, climbing trees, and chasing one another, but Paati's stories never came up. We didn't ask for them, neither did she ask if we wanted to hear them. Without Aru, the enthusiasm for video games died down. After a few days of chasing one another and some fights, we went our own ways. I liked sitting down somewhere in a corner with books, and Lila and Abi did their own thing.

After another summer in Chennai, I bribed my way out of the next one. Why couldn't I read my books in Pune?

'I'll go for classes. Whatever you want. And I will not bug you at work.'

'You've always loved visiting Madras!'

'Madras is boring!'

Amma raised her eyebrows but didn't push. I'd said 'Madras' and boring in the same breath. I never spent a summer in Chennai again.

⁂

Paati fell ill when I began my first job. I couldn't spend much time with her as I no longer had the luxury of long leaves. I went down for a weekend and she had changed so much from the last time I'd seen her. She was much older now, her face was lined with wrinkles and grey hair sprouted from moles on her face, moles I hadn't noticed before. Her thick coil of hair was no longer wound at the nape of her neck but lay limp in a thin plait. As she slept that afternoon, I stood in front of a wall of family photographs. There were photographs from her entire life: my grandparents at their wedding; with their first grandchild, Aru; with five of us one summer; another with everyone smiling and laughing in a typical USA studio photoshoot with that sterile backdrop; and one from a few years ago, at a family reunion.

'Kanna, dear one,' she called out.

I went to her, 'Is there anything I can get you, Paati?'

Her voice was a gentle wheeze and her breath stumbled over a short sentence. She coughed through the few words. 'My skin is very dry. Can you apply some cream?' I took out a box of the latest new-age youth serum from my bag. I rubbed a bit on my fingers and then gently applied it to her face. Her skin was soft, tender, each wrinkle collapsing into another. She lay there on her back, content, eyes closed, as I smoothed out each wrinkle, feeling my way around the lines that now marked her face. There was a smell about the room, a smell of old age and decay. When had she aged? I couldn't remember. By the time I finished, she'd fallen asleep. Her eyes were loosely shut, her lips upturned in a small smile and her hands were interlocked over her stomach. I covered her with a light sheet and stepped out.

She died one day without anyone present in the room. It was a few years after my visit. I was working away from home when Amma called me, sobbing. Amma was sixty years old and her mother eighty, yet she was frantic, lost. Paati had suffered a heart attack. It was sudden, quick, and decisive. Thatha had gone to the bathroom and came back to find her lying on the floor next to her bed, her eyes shut, her hands spread out and her head tilted to one side. That was it. It felt like an ideal death, quick, with no drama.

Some months later, I found out I was pregnant. After a long nine months filled with intense nausea, Ari was born. He had a crop of black hair and wide eyes that were constantly moving as if searching for something.

∽

'Amma, can you look for some stories? Maybe some book, somewhere. That Maami, who is your neighbour, maybe you can ask her? Ari would like them. He is now listening to stories, you know. He is just a year old, but so responsive! It would be nice to listen to Tamil ones like the ones Paati told us, instead of the ones I'm reading out from books written by Western authors. Maybe you can ask....'

I asked my husband's mother too if she knew any stories that had been passed down through the generations in her family. She sent me a Google search that threw up links to YouTube videos of the best children's stories from around the world. None of those stories gripped me like Paati's had. None of them felt like they could be mine.

∽

Behind the wooden study table that was Thatha's through the hole-in-the-wall window with thick grills running across, a ray of light from the street light outside the compound wall filtered in and fell on her nose. The mookkutthi or diamond nose stud that was a part of her wedding trousseau from eons ago shimmered in the light, showing its multiple facets. As the gathering darkness settled around us, the mosquitoes buzzed, briefly claiming our attention and receiving quick swats; but our eyes remained glued to her face, her bright eyes illumined in the light that ricocheted off her diamond nose stud. We followed every movement of those expressive eyes, jet-black orbs that seemed to grow or narrow down as she moved through the flow of the story.

Paati told a story like no other.

7

EGGS KEEP FALLING FROM THE FOURTH FLOOR
BHAVIKA GOVIL

On the fourth floor, an auntie lives. She calls out to the kids passing by and whistles at us and shouts, Hellooo, get me a shikanji, will you? But all the parents, the good ones, the bad ones, have told us to look away when she's shouting. She doesn't really need anything, don't go to her when she asks for things. And when she's crying or wailing, they say, it's fake. But it's hard not to look, because when she shouts, it sounds almost like she's singing. She has a voice like that—a little like imli—khatta meetha. Or like honey with lemon when you pour it into a scratchy throat and it feels bad at first and then goes down smooth, like plonk! and you fall asleep. Auntie's voice is like that.

When Papa started hitting Amma more often, they made so much noise that they couldn't even hear it when a gunshot went off on TV or when some boys set off firecrackers outside the house or when the watchman's mad wife was so angry with him for looking at another woman that she shrieked like she had seen a huge spider, for days and days and days. So, I started slipping out of our flat and going to Auntie's house. Her door was always open which was funny because most people in our building keep their doors shut, then double-shut with locks and bolts and all sorts of things like that as though they are rich and have plenty of things to lose.

When I complained to Auntie about my parents, she fixed me with her gaze and grinned widely and said: There are three ways to get their attention. You know, na, what to do. When you think they're not listening to you, you can jump out of a window.

I said, But I'll break my head.

She continued, scratching her hair which was a little grey and a little brown in places, That's right, the problem is that you'll break your head.

Yes.

When you go falling down down down.

Like an egg? I asked.

Like an egg, she confirmed.

So we dropped the idea.

The next time I was at her house, Auntie said, Let's move on to option number two. She said, I can run away from home and run faster than everyone and go to a place where everybody listens to me.

I said, You mean *I* can?

She looked at me blankly and nodded. Yes, of course. You can.

But my legs are shorter than Papa's, I said.

She scratched her head and said: Ah.

Then her eyes, which before this were sleepy and weepy, and even a little bit crusty, became big and brilliant, and she said, But this one will work. Then she whispered in my ear and grinned. Yes, this one *will* work.

∽

Misi at school still can't believe I had the guts to go to Auntie's house all alone but that's because Misi gets scared easily. I told her that Auntie looks like a monster from way way way below—with scraggy hair and big bulbous eyes and a little goop that always hangs from the side of her mouth. But she isn't really like that.

No one thought Misi and I would ever become friends either. We are so different. For one thing, she has many siblings and I have none. She has parents that don't hit each other, in fact, they don't really talk at all, and I have ones that bash and beat each other up like they are villains in a movie. Misi lives in a big house with one whole floor all to herself and many big windows to look out of. I don't. *I* have to climb on top of the cupboard in our one-room flat and then peer out the tiny, dirty window that we never clean because Amma always says What's the point? There's nothing outside to look at anyway.

Plus, Misi has long hair that never get lice. Mine get lice. Mine have got lice twice. But we still became friends.

Whenever I go to school after a whole night of drama in our house, I have big, puffy eyes. I try to keep quiet and not say anything even when the teacher asks us to because if I do, I'll cry. So I keep my feet tap-tapping and roll my head into my top like a turtle and put my head on the desk. And whenever I feel like I need to see people I just pop my face out and there I am. And although Misi is rich and Amma and Papa and Auntie and everyone says that rich people don't understand much and can't think outside of themselves, Misi still does. When I'm in my turtle home, she knocks on my shell and comes sits next to me and holds my hand. And if there's nothing to say, she braids my hair and says it doesn't matter if I have lice or not. That's Misi for you.

Amma and Papa didn't always hit each other. When I was four, maybe five, they told each other things like I love you and No I love you more. When they hugged, they took me into the centre of their hug and wrapped themselves around me until I couldn't see or smell anything but them. And when they thought I couldn't tell, they held hands under the blanket but we shared a bed and, of course, I could tell what they were doing by the lump. But when Papa stopped going to the factory and Amma started coming home late from the building she works in, they began spending more time fighting and hating everything: our house, each other. Even me.

When Auntie whispered the third idea to me, I didn't understand at first what she was talking about.

Get me the pills, the pills, she said, and began rubbing her eyes fast.

I looked at her blankly, wondering if she had a tummy ache and wanted the pink Digene medicine which tasted horrible but always worked.

No, no, Auntie said, irritated. The pills that make your mouth foam up like someone washed it out with soap. They make your body act as though an earthquake is taking place inside you.

You can get the pills from the man in the striped shirt behind the market. Then she added, If you ask nicely enough.

I stared at her.

She continued, Eat enough of the pills and everyone will notice you.

Everyone? I asked. I was thinking of Amma and Papa.

Everyone. And you'll share them with me, won't you?

People in the building say a lot of things about Auntie. That she used to be married to a woman. That she's a witch. That she was rich. That she drinks her face off. Drink what? I once asked, but they just laughed. That she came here from Pakistan. That she secretly owns a big van. They say a lot of things, but they don't say one thing for sure—she's smart as hell.

∞

Misi is not coming to school nowadays. The girls are saying lots of things—that Misi has moved schools, which can't be true because she'd never do that without telling me; that she has fallen down and broken her neck and legs and teeth all at once; and, worst of all, that her parents died, which is a very bad thing to say when it's false but even more so when it's true.

The teacher shushed them all and said, not die, they got *divorced*. Everyone sniggered. Later, I told Auntie the die-divorce thing, and she muttered that sometimes it means the same thing. Then, she roared with laughter. I asked her if she was married once and she said, Yes, perhaps. Perhaps, I was.

∞

The guy behind the market exploded with laughter when I went to him. He looked at me like I was joking. And even though my legs were shivering and I wanted to escape into my turtle home, I asked again loudly, pointing vaguely towards Auntie's flat. The man creased his eyebrows, and said, So, she's sent you this time, has she?

Then, he asked, Got the money?

When I said no, he said, There are other ways to pay, you know. Surely, your auntie must have told you that. He looked at me in my school uniform from top to bottom, slowly, licking his lips as he did. I ran away to my house as quickly as I could, thinking the whole time that Misi would *never* believe I had the guts to do this.

∞

Today, after ages, Misi came to school. I asked her what happened. Why was she gone for so long without telling me? But this time she was the one who was shivering, not me, so I took her to a corner in the girls' bathroom. She said that her mother didn't love her father any more. It was true, what the girls said, they were getting divorced. In fact...Misi began, But you can't tell anyone this. She paused, her words hanging in the air. So, I nodded violently and promised.

I don't know if it's true or not but Misi says that she saw her mother kissing her best friend.

Kissing? I asked, opening my eyes wide.

She nodded. Apparently, her mother never loved her father very much at all, and now she goes around kissing her best friend who's a woman.

At least that's what Misi says.

∽

Auntie with the imli voice fell from her balcony two days ago. She fell falling splat and made such a mess that people around complained that they had to pay money to get the courtyard scrubbed. Her head broke and cracked like an eggshell, but instead of yellow, red blood spilled out, and kept on flowing and flowing and flowing. I thought a lot of police people with their big cars and red rotating lights would come like they do in the movies to see a body crumpled on the ground. But only one man came and he was wearing loose brown trousers and honestly, I swear, he looked like he also didn't want to be there.

Misi at school says that it's not possible that Auntie just fell. People don't simply fall out of balconies. Sometimes, I think maybe Misi's right. But other times, I think that maybe what people said *is* true. Maybe Misi doesn't understand these things because she is too rich. And even if I'm not, I think, at least I'm better than Misi. At least my Amma only kisses my Papa when she does and not strange women, and at least lice like me enough to come stay in my hair. And at least my building has four floors, not two, even if people fall out of it like eggs sometimes. At least.

8

AIR

DILSHER DHILLON

There was no dignity in the night shift. Waving away beggars from the securely locked glass doors and watching them slowly asphyxiate on the pavement. Conducting an audit of every single oxygen tank in the storeroom. Maintaining the ledger and making sure the accounts were in order. Putting the day's earnings in the safe while being closely monitored by the CCTV. Haggling with loyal customers who were down to their last thousand rupees. Every single night.

As Arya's long shifts blurred into dreary days marked by inadequate sleep and fever dreams, he knew he was inching towards the threshold of his sanity. However, he was bound to the routine of his solitary existence.

Working in oxygen supply was one of the more stable jobs in Delhi. Ever since the concentration of pollutants in the air barrelled past the upper limit of the Air Quality Index, the city had imploded. Rioters ran helter-skelter, burning government buildings and looting malls. Most of the middle class, the erstwhile backbone of the economy, moved to other cities, driving up rents and prices and increasing pollution wherever they went. The business elites shifted base to other countries while the politicians holed up in airtight castles. The manual labourers, who could not afford to leave, continued to work in wretched conditions, breathing the deadly air.

Those who stayed tried to find reassurance in the government's vague declaration that, due to the mass exodus, Delhi's air would return to sufficient breathability 'within years'. Until then, the city's residents would have to rely on the 24x7 convenience stores selling state-subsidized oxygen tanks which had sprouted all over the city. Despite the subsidy, these were well beyond the means of wage labourers, so it wasn't uncommon to see groups of workers and families purchase just a single tank every week—to be rationed amongst them. The downside to this, inevitably, was that members of these groups began to fight among themselves over the amount of oxygen they were getting. People began to kill each other for oxygen.

The streets were filled with soldiers—they would round up and detain anyone who was disturbing the peace. In the midst of all this, Arya, out of a job and without anywhere to flee to, decided to leverage his ten years of experience working in electronics sales and applied for a job at all the oxygen-supply stores in the vicinity of his Saket apartment. After being rejected outright by all of them, he extended his search and was finally invited to interview for the position of night manager at a store in Gurgaon.

The proprietor, a surly man in his fifties, asked him what he hoped to get out of the job. In an attempt to humour him, Arya eschewed the obvious response, and stated that he wished to open his own oxygen-supply outfit one day. Perhaps taken with the thought that people could still harbour ambition in a city beyond repair, the owner hired him on the spot.

And so, Arya began to live out a dreary, unexciting existence with nothing to look forward to beyond his pay cheque. He had no immediate family and all his friends had left the city. The only bright spot of his day was when he came to work at sunset and watched his employer's daughter leave the building. She was beautiful, and he sensed a certain sadness in her that made her seem like a kindred spirit. He constantly fantasized about their occupying the emptiness in each other's hearts.

On most days she would smile at him. On better days, they would talk for a few minutes.

Everything changed one evening when she asked him if he wished to have a meal with her before his shift started. There had been a supply shock due to government inefficiencies and the price of oxygen tanks had risen manifold. This, in turn, had reduced the footfall in the store considerably and had led to more derelicts clamouring outside. Arya was easily convinced to steal an hour away for dinner.

For the first time in a while, he was able to open up to another person. As they sat down in the air-locked delicatessen on the corner, they exchanged notes on their lives. They competed for each other's sympathy and had the self-awareness to laugh about it. After the meal, as they strapped on their oxygen tanks in the establishment's vestibule, she kissed him on the cheek before putting on her gas mask.

One dinner led to another, and soon a courtship began. He began to envision a life for himself beyond the smoky, neon-drenched nights and sanitary white walls of the store. In his mind, their relationship had blossomed as a direct consequence of their mutual desire to find beauty amidst the squalour of the city. He had expected the sensation of love to be a lot more tranquil. However, it had hit him like a surge of electricity. It made him feel invincible and in control of his destiny. He knew, somehow, that everything about his life was going to change.

They began to spend a lot more time with each other. They began to discuss a future together. Just then, there was another massive financial crash; the government raised the price of oxygen tanks in order to pay for all the new costs it had to incur. Supplies began to become sporadic. She had been spending nights at his place and one morning, before heading off to work, she told him that she couldn't see a life for them at the store, given the constant fluctuation in supplies. When he said he was open to alternatives, she suggested that they run away to another city. He felt they couldn't afford to flee on their current savings. She then said she had an idea of how they might raise the funds they would require.

She knew a local politician, rumoured to be the scion of a crime family, who was interested in building a stockpile of tanks. As it seemed likely that the government's supplies would be exhausted indefinitely in the near future, he would be sitting on a veritable goldmine. She left it to Arya to guess the rest of the plan. He didn't hesitate for too long. Anything to ensure a comfortable future together.

He went by himself to meet the politician the following week. He drove to a huge estate in Sultanpur that was enclosed in a transparent silicon dome. The politician, a louche man with an intense gaze, dictated his terms imperiously. Arya, visibly nervous and lacking a pre-planned negotiation strategy, accepted his offer. For the cost of delivering regular shipments to this man's associates, he would be paid a generous monthly sum. Upon leaving the estate, he shook off his guilt at having struck a Faustian bargain with a gangster. The real crime would have been to not take advantage of this opportunity, condemning him and his girlfriend to a bleak and hopeless life.

He started siphoning off supplies through the fire exit in the storeroom, a blind spot for the security camera. He made drop-offs once a week, accounting for the difference in sales in the ledger upon payment at the end of each month. He'd pocket the difference between the retail price and the politician's price and deposit the rest of the funds in the store's account. In this way, he convinced himself that he wasn't really stealing because the accounts showed that the tanks were still being sold at their legitimate price. Of course, this would result in him routinely telling regular paying customers that they were out of stock—an understandable excuse given the economic environment.

When the money began to pour in, they decided to buy a safe to keep it in. The safe was placed in her apartment as the building she lived in had better security than his. Arya didn't spend his earnings on anything other than his daily necessities, only splurging a little every now and then on a bar of chocolate or a bouquet of natural flowers. His girlfriend, on the other hand, had different ideas. As their finances improved, in addition to trading in her old phone for a newer, multiscreen monstrosity, she bought herself a gold necklace. After a round of bitter arguments wherein Arya tried to impress upon her the need to keep a low profile and not show signs of sudden wealth, she broke down in a torrent of tears and apologized for her profligacy. Unable to bear the sight of her crying, he hugged her and apologized for being harsh. She made him promise that he would never let them be caught, and he would do whatever it took to protect her. Rashly, in a fit of ill-advised gallantry, he promised that if they were ever caught, he would shoulder all responsibility. She had saved him from the purgatory of his life, and in return he would be her saviour.

His promise was tested sooner than he expected. The proprietor of the store was not a believer in coincidence. First, during a routine check of the accounts, he had noticed the high level of month-end sales. Second, given that he hadn't increased his daughter's salary in years, her new high spending habits made him suspicious. This led him to view the security camera footage, which had recorded her regular meetings with Arya during his shifts.

After waiting outside the storeroom for three consecutive nights, he finally apprehended Arya as he wheeled out the tanks in the early morning— on his way to make a delivery. As Arya wasn't exactly gifted with a fertile imagination, he had trouble coming up with a suitable explanation. His attempts at equivocation failed as soon as his employer summarized his understanding of their crime and made a reference to the collusion between Arya and his daughter. Arya proclaimed that he was singularly at fault and that she had nothing to do with the operation. The owner, resisting the impulse to exonerate his flesh and blood, declared that this was now a matter for the authorities to decide. At that point, Arya's instinct for self-preservation as well as the promise he'd made his girlfriend came together in a potent combination—and he lunged at his employer in a fury. A violent tussle ensued, during which he overpowered the older man easily, tearing off his gas mask and strangling him to death.

Soon after, Arya landed on his girlfriend's doorstep in a state of panicked exhilaration. It was time for their great escape. When he relayed the events of the previous hour to her, she withdrew from him, repulsed. She said she never wanted to see him again. His repeated cries of 'I did it for us' had little effect. Broken, dejected, and wracked with guilt, he left after telling her that their money was hers to keep.

He rushed to his apartment and packed his things. Before driving towards the city's outer limits, he decided to make a final stop. In preparation for a life in hiding, he would need all the oxygen he could carry. In the dense night smog, the street lights resembled a swarm of spirits standing aside for him, complicit in his descent. About a block away from the store, he could see a crowd of white vehicles belonging to the gendarmerie. He got out of his car and stealthily made his way forward. As he got closer, he was shattered by what he saw outside the store. Weeping profusely, his girlfriend was making a statement to the police. Someone was by her side, holding her hand. It was him. The politician. The dealmaker.

He took a deep breath. Tried to calm himself. The indignity of being cuckolded. The humiliation of being a pawn in their game.

As Arya staggered back into the shadows, he realized there was only one thing left for him to do. A permanent escape would be the best revenge. He took off his mask and tank and gifted them to a group of squatters at the nearest traffic light. He then started walking east towards the smudged dawn, leaving behind the ugliness of a doomed world. He felt in control again. As the sun began to slowly rise, he drifted away with the remains of the night.

9

THE TEETH ON THE BUS GO ROUND AND ROUND

DINESH DEVARAJAN

About a week after he died, Appa sauntered towards Amma's closed second floor window and whistled loudly with his fingers in his mouth. Still whistling, he clambered up the ladder, leapt lightly into her dreams and began to do improbable things: mixed martial arts fights to the death in a cage; driving a blood red Ferrari through a stop light with a hooker on his lap; sitting in the audience of a reality TV dance show, cheering and clapping as young children onstage, with excessive make-up and bling, sang, danced, and thrust their hips suggestively at the camera. He rested on his haunches while gnawing at the entrails of a groaning, dying deer, pausing from time to time to look up, smile, and wink at her through blood-soaked bifocals.

'It was disgusting,' Amma woke me up and told me. 'Your father is now a repulsive man.' Then she went back to sleep, the pills quickly pulling her under. I lay awake and uncomfortable. The Appa I knew had been very different.

He had been fifty when he passed away. A physics professor at the University of Pondicherry for the last twenty-three years of his life. He spent Monday to Friday living alone in Pondicherry then came home to us in Chennai for the weekend. He had wanted us to stay back in Chennai because it was a bigger city—the schools were better and his family was close by. He was a simple man with simple needs: a good book, South Indian vegetarian cooking, intelligent conversation with a few close friends, and visits to his mother and brothers on Sunday.

Squinting at me through thick lenses, he would bleat out long lectures on the dangers of smoking and drinking. He was forever chiding me to master high school physics, chemistry, and mathematics because there was no future in the world for a middle-class Indian boy who did not excel in these subjects. He wouldn't buy a scooter and brave the roads of Chennai because he did not want to die from a head injury. How ironic that he died from a brain tumour in the end.

You would think that such a man would, in his younger days, have quietly waited for his parents to find him the right girl from the same community and then marry her. Instead, he ran away with my mother, much to the displeasure of her parents and to the surprise of his. After doing one bold thing in his life, he felt he had used up his quota of luck. His life after his wedding was completely devoid of risk.

Now he was dead.

Later that night he visited Amma again—this time with a Panama hat placed at a rakish angle on his head, smiling and winking as he smoked a cigarette. He blew a heart of smoke in her direction and followed it up with an arrow. He then squatted and ground out the glowing tip on a used condom that lay on the floor. The burning latex smelt of everything forbidden. Middle-class vegetarians in Chennai never did anything forbidden. Amma woke up and nestled close to me.

'Hold me,' she whimpered, and then told me about the condom. I blushed. She placed her head on my chest. I put a self-conscious arm around her shoulder and executed the series of instructions that my brain gave: raise one hand, place it on her shoulder, and gently pull her in. I stared at the ceiling fan.

A car growled softly as it entered the street, its headlights directed momentarily at our second floor bedroom window as it negotiated a speed breaker. The beam projected the shadow of the window grill on to the opposite wall—a black lattice on a yellow background. Nine along the length and six along the breadth made fifty-four squares. There was a time when I would have counted each individual square. Now I simply multiplied the row and the column and felt evolved.

Who was I kidding? The holy trinity of physics, mathematics, and chemistry made me feel like an idiot. The board exams were less than three weeks away and I still knew nothing. My classmates would blaze down the runway and take off towards countries with clean roads, low but educated populations, and high standards of living. I would splutter towards the end of the runway and then sit there blinking, dazed, and confused in the sunlight.

As the light of the car faded, I noticed a curved smudge of dirt on the face of the ceiling fan. As the fan whirled, it looked like a brown street dog furiously chasing its tail. My perfectionist mother, the one who spent her weekends up on the stepladder cleaning the fans with gritted teeth, was now shaking soundlessly in my arms.

She had always been the more alive of the two of us. She quivered at the world's injustices like the plucked string of a sitar. She was sensuously aware of life's pleasures and equally horrified at its capacity to maim and hurt. She would fight and demand what was rightfully hers; be triumphant in her success and bitter in her failures.

I led a more anaesthetized existence, unwilling to thrust myself into the world. I preferred the shadows where I was less likely to embarrass myself.

I remembered when I was not more than eight, a man had thrust his hand into my mother's purse on a crowded bus. She caught hold of his wrist, boxed his ears, kneed him in the groin, and tore his collar while I stared at the floor embarrassed by the unblinking stares of other men. Then she yelled at the same men while the other women roughed up the pickpocket a little more and kicked him off the bus.

I remembered an earlier time, perhaps when I was six, when my mother was up on the stepladder cleaning the blades of the fan in the hall. I was in the bathroom watching with strange fascination as my grandmother's maroon nine-yard sari churned inside the top loading washing machine.

The nine-yard sari is different from the more common six-yard sari. The six-yard sari is a multipurpose miracle. It can be worn to high-powered meetings at the office, to tend to the pressure cooker in the kitchen, to go shopping at the market, or to work in the fields. Worn a certain way, it can play havoc with the male mind: a gossamer curtain fluttering coyly over the navel; draped sensuously around the body, outlining the bosom and the buttocks while revealing the delicious curve of the waist. The nine-yard sari on the other hand, sent out only one message: I am a respectable, pious woman with only God on my mind.

My father's mother only wore the nine-yard sari. It wrapped around the body and shoulders completely obscuring the curves beneath. Too large to be washed with the other clothes, it had its own private forty-five-minute cycle. I watched the sari—thick, wet, and heavy—as it groaned and drowned in the washing machine's barrel of soapy water. There was something hypnotizing about the hum of the washing machine and the slow, weary revolution of sodden cloth. On an impulse, I dipped my arm up to the elbow into the warm, sudsy water of the barrel. The bubbles fizzed on my arm. I smiled. Then the sari, so placid until then, suddenly gripped my arm like an anaconda. It slithered and coiled around my fingers, my wrist, my forearm and then slowly but surely began to twist. I screamed as the cloth wrenched my arm. Amma fell off the ladder in shock and twisted her ankle.

'Aiyyo!' she cried.

'Aiyyayo!' I yelled as my grandmother's sari began to swallow me.

She scrambled to her feet, limped hurriedly to the bathroom, and yanked the plug. The machine stopped with a jerk. I whimpered, shoulder deep in my grandmother's sari.

'Are you okay?' she gasped.

I nodded. She stroked my cheek and then tapped me lightly on the side of my head. 'Idiot!'

She hopped on one leg and uncoiled the sari from my arm. I shook and inhaled a mixture of snot and tears.

Now, as I held her, I could feel a nameless dread snake its way through her body. The keening desperation of loss. The total annihilation of her life as she knew it. I sensed it all and felt weak inside. There my mother was, a child crying in my arms. I was at the moment protector, provider, and navigator. The role felt uncomfortable—artificial. A mask of responsibility pressed against my unwilling face. Seventeen is not a good age for manhood.

There was a ceremony on the thirteenth day after Appa's death, a ceremony that signified that he had finally left earth to join his gods and his Brahmin ancestors at Vaikuntam. Amma had stumbled through it in a daze, clutching the hands of those who came, weeping by herself in the balcony, or silently staring at the clock in the hall. Then, the day after the ceremony ended, everyone who had remained left, muttering excuses about work, children, and exams. Each departure caused Amma heartache and tears. The last one to leave had been Govind Chitappa, my father's younger brother. His departure had particularly disturbed Amma. Govind Chitappa shared Appa's mannerisms. He had his smile and his gait. He had been with us for over a month. She held his hand and asked him to stay longer. He shook his head sadly and picked up his bags. He was a dentist in Goa and he had patients waiting.

'Stay, stay another week,' she whimpered and tried to drag him back.

'I'll visit soon; I promise,' he mumbled and pulled his hand away. The door closed. Then it was just Amma and me.

I went back to my room, opened a few textbooks and stared at the writing. I wanted to purée the pages and drip-irrigate the dry, dusty plains of my brain. I was the son of a school biology teacher and a college physics professor, yet my intellectual inheritance was an empty wind whistling between my ears. My crotch stubbornly demanded that I masturbate. Masturbate because it was pleasurable. Masturbate because it could be done on autopilot. Masturbate because for five minutes it let me forget my difficulties. Therefore, I masturbated, willing imaginary attractive women to bend and curve to my pleasure. They came hesitantly and flickered the entire time they were there.

When it was over, I washed my hands and dried them as best as I could on the damp towel on the rack that had not been changed in weeks. The eyes that stared back at me from the mirror were dull. Reality started throbbing at the back of my head. Death. Death. Death. Exams. Exams. Exams.

My mother taught in the same school I studied in from the sixth standard all the way to the twelfth. It was pure torture for us. Nothing my teachers told me seemed to get through or feel important enough to retain. Paralysed by doubt and insecurity, I drifted listlessly towards my final board exams.

For a brief period, my parents sent me to tuition classes. That did not help. I wafted along, embarrassing my mother—whose colleagues made comments behind her back—and scaring my principal with the very real prospect of being the first student in the long, glorious history of the school to fail the board exams. In the past, similar students had been shoved towards the door and roughly asked to try another school, but because my mother was beloved, I was reluctantly allowed to carry on. Did I miss my father? I did not know. The question seemed too large, too complicated to answer. Was I going to disappoint him in the board exams? Most definitely so.

The evening before I returned to school, my grandfather sent for me. Relations between my mother's parents and my father's had always been frosty. They had wanted her to marry the son of a prominent industrialist and she had run away with a small town physics professor. I was the idiot product of that union. My grandmother had stayed home but my grandfather had come to the cremation and not uttered a word. He was a thin, stern man with an erect military bearing, who believed that discipline and hard work were all one needed to manage the difficulties the world threw at you. Orphaned at the age of three, and passed from relative to relative until he was sixteen, he found a job at BSNL and climbed the government corporate ladder until he headed the local telephone department. When he built his house with his own money, he did not trust the mason with the cost of the raw material. He bought the cement and sand after negotiating with the wholesaler himself, and would travel fifteen kilometres back and forth each day with the sacks piled up on his bicycle carrier until the house was completed. He had no patience with people who dilly-dallied, made mistakes, or did not follow orders.

Now he sat me down.

'How are the preparations for your exams coming along?' He stared at me with his piercing eyes that sat below two formidable, wiggling, cotton caterpillars that he used for eyebrows. A deep groove ran between his brows. I grinned uncertainly. He did not smile back.

'Do you expect to score a hundred in each subject? Because nothing less than a centum will do.'

I made a non-committal noise. He rubbed his palms and looked up at the ceiling fan. 'I've been thinking about your mother.' He stood up and went to the bedroom window. He wore a blue cotton shirt and an elegant veshti. He gazed outside and said nothing for a few minutes. Then he turned around. 'Your mother needs a distraction, something to do so that she does not go out of her mind.'

My grandfather stuck his hand in his mouth and pulled out his teeth. I stared at him horrified. His face had deflated in front of my eyes. He was an old man with a soggy, spent balloon for a mouth.

'Does not fit as well as it used to,' his mouth gulped, slurped, and quivered gummily. 'Hurts to talk or eat.'

The skin below his jaw hung slack, then jiggled. He put the dentures back into his mouth and it was like watching a video of a collapsing building in reverse. Once again his face had lines and edges.

'I had my dentist fit me out for a new pair.' He rubbed his jaw and winced. 'Bloody expensive. I looked at the bill and asked him whether my teeth had been cast from melted gold!' He grimaced and shook his head.

'I want your mother to pick them up from the dentist this week. It took him over a month to get them ready. I want her to pay me a visit with my teeth. Then we will talk about what she wants to do now with her life. Can she run the house on a teacher's income? Can she pay for your college? Your father was not a rich man. I do not want her to suffer.'

'I never knew you had dentures,' I blurted. He paused and considered my question.

'Have had them for twenty years. With these I can gnaw the bark off a tree if I want to.'

'Can I see them?'

'Here.' He pulled them out again, wiped them with a towel, and handed them to me. I took them in my hand and examined them closely. Each incisor, canine, premolar, and molar was a work of art, each tooth a white gem set in a roseate foundation. I wanted to ask him how he brushed his teeth and whether he could tell if there was a strand stuck between them. Why did he never smile even when in possession of such perfection?

'Very nice!' I looked at them one last time, and as I handed them back, the dentures slipped from my palm, fell soundlessly through the air, and shattered on the ground. Lacquered pieces of pink and white littered the floor. A single jagged tooth scooted out of the door and into the hall where my grandmother stepped on it and yelped.

My grandfather looked sombrely at the floor, his mouth a dour, listless mass of flesh. He shook his head and mumbled. 'Please ask your mother to hurry.'

I relayed the request to my mother and it was as if a tiny ray of sunshine had been allowed to penetrate the gloom. 'Appa,' she whispered, 'my appa will help me.'

She went to school the next morning, her first day back after Appa died. She came back in the evening in a rage, 'There's nothing worse than the sympathy of married women!' she spat. 'I couldn't bear the looks on the faces of the teachers!'

I looked up from the practice test paper and gave up trying to answer the question it posed.

She simmered for a few minutes and then went to freshen up. She drank her coffee and then took the bus to the dentist's office. She picked up the wrapped dentures, thanked him, and walked to the bus stop. She got into the bus, stared listlessly out of the window, missed her stop, and then got off the bus. She walked back home in a daze, prepared dinner, and opened the handbag. The teeth were missing.

When at home, my father would wear a faded white vest with faint stains and a white veshti below. The veshti was almost transparent from overuse and it gently brushed the floor as he shuffled around the house.

'Shall I ask the maid to stop coming?' my mother would hiss through gritted teeth. 'Why pay her salary when you can walk around the house and swab the floors clean?'

In response, Appa would shrug and attempt to tighten the veshti. In order to do this he would first lift his vest and tuck the bottom edge under his chin, before opening the veshti so he could tie it better; when he did this he would flash whoever was in the house, affording them a brief glimpse of his underwear. He would then wrap the veshti higher and tighter around his stomach. Then he would let go of the vest. The veshti would hold for a few minutes before making a slow but determined journey back towards the ground. I never dared to wear a veshti as I associated it with a certain middle-class, middle-aged tiredness. I also carried a deathly fear that it would unravel around my pencil waist, slither down my legs, and leave me exposed in front of an unimpressed audience.

Yet when Appa came to me to my in dream that night, he wore a black cowboy hat, black cowboy boots, shiny leather pants, white suspenders stretched over a taut, muscular body, and a tattoo on his back, of a winking hooded cobra whose tongue pleasured a woman. On his ears were concentric rings that jingled in unison with the spurs on his boots as he walked around the house. I heard him and felt comforted. He came into my room and sat down next to me. This ridiculous caricature was now my father. It felt good to sit next to him. Perhaps that is how I knew I missed him.

'Ah! Have to use the bathroom!' he grinned and left. I did not want him to go away so I stood outside the bathroom door. I heard him unbuckle his belt and sit down. He whistled and then stopped. 'I often wondered you know...' his voice came to me muffled through the door. 'Is a good satisfying shit the same as anal sex? '

He came out and I knew he had not bothered to wash his hands. He walked back into my room, picked up my mock physics exam paper and studied it with a sardonic smile on his face. He pursed his lips, dropped the paper on the floor, then stood up and began to walk out of the room. 'You're going to fail....'

Darkness began to swirl around me. I called out to him and beseeched him to come back. He turned around and smiled evilly. His teeth glowed white and the darkness dissipated 'unless you make a simple phone call'.

∽

The telephone rang the next evening and I heard my grandfather's voice snuffle wetly through the speaker. 'I drank a dosa chutney milkshake for dinner because of you. Do you know what it is like to consume something that is meant to be hot and crispy through a tumbler? Where are my teeth?'

'Tomorrow. She will come tomorrow,' I quavered.

My mother blanched.

The telephone rang again the evening after. 'Your grandmother is limping around the streets telling the neighbours that I bit her foot. Where are my teeth?'

My mother sagged. She stared intently at the floor as if trying to make up her mind. Then she stood up straight. 'Come with me.'

'The physics exam is tomorrow.'

'What are you going to accomplish in two hours that you haven't in seven years? Come. I cannot do this alone.'

I went with her.

Depending on how you looked at it, Amma's plan was either bizarrely straightforward or straightforwardly bizarre. She had taken the 23C bus from the dentist's office. Therefore, she would board every 23C bus in the city and search both over and under the seats until she found the teeth.

I tried not to turn away when she explained her intention in strident tones to the bus conductors and drivers taking their rest at the terminus. They scratched and shook their heads. She turned around without waiting for anyone's permission and made her way towards where the buses were parked.

The driver closest to me caught my hand as I began to make my exit. 'Listen, brother. How do you know it is on the bus in the first place? What if there had been a pickpocket on the bus that day? Some rash idiot who did not know what he had stolen?'

'I don't know,' I mumbled and pulled away.

His voice followed me on the way out. 'The numbers on the buses are not fixed. You could stick your head under the seat of a 23C sitting in the Adyar terminus right now but someone could be having his arse bitten on a 47A in West Mambalam as we speak....'

I walked to the 23C bus and climbed inside. Passengers stared curiously at Amma as she crawled along the floor of the bus on her hands and knees. I joined her. We crawled along the dusty length of the bus and prayed for a skeletal smile to greet us in the darkness.

'What has my life come to?' she whispered to me as I craned my neck. 'Why am I here?'

'The dentures.'

'No. Where is your father now? What is he doing? I need to know!'

The passengers stared at us.

'He was supposed to retire in a few years! Supposed to stop this mad back and forth between Chennai and Pondicherry! Twenty years spent sitting on a government bus. He should have come home. He should have lived in a house where he could have been looked after. We had plans to travel, buy a car—to finally start living our lives after two decades of living apart. And now what is left? Where did all that slogging take us? He is dead and I am alone!'

Perhaps I should have held my mother, maybe given her a hug, but she was so fierce, so angry, so bursting with rage that it made more sense to hug an exploding gas cylinder. I sat there on the floor and screwed my face into an expression of virtuous understanding. The conductor boarded the bus and threw us out. We walked back home slowly and now I thought of what Appa told me in that dream.

The next day we took the evening bus to my grandfather's house. My mother was nervous. I held her hand, stared out of the window and felt a strange, fierce joy in my heart. My grandfather sat outside on the veranda, hidden behind the evening paper. The headlines read: *Papers leaked! Board exams across the country to be postponed by six months!*

In tinier font: 'Late last evening the Central Board of Secondary Education received an anonymous phone call that all copies of all the papers had been leaked.'

We heard the sound of grinding and chewing. My grandfather abruptly folded the paper and saw us. He smiled and dazzled us with his teeth. He nodded at the two chairs next to him. We sat down confused.

He offered us a plate of murukku. 'Freshly made by your grandmother. Nice, hot, and crisp. Enjoy!'

'The dentures...' I began.

'Left at the counter of the dentist's office. I went and picked it up myself. The state of mind your mother was in, I don't blame her.'

My grandmother limped out of the house and looked at us with approval. My mother leaned into her father. He put his arm around her and together they were silent.

10

THE ADIVASI WILL NOT DANCE

HANSDA SOWVENDRA SHEKHAR

They pinned me to the ground. They did not let me speak, they did not let me protest, they did not even let me raise my head and look at my fellow musicians and dancers as they were being beaten up by the police. All I could hear were their cries for mercy. I felt sorry for them. I had failed them. Because what I did, I did on my own. Yet, did I have a choice? Had I only spoken to them about my plan, I am sure they would have stood by me. For they too suffer, the same as I. They would have stood by me, they would have spoken up with me and, together, our voices would have rung out loud. They would have travelled out of our Santhal Pargana, out of our Jharkhand, all the way to Dilli and all of Bharot-disom; the world itself would have come to know of our suffering. Then, perhaps, something would have been done for us. Then, perhaps, our President would have agreed with what I said to him.

But I did not share my plan with anyone. I went ahead alone, like a fool. They grabbed me, beat me to the ground, put their hands on my mouth, and gagged me. I felt so helpless and so foolish.

But we Santhals are fools, aren't we? All of us Adivasis are fools. Down the years, down generations, the Diku have taken advantage of our foolishness. Tell me if I am wrong.

I only said, 'We Adivasis will not dance any more'—what is wrong with that? We are like toys—someone presses our 'ON' button, or turns a key in our backsides, and we Santhals start beating rhythms on our tamak and tumdak, or start blowing tunes on our tiriyo while someone snatches away our very dancing grounds. Tell me, am I wrong?

I had not expected things to go so wrong. I thought I was speaking to the best man in India, our President. I had thought he would listen to my words. Isn't he our neighbour? His forefathers were all from Birbhum district next door. His ancestral house still stands in Birbhum, where Rabin-haram lived in harmony with Santhals. I have been to that place Rabin-haram set up. What is it called? Yes, Santiniketan. I went there a long time ago, to perform with my troupe. I saw that we Santhals are held in high regard in Santiniketan. Santiniketan is in Birbhum and our President is also from Birbhum. He should have heard me speak, no? But he didn't.

Such a fool I am! A foolish Santhal. A foolish Adivasi.

My name is Mangal Murmu. I am a musician. No, wait...I am a farmer. Perhaps it should be: was a farmer. Was a farmer is right. Because I don't farm any more. In my village of Matiajore, in Amrapara block of the Pakur district, not many Santhals farm any more. Only a few of us still have farmland; most of it has been acquired by a mining company. It is a rich company. It is not that we didn't fight the acquisition. We did. While we were fighting, this political leader came, that political leader came, this Kiristan sister came, that Kiristan father came. Apparently to support us. But we lost. And after we lost, everyone left. The leaders went back to Ranchi and Dilli or wherever they had to go. The Kiristans returned to their missions. But our land did not come back to us. On the other hand, a Kiristan sister was killed and our boys were implicated in her murder. The papers, the media, everyone blamed our boys. They reported that the Kiristan sister was fighting for our rights and yet our boys killed her. No one bothered to see that our boys had been fighting for our land and rights even before that Kiristan sister came. Why would they kill her? Just because our boys did not have reporter friends, their fight went unseen; while the Kiristan sister, with her network of missionaries and their friends, got all the attention. Now that our boys are in jail on false charges of murder, who will fight for us? Where are the missionaries and their friends now? If the missionaries are our well-wishers and were fighting for us, why did they run away? Kill a well-known Kiristan sister, accuse a few unknown Santhal boys fighting for their lands of her murder, move both obstacles—the Kiristan sister and the Santhal boys—out of the way, grab as much land as possible, dig as many mines as possible, and extract all the coal. This is how this coal company works. Is this scenario so difficult to understand that the media does not get it?

If coal merchants have taken a part of our lands, the other part has been taken over by stone merchants, all Diku—Marwari, Sindhi, Mandal,

Bhagat, Muslim. They turn our land upside down, inside out, with their heavy machines. They sell the stones they mine from our earth in faraway places—Dilli, Noida, Panjab. This coal company and these quarry owners, they earn so much money from our land. They have built big houses for themselves in town; they wear nice clothes; they send their children to good schools in faraway places; when sick, they get themselves treated by the best doctors in Ranchi, Patna, Bhagalpur, Malda, Bardhaman, Kolkata. What do we Santhals get in return? Tatters to wear. Barely enough food. Such diseases that we can't breathe properly, we cough up blood, and forever remain bare bones.

For education, our children are at the mercy of either those free government schools where teachers come only to cook the midday meal, or those Kiristan missionary schools where our children are constantly asked to stop worshipping our Bonga-Buru and start revering Jisu and Mariam. If our children refuse, the sisters and the fathers tell our boys that their Santhal names—Hopna, Som, Singrai—are not good enough. They are renamed David and Mikail and Kiristofer and whatnot. And as if that were not enough, Muslims barge into our homes, sleep with our women, and we Santhal men can't do a thing.

But what can we do? They outnumber us. Village after village in our Santhal Pargana—which should have been a home for us Santhals—are turning into Muslim villages. Hindus live around Pakur town or in other places. Those few Hindus here, who live in Santhal villages, belong to the lower castes. They, too, are powerless and outnumbered. But why would the Hindus help us? The rich Hindus living in Pakur town are only interested in our land. They are only interested in making us sing and dance at their weddings. If they come to help us, they will say that we Santhals need to stop eating cow meat and pig meat, that we need to stop drinking haandi. They, too, want to make us forget our traditional religion, convert us into Safa-Hor, and swell their numbers to become more valuable vote banks. Safa-Hor, the pure people, the clean people, but certainly not as clean and pure as themselves, that's for sure. Always a little less than they are. In the eyes of the Hindus, we Santhals can only either be Kiristan or the almost Safa-Hor. We are losing our traditional faith, our identities, and our roots. We are becoming people from nowhere.

It's the coal and the stone, sir; they are making us lazy. The Koyla Road runs through our village. When the monstrous Hyvas ferry coal on the Koyla Road, there is no space for any other vehicle. They are so rough, these truck drivers, they can run down any vehicle that comes in their way. They can't help it, it's their job. The more rounds they make, the more money they earn. And what if they kill? The coal company can't afford to have its business slowed down by a few deaths. They give money to the family of the dead, the matter remains unreported, and the driver goes scot-free, ferrying another load for the company.

And we Santhals? Well, we wait for when there is NO ENTRY on the Koyla Road, the stipulated time when heavy trucks are not allowed to ply on the road so they have to stop somewhere. For that is when all our men, women and children come out on to the road and swarm up these Hyvas. Then, using nails, fingers, hands, and whatever tools we can manage, we steal coal. The drivers can't stop us, nor can those pot-bellied Bihari security guards posted along the Koyla Road by the company. For they know that if they do not allow us to steal the coal, we will gherao the road and not let their trucks move.

But a few stolen quintals, when the company is mining tonnes and tonnes, hardly matters. They know that if we—the descendants of the great rebels Sido and Kanhu—make up our minds, we can stop all business in the area. So they behave sensibly, practically. After all, they already have our land, they are already stealing our coal, they don't want to snatch away from us our right to re-steal it.

It is this coal, sir, which is gobbling us up bit by bit. There is a blackness—deep, indelible—all along the Koyla Road. The trees and shrubs in our village bear black leaves. Our ochre earth has become black. The stones, the rocks, the sand, all black. The tiles on the roofs of our huts have lost their fire-burnt red. The vines and flowers and peacocks we Santhals draw on the outer walls of our houses are black. Our children—dark-skinned as they are—are forever covered with fine black dust. When they cry, and tears stream down their faces, it seems as if a river is cutting across a drought-stricken land. Only our eyes burn red, like embers. Our children hardly go to school. But everyone—whether they attend school or not—remains on the alert, day and night, for ways to steal coal and for ways to sell it.

Santhals don't understand business. We get the coal easy yet we don't charge much for it; only enough for food, clothes, and drink. But these Jolha—you call them Muslim, we, Jolha—they know the value of coal, they know the value of money. They charge the price that is best for them. And the farther coal travels from Matiajore, the higher its price becomes.

A decade earlier, when the Santhals of Matiajore were beginning their annual journey to sharecrop in the farms of Namal, four Jolha families turned up from nowhere and asked us for shelter. A poor lot, they looked as impoverished as us. Perhaps worse. In return, they offered us their services. They told us that they would look after our fields in our absence and farm them for a share of the produce. We trusted them. They started working on our fields and built four huts in a distant corner of Matiajore. Today, that small cluster of four huts has grown into a tola of more than a hundred houses. Houses, not huts. While we Santhals, in our own village, still live in our mud houses, each Jolha house has at least one brick wall and a cemented yard. This tola is now called the Jolha tola of Matiajore.

Once, Matiajore used to be an exclusively Santhal village. Today, it has a Santhal tola and a Jolha tola, with the latter being bigger. Sometimes I wonder who the olposonkhyok is here. These Jolha are hard-working, and they are always united. They may fight among themselves, they may break each other's scalps for petty matters, they may file FIRs against each other at the thana, they may drag each other to court; but if any non-Jolha says even one offensive word to a Jolha, the entire Jolha tola gets together against that person. Jolha leaders from Pakur and Sahebganj and elsewhere come down to express solidarity. And we Santhals? Our men are beaten up, thrown into police lock-ups, into jails, for flimsy reasons, and on false charges. Our women are raped, some sell their bodies on Koyla Road. Most of us are fleeing our places of birth. How united are we? Where are *our* Santhal leaders? Those chor-chuhad leaders, where are they?

Forgive me. What can I do? I cannot help it. I am sixty years old and, sitting in this lock-up after being beaten black and blue, I have no patience any more. Only anger. So, what was I saying? Yes, there are no shouters, no powerful voice among us Santhals. And we Santhals have no money—though we are born on lands under which are buried riches. We Santhals do not know how to protect our riches. We only know how to escape.

That is probably why thousands of Santhals from distant corners of Pakur district and elsewhere in the Santhal Pargana board trains to Namal every farming season. They are escaping.

Did I tell you I was once a farmer? Once. My sons farm now. The eldest stays back to work our fields while the other two migrate seasonally to Namal, along with their families. I used to compose songs. I still do. And I still maintain a dance troupe. Though it is not a regular one, the kind I had earlier, some fifteen—twenty years ago, when I was younger and full of energy, enthusiasm, and hope. Matiajore, Patharkola, Amrapara—I had singers and dancers and musicians from all these villages. I used to compose songs and set them to music. And my troupe, young men and women, they used to bring my songs to life through their dances, through their voices, through the rhythms of the tamale and the tumdak, and the trilling of the tiriyo and the banam.

At that time, our Santhal Pargana was not broken up into so many districts. Today, the Diku have broken up our Santhal Pargana for their own benefit. If it suits them, they can go on breaking down districts and create a district measuring just ten feet by ten feet. At that time, when I was younger, even Jharkhand had not been broken off from Bihar. There used to be so much hope. We used to perform in our village, in neighbouring villages, in Pakur, in Dumka, in Sahebganj, in Deoghar, in Jamtara, in Patna, in Ranchi, even in Kolkata, and in Bhubaneshwar, where we were taken to see the sea at Puri. What a sight it was! We performed in Godda, too. Godda, where my daughter, Mugli, was married. We used to be paid money. We used to be given good food, awarded medals, and shields, and certificates. We used to be written about in the papers.

All that has changed now. First, all the members of my troupe are old. Some have even died. Many have migrated, or migrate seasonally. The ones who remain hum songs, sing to each other, but a stage performance? No, not again. Like me, even they are tired, disillusioned. All our certificates and shields, what did they give us? Diku children go to schools and colleges, get education, jobs. What do we Santhals get? We Santhals can sing and dance, and we are good at our art. Yet, what has our art given us? Displacement, tuberculosis.

I have turned sixty. Perhaps more. I am called Haram now. Haram, respectfully. I have started wearing thick glasses. Even my hearing has weakened. Though my voice is still quite good. People in my village say that my voice still impresses them. Sometimes they ask me to sing. I sing some of my old compositions. It makes them happy. I still compose songs. Not many. Maybe one song every six or eight months. One song of just six to eight lines. And because I had some fame in the past, I am still invited to perform at public functions in Pakur and Dumka and Ranchi.

I keep putting together new troupes, though the members constantly change. I have a dancer today, tomorrow he is growing potatoes for some Bangali zamindar in Bardhaman. So I have to replace him with some other dancer. Two days later, the original dancer returns. So I have to replace the substitute. This is how my troupes work nowadays. But I keep it going because it brings us some money. And when we are hosted in towns, we are usually fed good food. So we perform.

Our music, our dance, our songs are sacred to us Santhals. But hunger and poverty have driven us to sell what is sacred to us. When my boys perform at a Diku wedding, I am so foolish, I expect everyone to pay attention. Which Diku pays attention to our music? Even at those high-profile functions, most Diku just wait for our performance to end. Yet, be it an athletic meet, some inauguration, or any function organized by someone high and mighty—in the name of Adivasi culture and Jharkhandi culture, it is necessary to make Adivasis dance. Even Bihari and Bangali and Odia people say that Jharkhand is theirs. They call their culture and music and dance superior to those of us Adivasi. Why don't they get their women to sing and dance in open grounds in the name of Jharkhandi culture? For every benefit, in jobs, in education, in whatever, the Diku are quick to call Jharkhand their own—let the Adivasi go to hell. But when it comes to displaying Jharkhandi culture, the onus of singing and dancing is upon the Adivasi alone.

So how did I land up in front of the President, you ask. Some three months ago, an official letter came to my house in Matiajore: a thick white envelope bearing the emblem of the government of Jharkhand. The paper on which the letter was typed in Hindi was equally thick and crisp. In fewer than five sentences I was told that the government of Jharkhand sought the pleasure of my musical performance at some event, the identity and venue of which would be communicated to me later, and that I should gather a troupe for a fifteen–twenty-minute performance, and that all participants would be paid well. The letter was signed by some high-ranking IAS officer in Ranchi.

What does a hungry man need? Food. What does a poor man need? Money. So, here I was, needing both. And recognition, too. We artistes are greedy people. We are hungry for acceptance, some acknowledgement, something to be remembered by. So, without thinking, I sent back a reply the very next day saying that, yes, I would be happy to perform. I was so happy, I went to the big post office in Pakur, more than twenty kilometres away, all by myself, to register that letter. I went in a Vikram, packed with many other Santhals like me, all going to Pakur. Nearly all of us travellers were blackened by the dust from the Koyla Road. Yet I was so happy that I did not notice it at all.

Around the time that I was preparing for our performance, selecting young men and women for my troupe, digging up old songs from memory, I was faced with a strange situation. I told you that Mugli, my daughter, is married into a family in the Godda district, didn't I? Well, she began calling me regularly on my mobile phone. I couldn't understand the situation clearly at first but it seemed to me that it had something to do with their land. Her husband was a farmer—they are a family of farmers—as are all the Santhal families in that village. There are more villages nearby, populated by Santhals, Paharias, and low-caste Hindus.

What had happened was that the district administration had asked the inhabitants of all the villages to vacate their land—their village, farms, everything. Eleven villages! Can you imagine? The first question everyone asked was: what will the sarkar do with so much land?

Initially, I thought they were all rumours. And, I thought, how can anyone force Santhals to vacate their land in the Santhal Pargana? Didn't we have the Tenancy Act to protect us?

Still, when the rumours started floating about, I went to Godda. We all marched to the block office in a huge group. The officers there assured us that they were all just rumours. The lands were safe. The villages were safe. Yet, later, police were sent to the villages. They came with written orders from the district administration. The villages would have to be vacated to make room for a thermal power plant. The villagers refused outright. Santhals, low-caste Hindus, Paharias, everyone began fighting for their land.

The district administration fought back. The agitators were all beaten up and thrown into police lock-ups. I called my daughter and her small children to Matiajore after her husband was taken away. Mugli arrived, her children and in-laws in tow. It was strange: a village which annually empties itself every few months was suddenly providing shelter to immigrants.

How would I manage to provide for all these people who were dependent on me now? How could the members of my troupe feed all those who had come to seek refuge in their houses? We needed money.

And our current—mysterious—assignment was our only hope. Despite our troubles, we kept practising.

In the meantime, some people arrived to help the villagers facing displacement in Godda. They wrote letters to the government, to people in Ranchi and Dilli. They even wrote letters to the businessman who was planning to build that thermal power plant in Godda. We heard that he was a very rich and very shrewd man. He was also a MP. We also heard that he liked polo—some game played with horses—and that his horses were far better off than all the Santhals of the whole of the Santhal Pargana.

News about the displacements taking place in Godda began to appear in newspapers and on TV after a few days. All of us tried to concentrate on our practice, but how could we sing and dance with such a storm looming ahead? In between, I received phone calls from several officers in Ranchi and Dumka and Pakur. They asked me to keep working for the show. They never forgot to remind me that this show was of the utmost importance, that we were going to perform before some very important people. Some officers from Dumka and Pakur even came to Matiajore to see if we were really practising or not. When they saw that we were really working hard, they were happy. They smiled and encouraged us, they talked to us very sweetly. So sweetly that we all wondered if they could really not see how troubled we were feeling. Many times, I felt like asking them: 'How can all of you be so indifferent? How can you expect us to sing and dance when our families are being uprooted from their villages?' At other times, I felt like asking: 'Which VIP is coming? The President of India? The President of America? You are making us Santhals dance in Pakur and you are displacing Santhals from their villages in Godda? Isn't your VIP going to see that? Doesn't your VIP read the papers or watch news on TV? We foolish Santhals can see what damage is happening around us. Doesn't your VIP see all that?'

But I stayed silent.

Reality started dawning on us three weeks before the date of our performance. First as floating rumours which were gradually confirmed by newspaper reports.

The reality was that the businessman was certainly going to set up a thermal power plant in Godda. That plant would run on coal from the mines in Pakur and Sahebganj. If needed, coal would be brought from other places. That businessman, in fact, needed electricity for the iron and steel plants he was planning to set up in Jharkhand. The plant was to be set up for his own selfish needs; but if he were to be believed, the whole of Jharkhand would receive electricity from his plant. Whole towns would be lit up non-stop, factories would never stop working for lack of power. There would be development and jobs and happiness all over. And, finally, news also reached us that the foundation stone of the plant would be laid by the President of India. We would be performing for him.

Yes, I was shocked. All of us were. Shocked and sad, but also surprised and delighted. We couldn't believe our luck. We had performed before ministers, chief ministers, and governors. But never before the President of the country!

Then we heard more news. People demonstrating and agitating against the forcible acquisition of land were being beaten up by the police, they were being thrown into lock-ups. Paramilitary forces, the CRPF, had been called in to control the situation. Four villages out of the eleven had already been razed to the ground by bulldozers to make room for the foundation-stone-laying ceremony.

But the papers carried glowing reports, along with pictures, of the roads which were being repaired or rebuilt in Ranchi and Dumka. Breathlessly, they reported that the President would stay in Jharkhand for three days. He would spend day one in Ranchi. On day two, he would preside over a university convocation in Dumka. On day three, he would visit Godda, lay the foundation stone, and fly out of Jharkhand.

We received official intimation of the event a week before it was to take place. One day before the event, we were taken to Godda by bus. The entire district, the district headquarters, was unrecognizable. A football ground had been converted into a massive helipad. There were hundreds of policemen and CRPF jawans. And everywhere we turned our heads, all we could see was a sea of people. I knew they had come to see the helicopter. Tucked away in the papers had been reports that all protestors had been detained and were being held somewhere. Perhaps my son-in-law, too, was among them.

From where I stood, the stage looked massive, but still not big enough for all the people who had climbed upon it. Ministers from Dilli and Ranchi, all dressed in their best neta clothes, laughing and chatting among themselves. All very happy with the progress, the development of the area. The Santhal Pargana would now fly to the moon. The Santhal Pargana would now turn into Dilli and Bombay. The businessman was grinning widely. Patriotic songs in Hindi were playing from the loudspeakers placed at all corners of the field. 'Bharat mahaan,' someone was shouting from the stage, trying to rouse the audience, his voice amplified by numerous loudspeakers. What mahaan? I wondered. Which great nation displaces thousands of its people from their homes and livelihoods to produce electricity for cities and factories? And jobs? What jobs? An Adivasi farmer's job is to farm. Which other job should he be made to do? Become a servant in some billionaire's factory built on land that used to belong to that very Adivasi just a week earlier?

Reporters with cameras swarmed all over the place. Three vans with huge disc antennae on their roofs were parked near the venue. I identified the logo of a popular TV channel painted on the sides of one of those vans. I wondered if any of its reporters had visited the place where the villagers were being detained by the police.

My troupe was waiting in an enclosure built specially for the performers at that event. All the women were wearing red blouses, blue lungis, and green panchhi, and huge, colourful plastic flowers in their buns. They were carrying steel lotas with flowers and leaves put inside them. All the men were wearing red football jerseys and green panchhi and had tied green gamchas around their heads. We all looked very good.

The helicopter arrived...thud thud thud thud.... Its rotors swirled up dust from the playing field. The crowd was excited and a slow roar began.

The President was accompanied by his security staff to the stage. He was a short, thoughtful man. All Bangalis look learned and thoughtful. Why should this Bangali President be any different?

The festivities began. The man who had been shouting 'Bharat mahaan' announced how fortunate the land of Jharkhand was that the iconic billionaire had deemed it suitable to set up a thermal power plant here. He didn't mention how fortunate the billionaire was that he got to come to Jharkhand, a place rich with mineral deposits beneath its earth; a naive population upon it; and a bunch of shrewd, greedy thief-leaders, officers, and businessmen who ran the state and controlled its land, people, and resources.

The 'Bharat mahaan' man announced the welcome dance and my troupe was ushered into the open space before the stage. We entered with our tamak, tumdak, tiriyo, and banam. The President seemed impressed. The businessman looked bored.

When we had taken our places before the stage, I took the mic in my hand and bowed to the President. Then I tapped the mic to check if it was working and began in Hindi, as good Hindi as I could muster at the height of my emotions. Actually, it was a miracle that I did not weep and choke up.

'Johar, Rashtrapati-babu. We are very proud and happy that you have come to our Santhal Pargana and we are also very proud that we have been asked to sing and dance before you and welcome you to our place. We will sing and dance before you, but tell us, do we have a reason to sing and dance? Do we have a reason to be happy? You will now start building the power plant, but this plant will be the end of us all, the end of all the Adivasis. These men sitting beside you have told you that this power plant will change our fortunes, but these same men have forced us out of our homes and villages. We have nowhere to go, nowhere to grow our crops. How can this power plant be good for us? And how can we Adivasis dance and be happy? Unless we are given back our homes and land, we will not sing and dance. We Adivasis will not dance. The Adivasi will not—'

11

SWIMMER AMONG THE STARS
KANISHK THAROOR

As a rule, the last speaker of a language no longer uses it. Ethnographers show up at the door with digital recorders, ready to archive every declension, each instance of the genitive, the idiosyncratic function of verbal suffixes. But this display hardly counts as normal speech. It simply confirms reality to the last speaker, that the old world of her mind is cut adrift from humans and can only be pulped into a computer. She finds it strange to listen to the sounds of her mouth. Inevitably, she mingles a more common language with her own. That common language, after all, is the speech that now keeps her company, that leads her through the market, that sits with her in the evenings by the television, that gives her the terminal diagnosis at the clinic, that pours through her letterbox, that comes in a crisp nurse's outfit to wash her feet. Her own language does nothing of the sort. It is nowhere to be found. She pauses, silent now, staring incredulously at the microphone. How am I the last speaker of my language? How can I be its keeper? My language left me.

She apologizes to the ethnographers. You must understand, she says, that though my memory is preserved better than a lemon, it is still difficult to remember which words are my own and which words are not.

Please speak as it comes naturally to you, the ethnographers say.

Thank you, I will try.

In any case, we can help you remember.

The last speaker looks up, puzzled. But if you know already, then why do you want to hear it from me?

It means something more if it comes from you.

Do you speak my language, then? Do you understand me when I say this, when I say that, and even now, when I am singing this song that my father sang every day as he disappeared down the valley? She sings and her alien words crackle about the room.

No, we do not understand, the ethnographers say. Or if we do, it is only distantly, as if we were reading shapes in a raincloud.

Oh, that is a shame, it would be nice to sing that song for someone.

Please, madam, sing it for the microphone.

She grins. So the microphone understands, does it?

Yes, it understands.

If only you could get microphones to talk! She laughs and then feels a little sorry for herself. She does not mean to sound sardonic, no one could accuse her of being indifferent to her plight. Some years before, it had occurred to her that she was no longer in the habit of hearing her own tongue. Everybody in the town seemed to be speaking the common language. She did not mind using their language since she had dwelled in it for a long time, almost as long as she could remember, and had kept it clean and given it a good airing, rearranged the furniture so it suited her just right. It was the language of her husband and her children, and she had made it hers. But always, in the darker corners, she placed mementos of her own, a proverb, a snatch of a rhyme, some light daily expressions the glimpse of which would startle her family. With nobody to speak her language to, she began talking with objects, the pots and pans, a creaking door, the sharp corner of a table. She never spoke it with animals because—and here, a foreign kind of pride sparked within her—it was never a language to waste on goats. Once, on a rare visit, her son came upon her in the living room, speaking in tongues with a teacup. He told her she was going mad. No, she sighed, you don't understand, this is what a conversation sounds like.

Would you like a cup of tea? the last speaker asks the ethnographers. They would. Let's have some tea and then I'll sing for you. She rises from her seat and waits as they shift their equipment, the light-stand and camera, the microphones, the attendant knots of wires. Brushing away their offers to assist her, she lights the stove with a match and stares out through the kitchen window. Poplars nod in the breeze over the mustard field. Someone's boy is loitering at the front gate, his hands in the pockets of his jeans. At each half-step, his sneakers light up red. She thinks he must be here to look at the visitors, but she is wrong. He follows her movements with open and unblinking curiosity, as if there were something surprising about the way a kettle boils. She smiles: that's the matter with strange guests, they turn you into a stranger as well.

The tea warms her voice. When she sings, her eyes close and her chin, with its gentle down of hair, thrusts forward into the lamplight. The ethnographers cannot help but admire her strong set of teeth, a rare sight in so much of their fieldwork. They are used to thinking that there is half a relationship between dental health and endangered languages; languages, like people, become toothless. In her case, of course, a full mouth of teeth won't make any difference. She is the last, the very last. After her, the language has only a ghostly future. Its memory will haunt scholars and graduate students. Nobody misses it in the places where it was once spoken. Few even remember the time when its clambering rhythms united the valley and the uplands. Clinically speaking, it is already dead. A language cannot be alive if it exists alone in the mind of an old woman, no matter how fine her teeth.

The song is about a wedding. At the end of the festivities, the bride leads the groom out from the town, through the fields, and up the slope of a mountain. Where will it happen? the groom asks. The bride kisses him and beckons him to follow. He does. She allows him another kiss after a hundred steps, and another after another hundred, and so on until they can walk no further and are forced to start climbing. Perturbed, the groom grabs her wrist: Why not here? She shakes her head and slips out of his grasp, removing a scarf and draping it over his shoulder. She hoists herself up the face of the mountain. The groom can see the stars shining through the black of her hair. As they climb, she leaves bits of clothing and jewellery for him to gather: bangles, her belt, a necklace, a vest, socks. When he reaches the top, he finds her naked and motionless. Only when he touches her does he realize that she has turned to stone.

The last speaker stops. She apologizes again. Our songs are sad songs. Nobody ever gets to have sex.

The ethnographers smile vaguely. Even the most capable among them can understand at most a handful of her words, an occasional phrase. The full meaning of the song awaits its patient digestion in a computer lab. For now, their responsibility is only to the collection of raw material and the husbanding of its source, a happy task. They are growing fond of the last speaker, softened by her unabashed, tuneless singing. Privately, they all feel the stirrings of great affection, the sort that civilians might call sympathy but they know to be truer still, the love of the student for the studied.

Can I sing it again? the last speaker asks. I would like to change the ending.

By all means, they say, whenever you are ready. The ethnographers, after all, are modern enough to know that nothing can be totally genuine. Traditions are invented to be reinvented. If the last speaker wants to sex up a folk song, so be it. In any case, it's the form of the words that matter, the syntax and structure of her speech. Everything else is just pleasant air.

This song departs entirely from the previous version, but the ethnographers cannot sense the fullness of the difference, nor can they tell that she is improvising fresh phrases. The bride eludes the groom and disappears from the wedding festivities. She journeys to the mountain. At its summit, she finds a rocket (here, the last speaker pauses to construct a suitable compound for the noun 'rocket,' which she renders with verbal suffixes as 'fiery flight in void into void'). The bride enters and sets off up to the heavens. Everything recedes beneath her. The bride has never wanted to be a bride, but rather an astronaut ('swimmer among the stars'), and fair enough, why should brides be brides when they can be astronauts? In space, the astronaut dances between satellites ('invisible lightning moths') and befriends the moon. They drink wine and watch TV ('chaos of shadows in stillness') together. The sun grows jealous, since the moon is its bride. It asks mankind to fetch the astronaut back: Why do you let her be up there? If your women become astronauts, who will be your brides? Mankind agrees: this is a worrying situation. The prime minister ('temporary rent-collector') is sent to the moon to reason with her. He sets up a table on the surface and waits for her to appear for negotiations. He waits and waits, not knowing that the moon has whisked the astronaut to its dark side. The vastness of space inspires only a deep tedium in him. But he has a mission to fulfil, so he remains seated on the surface of the moon, facing an empty chair, expecting a woman who will never come.

Look what I've done, the last speaker says after finishing, I'm such an old fool, I haven't changed the ending at all.

The ethnographers chuckle. There's no sex this time either?

Not a drop, she shakes her head, not a drop. She falls silent, her jowls sinking. The ethnographers think she must be tired—it is always a little unfair to bustle into the homes of lonely pensioners and force them to talk. Indeed, the last speaker is tired, but not from the physical exertion of speech. If anything, inventing within her language is invigorating. Why haven't I done this before? she wonders, why haven't I played with my language?

But another realization exhausts her: there is no simple direct way in her language to express the idea of a 'tractor'. Perhaps there was a time long ago, before she was born, when her language could tackle all concepts of the fields and towns, when it was savvy enough to run its world. In her life, it has only ever been in retreat. She grew up hearing it at home, in the living room and around the stoves and in the whispering dark of the bedroom she shared with her sisters. At school, they made her speak the common language. The teachers slapped her wrists if she ever misspoke and emitted the unwelcome sounds of her own tongue. As she grew older, the living room was overtaken by the radio, then the TV. She lost her bedroom and gained her husband's. The language survived a little while longer in the kitchen, nourished by the memory of food. Then her sisters passed away. For most of her life, funerals were the only occasions she would hear her language outside the home. Now there is no one else left to die.

When it comes time for her funeral, she will be remembered by common people, in common words, with common ideas.

One way to represent 'tractor', she thinks, could be 'making absence of presence', but surely that is a bit vague. 'Tilling with power of many men' seems too literal and inelegant for her liking. Piling on the suffixes to a verb, she settles on an image, 'smoke mowing through grass'. That might do for 'tractor', but this is an impossible task. She looks at all the equipment brought by the ethnographers. Her language has no natural way of referring to a camera, a microphone, a digital recorder. It has been in exile from this world, and so it is no longer of this world. She could come up with phrases for all of these objects, but what would be the point? No matter how innovative she is with her language, it does not have the force to take possession of an idea. In later years, they will say that her term 'swimmer among the stars' means 'astronaut'. They will never say that 'astronaut' means 'swimmer among the stars'.

Have you done this before? she asks the ethnographers. Have you listened to other old women sing?

Yes, they say, but none sing as magically as you.

You shouldn't flatter me. The ancient know their weaknesses better than anybody else.

When you are rested, we'd be happy to record more of your songs.

I don't need to rest. What do you do with these recordings? Where do they go? Who listens to them?

We'll take them to our university, the ethnographers say, we'll study them, we'll write about them, we'll archive them. We'll organize them such that all future generations can learn about you and your language.

It must get noisy over there, with all those voices of old people trying to make themselves heard. She laughs. She knows how computers work, how she can be skimmed into light, vanished into the whirring darkness of a hard drive. That's what will happen to me, she thinks, what a drab afterlife. Technology has so little romance.

She chooses instead to imagine a cavernous exhibition hall, its walls lined with screens. Old women and men stare out of each one, speaking their lonely languages in an unending loop. During the day, visitors come to marvel at the spectacle of so many lost tongues. Inevitably, they feel sad and perhaps light candles or leave flowers, as if they were at a mausoleum. The figures in the screens wait patiently for the visitors to leave. At night, after hours, they interrupt their own digitized soliloquies, listen to one another, and laugh at all the jokes.

Where is your university? she asks.

In our country, very far away from here.

She squints at them—though the creases around her eyes make it hard to tell when she is not squinting—and makes no attempt to veil her disappointment. Why didn't you take me there? It would be much easier. When you do this again, fetch the next old woman to your university. All of you wouldn't have had to go through this hassle or had to bring your van into our narrow streets. I would have got to see your country. Maybe I would have even recorded the way your people speak. Then, I could return home with your words and study you!

The ethnographers look at each other. In our work, they say a little hesitantly, it's best to talk to our informants in their native surroundings. In any case, we were worried about your health, we weren't sure if you would cope with the rigours of travel.

She straightens. I'm well aware that I'm on my way. It makes no difference to me where I die, in this chair, or on a plane, or in your university.

Why don't we let you rest for a bit? The ethnographers feel wretched for making her morose.

No, no, she waves them away. You're not tiring me. It's just…until you came, I never thought of my language as a burden, but that's what it is, isn't it? You want to take it from me so I no longer have to carry this weight.

It should not be just yours to bear.

Will you do me this favour? Whatever recordings you make of me speaking my language in the coming days, please put together a little package and have it played at my funeral ceremony.

The ethnographers melt a little. Their words seem to come through a mist. We can do that, they say.

I'm much obliged to you, she says, I'm very grateful that you have come here to see me and let me feel old in my language. She means it, too—to whom else can she pass this inheritance? Her children may have known a handful of words when they were young, but their mother's tongue was always too much of a responsibility. They shed what little of the language she gave them. Her son now farms in his wife's town on the other side of the valley, not far, but far away enough that he does not see his mother often. Her daughter was always the cleverer of the two, destined for the city and its indispensable comforts: air conditioning, good coffee, the admiring glances of strangers. Every month, her daughter sends her some money. They speak often on the phone, and their conversations are loving and repetitive as all loving conversations should be. She is proud that neither of her children are vulnerable to false nostalgia, that they find full satisfaction in the present of their lives. She would not have them bound to her relic. She would never wish that loneliness upon them.

In my language, she tells the ethnographers, words for gratitude are much different than in the common speech. We have many kinds. This, for instance, is used to express a very dark kind of gratitude, to be thankful for the loss of something. This means to be grateful despite yourself, with a hint of bitterness. This is used to describe a sudden, overwhelming feeling of gratitude. This is the feeling children have when they receive small treats, like sweets, or when they are lifted by an adult and spun and spun: a child's thanks.

The ethnographers take notes. Nobody ever compiled a complete grammar of the language, so part of their mission is to attempt to reconstruct the language in its fullness. They will never know that in her language there were more than a dozen ways of indicating and describing gratitude. Here are a few more: the gratitude of natural things for one another, like the hive for the branch, the tree for the bees, the cloud for the sun; collective gratitude, the thanks of a family or a town or a people; gratitude—directed to the cosmos—for superiority, for knowing that one is better than everybody else; the gratitude of one saved from death by starvation.

Her language boasted many verbs for which no simple equivalents exist in the common language. For example, this means to be afraid of seeing time pass. This means to tell bedtime stories in the depths of winter. This is the action of stirring a kind of gravy in a pot; this also denotes the motion of a pig rooting around in the mud. This refers to the way light splinters against a range of mountains at dusk. This describes in one word how mountains gain mass and shape at dawn. This means to feel strange in an unfamiliar place. This means to be patient for spring. As does this. And this.

If she remembered all or some of these words, the last speaker's testimony would be a little more elegant. Unfortunately, she doesn't remember them. Some she never knew in the first place. It's not her fault, no measure of her intelligence or sophistication. When the number of speakers of a language shrinks, so does the language itself. She grew up with an impoverished vocabulary, a skulking tongue, never with the means to recover those lost words. The ethnographers, despite their best efforts, won't be able to restore her language. How can anybody learn that which has never been written down, that which nobody knows any longer? It is sad, but sad in an unremarkable way. Humans always lose more history than they ever possess.

Speech, however, can be enriched, no matter its condition. When she cannot find the word she wants in her language, she builds compounds with the words she does have. Occasionally, she imports one from the common language. In this way she sketches her life for the ethnographers, narrates in her language the sequence of events and relationships that brought her to this chair before their camera and its severe lamp. Our father raised us in my mother's absence, which means that we raised ourselves, because he was away during the days, and often for many nights. My favourite thing to do in the summers was to wade into the irrigation channels and feel the chill of the mountain water on my ankles. I don't remember anything from my wedding night, you see, I got very drunk. Neither of my children like eating cake, which is a real pity; life isn't complete without confectionery. The army installed solar ('fed by sun') street lamps—look, they just came on!—in the village so now it's never dark at night-time in the way our nights were once so totally dark. I miss that darkness, I miss angling lanterns and torches around corners. I only recently learned that I was the last. I had assumed there were others elsewhere, just not where I was, not here.

A neighbour interrupts the recording with a platter of pastries, a generous pretence with which to inspect the visitors. The ethnographers are ravenous. For a few moments, the sounds of grateful munching overwhelm all conversation. The neighbour studies the ethnographers and their equipment, and then, for a long while, her. How quickly something familiar becomes strange when it takes shape in another language. He makes his excuses and leaves. At the door, he passes the loitering boy, who is still poking about at the threshold. The last speaker beckons to the boy. Why don't you come in? The boy shakes his head, backs a few steps away, and stares.

It is getting late. Stray dogs growl in the dust. Bicycles rustle down paths. The most popular soap operas blare from the televisions in nearby houses where families assemble for dinner in the glow. My nurse will be coming soon, the last speaker reminds the ethnographers, and she will want to settle me for my bedtime. She won't be happy that I've strained myself like this.

Oh no! they protest. You should have allowed us to give you a break.

That's all right, I'm beginning to enjoy myself. It's coming back to me. Tomorrow, I hope I'll be able to tell you even more.

We'll return after breakfast. In fact, we'll return *with* breakfast.

How sweet, but don't go just yet. I'll sing you one more song today. Make certain your recorders are working, are they properly plugged in? Are you sure? I want an example of my singing played at my funeral, too.

Eager to please her, the ethnographers vigorously double-check all the controls and settings before signalling for her to begin. She sings, tuneless and a bit rasping, but a voice still captivating to men who have heard so many others.

On their wedding night, the bride and the groom retreat to the chamber prepared for them. He undresses and rushes to get under the covers. Awaiting her arrival in the pregnant darkness (a rough translation of one of many kinds of darkness in the last speaker's language), he realizes that he has not heard her talk at any point during the day. She must be shy, he thinks, she must be as nervous as I am about this moment. Is she? He feels her weight on the bed, her fingers now on his shoulder, her knee in the space between his knees. Her face looms above him, all light concentrated in the teeth. He moves to bring her mouth to his, but she pushes away and raises her torso, her hands firmly on his neck and chest, straddling him.

The last speaker stops. Thinking that she is done, the ethnographers start to commend her singing and to turn their thoughts towards dinner. She has not finished. Her eyes search the camera lens. She sings again, not quite song, more like an incantation, urgent in its rhythm, her feet tapping a measure on the floor. The ethnographers strain to discern the sequence in the flow of words. Weeks later, in the computer lab, they will discover that there is no order at all in this passage. It is merely a list of unconnected phrases, shards of speech, jagged and inscrutable, the debris of a language swept clean. But in the moment, in her living room, it rises in pitch and volume and dissolves the ethnographers' scholarly attention. They surrender to the unlikely beauty of it. She looks up when she finishes. Was the song racier this time? the ethnographers grin. Was there sex? She smiles, exhausted.

Her nurse enters and looks balefully upon the scene. I'm afraid your interviews are over for the day, the nurse says, it's time for me to take care of her. The ethnographers pack up their things. They linger at the door, watching the last speaker as she settles into an armchair, puts up her feet, and turns on the TV.

Until tomorrow, they say.

Until tomorrow, she replies, staring closely at the buttons on the remote. The ethnographers sputter away in their van. While the last speaker watches TV, her nurse does all the required nursely duties, checking blood pressure and temperature, feeding her the nightly quota of pills, talking to her about the antics of celebrities she only pretends to recognize. Restless, she eventually goes to the kitchen and insists on preparing dinner for both of them. What is the point of living if I can't exert myself? The nurse, who knows this routine well, protests and then acquiesces, expressing her earnest, simple gratitude. While the last speaker cooks, she sinks into the armchair and starts to channel surf on the TV.

The last speaker turns to the stove. The pots begin to murmur. She whispers in her language to a smattering of onions and garlic and greens and lentils: soon you'll become delicious and then, I'm afraid, I'm going to eat you…don't worry, there's much more of you where you came from. Through her kitchen window, the wheezing solar lamps cast a light gloom over the village. She is surprised to see a hunched form sitting on her courtyard wall. It is the boy from earlier. He's been here the entire time, she thinks. Whose son is he? At her gaze, he drops from the wall and runs down the village path, red flashes in the dark, leaving her wondering if there was ever a time when she knew his name.

12

PUBLIC RECORD

KARAN MADHOK

The lady drops her handbag climbing the steps outside the station. She bends down to pick it up off the dusty floor, and groans weakly as she straightens up. I wait a few metres away, until she's back on the move again. She walks with a slight hunch in her back, favouring her right leg. Early sign of kyphosis. She's in her late sixties, I deduce, basking in the glow of calcium deficiency. Weak, brittle bones. Almost painful to watch. I decide to follow her.

The crowd of commuters is sparser than usual at the Mandawali station this morning. I step into the security check queue for men, where a uniformed officer waves his handheld metal detector. The officer is a familiar face, with pockmarked, sweaty cheeks and a bushy moustache. I wonder if he recognizes me too, or if I'm just one among the hundreds, thousands, he waves past every morning.

The old lady is tiny: four-feet-seven, four-feet-eight. Considerably smaller than Wife.

She wears a red sari with pink and orange floral designs. She beeps her card into the AFC gate and goes through, and I do the same nearby. She's taking the Pink Line, heading in the same direction I would usually take to work this time of day. The train arrives and she walks into a near-empty coach. She takes a seat, and I take one opposite her.

The PA announces the IP Extension station next. I resist the practised reflex to exit here: after years of this short, one-stop journey, I need some unlearning to stay seated. The platform triggers a smell of the hospital, of antiseptic and orange-scented room fresheners, of burnt hair and metallic blood. I shudder and sneeze.

More commuters enter. I wonder about the chances of coming face to face with a colleague from work, or a patient. I wonder what I would say if they asked why I wasn't in my uniform, why I wasn't wearing my scrubs, my clogs. But then the doors shut and the train zooms away.

At the next stop, the old lady stands and waddles out the door. I follow her down the escalator, across the platform, down another escalator. I slow down to her pace, ten to fifteen feet behind, brushing past other busybodies zigging and zagging between us. She gets into a waiting train, I don't check to see where it's going before getting into the crowded coach. A man stands up to offer the old lady his corner seat. She accepts, clutching at a nearby handle to steady herself, ensuring to balance herself with the poles as the train suddenly accelerates forward. She sits down and closes her eyes, taking a mini nap to the hum of the train's movement.

It's dark outside, under the earth of New Delhi, and the train lights are dim. We feel reverberating engines, hear a zooming drone, smell each other's underarm sweat. But we avoid eye contact, looking everywhere except at each other.

There is a young woman seated a few spaces away from me, looking ahead at nothing, lulled by the train's rhythmic movement. She's in her early thirties, with voluminous black hair, a sharp nose. She reminds me of my last patient—the woman from the hospital, the fibroid surgery. But many Delhi women have these features. The one from the surgery had a mole on her forehead, a protruding black spot permanently blocking the spot where she would've otherwise dotted a bindi. The one from the surgery is dead.

Twenty minutes pass before the busiest stop on the route, Rajiv Chowk. The old lady in the red sari creaks up to her feet, as does almost everyone else in the coach. They crowd the exits. When the doors open, the lady is pushed by the momentum of men behind her; for a moment, I consider reaching out to grab her before she loses her balance over the gap. But she is experienced in these matters; she elbows, pushes, manages her steps, and is out and walks on.

For those who spend their transit lives underground, the Rajiv Chowk station is the core of the city, the largest interchange hub, the beating heart of the metro's central nervous system connecting the wide breadth of the capital and its suburbs. People cross paths in varying directions, going up escalators and down stairs, waiting on trains, waiting at food kiosks. The lady heads deeper underground on another set of escalators. The Yellow

Line train is already there. She walks in, and for the first time that morning, I have to break into a little sprint, jostling past others on my way down the escalator. I jump into the coach just in time before the doors shut behind me.

She exhales a soft grunt as she folds herself down on to a seat. Despite her obvious decrepit condition, she has remarkable control over those creaky, old joints. I've seen something similar in athletes, the ones who have had ACL surgeries on their knees in the past, and yet have continued to play their sport. They have a familiarity with their weakness, and they make the most of the body's more durable parts to function.

Such an interesting machine—the body—vulnerable to every hazard in the environment: to viruses plaguing the lungs, to cholesterol clogging the heart, to sharp objects piercing through skin, to blunt ones thrashing against bone, and to a cocktail of radiation. A machine evolved with intricate, delicate parts, of organs that fail, tissues that tear, veins that rupture. And yet, a machine often capable of survival, too, of taking a beating and getting back up.

The lady walks out the doors at Lok Kalyan Marg, into a spacious, pristine platform. I follow her up the escalator and out the AFC gate. My card has been reduced by forty rupees. Wife won't pay attention to a small spike in my weekly commuting costs; the difference is no more than a sandwich at the station, a magazine off the rack. But the numbers will add up exponentially if I continue to wander. There's no more work to return to. And when my salary doesn't arrive on the first Monday of next month—well, then what?

Up another set of escalators, and finally, we are back on earth-level, back in sunshine. This is Lutyens' Delhi, clean and green, with well-paved footpaths and wide roads. The lady steps into the first autorickshaw by the curb, and I get into the one behind. My driver is a tall, lean man, with a sharp nose, a bidi in his hand, and thin, scrawny wrists. *Follow the rickshaw ahead*, I say.

My actions this morning—tethered behind the stranger—are no longer mine alone, but are now a matter of public record. The autowallah takes one more puff of his bidi and revs his three-wheeler to life. *Phut-phut-phut.* We're on the road.

I've hardly had a chance to visit this part of Delhi. There is so much of the city waiting to be seen. Rows of pruned flowering shrubs pave the side of the roads. Fresh paint on the road dividers, black and yellow. Green parks and gardens, vast embassy buildings. Delhi seems simultaneously older and younger here, ancient in its heritage architecture, youthful in the untarnished green and undefiled air. I chuckle at this irony: my flat in Mandawali is technically a newer settlement, built for young families seeking opportunities in the city's ever-expanding margins. And yet, our neighbourhood has aged quickly in neglect, past its expiry date within a decade of its expansion, already bathed in dust and grime.

The auto ahead turns right. So does ours. Around a vast roundabout. The destination is a block of large properties in a crescent-shaped block hugging a park full of trees. I tell the autowallah to stop outside the crescent, but I don't get out. The lady pays her driver and walks up to a large black gate.

A maid, I assume. She must be a cook, a cleaner, a babysitter—someone who serves someone richer. An armed security guard opens the gate, and she hobbles inside on her shaky knees, and I tell the autowallah to take me back to the metro station.

I never see her again.

Wife drives to her office every day; it's safer for her away from the leery eyes of men in the metro. It's far more expensive, of course—the petrol prices could send the best of us to a cardiologist.

After she picks me up outside the station, she reminds me that my birthday is coming up. She asks me if I want anything special, and I insist that I don't like gifts.

But it's your birthday. A sweater, maybe? It will get cold soon. Or a tall coat? Those are fashionable.

Sure, I say.

We only have time to speak in the ten minutes we spend in the car together without our son, between the metro station and home. She is inquisitive about my job. I tell her that I'll be performing surgery, without the supervision of Dr Khare.

They allow nurses to perform surgeries?

Yes, for routine procedures. Dr Khare is busy. She performs bariatric surgeries on Bollywood stars and MLAs. She can't deal with every chhotu-motu that comes into her office, can she? People like me do liposuctions for the usual fatsos.

Wife flashes a cheeky smile, spreading her dimples wide, *Liar, there are no Bollywood stars in Delhi!*

With vivid details, I elaborate manifestos from past surgeries. I share graphic descriptions of bloodied hands and pulsating organs. There is a darkness inside the human body, an inverted world oozing in sable, crepuscular colours I don't yet have names for.

I don't tell Wife about the woman who died.

∽

I see youngsters in the metro, college-going types in a big group, boys and girls speaking to each other loudly, playing music on their mobile phones with carefree confidence. I was young like them, too, not so long ago. And yet, the past six or seven years have accelerated me eons away from these students, as if I'm now an anachronism, born without youth, with no relation to the past.

I watch a younger couple, teenagers. Both have thick, bushy eyebrows, and they stare around the train impatiently, as if each moment that they are sitting still is a moment being wasted. We're underground. Instead of staying put in their coach, the couple get up and brush past the standing crowds in the coach and walk through the linking gangway into the next coach. I follow.

The train gets going. The boy reaches out and holds the girl's hand, pulling her gently through the next gangway to the next coach, passing more faces, balancing themselves to the train's uncertain sway, walking under the bluish, dim lights.

They walk to the far end of the train—the women's only coach—and settle in the gangway space. The girl walks into the women's section and the boy stays on the general side, a few feet away. I stop close to the boy and lean against a pole.

They murmur to each other, but in the hum and din of the train, I am unable to eavesdrop. The boy turns, briefly catching my eye. I avert my gaze and look away, out the dark windows.

I watch my fingers wrap tightly around the handlebar, afraid of slipping, of making a mistake. Surgical hands—I remind myself; hands that save lives, mistakes that take them away.

The couple step off at Mandi House, and I follow them out through the station, and down again into another train. Each one is now lost in their respective phones. They have the same flat, wide shape to their nose, and I realize then that they looked alike in other ways, too: the oval shape of their eyes, the light gait with which they moved.

They're siblings, I conclude—brother and sister out on an errand.

They get off at the Jama Masjid station and take a turn towards the ancient mosque. Under the harsh afternoon sun, the air here is thick. Filled with the musk of frequent human congregation. I have never visited this mosque. I haven't visited any place of worship—mandir, masjid, gurdwara, church—in decades.

I still hear Dr Khare's voice in my head. *Real surgeons*, she would say, *Real surgeons are too busy with operation halls to worry about prayer halls.* I agree. The day after the woman with the mole on her forehead was declared deceased, Virender from the east wing told me this accident could even make the biggest agnostics turn to prayer. I could only shrug on my way out of the hospital for the very last time.

The path to the mosque is lined on both sides with peddlers selling various wares: pots, pans, gold-painted chains, jewellery, and food—lots and lots of food. Chhole sizzling next to puffy baturas, parathas with melted butter, and many many kebabs on many many sticks. My mouth waters as I pass by. The siblings take a right turn before the mosque, and then left and right again, until they walk into a narrower alleyway. This gully houses stores filled with decorative material: colourful wall hangings, beads, and cheap jewellery. They open a narrow, greenish door next to one such shop, and then climb up a dark flight of steps.

They disappear.

I wait. I browse through the wares of the shop below, pretending to be interested. The shopkeeper is a thin, eagle-faced man, with well-oiled and pressed grey hair, and a grey beard that sprays out with the wild abandon of a learned cleric. I ask about the garlands, and he quotes me some prices. *Who's getting married?* he asks.

Me.

And you're shopping for your own garland?

I nod. I can't help but smile.

A buzzing in my pocket. Phone call from Wife; it must be her lunch break.

Hi, she says. Her voice is cheery. *Where are you?*

Work. A little busy. The doctors have a big case, so I'm taking over the appendectomies today.

Oh, again?

I wonder if she can hear the groaning engines of scooters behind me, or the sharp sizzle of a welder working on a rusted sheet of metal nearby.

You don't have a Sunday shift this week, do you? Sandip is excited for the Planetarium.

Sunday. *I won't forget.*

She hangs up before I do.

An hour passes. I don't see the siblings exit. My feet are restless to be on the move again. These are the hours of my day I would usually be on high alert, with not a moment to pause, passing silver steel instruments, pumping up hearts, pumping in oxygen, ready to assist, blades and forceps in hand, a perforated human body before me, a petri dish of organs and vessels waiting on me, pulsating, bubbling, mucus and blood and muscle, flesh alive and flesh lifeless. My hands jitter to hold something, to move something.

I walk back around the corner to find the parathawallah I had passed earlier. Electric wires hang low above me, intertwined with the complexity of a nervous system, somehow keeping this neighbourhood lit. I order a paratha stuffed with potatoes and onion, slathered with butter. I eat standing up and wipe my hands on my trousers when I'm done.

I feel disoriented. New streets, new shops. A smell of grease, then petroleum. Perhaps I have taken a wrong turn somewhere. I pass by another thela selling kebabs, and I buy a warm, thick stick of meat. Twenty rupees. At least I can still afford these second lunches, these wanderings around town, the top-ups on my metro card. The savings will last a few months. And then, we'll make do with Wife's salary, won't we? Perhaps she, too, will have to ditch the car and ride the metro like the rest of us. A government school for Son, perhaps. Cancel the holiday to Jaipur. No more birthday gifts.

The kebab is delicious, melting quickly in my mouth. I wander with the kebab stick in my hand, drowsy under the authoritarian afternoon sun, passing more shops carved out of small holes in the walls until I find a nook populated with dozens of small cages filled with fluttering, twittering birds. Parrots. Cockatoos. Parakeets. Around another corner, pigeons—many, many pigeons. Some fly in circles in their cages. Some are free but stay near the cage. A group of men in multicoloured kurtas sit near the free birds, clapping their hands. The birds hover low with practised obedience.

I stand there long after my second lunch, watching a small, chubby pigeon cooing and circling around a man in a white kurta, round and round with meaningless determination, safe inside the bird shop.

The surgery was routine. That's what I told the patient. Her husband was by her side. He was a tall, broad-shouldered man, at least half a foot taller than me, with glowing, light skin.

The woman had a pedunculated fibroid growth in her uterus. After trying out a couple of other procedures, Dr Khare recommended a myomectomy. She let me handle it on my own; that wasn't unusual. *A standard procedure,* I told the patient.

And then, the error.

My fingers slipped, perhaps; or perhaps it was my wrist that slipped first, or perhaps it was the moisture in the hall; or the loose latex of my scrubs; or a breath untimed to the beat of surgery, an exhale gone wrong. I cut open her bowel.

I exhaled. She was asleep.

I cleaned her up with a superficial stitch and when she woke I told her the news—and later, in Dr Khare's office, told her husband, too, seated across from me at the desk. I told them it would be all okay. Dr Khare wheeled on the rolling chair beside me. *You'll be fine. Thirty-four? You're so young, and you can recover quickly,* she told the woman with the forehead mole, with the soon-to-be-inflamed peritoneum. They were back at the hospital early the next morning, the husband and wife. I'd just soaped my hands in the sink down the hall when I heard her. A growl; then, a baritone, low moo; and finally, screams of desperation. Moans are common here—uncomfortable, animalistic sounds of human vulnerability.

Overnight, the woman's bowels had opened up into her body. She turned her head from side to side on the stretcher, sweat beading down her forehead, hair sticky with perspiration, eyes looking at the fans on the ceiling, one hand holding on to her husband. Her husband's nostrils flared and snorted as he spoke. He recapped the pain of the previous night. She could only emit more of those wild roars. Dr Khare put her on morphine. I read the scan results, and Dr Khare explained them to her husband. *Her organs are shutting down due to the faecal matter in her body. We have to cut her open again and repair her bowel. You brought her here just in time.*

The woman's face changed colour, brown to milky pale.

I don't want to die, she said to her husband. Her voice was throaty, weak.

It'll be okay, he said.

Who is with Raghav?

Your mom's watching him. Don't worry.

He lost his voice too, like teenagers when their vocal cords first give way, when they are about to transform into someone else.

Tell her I'm sorry about dinner last week, she said. *There was too much ajinomoto.*

Don't worry about it.

It's not fair.

You'll be okay.

Who is watching Raghav? Raghav? Raghav who is with Raghav? Raghav?

We wheeled her into the operating room, and it was not a complicated case at all, because it was too late to save her, and she died.

Dr Khare had another appointment. *It shouldn't be a problem,* she told me. *This is what they sign all those waivers for.* On her way out, she stopped in the hallway to explain the matter to the husband. She liked to have this personal connection with patients: she stressed that it always helped them to have a more fulfilling experience. Even their sobbing faces didn't dampen her mood, and she would always leave work in the evening with a smile on her face. It was one of her superpowers.

I noted the time of death, discarded my scrubs, and walked out. That night, in the flux between consciousness and dreams, I heard the woman apologizing for the ajinomoto.

I quit my job the next morning.

After a change from Pink to Blue, I find myself at the Rajiv Chowk station. After weeks of movement, I decide to stay still and observe the rest of the world move past me. This place is a grand, manic mela of movement, from the opening hours to the last train at night. I drift around, changing vantage points through the course of the day. I sit on the dusty floor on a footstep, lean against the wall outside a busy coffeewallah, or stand still on moving escalators. There are old people and young people, men and women here. They mostly walk fast, in a rush to get to the next point in their diagrams, joining the dots without experiencing the gaps of life to be lived between the commute.

On my way back home, sandwiched tight in a crowd of chattering passengers, I stare out the window overground. I love to see the city from this elevated line. We pass a construction project for a mammoth sports stadium, and small jhopris underneath the flyovers. We pass large forested areas and barren fields, surprisingly situated here in the middle of the urban expanse. I remind myself to explore these forests someday. Why shouldn't I? I'm alive—I should live.

Often in these barren fields, I see people in the distance, loitering, waiting for another day to pass. I can't see their faces from so far away, but I can see their shapes. Some sleep on the grass, some walk at a leisurely pace across dusty paths; some sit and wait. I wonder how they pass their days, their lives, how they can be so free, so brave, to do anything they wish with their time.

Now, on some days, I get off the metro and visit parts of my city usually only sought out by tourists: Humayun's Tomb, Qutub Minar, the Red Fort. I don't enter any monument that requires a ticket—the stamp, I feel, would make the trip unwelcomely purposeful. Instead, I wander alone through the public parks, amble under shaded trees at Lodi Garden I watch young couples looking for a private corner to rub their bodies against each other, mothers chasing after hysterical toddlers, balloon sellers and chaatwallahs, the security guards with loyal stray dogs for company.

The next payday is two weeks away. I still have time to let time pass.

I see patterns in the closely packed homes of middle-class colonies, the high-rising apartment buildings, narrow gullies, and the unsteady structures of flats in the smallest corners, the holes beside bigger apartments that lead to smaller basement homes, the grand green crescents where mansions lie under the shade of neem trees. I continue to wander. Some of these homes look like my own—balcony after balcony behind metal railings with clothes on racks and mini gardens, with blocks of AC units protruding out of their buttocks.

No matter which direction of the city the trains take me, I always find groups of men in army colours—soldiers, policemen—huddled in a corner, rifles hanging over their shoulders, pistols holstered at their waists, rucksacks in hand. On one long journey, I fall asleep on my seat, and I dream of a coach full of soldiers, and when I ask for their attention, they are deaf to my cries. Then, the colour of their khaki uniform blends into the reddish-grey of the woman's insides, of the last pulsating breaths of her organs. I think about the mole on her forehead. I see her being alive and then being colourless. I see a kidney dish and forceps and surgical scissors. Stainless steel, shining silver.

One day, perhaps out of instinct, I leave the train—at IP Extension, my former work stop—and quickly remembering my mistake, run back inside before the automatic doors slam shut behind me. I find myself alone in this coach as the train rumbles ahead. I put a hand on an orange plastic seat, and rapidly pull it back. This seat looks different under a familiar light, as if it were a discarded organ, useless unless I prescribe some use for it. It's a seat, I murmur to myself.

Around one in the afternoon, faces bubble up at Rajiv Chowk, appearing, disappearing. A mass of humanity in different shades of grey. Then I see him: towering over the rest, broad shoulders, wheatish skin, those wide nostrils I remember from the lobby outside the surgery halls.

The husband.

I'm standing between the samosawallah and the magazinewallah. He walks towards me at a rapid pace. A leather laptop bag hangs like a saddle by his waist, its strap over his shoulder.

He looks beyond me to the samosa counter, where he asks for a bottle of water. There is a certain fragility to his movement; his shoulders hang loose, he covers his mouth as he speaks—as if he's afraid of revealing the weak quiver of his lips. Out of the corner of my eye, I can see how much he has changed: his cheeks are puffier, his hair thinner, his eyes darker.

His lips barely move when he speaks. *Thank you*, he says and darts off. Blue Line.

I follow.

The blue collared shirt he wears is at least a size too large. He's thinner than I remember.

The train is crowded, with barely any place for either of us to find our footing. We are separated by three or four bodies. He grabs a handlebar and falls into his phone. I grab a handlebar to watch him.

The train moves west. We emerge overground soon into the welcoming, blinding light of the sun. The next stop causes a mass exodus—half the train departs, leaving a number of seats free on both sides. I sit down. He remains standing.

He tucks his phone away into the front pocket of his shirt and looks out at the passing city. I do the same. Apartment buildings. Water tanks under corrugated tin sheds on the rooftops. Solar panels. Double-dish antennas for internet and cable. He ignores the sound of the PA system, stop after stop.

His black leather bag is fattened to the brim. I wonder if he has a laptop inside. Or books. Folders. Or a change of clothes.

I haven't taken the train this far on the Blue Line before, out to the sparsely populated suburb of Dwarka. Empty malls on both sides, with faces from Bollywood gracing mammoth film posters on the banners. Little traffic to be seen from our train. Trees line the sides of the footpaths. Empty lots sit unattended, waiting to be claimed and made into more residential space.

When the train comes to a halt at Dwarka Sector 9, he gets off. I jump up off my seat, too, and follow him outside to a vacant, spacious platform. The husband takes the escalator down, swipes his card and exits. Outside, he ignores the cacophony of voices from a dozen or so autowallahs lined up on the road, all offering to take him wherever he wants to go. He walks on the footpath towards what seems like a residential neighbourhood. It's hot and humid; a threat of rain without the relief of rain itself.

It's the middle of the day, a working weekday.

Is he unemployed, returning home? Or does he have the type of work that takes him to the homes of other people? Is he a maths tutor who teaches kids at home? A guitar instructor? An architect called to inspect the blueprint of a new apartment? A plumber called to fix someone's busted drain? No—that would be ridiculous. Who would call someone living an hour away on the metro? Unless he was Delhi's greatest plumber. Is he the greatest plumber in New Delhi?

The footpath is shaded by old trees; their voluminous branches make intricate designs when their shadows hit the earth below. We pass a large banyan tree on our left. The husband takes a right into a gate. When I catch up, I see that behind the gate is a driveway diverging in different directions to three or four tall apartment buildings. There is a guardhouse here with a man in a blue uniform. The guard looks at me lazily and scratches his beard.

My presence is realized. I turn around and leave.

I return to Rajiv Chowk at noon the next day and take my place between the magazines and samosas. I see a number of faces, but I can't study them any more—they are only a blur of varying shades of brown. Time passes, but the husband doesn't appear.

The following day, I do the same, and this time I spot him.

He wears a brown overcoat and carries the same laptop bag over his shoulder. I follow him to Dwarka again. I wonder where he has come from; Rajiv Chowk is a massive interchange station, connecting nearly every important corner of the city. Five crore people live and move through Delhi and its adjoining suburbs, a population larger than most European nations. How many Delhiites take the metro every day? How many pass through this station? What are the chances of seeing him again?

The next day, I arrive at Rajiv Chowk even earlier in the morning, but instead of waiting by the samosawallah, I take the elevator up and outside the station to the Connaught Place area. Here, circles of commercial space surround a park, and in the park stands the country's largest tiranga flag, fluttering whenever the wind allows it an occasional sense of pride.

There's no wind today. It's muggy and still. It needs to rain.

I walk around the blocks until I find what I'm looking for: a travel accessories shop. It smells of leather and agarbatti from the morning's prayer. I pay 2,900 rupees and walk out with a black laptop bag, strap hanging over its shoulders. Wife, of course, will notice. Perhaps she'll imagine I'm celebrating a financial bonus at work. Perhaps, she'll believe it if I told her it was a gift. But who is there to gift *me* a bag?

Back at Rajiv Chowk, I spot a tall man in a long, brown overcoat, but upon closer review, it isn't the husband. It's a different man, sporting large, round-rimmed spectacles and a moustache. The overcoat is almost exactly the same as the husband's. I wonder if this is the latest fashion for men in the city.

Monday, he isn't there.

Tuesday, he isn't there, either.

On Wednesday, I take the route to his stop at Dwarka Sector 9. I go all the way up to the blue-uniformed guard at the gate, turn around, and head back home.

It's my birthday on Saturday and I unwrap the gift from Wife. A thick, long brown overcoat. Not unlike the one the husband wears, but—I'm convinced—of cheaper material. An older used copy.

You shouldn't have, I say. *This looks.... This looks pricey.*

She smiles. *Don't worry. Your birthday only comes once a year.*

She suggests that we have lunch—the three of us together, but as she continues to speak, I feel her voice fading away, as if her words are now mere whispers; and then, her whispers become mere whiffs of the passing breeze. *No lunch,* I say and look away from her. I tell her that I have another shift, I will have to fill in at the last minute for a colleague who fell ill.

On the metro, I worry if she has seen through this lie. I wonder if she still knows me as well as she once did. I wonder if she still cares enough to do so.

I wear the new overcoat on Monday and sling the strap of the laptop bag over my shoulder while I wait for him. When the husband doesn't appear, I begin my walk down the stairs for the Blue Line to Dwarka. I rub shoulders against strangers and smell their socks and their sweat. As the train moves forward, I watch the blur of time passing by, station to station, underground and outside, building after building, civilization and all those who occupy it. I slump into my seat and sigh.

An hour passes, more, and I'm there.

Past the autowallahs, the temple, the giant tree. Right to the gate, but before I do that—

The banyan tree on my left. A figure seated on the concrete circle of space around its circumference. The husband sits there alone, in his long overcoat, laptop bag by his side. His face is buried in his palms.

Hey, I say.

He looks up and wipes his eyes. His eyes are sparkling red.

Hello, he answers. His voice is slightly high-pitched. I imagine that is how I must have sounded to him, too, my voice hesitant and out-of-shape, unpractised from regular use with other humans.

The air is heavy, water particles packed close together, heating up in the atmosphere, rubbing and ribbing, their last stand before the big burst of rain.

I...I'm the surgeon, I say.

The surgeon?

Not the surgeon, I correct myself. *The surgical nurse. From Atlas Hospital.* I find myself covering my mouth with my hand as I speak. The words I emit are muffled, weak.

He stares at me without recognition. What have I done? I have caught a vulnerable man at a vulnerable time. I have seen him when he didn't wish to be seen.

I have an urge to reach out and embrace him. To let him cry on my shoulder. Perhaps he would allow me to cry on his shoulder, too. I imagine we could be nearly the same height. I thirst for his touch, overcoat on overcoat, warm body on warm body.

Who are you? he asks.

I feel shame jolt through me. This jolt is specific, with a particular aftertaste. What is a hug, anyway, but the mind fooling the body about an oxytocin shortage? This tree, this metro stop is *his* space. This route

is his—on the Blue Line. This city is his. What am I doing here?
The surgery, I say. *Your wife. It was me.*
I feel that I should repeat myself.
It was me.
His eyes peer up in confusion.
You're mistaken, says this man. *I have no wife.*

On the way home from Dwarka, I cradle the laptop bag in my arms and rest my head against the glass behind me. Two elderly women sit close together in a corner, sharing a pair of headphones between them, frowning down into a phone. A slim, turbaned man sways while standing between poles, a solemn dance to a tune in his head and the rhythm of the train. In the far corner sits a tall, sinewy man. He has glowing light-brown skin, a clean crew cut, and a backpack by his feet.

The PA announces the next stop. It's too muffled for me to hear, but this tall man springs up to his feet, gathers his bag, and goes to the door. I get up and posit myself next to him.

I know him.

I have been wrong all along. I had expected sorrow in the husband's eyes, so I had only hunted for sorrow. Perhaps, I should have looked for something else. This man—this tall man with the crew cut—seems to know exactly where he's going. He has a decisive strength in each step: out the coach, past the other rushing passengers, up the stairs. He ignores the escalators to favour the staircase. Two at a time.

It's near the end of the month. The salary won't arrive on Monday. Wife will know. There are unread messages on my phone, birthday greetings Wife has forwarded from her parents and cousins. I don't stop to read them. I don't stop to read the name of the station.

I follow.

13

THE GREAT INDIAN TEE AND SNAKES
KRITIKA PANDEY

The girl with the black bindi knows that she is not supposed to glance at the boy in the white skull cap but she does. The boy moves restlessly on a stool as he cradles a cup of chai in his hands. The girl has flavoured it with cardamom for no extra cost before swallowing the leftover pod so her father won't find out. He is the moustachioed owner who cleans his ears with Q-tips at the cash counter. The girl looks up from the boiling contents of the saucepan, pretending to notice new customers while examining the contours of the boy's stubbly chin, the kite-shaped birthmark on his neck. He mostly watches the speeding vehicles on the road. Once in a while, he meets her gaze and his ears turn crimson. At such moments the girl and the boy realize that they must immediately look away but never stop noticing each other wherever they go.

∽

It is September. Hawkers appear with baskets of tomatoes. They are overpriced but surprisingly red. The girl's father asks her to buy two kilos. They would keep tomato chutney on the menu until tomatoes become wholly unaffordable in the winter. She squats at the water pump outside the stall to wash the tomatoes, facing the boy, gazing at the stubbed toe sticking out of his sandals. He is one of the few customers who prefer eating keema samosas to aloo samosas but it is the least of the girl's concerns. Their stuffings are somewhat different but the girl makes both types of samosas with the exact same batter. They are the same thing unless one absolutely wants to differentiate, which most people do, including the girl's father who has strictly warned her against eating keema samosas.

A chilly breeze leaves the girl covered in goosebumps.

'Why does it have to get cold?' she says to no one in particular.

'Seasons change,' says one of the men sitting next to the boy. They are daily wage labourers who ask for aloo samosas with their chai, not keema samosas, never keema samosas. They carry grimy shovels and miss no opportunity to talk.

'Because this is how it is.'

'Because this is how it's always been.'

'Because the earth moves around the sun,' says the boy.

The girl breathlessly punctures a tomato, then washes the red mush off her fingernails. She has never heard him speak before.

A man eyes the monogram on the boy's shirt. 'Go to school?'

He nods yes.

The girl's father had pulled her out of school after a couple from Class 10 eloped to Bombay.

The man chuckles. 'I went to school myself. Now I shovel cement and sand.'

Later that night, the girl can't stop wondering if the earth really moves around the sun. Why had no one told her that? Who was making it move? She sits up in bed and thinks about endless fields of cauliflower and tries not to throw up, like she has to do on the giant wheel at the funfair. Dreams take over when she falls asleep. She grabs the boy's stubbed toe as they fly off the face of the earth.

∽

The town is on a plateau formed by colliding land masses when the dinosaurs were still around. It is big enough to have a Domino's but too small for traffic lights. The traffic policemen take breaks from signalling vehicles to rub lime and tobacco in the palms of their hands until drivers yell at them to regain control. The girl's father had moved here when growing onions in the village farmlands stopped being profitable. It was raining less and less each year. For a while, he tried to find work at the department store with glass walls, live in a house with bedrooms. Then he gave up. He got bamboo sticks and tarpaulin and set up the stall outside their shack. It unsettled him to include keema samosas on the menu but he wanted to make whatever profit he could. A painter demanded five hundred rupees for adorning the aluminium anterior of the table where the chai was prepared on a coal stove. 'It better be a nice and important name,' the girl's father had told the painter, who could hardly spell, and so the tea and snacks stall was christened *The Great Indian Tee and Snakes*. The painter had promised, 'Anyone who loves this country will love this name.' Some passers-by point out the sign to each other and have a good laugh. Others nod in admiration of what they take to be high literary nonsense. Many click pictures.

∽

The girl is frying samosas. Today the boy is being questioned by the men with grimy shovels about what brings him to this part of town every weekend.

'I water an old man's geraniums,' he says.

'Gera-what?'

'Flowers.'

Thanks to the labourers' interest in him, the girl can now hear the boy talk.

'Germium,' she says to a golden samosa floating in the oil, pleased that the boy knows such words. Her father glares at her. She sighs. If only she were allowed to talk to the boy, she wouldn't have to talk to the samosas.

'Pays well?' a labourer asks.

'Six hundred per month,' says the boy.

'For watering flowers!'

'Kya kismat hai.'

'Lucky bastard.'

The boy says that his wealthy employer lives by himself and reads magazines with high-definition photographs of wild felines. When someone brings up the new prime minister's yoga moves, the boy silently nibbles on his samosa. The girl mumbles things that she wishes to say aloud to him.

'Plants make their own food. I know because I used to go to school as well.... I also know that we can't see air but it's there.... Do you like summer or winter? I like summer for the mangoes. I don't like winter because the cold makes me feel more feelings.... I don't care if you eat this samosa or that samosa. Just saying. People should eat whatever they want to. Why is it a big deal?... You have nice fingers, you know...every morning, some men gather in the park with Gandhi's statue and force themselves to laugh. If you look at them, they'll make you laugh too. They say it makes you happy....You have really nice fingers.... Do you like me?'

The girl's father wants the boy to be served chai in stainless steel cups only. If the girl mistakenly serves him in ceramic, her father waits for the customers to leave, then smashes the cup. 'Steel can be washed with soap and water,' he says, 'But you can't wash a keema-eater's saliva off of clay.' The girl used to follow her father's orders and throw away the ceramic pieces. But now she collects them as if they are artefacts. When her father is snoring at night, she steps out of the house, glues back the broken cups under the street light, and hides them among the tangled roots of a banyan tree.

The girl believes that her father is kinder than he appears to be. He could have tossed her into the river after discovering that she was not a boy but he did not. Not even after her mother, his wife, died a week later from excessive bleeding. The girl obviously doesn't like that he expects her to be up around five in the morning to open the stall, calling her the 'Queen of England' when she sleeps in. However, he lets her spend on nail polish and newspapers from which she cuts out pictures of the oval-faced woman with shimmery eyelids. The man at the newspaper stand says that her name is Beyoncé. The customers at the stall eat samosas from scraps of newspaper with Beyoncé-shaped holes in them.

At times when the girl gets a bridal mehndi assignment—she is a decent henna artist—her father takes care of the stall so she can spend hours painting the hands of brides. She hides the names of their future husbands amid swirly, intricate henna patterns.

Nevertheless, as far as the keema-eater is concerned, the girl must not get ahead of herself. Her father doesn't need to tell her that girls with black bindis are not supposed to feel this way about boys in white skull caps. She knows.

The girl wakes up with cold toes. She gathers twigs, leaves, bits of paper, cloth, and empty Lipton cartons before setting them on fire. Her father fans the flames. The girl, the boy, four of the labourers, and the girl's father sit around the fire with their chai, yawning. Sun rays are trapped in fog. The morning feels like evening. The unbroken-broken cups hidden among the banyan's roots must be covered in frost, the girl thinks, wondering if she should show them to the boy. But what if he has a girlfriend at school? What if he has held her hand? When a labourer coughs, the boy says that his mother coughs all the time. Something is wrong with her lungs.

'I'll become a doctor and treat her,' he adds.

'Treat us also,' jokes the labourer.

The boy smiles. 'I will.'

The chai has finally awakened the men. They won't stop talking now.

'People should be able to become whoever they want to be.'

'But the problem is that there are too many people.'

'And too few things one can become.'

'And fewer things one can sell to buy rice.'

Their laughter is followed by silence.

'I want to become Beyoncé,' the girl says.

'Who?'

∽

The new prime minister's face is everywhere. On telephone poles and park benches and garbage cans and the backs of cars and even on the faces of so many people who wear masks of his face with tiny holes for eyes. The girl doesn't know how his face appeared on the water pump outside the stall. Sometimes she is unable to flavour the boy's chai with cardamom for fear of the prime minister watching her. Other times she skips the cardamom because, for all she knows, the boy doesn't even care.

∽

The Great Indian Tee and Snakes is out of sugar. The girl walks to the grocery store. Tiny rocks push into the soles of her feet through the cracks in her chappals. Once she had stolen a pair of cat-printed chappals from outside the temple, but they have been lying under her bed ever since. She worries that the owner may spot them and take them away.

The grocer is an old man who is partially deaf. The TV in the store needs to be pounded from time to time to keep the images from splintering. The place is packed during the cricket season when people stop by to watch an over or two, praise or curse Dhoni. After purchasing the sugar, the girl is too caught up watching on TV the magnified insides of somebody's mouth being cleansed by a toothpaste that tastes like turmeric to notice when the boy appears next to her. He asks the man for chewing gum.

'Hello,' he says to the girl.

'Arrey, tum?'

The boy is standing right next to her in a place where her father's gaze is not upon them. She can touch the kite-shaped birthmark on that neck if she wants to. The man has left a pack of gum on the counter before returning his attention to the TV.

'Nice to see you outside the stall for a change,' the boy says.

'Same.'

'You'll make a good Beyoncé. Probably better than Beyoncé herself.'

The girl touches her bindi, smiling, telling herself that she was wrong about the boy having a girlfriend at school. 'Won't you offer me chewing gum?'

'Absolutely.'

The girl chews the gum until it's time to go to bed, then she swallows it.

෴

The girl examines ordinary objects with newfound fascination—a matchbox, a potato, freight trucks on the road, the ground beneath her feet—thinking that nothing is bigger or smaller than it should be. Everything is the perfect size. She air-dries her shampooed hair in the afternoon sun instead of twisting it up in a towel. She wonders if this is how girls become women. One night when she is putting a broken cup back together, soiled with the keema-eater's saliva, blood gushes out of her finger like water from the pump. Nevertheless, unlike the brides whose hands she paints with henna, she feels no need for a husband and a house and a washing machine and a baby and a mixer-grinder to be content. All she needs is for the boy in the white skull cap to drink chai and eat samosas at the stall so she can watch him watch her.

෴

The labourers are talking about an upcoming cinema hall in town that will play three movies at once. The boy is eating a keema samosa, waiting for his chai. Around a dozen young men with saffron bandanas arrive on motorbikes. They order chai and aloo samosas. The girl's father tells them to leave because they never pay.

'This isn't a wedding you can crash any time,' he says.

'Don't be so touchy now,' says a young man. His T-shirt is just as saffron as his bandana. He looks like a carrot.

'Extra spicy samosas, please,' another young man tells the girl.

When the girl's father stands up to protest, the young man who looks like a carrot pushes him into his chair before noticing that his companions are still struggling to park their motorbikes.

'Who the fuck left this bicycle here?' He hollers.

'It's mine,' says the boy in the white skull cap. He starts moving his bicycle but the young man stops him.

'You think this is the fucking Olympics?'

'I am sorry. I'll move it.'

'Sorry won't do. Say, "chai is great".'

'Haan?'

'Say it.'

'Chai…chai is….'

'You don't like chai?'

'I drink it every day.'

'So say it! "Chai is great"!'

'Chai is…great.'

The girl whips the batter slowly. She would poison the samosas if she could.

'Good. Now pick up your disgusting samosa and throw it away.'

'What?'

'You deaf?'

'No more keema samosas for you,' says another young man. 'Only aloo samosas from now.'

'But I like keema samosas,' says the boy.

The young man who looks like a carrot slaps him. The girl stops whipping the batter.

'Throw your samosa away or we'll boil you with the chai.'

The boy does as he is told.

The young man takes off his saffron bandana before handing it over to the boy. 'Now get rid of that dumb skull cap and put this on.'

'I won't.'

'You won't?'

This time the boy looks into the young man's eyes.

'I will not do that.'

The young men beat up the boy, calling him a fucking keema-eater, asking him to go back to his keema-country as one of them makes a video on his phone. The girl's father and some of the labourers try to intervene unsuccessfully. The girl begs the men to let the boy go. 'All he does is water flowers!' she screams. Nobody listens. A couple of labourers join in after some time, calling the boy names, thrusting their shovels into his stomach. 'But he is going to become a doctor and treat you!' the girl pleads. 'How could you forget?' Her father yells at her to go into the house. The boy looks like a punctured tomato and dies.

∽

December is almost over. The girl with the black bindi weeps when she is cold. She cannot stand straight. She cannot hold her head high. She cannot feel her nose. When her father wakes her up in the mornings, she turns her back towards him. 'No,' she says. She sneaks out keema samosas from the stall before eating them hidden behind the kangaroo-shaped trash cans at the park. She has never eaten anything with keema before. It tastes like tears until she realizes that she needs to stop crying while eating. After that, it tastes like food. Newspapers carry front-page pictures of the boy in the white skull cap, sitting against a plain grey background, in even lighting, unsmiling, but alive. He looks straight at her. Now, instead of Beyoncé's pictures, the girl cuts out every picture of the boy from every paper before burying them under her mattress. She wipes the frost off the unbroken-broken cups under the banyan tree.

∽

When the wedding season arrives, the girl has too many henna assignments and not enough time to grieve. The brides talk while getting their hands painted because the girl listens. One of the brides points to a picture on the wall. Her fiancé is holding the Taj Mahal in the palm of his hands. Another bride tells the girl that her fiancé's name is Adithya with an H. She wants his name on both her hands, front and back. Another requests her to feed her chocolate after her hands are covered in mehndi. Yet another suggests the girl play hard-to-get if she ever wants her boyfriend to propose for marriage. 'Love requires you to be something of an asshole,' she says. And yet another woman looks uninterested in all such matters despite her Banarasi sari and eye make-up, despite the jasmine flowers in her hair, as she spreads her hands before the girl. She doesn't even remember her fiancé's name. The girl tells her that it doesn't seem like she wants to get married.

'I don't.'

'What do you want to do then?'

'Paint pictures of the sky.'

'You can do that even if you're married.'

'I can do that even if I'm not.'

'But why the sky?'

'Because it is infinite.'

∽

Newspapers are covered in pictures of a high-speed train by the time the weddings are over. There's a nationwide ban on keema samosas, keema naan, keema parathas, keema pakoras and, basically, keema everything. The girl loiters in the park with Gandhi's statue.

In the mornings, a group of men stand in a circle and force themselves to laugh. They are loud and self-assured, the type that eat aloo samosas. At first, they go, 'Ho-ho, ha-ha, ho-ho, ha-ha'. Before long, however, they are laughing uproariously, teeth bared, arms raised in the air. The girl wonders if they had seen the front-page pictures of the boy in the white skull cap. In the evening, young men and women take too many selfies against the fountain. The young women wear lipstick, the young men have their hair sticking up. Their faces change when they point their phone cameras towards themselves. The girl wonders if they have ever tasted a keema samosa.

Men in blue uniforms water the plants in the park. One of them is watering a bed of flowers. The petals are more purple on the inside than the outside. She walks up to him.

'Sir, are these germiums?'

'What are you talking about?'

'Are these germium flowers?'

'There are no flowers by that name.'

She walks up to another man who is watering potted yellow flowers with long, spaced-out petals, and repeats the question.

'No,' he says, 'but nice tits.'

∽

The girl sits on a park bench and tries to fall in love again. She tries to fall in love with the boy in an oversized T-shirt who is kicking a football, or the one who is doing push-ups, or the young man with the shocking blue earphones, walking with his hands in his pockets, or the boy who is holding hands with a girl who has streaks of red hair, or the one lying on his stomach, reading a book, or maybe even the one who is ogling the women practising yoga. Nothing happens.

Then she lies on her back and stares at the infinite sky. She hopes the woman who didn't remember her fiancé's name is painting as many pictures of the sky as she wants to. But infinity is not the girl's type. She needs something more measurable than that, something smaller than the sky but bigger than a samosa.

It is a pleasant April morning. The men who force themselves to laugh are laughing like there's no tomorrow. One of them notices the girl sitting by herself and invites her to join them. 'Guaranteed to make you happy,' he says. She reluctantly accepts. In the beginning, she stands there, wanting to disappear. Then, encouraged by the men, she smiles a small, confused smile. Then she laughs softly because everyone else is laughing. For a few minutes, it feels insincere, but after that, she is actually laughing aloud. She bookmarks this as an important skill.

A man turns to her when it's over.

'So, young lady, are you happy now?'

She looks at the beads of sweat on his forehead, laughter lines around his mouth.

'Are you?' she asks.

14

THE ACCOUNTS OFFICER'S WIFE

LAKSHMIKANTH K. AYYAGARI

Many years ago, in a village called Uttarapuram, there was a Brahmin settlement. Houses with red potsherd roofs, common walls, and wide verandas stretched for about half a kilometre. At one end stood a peepul tree, and at the other a wall, with red and white stripes, enclosing a temple dedicated to Sri Venkateswara Swamy. Dhanalakshmi came here after her marriage to Kutumba Rao. She was sixteen. She had spent most of her childhood skipping stones across the pond and chasing puppies in the coconut plantations. Her education comprised a few poems her mother taught her, and she sang them aloud as she walked along the goat trail by the pond, stopping wherever she found a pebble promising enough to trump nine bounces, her unbeaten record.

One day, her father announced that she would marry Kutumba Rao, the accounts officer from Uttarapuram, and she didn't quite understand what it meant. Leaving her mother and her village and moving to Uttarapuram with Kutumba Rao was too much to wrap her head around at once. Her mother-in-law, Ramayamma, was a stout woman, five feet tall, with a large face and probing eyes. She wore a spot of dense vermilion between her thick eyebrows, which Dhanalakshmi found unsettling. Ramayamma had waited a long time for a daughter-in-law; when she got one, she declared that she would relinquish her responsibilities and dedicate the rest of her life to serve her gods: her husband and Sri Venkateswara Swamy.

Dhanalakshmi's lessons began from her first day at Uttarapuram. Ramayamma expounded the ways of a married woman, both as a daughter-in-law and as a wife. Dhanalakshmi imbibed her new life by degrees. At first, she was silent and contemplative, often staring at objects with a vacant expression that belied the train of thought that chugged on in her head.

With time, the clamour subsided. She perfected the routine of waking up before sunrise, fetching two pails of water from the community well, bathing, cooking while her clothes were still damp, and maintaining all the rules she was expected to. She learnt what spices were allowed on what days. She noted how many spoons of sugar her husband and her father-in-law preferred in their coffees. There were precise timings for serving breakfast, lunch, and dinner, and all were met with impeccable punctuality. She learnt the required propriety when conversing with the men in her family.

'Never ask men where they are going. It will jinx their purpose.' Ramayamma told her when she stopped Kutumba Rao at the door one day.

Many mornings, when they sat in front of bronze and silver idols, long lists were committed to memory: what offerings for what gods, which flowers for which goddesses, what rituals for male children, which days to fast on for a husband's longevity.

But dawn after dawn, the crowing of roosters brought days that felt longer, more tiresome. Chores multiplied and appeared out of nowhere. She began feeling hauled through the hours of the day by an invisible force. As the sun sank below the horizon, a strange weariness descended upon her. Was it exhaustion? Was it her mother-in-law? Was it because she wasn't able to befriend her neighbours? She didn't know.

Sometimes, after serving lunch, she would croon, her mother's poems on her lips, under the cool of the guava tree in the backyard. Sometimes, she spent a while longer at the well and skipped stones, although the well limited the bounces to two. When she missed her mother, she suppressed her tears by grasping tighter the handle of the pail, or the wood of the millstone, or the strip of husk she was peeling off a coconut. Some evenings, a mixture of confusion, fear, and gloom stirred her stomach. She was someone else in a place she couldn't recognize no matter how hard she tried.

One such evening, Ramayamma found her in the backyard, gazing at the horizon, lost in its dim hues. When she turned, Ramayamma saw her misty eyes. She went to her and held her by her shoulders.

'What is this? Are you crying?' she asked.

Dhanalakshmi lowered her head and remained silent.

'You are not your mother's little girl any more. Do you know who you are now?'

Ramayamma placed two fingers under Dhanalakshmi's chin and lifted her face. 'You are the wife of Kutumba Rao! You are the accounts officer's wife! You understand?'

Ramayamma's vermilion appeared more menacing from this close. But a hint of a smile that for the first time lingered on the otherwise stern face lightened Dhanalakshmi's heart.

'Do you know how many accounts officers there are in this district?'

Dhanalakshmi shook her head. A faint 'No' slipped past her quivering lips.

'Only one! And that one is your husband!'

'Now, say it aloud.... I am the accounts officer's wife!'

Dhanalakshmi hesitated.

'Come on!'

'I am the accounts officer's wife,' she said, trembling.

'Louder now!'

'I am the accounts officer's wife!' she said, her voice still faint.

'That's right. Now go. No more crying like a little girl.'

These words calmed her. Like in one of the poems she recited that extolled the luminous image of Sri Ram, she imagined her soul take the form of a warm flame and travel across the sky to fuse with a luminous image of her husband, Kutumba Rao. Albeit inchoate, a new determination took root in her, and she refused to be a young girl in a strange place. She accepted, at that moment, that she belonged to a different family and welcomed with new-found confidence her responsibility to this family.

∽

Kutumba Rao was kind to Dhanalakshmi. Like many women in Uttarapuram, she too was struck by his handsomeness. With perfectly combed hair, thick-rimmed spectacles, a golden pen in the front pocket of his crisply starched shirt, and a stark white dhoti, he exuded an officer's dignity and grandeur. Every day, after returning from his office, he would ask Dhanalakshmi about her day and whether she'd had lunch. Although that was almost the extent of his conversation with her, we must note that a certain aloofness and reserve in husbands were common those days and often was what was expected of them.

For a while, Dhanalakshmi felt better. The disquietude that had once been a constant feature of her evenings dwindled to mild yearnings for her life before marriage. But soon, a new concern distressed her. It was the end of the first year of her marriage, and she was still without child.

Her visits to the temple along with Ramayamma increased in number and duration. She could discern the disappointment in Ramayamma. She felt stifled, shunned. Wives and grandmothers whispered in her ears and gave her powders. She stacked their little bottles in her trunk. Some of these could have been useful, but her problem was different, and she couldn't tell anyone about it.

The act itself was, to her, painful. Kutumba Rao was gentle, still, she couldn't help but protest when her skin felt lacerated. Some nights, when he gave up, she was relieved. Other nights, when he persisted, the subsequent mornings were so painful that she wished she could go back in time. She often wondered how other women felt, how her mother felt, if something was wrong with her. These questions remained unasked. With each of these nights, she built endurance, but it didn't help enough.

As she despaired, a letter from her mother arrived, bringing relief. It requested Kutumba Rao to send Dhanalakshmi back to her natal village for her father's sixtieth birthday. Kutumba Rao and his parents agreed, and Dhanalakshmi packed her trunk with much excitement. A bullock-cart ride to the nearby bus station and a three-hour journey in a state transport bus took her to her village.

After the celebrations were over, she spent time with her mother in the kitchen. Besides flaunting her newly honed culinary skills, she managed a few whispered conversations. With a pleasant smile and tender words, her mother assured her that nothing was wrong with her and that everything would get better with time. Vague and heavy guilt lifted off her bosom. Her gait took on the cheerful bounce that was once hers. A day before her scheduled departure, a smooth flat pebble bounced nine times and fell on the other side of the pond. After all these months, she was still the same girl she used to be. She smiled a childish smile, but immediately replaced it with a collected expression befitting an accounts officer's wife.

That evening, when she returned from the pond, a telegram arrived from Kutumba Rao's father. It assured the good health of everyone, yet urged Dhanalakshmi's father to visit Uttarapuram at once. It said nothing about Dhanalakshmi.

༄

The next day, Dhanalakshmi and her father journeyed to Uttarapuram. As they entered the house, Ramayamma asked Dhanalakshmi to go into the kitchen and wait till called. Dhanalakshmi obliged, although her eyes questioned the silence that engulfed the hall and the presence of strange persons there. Kutumba Rao stood straight, with his hands crossed. An old man with a freckled face and two other elderly men stood opposite him. Beckoned by Kutumba Rao's father, the elders sat in their chairs.

Dhanalakshmi tarried in the kitchen, sliding her palm over the steel jars lined up on the shelf. Questions flooded her mind, and the silence unnerved her. Sunlight streamed in through the window and reflected off the jars, blinding her. When she heard her father shout, a shiver traversed her spine. She had never heard her father speak above a whisper. Ramayamma appeared and asked Dhanalakshmi to make coffee as if to distract her from what was transpiring in the hall.

The milk began to boil and the firewood burnt with a heavy smoke. She was blowing air through a sooty iron pipe when, through the window, she saw a young woman in the backyard with someone who looked like her mother. They stood next to the guava tree. The mother had covered her head with her sari, and her daughter stood with one hand resting on the lower branch of the tree. She was remarkably fair with a beautiful face, elegant, almond-shaped eyes, and a finely shaped nose that sported a glittering ruby-studded nose ring. Her hair was jet-black and braided into one long plait that hung till below her trim waist. She stood there with apparent breathlessness and a tremble which, though visible, did not betray the grace she seemed to possess. Dhanalakshmi stared at her for more than a minute, wondering if she was indeed as delicate as she looked.

The milk spilled over. Dhanalakshmi took the pot down with her bare hands and her fingers turned a deep pink. As she dipped them in a pail of water, Ramayamma appeared again and asked her to join her father in the hall. She also called in the mother and her daughter from the backyard. Everyone assembled, and, for a moment, everyone was silent.

In the next few minutes, truth, like an executioner's whip, lashed Dhanalakshmi. Her husband had slept with the young woman in the backyard, and she was pregnant with Kutumba Rao's child. And, after all the deliberations that had happened without her in the hall, it was agreed by all, including her father, that Kutumba Rao would marry this woman, and they, that is, Kutumba Rao, this woman, and Dhanalakshmi would enter into this arrangement under the blessings of Sri Venkateswara Swamy, who was wed to both goddess Sridevi and goddess Padmavati. It was also announced that the wedding ceremony would take place the coming Thursday in the very same Sri Venkateswara Swamy temple. Dhanalakshmi looked at her father. On hearing nothing from him, she wobbled a bit, regained her balance, and ran out of the house towards the well and jumped into the water with a heavy splash.

And that is when, some said, Dhanalakshmi became a little odd. What went on inside her head is something we, of course, cannot be sure of. It is indeed true that ever since that day the local doctors visited her house frequently. Then again, the causes behind these visits, to the extent we can adduce, were more to do with the frailty of her body than of her mind, for both the doctors were physicians and not psychiatrists.

∞

After she was brought home, Dhanalakshmi slept all day. Her father, who had not yet left, tried to persuade her to eat, but she refused. He sat by her side throughout the day and throughout the night, and at some point during the night, he fell asleep in the armchair he had been sitting in. Next morning, before the roosters crowed, when Ramayamma entered the room, Dhanalakshmi wasn't there. Ramayamma woke Kutumba Rao up. He ran to the well, dived into the cold water, and searched for long, but nothing indicated her having drowned. A search party consisting of Kutumba Rao and a few able men went out with their torchlights. They split into two groups and searched in different directions, one along the track leading to the bus station by the highway eight kilometres away, and the other along the muddy road that went through Uttarapuram to the adjacent village twelve kilometres away. At noon both parties returned without success despite enquiring with everyone they met on their way.

They assembled in front of Kutumba Rao's house. Dhanalakshmi's father grew frantic by the minute. Ramayamma tried a few pacifying words but was quickly silenced by her husband, who stood stiff and straight on the veranda, tapping his knuckles with his fingers. Dhanalakshmi's disappearance caused much stir in the settlement. It couldn't be contained, unlike the news of her jumping into the well. Consumed by guilt and standing in the presence of his wife's father, whom he felt answerable to, Kutumba Rao explained to the men why Dhanalakshmi had disappeared. Everyone had questions. Could she have boarded the bus to her village? Are there any morning buses to her village? Did she carry any money on her? Kutumba

Rao replied patiently to all. When the questions petered out he sat down on the veranda step, his head in his hands.

About half past noon, Dhanalakshmi appeared, coming out of the Sri Venkateswara Swamy temple merely yards away. After the initial shriek from a young man who first spotted her, everyone remained silent and stared at her as she neared, carrying a baby turtle from the temple tank in her hand. It had never occurred to any of them to search the temple. Regular temple-goers wouldn't have spotted her, for the pillars limited their view. Only a thorough search could have revealed someone sheltering there, but no one, even once, suggested searching for her in the temple. And when they saw her walk out of the gate, they gaped in silence. Some said that, as she came out, she was talking to the turtle with much animation. Some claimed that she was sweating profusely and that her countenance showed wild excitement interspersed with ghastly frowns. Both could have been right. But what everyone remembered clearly was the answer she gave her father near the porch.

As she approached, she appeared utterly oblivious to everything around her. Kutumba Rao was relieved. He kept looking at her, hoping for some sort of acknowledgement. His parents stared at her like the rest of the crowd. Her appearance appeased her father's pounding heart and dissolved the stone that was stuck in his parched throat. He was angry with her but didn't know how to rebuke her. She walked up to the house unconcernedly.

'WHAT were you doing in the temple since daybreak?'

'Oh,' she replied, 'I was sleeping with the pandit.'

∽

Dhanalakshmi went to her room and slept. Kutumba remained at the door and didn't step in as if thwarted by an invisible line that would burst into flames were he to cross it. For a long while, he watched her sleep. Later, he returned to his room and tallied his accounts. Her father sat by her side, like the previous day, in an armchair. As his fatigued nerves relaxed, he descended into a deep slumber. Ramayamma went into the room the following morning, and again, Dhanalakshmi wasn't there.

Ramayamma was furious. The sympathy she'd had for her daughter-in-law vanished. She decided that she wouldn't care any more. It was better her son slept. There was no point searching for this woman in the chilly morning. It was her karma; there was nothing one could do about it. Half an hour later, Dhanalakshmi's father woke up. He stormed out of the room, saw Ramayamma sweeping the backyard, and enquired about his daughter. At her reply, he slapped his forehead, rushed to Kutumba Rao's room, and woke him up.

Kutumba Rao went to the well first. He walked at a measured pace and was less agitated than the day before. From the well, he went to the temple and searched behind every pillar and enquired with the pandits. She was not there. Walking back to his house, he wondered if the neighbours would be willing to assist him again. Choosing not to take their help, he walked eight kilometres to the bus station, making enquiries along the way. Unsuccessful in finding her whereabouts, he returned at about quarter past seven in the morning. His mother served breakfast. He was hungry, but when Dhanalakshmi's father refused to eat, he followed suit. This enraged Ramayamma further. Muttering inaudibly, she took both plates back into the kitchen.

Kutumba Rao was leaving the house to search in another direction when, at the end of the street, below the peepul tree, he saw Dhanalakshmi. She was carrying a stray puppy and was swaying sideways as if drunk. The street dogs were barking, jumping, and howling. They were so riotous that everyone rushed out to see what was happening. Kutumba Rao stood on the porch steps as motionless as the day before.

Ramayamma was thoroughly scandalized. She dropped a copper bowl, and it tumbled down the porch steps. Her face contorted. Cursing loudly, she went back into the house with heavy, resounding steps.

Dhanalakshmi's father looked resignedly at his daughter as she approached him. This time, it was clear that she was talking to the puppy. She staggered, stumbled, and zigzagged up to the porch. The stench of palm toddy was pungent, and everyone took a step back involuntarily. She almost fell when, with a swift manoeuvre, she regained her balance and stood, puppy in arms, in front of her father, smiling a broad smile. Neighbours stood on their verandas, their mouths betraying their inner excitement. The dogs followed her, barking incessantly. Ramayamma paced about in the kitchen, vexed by the intolerable growls that now echoed from the hall. She threw a steel plate from the kitchen into the hall, expecting it to silence the dogs. The dogs didn't stop.

Dhanalakshmi fell forward and her father caught her in time. She stood erect again and pushed the puppy towards him. He took the puppy with a downcast face and was about to put it down, but it looked like the dogs would tear it apart. Confounded by everything around him, he went to place the puppy on the veranda when she stopped him, saying, 'No, Appa …take him to the backyard. I am marrying him tomorrow in the temple.'

⁂

Kutumba Rao's father postponed his son's second marriage by a month. Did he expect Dhanalakshmi to become normal by then? Dhanalakshmi left every day before dawn and no one could do anything to stop her. Her father wrote to his wife asking her to come immediately. However, she was sick and took two weeks to visit Uttarapuram. Meanwhile, Kutumba Rao resumed office work, the two old men read newspapers in their armchairs, and Ramayamma grew more and more furious by the day.

One day, Dhanalakshmi prepared a variety of delicacies: spiced dal with spinach, tender purple brinjals incised with precision and stuffed with a paste of fenugreek seeds, rasam, fried pumpkin crisps, thick curd, rice steamed to perfection, and a payasam made of rice, lentils, jaggery, cardamom, cashews, and thin wedges of copra. She made these the way Ramayamma had taught her, but at three in the morning. She feasted all alone and left for the toddy stalls, having exhausted quite a share of the monthly rations, and leaving behind many used utensils.

Another day, she returned with a stiff roll of tobacco sticking out of the corner of her mouth and seemed to have mastered the art of smoking tobacco the rustic way. Another morning, she took away both the water pails and brought them back filled with toddy. Ramayamma hurled abuse at her to no effect.

After two weeks, when her mother arrived, Dhanalakshmi wasn't at home. Ramayamma complained at length about all the scandalous behaviour she'd had to witness. Her mother listened silently, nodding at intervals. That day too, both the pails were missing. Dhanalakshmi returned after an hour, swaying more than usual, holding the toddy-filled buckets and puffing at her tobacco roll. She looked at her mother and paused. Her mother surveyed her with wide eyes and, for a moment, smiled—a gentle, cautious expansion of the cheeks, a soft inhale, an indiscernible parting of the lips, and a dimple of tempered surprise. Dhanalakshmi stood still, blinking.

A brief silence ensued, and then the frenzied voice of Ramayamma shattered the quiet: 'Look at her! This is her routine. What a disgrace!

This is unacceptable, madam, no matter the cause. Unacceptable by any standard! She must be thrown out of the house, but my son won't allow it! God help us with this abomination! Knock some sense into her. You are her mother; it's your....'

Dhanalakshmi dropped the pails. They fell with a heavy thud, shook, and lay still on the floor. Toddy splashed on Kutumba Rao's father's newspaper and on his clean-shaven face. He folded the soiled paper and went into the yard, wiping his face. Dhanalakshmi stepped up, stood in front of Ramayamma, peered into her face, and blew a wisp of smoke at her.

'What effrontery! Nasty woman!' Ramayamma screamed.

Dhanalakshmi's mother stood up in an effort to defuse the situation, but before she could take one step, Dhanalakshmi, with loud retching, vomited all over Ramayamma and collapsed.

Kutumba Rao came home with the local doctor. Dhanalakshmi was on her bed and her parents sat by her side. Her father-in-law was in the armchair, troubled by the smell of toddy that persisted despite his meticulous scrubbing of his face and body. Ramayamma was still bathing. Kutumba Rao stood by the doctor who was checking Dhanalakshmi's pulse. His mother-in-law's presence renewed his sense of guilt. The doctor unplugged the stethoscope from his ears and replaced it in his briefcase.

'Nothing to worry about...is she your wife?'

'Yes.'

'Congratulations! She is pregnant.'

15

LORRY RAJA

MADHURI VIJAY

What happened was that my older brother, Siju, got a job as a lorry driver at the mine and started acting like a big shot. He stopped playing with Munna the way he used to, tossing him into the air like a sack of sand, making him sputter with laughter. When Amma asked him anything, he would give her a pitying look and not answer. He stopped speaking to his girlfriend, Manju, altogether. He taunted me about playing in the mud, as he called it, breaking chunks of iron ore with my hammer. With Appa especially he was reckless, not bothering to conceal his disdain, until he said something about failed drivers who are only good for digging and drinking, and Appa wrestled him to the ground and forced him to eat a handful of the red, iron-rich earth, shouting that this was our living now and he should bloody learn to respect it. Siju complained to the mine's labour officer, Mr Subbu, but Mr Subbu dismissed it as a domestic matter and refused to interfere. After that, Siju maintained a glowering silence in Appa's presence. When Appa wasn't around, Siju sneered at our tent, a swatch of blue plastic stretched over a bamboo skeleton. Never mind that he was being paid half a regular driver's salary by the owner of the lorry, a paan-chewing Andhra fellow called Rajappa, because Siju was only fourteen and could not bargain for more.

Never mind that Rajappa's lorry permit was fake, a flimsy transparent chit of paper with no expiry date and half the words illegible, which meant that Siju was allowed to transport the ore only to the railway station in Hospet and not, like the other drivers, all the way to port cities like Mangalore and Chennai, where he'd run the risk of arrest by border authorities. Never mind that the mine's lorry cleaners, most of whom were boys my age, called him Lorry Raja behind his back and imitated his high-stepping walk. None of it seemed to matter to him. And, as little as I wanted to admit it, he was a raja in the cab of that lorry, and moreover he looked it. His hair was thick and black, and a long tuft descended at the back of his neck, like a crow's glossy tail feathers. His nose was straight, and his eyeballs were untouched by yellow. His teeth remained white in spite of breathing the iron-laden air. He seemed, when he was in the cab of that lorry, like someone impossible and important, someone I didn't know at all.

The ore went to the port cities, and then it went on to ships the size of buildings. I hadn't seen them, but the labour officer, Mr Subbu, had told us about them. He said the ships crossed the ocean, and the journey took weeks. The ships went to Australia and Japan, but mostly they went to China. They were building a stadium in China for something called the Lympic Games. Mr Subbu explained that the Lympic Games were like the World Cup, except for all sports instead of just cricket. Swimming, tennis, shooting, running. If you won you got a gold medal, Mr Subbu said. India had won a gold medal in boxing the last time the games were held.

The stadium in China would be round like a cricket stadium, except ten times bigger. Mr Subbu spread his arms out wide when he said this, and we could see patches of sweat under the arms of his nice ironed shirt.

The whole world worked in the mines. At least that is what it seemed like then. There was a drought in Karnataka and neighbouring Andhra Pradesh, and things were so bad people were starting to eye the mangy street dogs. Our neighbour poured kerosene on himself and three daughters and lit them ablaze; his wife burned her face but escaped. Then came the news of the mines, hundreds of them opening in Bellary, needing workers. And people went. It seemed to happen overnight. They asked their brothers-in-law or their uncles to look after their plots and their houses, or simply sold them. They pulled their children out of school. Whole villages were suddenly abandoned, cropless fields left to wither. Families waited near bus depots plastered with faded film signs, carrying big bundles stuffed with steel pots and plastic shoes and flimsy clothes. The buses were so full they tilted to one side. There wasn't enough space for everyone. The people who were left behind tried running alongside the buses, and some of the more foolish ones tried to jump in as the bus was moving. They would invariably fall, lie in the dust for a while, staring up at the rainless sky. Then they would get up, brush off their clothes, and go back to wait for the next bus. For months my family watched this happen. We didn't worry, not at first. Appa had a job as a driver for a sub-inspector of the Raichur Thermal Power Plant, and we thought we were fine. Then there was the accident, and Appa lost the job. He spent the next few weeks at the rum shop, coming home long enough to belt me or my brother Siju or Amma. After that was over he cried for a long time. Then he announced that we were going to work in the mines. All of us. Siju, who was in the seventh standard at the time, tried to protest, but Appa twisted a bruise into his arm and Siju stopped complaining. I was in the fifth standard, and to me it seemed like a grand adventure. Amma said nothing. She was pregnant with Munna then, and her feet had swollen to the size of papayas. She hobbled into the hut to pack our things.

Within a week, we squeezed on to a bus that was leaking black droplets of oil from its heavy bottom, and Appa bought us each a newspaper cone of hot peanuts for the journey. I flicked the burnt peanuts into my mouth and watched as the land slowly got dryer and redder, until the buildings in the huddled villages we passed were red too, and so was the bark of the trees, and so were the fingers of the ticket collector who checked the stub in Appa's hand and said, 'Next stop.' We lurched into a teeming bus station with a cracked floor, and I asked Appa why the ground was red, and he told me this was because of the iron in it. While Appa was busy asking directions to the nearest mine that was hiring, and Amma was searching in her blouse for money to buy a packet of Tiger biscuits and a bottle of 7Up for our lunch, Siju came up to me and whispered that, really, the ground was red because there was blood in it, seeping up to the surface from the miners' bodies buried underneath. For months I believed him, and every step I took was in fear, bracing for the sticky wetness of blood, the crunch of bone, the squelch of an organ. When I realized the truth I tried to hit him, but he held my wrists so hard they hurt, and he bared his teeth close to my face, laughing.

That afternoon, just about a year after we had come to the mine, I was working an open pit beside the highway, along with a few other children and a handful of women. I squatted by the edge of the road, close enough that the warm exhaust from the vehicles billowed my faded T-shirt and seeped under my shorts. The pinch of tobacco Amma had given me that morning to stave off my hunger had long since lost its flavour. It was now a bland, warm glob tucked in my cheek. Heat pressed down on my skin, and there was a sharp, metallic tinge to the air that made me uneasy. The women, who usually laughed and teased each other, curved their backs into shells and hammered in silence. The children seemed more careless than usual because I kept hearing small cries whenever one of them brought a hammer down on a thumb by accident. The horizon to the west was congested with a dark breast of clouds, but above me the sun blazed white through a gauzy sky. The monsoons were late, too late for crops, but I knew they would hit any time now. Over the past week, furious little rainstorms had begun to tear up the red earth, flooding various pits, making them almost impossible to mine. I remembered that during the last monsoon, a drunk man had wandered away one night and fallen into a flooded pit. His body, by the time it was discovered, was bloated and black.

Lorries crawled in sluggish streams in both directions on the highway. The ones heading away from Bellary were weighed down with ore, great mounds wrapped in grey and green tarpaulin and lashed with lengths of rope as thick as my ankle. The empty ones returning from the port cities rattled with stray pebbles jumping in the back. The faces of the lorry drivers were glistening with sweat, and they blared their horns as if it might make the nearly immobile line of traffic speed up. Now and then a foreign car, belonging to one of the mine owners, slipped noiselessly through the stalled traffic. I recited the names of the cars, tonguing the tobacco in my mouth: Maserati. Jaguar. Mercedes. Jaguar. Their shimmering bodies caught the sun and played with it, light sliding across their hoods, winking in their tail lights. The mine owners lived in huge pink and white houses on the highway, houses with fountains and the grim heads of stone lions staring from the balconies. I looked up as a sleek black Maserati went by, and in its tinted window I saw myself, a boy in shorts and a baggy T-shirt, crouching close to the dirt. And, standing behind me, the distorted shape of a girl. I stood up quickly, hammer in hand, and whirled around.

Manju flinched, as if I might attack her with it. A few days before, I had seen two kids get into a hammer fight over a Titan watch they had found together. One of them smashed the other's hand. Later I found a small square fingernail stamped into the ground where they fought.

'I'm not going to hit you,' I said.

Her slow smile pulled her cheeks into small brown hills sunk with shadowy dimples. She smoothed down the front of her dress, which was actually a school uniform. It had once been white but was now tinged with red iron dust. It wrapped around her thin body, ending below her knees and buttoning high at her throat. Her hair spilled in knotted waves down her back. She and her mother had arrived at the mine around the same time as we had. Her mother was sick and never came out of their tent. I didn't know what was wrong with her. For a while Manju had been Siju's girlfriend, saving up her extra tobacco for him, nodding seriously when he spoke, following him everywhere. Then he had stopped speaking to her. The one time I asked him about it, Siju leaned to one side, curled his lip, and spat delicately into the mud.

'Hi, Manju,' I said. We were the same height, though she was a few years older, maybe fifteen.

'Hi, Guna,' she said, and squatted at my feet. I squatted too and waited for her to do something. She picked up the piece of ore I had been working on and gave it two half-hearted taps with her hammer. Then she seemed to lose interest. She let it fall and said, 'He came by already?'

'No,' I said.

I liked Manju. Whenever journalists or NGO workers came to tour the mines, Manju and I would drop our hammers and prance in circles, shouting, 'No child-y labour here!' According to the mine owners, it was our parents who were supposed to be working. We simply lived with them and played around the mine. The hammers and basins were our toys. The journalists would scribble in their notepads, and the NGO workers would whisper to one another, and Manju would grin widely at me. Then, after we found out about the Lympic Games, we had contests of our own. Running contests, stone-throwing contests, rock-piling contests. The winner got the gold medal, the runner-up clapped and stomped the dirt in applause. I liked playing with Manju because I almost always won, and she never got angry when she lost, like the boys sometimes did.

'Manju,' I said now. 'Want to race? Bet I'll get the gold medal.'

But she just shook her head. She stared up at the lorries. She was thin, and the bones at the top of her spine pushed like pebbles against her uniform. I wanted to reach out and tap them gently with my hammer. One of the lorry drivers, a man with a thick moustache, saw her watching and made a wet kissing sound with his lips, like he was sucking an invisible straw. His tongue came out, fleshy and purple. He shouted, 'Hi, sexy girl! Sexy fun girl!' My cheeks burned for her, and I could feel the weight of the women's gazes, but Manju looked at him as if he had told her that rain was on the way. I busied myself with filling my puttu with lumps of ore. Each full basin I took to the weighing station would earn me five and a half rupees. On a good day I could fill seven or eight puttus, if I ignored the blisters at the base of my thumb.

I felt the other workers looking at us, the frank stares of the children. I carefully shifted the glob of tobacco from my right cheek to my left.

'You shouldn't be playing those dumb-stupid games anyway,' Manju said.

'No?' I said cautiously. 'Why not?'

Manju said, 'You should be in school.'

I didn't know what to say. It had been two years since I sat in a classroom. I had only vague recollections of it. The cold mud floor. Sitting next to a boy called Dheeraj, who smelled of castor oil. Slates with cracked plastic frames. The maths teacher who called us human head lice when we couldn't solve the sum on the board. All of us chanting in unison an English poem we didn't understand. *The boy stood on the burning deck.* The antiseptic smell of the girls' toilet covering another, mustier, smell. Dheeraj giggling outside. Then three, four, five whacks on the fleshy part of my palm with a wooden ruler, and trying not to show that it hurt. *The boy stood on the burning deck whence all but he had fled.*

'You used to come first in class, no?' Manju said. A grey gust of exhaust blew a wisp of hair between her teeth. She chewed on it. Her face was whiskered with red dust.

'How do you know?'

'Siju told me,' she said, which surprised me. 'Siju said you got a hundred in every subject, even the difficult ones like maths. He said you shouldn't be wasting your potential here.'

I had never heard him say anything like that. It sounded like something an NGO worker might say. I wondered where he had heard the phrase.

'But, Manju,' I said, 'I like it here.'

'Why?'

I was about to tell her why—because I could play with her every day and because the mine was vast and open and I was free to go where I liked, and, yes, the work was hard but there was an excitement to the way the lorries rumbled past, straining under their heavy cargo—but right then Manju dropped her hammer.

In a strained voice she said, 'He's coming.'

Siju's lorry looked no different than any of the others, except that it had been freshly cleaned. It had an orange cab, and the outer sides of the long bed were painted brown. The bed bulged with ore, like the belly of a fat man. Siju was clearly on his way to the Hospet railway station. The back panel of the lorry was decorated with painted animals—a lion and two deer. The lion, its thick mane rippling, stood in a lush forest, and the two deer flanked it, their delicate orange heads raised and looking off to the sides. Siju was especially proud of the painting, and I knew he stood over his lorry cleaner each morning, breathing down the boy's neck to make sure that all the red dust was properly wiped off the faces of the animals. His insistence on keeping the lorry spick-and-span was part of why the lorry cleaners made fun of him.

He must have seen us squatting there by the highway, but he kept his eyes on the road. I raised my hand and waved. When he didn't respond, I said, 'Oy, Siju! Look this way!'

He swivelled his head towards us briefly.

Manju's big eyes followed him.

Then one of the women working nearby, a woman with a missing eye whose eyelid drooped over the empty socket, spat out her tobacco with a harsh smack and said to Manju, 'Enough of your nonsense. Go sit somewhere else. Leave those boys to do their work.'

Manju didn't answer, so the woman said more loudly, 'You! Heard me? Go sit—'

Manju picked up a pebble and flung it at her. It hit the woman on the shoulder, and she yelped.

'Soole!' the woman hissed.

Manju turned her thin face to the woman. 'Soole?' Manu's voice trembled. 'You're calling me a soole? You old dirty one-eyed monkey.'

I looked at Manju, afraid to speak. She picked up my ore and began hammering at it.

'Manju—' I began. I thought she was going to cry, but then she looked up. 'I wish you had a lorry,' she said. 'Then you and me could drive to China.'

Later, I took my full puttu to the weighing station. On my way I passed Amma working with a group of women at the base of a slope. I stopped to watch her. She was shaking a sieve, holding it away from her body, a red cloud billowing around her. Dark pebbles of ore danced and shivered in the wide shallow basin. A few feet away Munna, naked except for an old shirt of mine, crawled in aimless circles. If he got too far or tried to stuff a fistful of dirt into his mouth, Amma or one of the women would reach out an arm or a leg and hook him back in. When Munna saw me, he stretched out his short arms, ridiculous in their baggy sleeves, and screamed with delight. Amma looked up. She put down the sieve and straightened her back. She was as small as a child, her hands barely bigger than mine. The other women glanced at me and continued working. The muscles in their forearms were laid like train tracks.

'How many?' Amma called up.

'Three,' I said. I held up the puttu. 'This is the fourth one.' There were still a few hours of daylight left. A few hours before the red hills of Bellary turned black and the day's totals were tallied and announced by the sweating labour officer, Mr Subbu, and no matter the numbers, how high or how low, the workers would be expected to cheer.

With her eyes on me, she put a hand inside her blouse to touch the small velvet jewellery pouch she kept there. Whatever jewellery had been in there was pawned long ago. I knew that now it contained a few hundred rupees, two or maybe three. This was what she had saved, in secrecy, for months, money that Appa overlooked or was too drunk to account for. It was for me, my school fees, and she liked to remind me it was there. She eyed me, her lower lip hanging open. I knew she was debating whether to speak.

'Guna,' she said finally. 'Tonight, when Appa comes—'

'Have to go,' I said. 'Lots of work. It's going to rain later.'

She sighed. 'You don't want to go back to school?' she asked. 'You don't want to study hard and get a proper job?' She lowered her voice. 'Such a clever boy you are, Guna. Such good marks you used to get. You want to waste your brains, fill your head with iron like a puttu?'

I made no reply. I remembered what Manju had said about my potential, and I saw myself flinging the entire contents of the puttu in Amma's face, iron flying everywhere, scattershot.

Amma was keeping half an eye on Munna, who was trying to climb into the sieve. 'Did Siju get a trip today?' she asked.

'You're asking about Lorry Raja?' I said.

'Don't act like those lorry-cleaner boys. He drives well.'

I hopped from one foot to the other, balancing the puttu like a tray. 'Lorry Raja tries to turn on his indicators and turns on the windshield wipers instead.'

'Guna!' Amma said.

'Lorry Raja is always combing his hair in the rear-view mirror.'

One of the women working next to Amma laughed. She had large yellow teeth and a gold stud in her flared nostril. Amma glanced at her, then at the ground.

Encouraged by the woman's laugh, I added, 'Lorry Raja's lorry doesn't even go in a straight line.' I waggled my palm to show the route Siju's lorry took.

Amma scooped up Munna before he overturned the sieve. She sucked the edge of her sari's pallu and scrubbed his cheek, which was, like her own, like mine, red with iron dust. The dust mixed with our sweat and formed a gummy red paste, which stuck to our skin and was almost impossible to get off without soap and water, of which we had little, except for whatever dank rain gathered in stray pits and puddles. It was easy to tell who the mine workers were. We all looked like we were bleeding.

Amma put Munna down, and he began to try to crawl up the slope to me. She held her small body very straight and looked at the other women. 'Siju is the youngest driver on-site,' she announced loudly. The other women, even the one who laughed earlier, took no notice.

'Only fourteen and already driving a lorry.' Amma was breathing heavily, and under her red mask she was flushed.

Munna slid back down the slope and landed on his bottom. He began to wail, his toothless mouth open in protest and outrage.

'He's your brother,' Amma said.

We looked at Munna. Neither of us moved to pick him up.

'I know,' I said.

I registered my fourth load at the weighing station and emptied my puttu into the first of a line of lorries waiting there. The weighing station was marked off from the neighbouring permit yard by a low wall of scrap metal: short iron pipes and rusted carburettors and hubcaps that sometimes dislodged and rolled of their own accord across the yard, stopping with a clang when they hit Mr Subbu's aluminium-walled shed. This shed, a square, burnished structure three times as big as the tent we lived in, was the labour office. Complaints were lodged there, and labour records were written down in a big book. How many labourers worked per day; how many puttus they filled; how many labourers were residents at the mine camp; how many were floaters, men and women who arrived by the busload in the mornings and stood in a ragged line, waiting to be given work. Mr Subbu would come out of his office and point at random, and those who were not chosen would shuffle back to the bus depot on the highway, where they would take a bus to the next mine to try their luck. Those who stayed were given a hammer and puttu. Most of them, used to this routine, brought their own. During the day Mr Subbu's shed could be seen from anywhere at the mine. All you had to do was look up from your hammering, and there it was, a sparkle on the rust-coloured hillside. His maroon Esteem was parked outside, a green tree-shaped air freshener twirling slowly from the rear-view mirror. I noticed the greenness of the air freshener because there was not a single green tree near the mine; they all bore red leaves.

Mr Subbu stood in the shade thrown by a backhoe loader, drinking a bottle of Pepsi. He was wearing a full-sleeved shirt with the top button undone, and I could see the triangle of a white undershirt and a few black tangles of hair peeping from the top. He sweated profusely, and there were large damp patches on his chest and lower back, and two damp crescents in his armpits, which swelled to full moons when he raised his arms.

I stood there, watching him. One of the workers, a young woman with two long braids, came up to him to say something. Mr Subbu listened with his head bent. Then he put his hand on the girl's shoulder and replied. The girl stood so still that her braids did not even swish. When he finished speaking, he let his hand fall, and she turned and walked away. There had been a rumour in the mine camp about one of the new babies, and how it had Mr Subbu's nose, and the mother, a rail-thin woman called Savithri, had been forced to sneak away from the camp at night before her husband came for her with the metal end of a belt. I had heard Appa call Mr Subbu shameless and a soole magane, but something about the way he stood all alone in his nice clothes seemed lonely and promising. And as I stood there watching him, it occurred to me suddenly that he might be able to help me. My heart beat faster, and I pictured myself standing in the shade with him, talking, him smiling and nodding.

I went over to stand by him, my empty puttu thudding against my thighs. He finished the Pepsi and threw the bottle under the backhoe loader, all without paying attention to me. Then he wiped his mouth with a handkerchief.

'Taking rest?' he said. He had seen me around the mine, but he didn't know my name, of course. There were hundreds of children running everywhere, and under that coat of red we must have all looked the same to him.

'Yes, sir,' I said. 'Only five minutes,' I added, lest he think I was shirking.

'Very good,' said Mr Subbu.

His eyelids drooped, and he nodded his head slowly. I waited for him to offer me a Pepsi, and when he didn't, I kept standing there. I wondered what a man like that thought about. I looked out over the mine, the land cut open in wide red swatches. Compared to the mine, the plain beyond seemed colourless, the trees sitting low to the ground, hardly different from the bushes, whose woody stems bore patches of dry leaves. In the distance there were hills that had not yet been mined, and they looked impossibly lush, rising and falling in deep, green waves against the sky. And the sun, the sun was a white ball that tore into everything, into the blistered skin on the backs of my hands, into the body of the backhoe loader, into the yawning red mouth of the mine.

I cleared my throat. Mr Subbu's mouth parted and closed, parted and closed. Long strings of spit stretched and contracted between his lips.

'Sir,' I said.

Mr Subbu's eyes snapped open. 'Hm?'

'Sir, I want to ask something.'

He looked at me. I took a deep breath and held his eyes. They were not unkind eyes, only a little distant, a little distracted.

'I want to become a driver, sir. Lorry driver,' I said, speaking quickly.

Mr Subbu seemed to be waiting for more, so I continued, 'I know driving, sir. My father taught me. He was the driver for the sub-inspector of the Raichur Thermal Station, sir. He drove an Esteem, sir, just like yours.' And I pointed to the maroon car that was parked outside his shed.

I didn't think of it as a lie. When Appa had driven for the sub-inspector, I had sat in his lap whenever the sub-inspector was in a meeting or on an inspection tour or at the flat of a woman who was not his wife. I would hold the Esteem's steering wheel, dizzy from the musky odour of the leather upholstery, while Appa drove us slowly around the streets of Raichur, his foot barely touching the accelerator, whispering in my ear, 'Left, now. Get ready. Turn the wheel slowly.' And his hands would close over mine, swallowing them, and I would feel the pressure of his fingers and respond to them, pulling as he pulled, inhaling the spice of the cheap, home-brewed daru that was always on his breath, waiting for those moments when his lips brushed the back of my head, and we would guide the car together, the big maroon bird making a graceful swoop and coming straight again. 'Expert,' Appa would whisper warm and rich into my hair as I frowned at the road to hide my pleasure. 'So young and already driving like an expert.'

I said nothing about the accident, about how Appa had been drunker than usual, how he had shattered the knee of the woman, how he had cried later because of the noise the woman made—a resigned sigh, oh— before she fell.

Mr Subbu's fingers kneaded one another.

'Please, sir,' I said.

'How old are you?' he asked.

I paused. 'Thirteen,' I said, rounding up.

'Thirteen,' Mr Subbu said. He squinted out into the sun, and then he pointed to one of the workers moving over the surface of the red, undulating plain. The sun shrank him into a black dot, no bigger than one of the pebbles I filled my puttu with. 'See him?' he asked.

'Yes, sir,' I said. And together we watched him for a while.

Then Mr Subbu said, as if posing a maths problem, 'What is he doing?'

'Working,' I said.

'Exactly,' said Mr Subbu. 'Smart boy. He's working.'

I watched a lorry wind its way to the bottom of a hill, heading to the highway, on an uneven road sawn into the hillside. Behind it trailed a hazy red cloud.

'Work hard, and you will get whatever you want,' Mr Subbu said, his voice louder than necessary, as if many people had gathered to hear him. 'That's the best advice I can give you, my boy. Your father would tell you the same thing.' And he touched me on the shoulder, a fatherly touch, at the same time pushing me lightly so that I found myself back in the sun again.

Instead of going back to the site beside the highway, I went to find Appa. Half-hidden behind a mound of earth, I watched him being lowered into a pit, a rope tied under his arms and passing across his bare chest. He had taken off his pants and wore only a pair of frayed striped boxer shorts. He carried a long-handled hammer like an extension of his arm. The loose end of the rope was held by three men, who braced their feet to hold the weight of Appa's body. And then earth swallowed him, feet first.

I often came to watch him work like this, when he didn't know I was there. I would count the seconds he was down in the pit, listening for the steady crash of his hammer, muffled thunder. I would wait, alert to the slightest sound of panic, the faintest jerking of the rope. I knew that no matter how many times one did a job, the worst could happen the next time. And just as the waiting became unbearable, and I was about to run into the open, to give myself away, he emerged, red-faced, dangling, gasping like a man being pulled from water.

They untied him, and he began rubbing his skin where the rope had cut into him. One of the men said, 'Nice weather down there?' and Appa said, 'Sunny like your wife's thullu.' The man laughed. Appa said, 'One day I want to tie up that bastard Subbu and send him down there.' The other man said, 'He'd get stuck, first of all. Second thing is he's too busy putting his fat hands all over girls. What else you think he does in that office all day?'

'Fat bastard,' Appa said. He raised his hammer and brought it down once, hard. Then he lifted it again and let it crash down, and then he did it again, the rise and fall of the hammer all part of the same smooth motion. I could feel the impact of each blow travel through the ground between our bodies, from the muscles in his arms to the muscles in my legs, connecting us.

'Thank god I have only sons,' Appa said, and the man laughed again.

When I returned to the site beside the highway, Manju had disappeared. The ground where she had been squatting was scuffed. I crouched over it and tried to make out the marks of her bare feet. A few women were still hunched over, their hammers clinking in rhythm. The woman with the missing eye pulled a pinch of tobacco from a large grey wad and handed it to me. I took it and chewed on it slowly. The bitter tobacco juice flooded my mouth.

The woman watched me chew. 'Want to know where that girl went?' she asked.

I tried to imagine what could have happened to her eye. I wanted to apologize for Manju throwing a stone at her, but I was angry at the woman for calling Manju a soole.

'She probably went back to her tent,' I said.

'Take another guess,' the woman said. 'Shall I tell you?'

'No,' I said.

'Smart boy,' she said.

Then she leaned forward and lowered her voice. 'Listen to me. That girl is not nice. Okay? Not nice. You should stay away from her.'

'Excuse me,' I said. 'I have to work.'

For the next few hours I worked without stopping. I pounded the ore with my hammer, the blows precise, never faltering, the ring of metal against metal filling my head. Sweat poured down my wrists, and I had to keep wiping my hands on my shorts. Lorries ticked by on the highway, marking time. Siju's lorry did not drive past again. After a while the women stood up and stretched their backs. They flexed their fingers and curled their toes in the dirt. The one who had given me the tobacco smiled, but with just one eye her smile looked insincere. They took up their full puttus and their hammers and walked off in the direction of the weighing station. As they walked, I noted their square backs, their strong thigh muscles showing through their saris, their strange, bowlegged gait, their gnarled feet caked with dirt. None of them owned shoes except for the odd pair of rubber or plastic sandals. Manju had been right, I thought. They looked less like women and more like monkeys, the muscular brown monkeys that would swarm our village outside Raichur. They were fearless and feral, those monkeys, grabbing peanuts from children's hands, attacking people with their small, sharp teeth. A pack of them would sit on top of a low, crumbling wall, chattering and picking lice from each other's fur, in the way that these women scratched their armpits and laughed in low, coarse voices.

The day ripened into purple and then rotted into black, the air sagging with the smells I never noticed when the sun was there to burn it all away, the stench from pools filled with stagnant water and buzzing with mosquitoes, the sweet whiff of shit drifting from the field we all used, furtively or defiantly, even the women and girls. I registered my last load of iron and returned to our tent, where Amma was preparing the coals for dinner. Clouds pressed down on the camp, our city of plastic tents, and we could hear the voices of the men coming down from the top of the rise where they gathered to drink after work every evening. I could hear Appa's voice above the others, his laugh the loudest. Amma glanced up every now and again, her face a shining red circle of worry in the light of the coals. I held Munna on my lap, and he blinked sleepily into the coals. When we heard Appa's singing, the notes warbling as he came down the rise towards us, Amma glanced quickly at me and began blowing at the coals. I pressed my nose into Munna's neck and smelled his sour baby smell. The coals pulsed brightly every time Amma blew, her cheeks puffed with the effort.

'Guna, the paan,' Amma hissed, and I rummaged in a plastic bag for the battered shoe-polish tin in which we kept a stock of crumbled areca nut and a small stack of betel leaves.

'Wipe Munna's nose,' she ordered, and I used Munna's sleeve to wipe away the shining thread of mucus that trickled out of one nostril.

'Guna—' and that was all she had time to say before Appa ducked his head under the tent and collapsed among us, creating a confused tangle of arms and legs. Amma smoothly moved out of his way and began pressing balls of dough between her palms and pinching the edges until the dough became round and flat, and she laid them over the coals to bake. She stared at them intently, as if they might fly away. Appa leaned on his elbow. He was no longer stripped down but was wearing his torn T-shirt that said *Calvin Kline* and his faded pants rolled up to his knees. In January, he had smashed his hammer into the large toe of his left foot, and it had healed crooked, like a bird's beak.

'Supriya,' Appa said, drawing her name out. Shoopreeya.

Amma said nothing.

'So serious you look,' Appa said. His face seemed to contract and expand, and his daru-scented breath filled the tent. 'Not happy to see me? Not even one smile for your husband? Your poor husband who has been working like a dog all day?'

Amma bit her lip so hard the bottom of her face twisted. She picked a baked roti off the coals with her bare fingers and laid it on a sheet of newspaper. Appa hiccupped.

I held out the shoe-polish tin. Appa took it, popped it open, and sprinkled some areca nut on a betel leaf. He folded the leaf into a neat square and began chewing it. Red juice came out of the side of his mouth. I watched it trickle down his chin.

'Guna,' he said then, his mouth red and wet. 'How many puttus today, Guna?'

I was about to say eight when I caught sight of Amma's face, looking engorged and pleading in the light from the coals. Without taking her eyes off the rotis, she slipped a hand into her blouse and touched her breast where the velvet pouch was.

I said, 'Six.'

'Six,' Appa repeated. 'That's all?'

'Yes,' I said. 'Sorry, Appa.' I waited for the sting of the slap.

But instead he reached out and slowly caressed the side of my face. He ran his hand from the top of my head down my cheek, over my chin, and to the soft spot on my neck, where my pulse had begun to race. His hand was like sandpaper, covered in scabs and blisters, some that had burst and scarred, some that were still ripe. I felt every bump and welt against my skin, every dip and hollow. It was as if he were leaving the living imprint of his hand on my face.

'No, no,' he said in a rich voice, his singing voice. 'Don't say sorry. I should be sorry. I should be the one saying sorry. It's because of me you are here. All of you. It is all my fault.' His voice trembled on the edge of a cliff, and his eyes were so dark.

I felt a pricking behind my eyes. My face was humming. There was a heaviness to my limbs. I wondered if this was what he felt like when he was drunk.

'My fault,' Appa said. 'I'm a bad father.'

Appa held out his hand, and I dropped my wages into it. All of it, even the eleven rupees I had just lied to him about. Appa's palm closed around the money, and he dropped it into his pocket. I tightened my arms around Munna. I didn't dare look at Amma.

I heard her body shift. She let out a breath she'd been holding.

'That is his school money,' she said.

Appa didn't turn to look at her.

'That is his school money,' she said again. 'We said this year he would go back. You have to keep some of that for tuition fees.'

He said, 'You're telling me what to do? In my own house you're telling me?'

Black spots appeared on the rotis, each accompanied by a small hiss.

'You're just one man,' Amma said, staring at the spots. 'How much daru will you drink?' She paused. 'I should have had a daughter.'

'What bloody daughter?' said Appa. 'Why you want a daughter? You want for me to pay dowry? Some snot-nosed fellow comes and says, I want to marry her, and I have to go into my own pocket and lick his bum? No, thank you.'

'Daughters help their mothers. And you'd drink all of her dowry anyway,' muttered Amma.

I thought he was going to caress her too, the way his hand went out, but then I saw he was pinching her, clamping down on the fleshiest part of her waist, right above her hip bone, the strip of bare skin between the top of her petticoat and the bottom of her blouse. She flailed, her mouth open without screaming. One of her hands caught Munna on the side of the head, and she kicked a stray coal so close to my foot that I could feel it scorch my toe. I drew my foot back and waited for Munna to cry, but he didn't.

When Appa let go, there were two semicircles of bright red on Amma's hip, the skin slightly puckered. She was moaning softly but did not let the rotis burn. She picked them off and put them on the newspaper. She was breathing hard through her teeth.

'Supriya, you know what problem you have? You don't smile enough,' Appa told her. 'You should smile more. A woman who doesn't smile is ugly.'

Then Amma's gaze travelled beyond the coals, beyond Appa's prone form, and I turned to see Siju standing at the entrance of the tent. He looked fresh. His hair was combed, of all things. He stood there, watching us, and suddenly I could see us through his eyes, the picture we presented, me with my toes curled in, Munna swaying with sleep in my arms, Appa reclining on his elbow, Amma hunched over the coals. I saw what he saw, and then I wished I hadn't seen it.

'What you think you're staring at?' Appa said. 'Sit down.'

Siju picked his way to an empty spot between Appa and me. As soon as he sat down, the tent felt full, too full. We were too close together, fear and anger flying around like rockets.

· 'Where did you go today?' Amma asked Siju. To my surprise, he didn't turn away like he usually did but looked at her with a distant sort of sympathy, as if she were a stranger he had made up his mind to be kind to.

'Hospet,' he said.

'Hospet,' Amma repeated gratefully. 'Is it a nice place?'

With the same careful kindness he said, 'Actually, I've never seen a dirtier place.'

'What the hell were you expecting?' Appa said, trying to provoke him. 'All cities are dirty. You want to eat your food off the street, or what?'

Siju ignored him, and I could sense Appa stiffening.

'How many trips did you get?' Amma asked.

'Trips!' Appa snorted. 'He drives that bloody lorry ten kilometres to the railway station. Ten kilometres! How do you call that a trip?'

Siju began to massage his feet. Amma put another roti on the coals. Appa glared at them both, their exclusion of him causing the pressure inside to build and build.

'So? How many?' Appa said. His head swivelled slowly in Siju's direction. 'How many trips? Your mother asked a question, can't you hear? You're deaf or something?'

'Three,' said Siju curtly.

'Don't talk like I'm some peon who cleans your shit. Say it properly.'

'Three,' repeated Siju.

'You're listening, Supriya?' drawled Appa with exaggerated awe. 'You want something to smile about? Your son got three trips to the bloody railway station in a bloody lorry. Three trips! What you want a daughter for? With a son like this?'

His glassy gaze never left Siju's face. Amma laid the last roti over the coals.

'Bloody lorry driver thinks he's a bloody raja,' muttered Appa.

I pinched Munna under the arm, hoping to make him cry, hoping to create a distraction, but he wouldn't. I pinched again harder, but he sat still, a soft, surprisingly heavy weight on my lap. One of the coals popped, and my heart jumped. I remembered the way the manager of the thermal station had come to our house after Appa's accident. Spit flew from the manager's mouth as he screamed, landing lightly on Appa's face, and I remembered how Appa didn't wipe it off. I remembered the way Appa had said, 'No, sir. Sorry, sir. No, sir. Sorry, sir,' like he didn't understand the words. Like they were a poem he had memorized. That night he went and lay down on the road, and when Amma went to bring him back in, he said, 'Supriya, leave me alone! I deserve this.' And I remembered the way she held his head, speaking to him softly until he dragged himself up and followed her back inside.

Now he waited to see what Siju would do.

For a second I thought he would hit Appa. Then he shrugged. 'Being a bloody lorry driver is better than hammering bloody pieces of iron all day.' He looked at me as he said this, and I looked away.

Amma used her finger to smear the rotis with lime pickle, rolled them into tubes, and handed them to us. She held her arms out for Munna, slipping her blouse down her shoulder, baring her slack breast with its wine-coloured nipple. Munna latched on, his black eyes shining in the semi-darkness, unblinking, gazing at us. The roti was warm and tasted of smoke, and the pickle was tart, the lime stringy and tough. I thought only about the food, about how it was filling my mouth, sliding tight down my throat, unlocking something. It was always this way. The food loosened something in all of us, a tightly wound spring uncoiling. I felt myself starting to relax. Food could do this, and warmth, and the approach of sleep. There were these moments of calm, when no one spoke, and there were only the coals and the insistent flapping of the plastic tent and the mumble of other families and the sky hanging low.

Then Siju, leaning towards me, spoiled it all by saying, 'I have something to say to you.'

I swallowed quickly. 'I don't want to hear anything,' I said. We kept our voices down because Appa seemed to have fallen asleep. He was snoring lightly.

'Listen just one second.'

'Oh-ho, Lorry Raja wants to say something,' I said.

'Don't—'

I put my fingers in my ears and chanted, 'Lorry Raja! Lorry Raja!' I knew it was silly, but I wanted to keep this fragile peace, to clutch it tightly in my fist like a precious stone.

'Guna, listen!' Siju said, louder than he had intended.

'What's the racket?' said Appa, coming out of his doze.

'Nothing,' said Siju.

'Nothing,' I repeated.

Appa closed his eyes again. Amma was still breastfeeding Munna, her head bent in contemplation of his placid sucking.

'That monkey woman called Manju a soole,' I said quietly.

Siju picked at a scab on his knee.

'What are you two talking about?' Amma asked.

Before Siju could reply, I said, 'Manju. His girlfriend.'

'The girl whose mother is sick?'

I nodded.

'Poor thing,' Amma said. 'Maybe I should go see if I can do something.'

But then Munna fell asleep, still making half-hearted sucks at her nipple, and her eyes went soft. She brushed her hand against the tuft of hair sticking up from his red-stained forehead.

'Don't bother,' Siju spat. 'She knows how to get what she wants.'

'I'm going to see if she's okay,' I said, standing up. To my surprise, Siju stood up too.

'I'll come with you,' he said.

'No!' I shouted.

'Yes,' said Amma. 'Both of you go.'

'Siju,' Appa said. He was still in that reclining position. His calves under the rolled-up pants were like polished cannonballs. I remembered the way I had seen him earlier that day, bare chested, bent at the waist, his long-handled hammer making smooth strokes, crashing against the ground. He was not a big man or a tall one, but he was a man who broke iron for ten hours every day.

Siju looked at him for a long moment, then nodded and reached into his pocket. He brought out a set of folded notes and pressed it into Appa's outstretched palm. Appa tucked it into his pocket, where my own wages nestled. He hummed something tuneless and closed his eyes.

Amma was watching us both. 'Here,' she said. 'Take something for them.' She made me wrap two rotis in newspaper. 'Come back before it rains.'

'You don't have to come if you don't want to,' I told Siju as we picked our way through the maze of tents. 'I won't tell.'

Instead of answering he was quiet, which made me nervous. A rat the size of my foot ran across our path and disappeared into the blackness to our right. The rats were a problem in the camp. They got into our food, chewed holes in our blankets, bit babies as they slept. Last year a baby had died from a rat bite. I thought of Munna asleep, of the whole camp silent, a ship of blue plastic afloat on these hairy black bodies that moved and rustled under it, restless and hungry as the ocean.

Manju wasn't in her tent. From inside came the loud, ragged breathing of her mother. Siju raised his eyebrows at me and jerked his chin in the direction of the tent's opening. I shook my head; I could just make out the shadowy figure wrapped in a blanket, smaller than a person should be. Then Manju's mother coughed, a colourless, wheezing cough, like wind passing through a narrow, lonely corridor. I took an unconscious step backward.

'She's not there,' I whispered.

'Smart fellow,' Siju whispered back.

'So now what?'

'We go back to our tent.'

'You go back,' I said. 'I'll wait for her here. She must have gone to the toilet.'

Siju gave me a long, searching look. 'Guna,' he said. 'Just forget her.'

'No!' I almost shouted. I felt the start of tears, burning in the ridge of my nose. Before I could stop myself, I said, 'She wants me to take her to China.'

'What?' His voice was flat.

'In my lorry,' I said. I knew I was babbling. I squeezed the rotis and felt the warmth seep through the newspaper. 'She said if I could drive a lorry, I could take her to China. To see the Lympic Games. I asked Mr Subbu, but he said no. He said if I work hard I'll get what I want.'

Siju let out a long breath. 'You asked Subbu?' he said. 'That fat bastard? You asked him?'

'Yes,' I said.

'My god.' My brother shook his head. 'Come with me,' he said.

Mr Subbu's Esteem was still parked outside his aluminium-walled shed. The shed was directly under a single lamp post, whose light cast it in a liquid, silver glow. The lamp post was connected to a generator, which growled like a sleeping dog. We crept up to the backhoe loader, which was just outside the shoreline of light.

Siju put his hand on my shoulder. 'Not too close,' he said.

'Why are we here?' I asked. He put a finger on his lips.

We waited, partly hidden by the massive machine. I leaned against it, and the cold of its metal body was a shock. Siju was standing behind me, very close. There was a strange calmness to the whole scene, the glowing shed, the purring of the generator, the still air.

And then, with a movement so smooth and natural that I forgot to be surprised, Manju stepped out of Mr Subbu's shed. She stood there for a moment, her uniform and thin legs perfectly outlined in the light of the lamp, her face lifted like one of the deer on the back panel of Siju's lorry. Then she turned and looked straight at us. I jumped, but Siju's hand was on my shoulder again.

'Be still,' he whispered.

But Manju had seen us. Her uniform seemed even bigger on her frame than it had earlier in the day. She was floating in it as she came over to us. Her feet were soundless in the dirt. As soon as she was level with the backhoe loader, Siju stepped out and pulled her behind it. She put her hands on her hips and looked at us for a long time without speaking. Behind her, the lamp post snapped off, plunging everything into darkness. Then the headlights of Mr Subbu's Esteem came on, and the car floated away, as if borne on an invisible river.

'So,' Manju said. As my eyes adjusted slowly, I noticed that her eyes were swollen. She had been crying. I thought of the shed, of Mr Subbu's hands kneading each other, of the cold bottle of Pepsi, of the way he'd put his hand on the shoulder of the girl with the braids. I thought of the woman with one eye saying, 'That girl is not nice.'

'How long have you been standing here?' Manju asked.

'Relax,' said Siju coolly. 'Guna felt like taking a walk.'

'A walk,' Manju repeated. She looked at me quickly, accusingly, and I felt a spike of guilt. 'And you just walked this way,' she said.

Siju shrugged. 'That's how it happened.'

I said, 'We came to give you these rotis.' I pressed the newspaper-wrapped rotis into her hand. She looked at them as if I had done something meaningless.

'Let's go back to the tent,' I told Siju. I wanted to get away from Manju's raw, swollen face. Her tears had made clear channels in the red paste on her cheeks.

'Just one minute,' Siju said. He leaned in close to Manju so that his face was barely inches from hers. He smiled. It was not a nice smile.

'Guna told me you want to go to China,' he said.

Manju looked at me, puzzled. I closed my eyes. 'What?' she said uncertainly.

'Still want to go?'

He had made a copy of the lorry key. In Hospet. He had waited in the lorry while a shopkeeper fashioned a new one, which was raw and shining and silver. It made me uncomfortable to look at it.

In the lorry yard, the smell of grease and diesel strong in my nose, I whispered, 'Mr Subbu will throw you out if he finds out. Appa will kill you.'

'Shut up,' Siju said in a normal voice. 'Mr Subbu! Appa! You think I care? Come with us or stay here and shut up. Your decision.'

He climbed into the high cab of the lorry. He reached over and held a hand out for Manju, who held it indifferently, as if she were being asked to hold a piece of wood. He let me struggle in by myself. When I had shut the door, he inserted the shining key into the ignition.

'They're going to hear us,' I said.

'No, they're not,' he said grimly. He turned the key and started the engine.

It sounded like thunder rolling across the plain. I closed my eyes and waited for a shout, a light shining in our faces, the relief of discovery. But no one came. The city of tents stayed dark, except for the glimmer of burning coals. The sky answered with thunder of its own.

Siju did not turn on the headlights, and the lorry drifted out of the yard, past the weighing station, past the permit yard, rounding the perimeter, the camp turning silently on its axis like a black globe, the dirt road invisible.

'On your marks,' I heard Siju say. He sounded calm. 'Get set. Go.'

And then I felt the pressure release, the lorry pick up speed, and we were driving downhill, and there was wind rushing in through the windows, filling my lungs. I could feel Manju's shoulder against mine, and there were Siju's hands curled on the wheel, and the floorboard thrummed under my feet, and I was suddenly awake, wide awake, filled with the cold night air.

Siju flipped on the headlights, and I saw that we were no longer within the boundaries of the mine, we had left it behind, and trees flashed by, their lowest branches scraping the sides of the lorry. There was no time to feel anything. All I could do was keep my balance, keep my shoulder from slamming against the door. We hurtled past rocks that were big enough to jump off. Siju drove leaning forward, without slowing for anything, and the lorry bounced and jostled, and its springs screeched, and in the yellow beam of the headlights I saw the ground jump sharply into focus for an instant before we swallowed it. The hills in the distance were getting closer, and I wondered if Siju intended to drive to the top of them, or even beyond. I wanted him to. I wanted him to drive forever. As long as he kept driving, we would be safe.

But then he stopped, let the engine idle, fall into silence. We were in the middle of the plains, far enough away from the mine to seem like a different country. The ground stretched away on every side. The trees provided no orientation. They simply carved out darker shapes in the darkness. Siju took his hands off the wheel and ran them through his hair. Manju's chest rose and fell under the uniform. She stared straight ahead, through the grimy windshield, even after we had been sitting there in silence for minutes.

'Gold medal,' I heard Siju whisper.

I opened and closed my mouth, each time to say something that crumbled and became a confused tangle of words.

'You shouldn't have brought Guna,' Manju said. The sound of my name made me shiver, as if by naming me she had made me responsible. For this, for the three of us here. As if whatever happened here would be because of me.

'Why not?' Siju said. 'He deserves to come, no? You know, he even went to Subbu today and asked if he could be a lorry driver. All because of you. Sweet, no? Bastard said no, of course. I could have told him not to waste his time; Subbu has his fat hands filled with your—'

'You think I like this?' she said. She spoke to the windshield, to the open plain. 'Begging for money? Sir, please give money for medicine. Sir, please give money for surgery. Sir, Mummy's coughing again. Doctor says her lungs are weak. Sir, please give money for doctor's fees. You think it's nice to stand still and let him do whatever he wants? And he gives too little money, so every time I have to go back. You think it's a big game?'

I could tell that Siju was taken aback. 'You could work—'

'Fifty rupees per day!' Manju said. 'Even if I work all day and night, it would not even be enough for food. Sometimes you're so stupid. Even Guna is smarter than you.' After she said this, she seemed to collapse. I could feel her shoulder sag against mine.

'Manju,' I said. For no reason other than to say her name.

Siju sat in silence for a while. Then he made a strangled sound in his throat, like he was coming to a decision he already hated himself for. He opened his door and jumped out.

'Come on,' he said to Manju.

I made a move to get out.

'No, you stay here,' Siju said.

'But—' I started to say.

'Guna, just stay here,' Manju said. She sounded tired.

I bit down on my lip. Manju put her arm around my shoulders and pulled me close. I could smell metal in her hair. It was the most vivid thing I had ever smelled. It was a smell that had a shape, edges as solid as a building. And then for no reason I thought of our neighbour's wife, the one who survived after her husband tried to burn them all. She lived in the temple courtyard after that, and the priests fed her. Sometimes she would take dried pats of cow dung and put them on her head like a hat and stare at passers-by, the skin of her cheek rippled pink. I don't know why I thought of that woman just then, but I did. And while I was remembering her, Manju was sliding away from me, into the driver's seat, her legs stretching to the ground. She dropped with a little grunt.

I heard them walk around the lorry, heard the clink of the chain and the rusted creak as the back panel was lowered. I felt the vibrations of their movements come to me through the empty lorry bed. A scraping noise, and I knew Siju was spreading a tarpaulin sheet across the back. Through the metal, through the fake leather of the seat, through the cogs and gears and machinery, I could feel their movements, the positioning of one body over another. I heard Siju say something in a low voice. I don't remember hearing Manju reply.

And then I didn't want to hear any more, so I listened instead to the whirring of insects in the bushes, the night-time howls of dogs from the villages whose fires hung suspended in the distance, the wind that travelled close to the ground, scraping dry leaves into piles. The darkness made everything vast, vaster than the mine, which in the daytime seemed so large to me. It was different in every way from the camp, where the sounds were either machine sounds, lifting and loading and dumping and digging, or people sounds, eating or snoring or crying or swearing at someone to shut up so they could sleep.

A light wind brushed my face, carried the smell of rain. Tomorrow the work would be impossible, the ground too wet to dig, the ore slippery and slick, the puddles swollen to ponds. The men would slide around, knee-deep, and curse. The children would push each other, making it into a rough game. The lorries would get stuck, their wheels spinning, flinging mud in all directions, and we would have to spend an extra hour digging them out. There would be red mud in the crooks of our elbows, in our fingernails, in our ears. The coals, in the evening, would refuse to light.

For a second I couldn't move, as if the coming days and weeks and months and years were piling on top of me like a load of ore, pinning me against the darkness, and then I found myself slipping into the driver's seat and taking hold of the shining key, which stuck out of the ignition like a small cold hand asking to be grasped. I tried to remember what to do, what I had seen others do. I carefully pressed the clutch. I needed to slide forward to the edge of the seat to do it. I turned the key, and the lorry rumbled to life. I waited for a second, holding my breath, and then in a rush I released the clutch and stomped on the accelerator. The lorry bucked, then jumped a couple of feet, and my temple hit the half-rolled down driver's-door window. I put my finger to my skin, and it came away wet with blood. The engine stammered and died, and everything went back to silence.

Siju wrenched open the door and dragged me out of the cab. He grasped two handfuls of my shirt and shook me.

'What's wrong with you?' he said. 'What kind of idiot are you?'

When I didn't answer, he let go of my shirt. His pants were unzipped, and I looked at the V-shaped flap that was hanging open. He saw me looking and said, 'What?'

'Nothing.'

'Just say it, Guna.'

'Nothing,' I said.

He zipped his pants.

'Then get inside,' he said. 'We're going home.'

'What about Manju?' I asked.

'She wants to sit in the back.'

'It's going to rain,' I said. 'She'll get wet.'

'Just get inside the bloody lorry, Guna,' Siju said. 'Don't argue.'

Inside the cab I hugged my body and tried to stay awake. The cold air was still coming in, and I wanted to roll up my window, but Siju had his open, his elbow resting on it, head leaning on that hand, the other guiding the lorry. He was driving slowly now, taking care to avoid the bumps and dips in the uneven ground. We passed a rock, ghostly white, that I didn't remember from the journey out. From the corner of my eye, I looked at him, my sullen brother. Not a raja but a fourteen-year-old lorry driver in a Bellary mine.

'What's going to happen now?' I asked.

He drew his hand inside. 'What's going to happen to what?'

To everything, I wanted to say. But I said, 'Manju's mother.'

He let a few moments go by before answering. And when he did, what he said was, 'Come on, Guna. You're smart. You know.'

'We could have given her the money from my school fees,' I said.

'For what?' He sounded like an old man. 'So she can die in three months instead of two?'

After that we didn't talk. The trees fell away, and the ground became smoother. The camp came into view, almost completely dark, just a few remaining fires that would burn throughout the night. Siju parked in the lorry yard and jumped out. I stayed sitting in the cab. A few drops of rain fell on the windshield and created long, glossy streaks as they travelled down. The camp would wake to find itself afloat. The rats would come looking for dry ground. Munna would need to be nursed. Amma would put her hand behind his soft, downy head to soothe him. Appa would bail out the water that pooled in the roof of our tent. Amma would tie an old lungi of Appa's to two of the bamboo poles to create a hammock for Munna that would keep him above the reach of the rats. Manju's mother would shift to a more comfortable position and wait for the rain to stop. There didn't seem to be a reason for any of it, a logic that I could see. There was repetition and routine and the inevitability of accident. Tomorrow Mr Subbu would drink a Pepsi, and we would dig for iron.

I heard Siju say my name, and I heard the panic in his voice. It was raining in earnest now, the windshield a silver wash. I pushed open the door and nearly fell out. My feet sank into the soft mud. Siju was standing at the back of the truck, the back panel open. His hair hung draggled around his face, and drops of water clung to the tips. He pointed wordlessly to the lorry bed. I forced my eyes to scan the entire space for Manju, but she wasn't there.

We stood there for what seemed like an hour, though I knew it was less than a minute. I pictured her walking across the plains, her face directed to some anonymous town. She would walk for hours, I knew, and when she got tired, she would sleep exactly where she stopped walking, her arms shielding her face from the rain. I imagined her curled up on the ground. I imagined that her hair would plaster her cheek. I imagined that her uniform would be washed back into white, a beacon for anyone watching, except no one would be.

Over the following months Siju began sucking diesel out of the lorries and selling it back to the drivers at twenty per cent below pump prices, and by the time the monsoons ended, he had earned enough money for one year of school fees for me. He gave it to Amma without telling me, and I never thanked him directly. We had spoken very little since the night of the lorry ride. I watched him closely for a while, worried that he would disappear too, but he came back night after night, sometimes after we had all fallen asleep, never smiling, never saying much. I knew he took the lorry out sometimes, but he never took me with him again. He stopped swaggering, and the lorry cleaners seemed disappointed. I went to school in the mornings and returned to the mine afterwards.

The next August, after the flooded pits were starting to dry out again, Mr Subbu arrived at the mine late one afternoon and announced that he was giving everyone the rest of the day off. He smiled at the responding cheer. Then from his Esteem he brought out a small colour television and a white satellite dish and hooked them up to the generator, setting them on a rickety table with the help of the one of the labourers. He fiddled with the antenna until a picture flickered on the screen.

We all gathered around to watch the magnificent round stadium in China fill with colour and light and music and movement. We watched graceful acrobats and women with feathers and children with brightly painted faces. We watched glittering fireworks and slender athletes in shiny tracksuits and flapping flags with all the shades of the world. We watched as the stadium slowly filled with red light, and thousands of people arranged themselves into gracious shifting shapes in the centre. Thousands more gathered in the seats, their faces reflecting the same awe we felt. We watched, all of us, in silence, stunned by the beauty of what we had created.

16

HOW TO HOST YOUR EUROPEANS
MEENA KANDASAMY

Your father does not know that this whitey exists in your life, let alone the absolute fact that said whitey is the love of your life. Your mother knows him—knows *of* him, actually—as an office friend. You've been dropping hints, retelling his jokes to her, talking to her of his general saviour-soul, his antifa, anti-war stance, that sort of thing—all in the feverish anticipation that your mother will want to find out more. Your mother is too clever to fall into your trap; you can give her that. Her universe will not entertain the idea of any non-Tamil, why, even any non-Jaffna Tamil boy in your life—so, instead of whitey, you could as well be describing a cat. This has been your situation for the last six months—and you've been sat on your ass, not trying to do much more about it, save the incessant chatter. You'd have let this go on—she does not ask, you do not tell, whitey stays in the closet—except that whitey has gone ahead and ruined it for you. Whitey's told his parents over the Easter break; they are coming to meet you right away.

You're secretly angry with whitey for not taking your permission but you don't fight especially when you see how grinny-happy he is about the whole invasion. As if exchanging a favour, you promise whitey that you'll break the news to your mother the night before the impending arrival, to put her on the spot, but mostly to let her make up her mind either way very quickly. She may ask to meet them, or she may curse you—all of you: her daughter, the whitey, the whitey's parents—to death under the garbage truck, one of two extreme scenarios. You channel your anxiety into battle plans—you'll pick them up from Eurostar, you'll check them into their Airbnb, you'll take them for a walk (weather willing) in Epping Forest. The next morning, you'll get them here to visit you in your natural habitat, Ilford. This is a running joke—here, in East Ham, and possibly fifty other pockets across London, whiteys will look out of place, like they need a passport to enter.

You've chosen Wanstead as their buffer-zone entry point—where old white people's care homes and hipster cafes coexist peacefully. They will still feel at home. You want to avoid what they call culture shock. The London that's home to you, the London you're taking them to, is not the tourist trap: Big Ben, Buckingham Palace, National Portrait Gallery, Thames cruise. You tell whitey that if they like you, *and* more importantly, if you like them, *and* rule out their being racists, you'll bring them here, to the south of the borough, where the colour gradient changes and loses its whiteness. You pretend not to hear when he says all white people are not racist.

You want to be as light-hearted as your whitey. You came from a place where bombs fell through the night, where death picked out random targets. Here, there are knives and, from not-so-long-ago, samurai swords. Tamil gangs once warred on these streets, one was even called the Tigers. You feel personally slighted; you feel everything here is just the mere husk of a life you left behind. You're superstitious, and think to yourself that you've carried the curse of sudden death with you across the seas. Some years ago, a five-year-old Tamil girl was shot in the chest walking distance from your home. Your British home. This March, on Ilford Lane, a man was stabbed ten times and left for dead on the snow.

You'll tell your whiteys all these stories—without a trace of fear, without making London sound unsafe or dangerous. You'll tell them there is going to be hot-spot policing and stop-and-search here, this is how Britain becomes Europe. You'll tell them you hate your journeys into the continent, being asked to show your papers, being considered a shoplifter, being avoided even by the beggars. You know that when you stand apart, you're going to be asked to step aside. Belong, belong, goes the voice inside your head. The same voice that in your mother tongue reminded you to stay defiant, that told you to not go weak in your knees at the sight of Sinhala army checkposts, that told you to be proud of who you are. You know that if your Europeans love you enough, and value your opinion, all of your rage will not offend them.

You'll take them out to Saravana Bhavan, teach them to eat with their hands, the way your whitey has loyally learnt to do. You'll give a haphazard tour—ruthless colonialism meets immigrant kitsch—Churchill uncle's statue, Murugan temple, fabric shops where all the brown girls go when they get married, Valentines Mansion, landmarks to show Redbridge as the birthplace of the East India Company. Your Europeans will find this fascinating, they happen to be from the country that slaughtered Congo.

You'll take a detour, go to an absolutely rundown place to show your whiteys the All Nations Church on Ley Street. You, and only you, know that it is right opposite your house. You'll tell them that you believe in God the way you believe in men: not to be taken at face value. You'll make it clear that this is not your church, you only pray in Tamil. This church has three billboards with fading words. *HOW DO I FIND GOD? AM I GOING TO HEAVEN? WHO WAS JESUS?* Your Europeans will probably laugh at these questions. You'll check their mood that moment, tally it with your mother's mood from the previous night, and if all goes well, you'll go, your European entourage in tow, and knock on your front door. If your whitey is lucky, your mother will make them tea. If you're lucky, she'll start asking you a lot of never-ending questions.

17

MRS NISCHOL

MEERA GANAPATHI

The day Navin Nischol died, a tomato sprang up in her garden. A luminous green jewel that sprouted shyly from a plant that hadn't blossomed in two years. She named the tomato Navin in memory of the actor who had once meant so much to her. A breeze swayed the tomato, and as it bobbed gently, she imagined that it was nodding in approval of its name.

'How did he die?' her husband asked her when she told him the news over lunch.

'Heart attack.'

As they ate in silence, she switched on the news, wanting to know more about the actor's sudden demise.

'He wasn't that famous or important,' Ajay offered by way of explanation when various news channels barely mentioned him. Sensing her husband's lack of interest in the matter, she decided to mourn privately, and felt a very deliberate loneliness for three whole days.

In those three days, the tomato stayed green, stubbornly refusing to ripen. The tomato showed some yellow on the fourth day.

'Mar jaayega yeh bhi....' cackled her husband from across the lawn, watching her kneeling beside her plant in the dirt. She frowned at him—his posture made his laughter seem obnoxious—as he sat splayed across two chairs, with his feet on one and his body pouring out of the other, a newspaper sliding off his knees.

His words stung because she couldn't manage to grow a single plant without it dying on her. Around her home in the senior citizen's colony they lived in, gardens gushed in praise of their nurturers, gifting them exotic flowers and canopies where a neat hedge and a few manicured roses should've done. Seeds were scattered optimistically, produce was grown and cooked, composting stories were giddily exchanged on WhatsApp groups, cuttings were gifted and sometimes stolen, eventually becoming the heart of tales of bravado narrated over cups of tea at the club. Gardening was the centre of life in the colony, and she, with her wilting excuse of a garden, never seemed to fit in.

She looked around at the grass on her lawn that rose up like it was doing her a favour—emerald in some patches but yellowing in others. Her roses were covered in mealy bugs, a bird of paradise drooped in some inexplicable sorrow, ambitiously planted orchids refused to bloom. Every plant—infested, dry, and brittle—seemed like an accusation.

'Don't get upset, Sujatha,' her husband continued from his perch, 'do you remember what Manoj told us? That our plot is probably built on barren land?'

Manoj, the contractor, had apparently shared this piece of information one afternoon when her husband had bumped into him. But how was it possible to have a few square feet of barrenness in the midst of this aggressive greenery? As usual, her husband was attempting to mollify her about her shortcomings with simplistic lies, and this was one of the things she couldn't stand about him. Each time his omelette was overdone, he offered to buy her a new pan, unwilling to blame her for not flipping it on time.

'Maybe I shouldn't have named it Navin,' she muttered. A dead man's name for a new life could only be a bad omen. She felt responsible, as though she'd wished death upon it.

'What's that? Navin?'

'Nothing,' she huffed and walked away, her mind full of guilt and sorrow.

∽

Sujatha Nischol
Sujatha Pratiman Nischol
Sujatha. N
Sujatha weds Navin
Mrs Sujatha Nischol
Mrs Nischol
Natasha Nischol, Arjun Nischol

The last page of her exercise notebook in college teemed with possibilities for her future. Within the confines of that page she blossomed from a timid

Arts student into a glamorous married woman—the wife of a famous film star. Each name promised evolving identities; some days, on the page, she chose to hold on to her maiden name, tucking it snug and safe within her new husband's surname; sometimes she became the mother of two children—a girl and a boy; and, on other days, she was simply an anonymous missus whose title carried weight.

She thought of her old friend Meenakshi, whose notebook had an identical last page. Despite the similarity of their desires, their dreams were so vague that they'd never considered the possibility of fighting over the actor. Instead, she'd passionately watched each of Navin Nischol's films with Meenakshi in Regal, beginning with *Sawan Badhon*.

In the dark of that theatre, each girl imagined herself as Rekha with her ample hips, soft, round cheeks, and big eyes, being tenderly embraced by the tall and gawky Nischol. Soon after the film, their flat, long braids rose to mid-sized bouffants, and each girl truly believed in her remarkable beauty and the very real possibility of a long-limbed man whisking them away from their ordinary lives. They began to scour film magazines for stories of him, they tore his pictures out and pressed them deep into the hearts of their books, adding an occasional homage of dried flowers to keep him company.

She wondered if Meenakshi had been sad to hear the news of the actor's demise. They had bonded over their affection for the actor at a time when their classmates had worshipped Rajesh Khanna.

'Do you remember when Rajesh Khanna got married?' she asked Ajay that evening. They were walking back from the market, their bags brimming with gourds, beans, potatoes, and onions. She didn't wait for him to answer, eager to share a memory. 'You know, a girl in my class heard the news, sat down on her bench and wept for a whole hour. She was heartbroken because Dimple was around our age.... "It could have been me!" she kept saying.'

She couldn't remember the girl's name, not even her face—only that her shoulders shook violently as she rested her head on the desk and wept noisily between her elbows. Some girls tried to console her, rubbing her back and offering their sympathy because many of them were equally disappointed, but most just laughed. Who was silly enough to believe they'd actually marry a film star? But Sujatha felt deeply for the weeping girl; even fantasies are built on a measure of hope.

When Sujatha met Ajay for the first time, he had stared at a spot between her neck and shoulder, unwilling to meet her eyes. 'You're a bit darker in person,' he'd said to her, before he could check himself. He took too-quick a sip of his tea and added, 'these photographers whiten everyone and no one looks like themselves.' He finally looked up at her face, and looked away immediately, as though to gaze at her so intimately would be an intrusion.

Ajay was fairly tall, with thick, bushy eyebrows and a handlebar moustache that hid most of his face. She wondered how he'd look if he smiled. She couldn't be sure if she found him attractive, he was too fidgety for her to take him seriously. But these things hardly mattered because she'd resigned herself to marrying him long before she'd met him. Her father had mentioned his many virtues quite a number of times, including his good family, his stable government job, and his ability to care for her in the future. It was as though these repetitions were meant to warn her that a refusal of his proposal would be a dismissal of their good intentions.

As they lingered on the balcony, sipping tea at a permissible distance from their families inside, she wondered if her darker skin tone would dissuade him from marrying her. For a brief moment, the thought of rejection made her want to fight for his favour. She straightened her back, lifted her downcast eyes, and gave him the full benefit of her every practised gesture. With a smile stolen from Rekha, a gentle toss of a long, thick braid borrowed from Jaya Bhadhuri, and the skilful adjustment of her printed silk sari courtesy of Sharmila Tagore, Sujatha was momentarily dazzling.

They were married soon after, but she continued to live at her parents' home in Bombay, as Ajay was transferred to a remote corner of Assam for the first year of their marriage. He wrote elegant letters to her in Hindi, addressing her quite formally as 'Sujathaji' but she rarely replied, never having much to say. On a trunk call every Friday, they would scream at each other, 'All OK?' and respond 'Yes, all OK here.'

Sujatha took up a temporary job as the receptionist at an office in Marine Lines, taking an early bus to work and returning home in time for tea. The tedium of her routine was sometimes broken when she met her old friend, Meenakshi, at an Irani café across the street from her office. Meenakshi was soon to marry an engineer, and they were meant to move to Canada. This move, more than her impending wedding, occupied every minute of Meenakshi's existence. Sujatha sometimes envied the ease with which Meenakshi had adapted to another part of her life while she still struggled to accept that she was married.

One afternoon, Meenakshi rushed into Sujatha's workplace, almost quivering with excitement. She was dressed in her favourite sari, a turquoise silk printed with a paisley pattern. Sujatha admired her friend, wondering if Meenakshi was planning to meet her fiancé.

'You look nice, where are you off to today?' Sujatha asked her friend.

'Come, come, we have to leave right away!' she gasped breathlessly.

'Where to? I can come after four when my shift ends....' Sujatha smiled at her indulgently, amused by Meenakshi's excitement.

'Tell them it's an emergency, Suj, I have the most wonderful surprise for you—we're going to the Taj for tea. Right now!' she insisted.

Sujatha did as she was told, but as they boarded the bus to the Gateway of India she wasn't sure if she'd have enough money for this rather extravagant date. Just this once perhaps, she told herself.

She decided she would have only one coffee and sip it slowly so they'd have an excuse to linger if they wished to.

But these concerns flew out of her mind when Meenakshi told her that Navin Nischol was at the Taj, promoting his latest film. Sujatha clapped her hands over her mouth in disbelief, suddenly concerned about her appearance—her sari was too plain, her hair too frizzy. But she was undeniably excited; she was about to see her one true love in the flesh.

Would he look at her? Should she say something to him? For a moment, she imagined pretending to not know him. She'd ignore him so pointedly that the actor himself would be curious about this one person who was unaffected by him.

'We're here...stop dreaming!' teased Meenakshi, as though she knew exactly what Sujatha was thinking. Both women laughed, overwhelmed by their unexpected adventure.

At the hotel, they lingered in the ladies' room, fixing their hair, adjusting their saris, reapplying lipstick and needlessly sticking on fresh bindis. Meenakshi dug into her handbag and pulled out a foreign perfume, muttering, 'Canada....' as an explanation. She liberally sprayed Sujatha with its rather overpowering scent and then added a dab to her own wrists with exaggerated sophistication. Sujatha found this impossibly funny and hugged her friend, both of them reeking of perfume and shaking with giddy, uncontained laughter.

At the glamorous Shamiana restaurant they grew quieter, self-conscious in a place full of wealthy businessmen and sophisticated ladies. They spoke in hushed whispers, unwilling to draw attention to themselves, Sujatha's voice growing even more muffled as she primly dabbed her lips with her handkerchief after every sip of coffee. For the better part of two hours they scanned their surroundings carefully, but were unable to spot a single Navin Nischol-like figure. A third of their coffees lingered at the bottom of their cups, untouched so they'd have an excuse to stay on. However, Meenakshi was impatient now; she gestured to a waiter and asked him if the actor was on the premises. 'He left after lunch,' said the waiter in a slow, unbothered drawl, making the most of this moment where he was privy to important information.

'When will he be back?' Meenakshi asked him, exasperated.

The waiter paused grandly and said, 'Any time now…but he doesn't come to the restaurant, he goes straight up to his room.'

They paid for their coffees and rushed to the lobby, holding hands and walking fast, their faces feigning a self-control they didn't feel. Meenakshi, who had been to the Taj about four times now, with her fiancé, guided Sujatha to a large, comfortable couch that had a direct view of the entrance. They sat there patiently, watching foreign tourists and hotel staff pour in and out of the revolving doors. When a tall, elegant-looking man walked in, they clutched each other's hands in anticipation, but it wasn't Nischol.

'It's 5.30 now, should we leave?' Sujatha asked her, finally.

'I suppose so…don't want you to miss your bus.'

'But I've already missed it,' Sujatha said, glancing at her watch. Some part of her wanted Meenakshi to insist that they stay back.

'Let's go, I don't think he's coming.'

They got up, and as Meenakshi adjusted her sari, Sujatha looked back at the hollows their bodies had left in the couch—some part of her was still here, she wasn't ready to leave.

They began to walk towards the entrance, dejected. Sujatha took in the scent of fresh roses placed in an ostentatious bouquet in the centre of the lobby. She felt the urge to pluck a rose and place it in her hair; she wanted to remember this day somehow. Meenakshi nudged her roughly, interrupting her thoughts, and when Sujatha looked up, she finally saw Navin Nischol saunter in through the revolving doors.

Was that really him? Sheltered within two panes of the door, he was visible but still quite unreachable.

They stopped to make sure it was him, unable to believe their good fortune, certain it was a trick, an illusion. But it was him—just as tall and lanky as they'd always imagined; in real life, his cheeks were an almost unnatural pink. When he entered, he seemed to carry a hushed silence with him, so much so that the busy hotel seemed to pause to watch the star. Everything slowed down to accommodate his presence, and to swallow every minute of his walk from the door to the elevator, so that nothing would be forgotten when anecdotes were repeated and regurgitated for ages to come. The air seemed heavy with an unspoken whisper that seemed to say, 'Is that really him?'

As Sujatha's eyes followed the actor, she felt tremulous, like her body was vapour and she would have to centre herself somehow to feel solid again. She briefly held Meenakshi's hand to find a connection to reality, but her hand was moist and uncomfortable to touch. She stood rooted to a spot in the middle of the lobby, soft, fragmented light from the chandelier fell pleasantly on her skin, her large, brown eyes were bright with anticipation. Perhaps in that moment she was more beautiful than she had ever been or would ever be again.

She felt pinned to her spot when the actor's gaze fell on her, and whether time had slowed down or he looked at her for a significant moment, she couldn't tell. But in that rushed minute or stretched second, the man she had imagined a whole life with, had finally seen her. She attempted to smile but found her mouth stiff and immovable. His gaze seemed to acknowledge something but then the elevator doors opened, he walked in, and left her frozen in the lobby.

A good five minutes after he'd left, Meenakshi and Sujatha walked in a trance to the door, chiding each other for not having spoken to him. But on the bus ride home, Sujatha could only think of one thing: Navin Nischol had wanted to look at her, for just a little longer. As the years passed, his gaze was embroidered in her memory into a long, lingering look, a look which eventually became a smile. And with each reminiscence, the last page of her notebook was no longer a childish dream, but a reminder of what could have been.

She plucked freshly laundered clothes from the line in the backyard. Crisp with sunlight, they folded with an almost audible crunch. She had left them out too long perhaps, a kurta was now a lighter maroon on one side than the other. These days were full of memories of the past and forgetfulness of the present, perhaps this was what getting older meant—you chose to remember what you wished to remember.

Her daughter had called that morning, with questions about Ajay and his diet and if his diabetes was under control. However, when she spoke to Ajay, she hadn't pressed him for details about her mother. One hot afternoon in Meerut, as Sujatha made a hurried lunch in their dingy kitchen, her daughter had walked in and asked her if she loved her husband at all. 'You never smile at him,' she'd said worriedly. Sujatha, preoccupied and startled, had not known what to say and scolded her daughter for being silly. But she supposed that old suspicion had never left.

She hadn't dedicated her life to pining for a film star, that was not the case. Sometimes when she remembered him in the lobby, looking at her, she felt cheated. But cheated out of what, she couldn't tell.

In the 80s and early 90s, Nischol had stopped appearing in the news, but she had continued to buy film magazines and would occasionally lose herself in gossip about some film star or the other. Except for the time she'd read about his divorce and the reasons for it; she'd been disappointed to note that the gossip columnists had denounced him viciously.

'Just imagine this is what he did, what if we'd married him?' she'd wanted to tell Meenakshi when she'd read the news. But Meenakshi was in Canada and their letters had dwindled until there were none at all.

∽

The afternoon her tomato showed signs of ripening, she found a packet of manure on the table; it appeared that Ajay was trying to aid her attempts at gardening. The packet made her think about an old birthday when he had bought her a pressure cooker. What she'd really wanted was a Garden Vareli sari—a coral pink dusted with summer flowers. She supposed she should've been grateful for getting what she needed, even if it wasn't what she had wanted. She dug the manure into the hard soil around the tomato plant and watched Navin again, did he look riper? Was there hope yet?

'I knew him, you know,' she'd told her eight-year-old daughter when Nischol had appeared on *Dekh Bhai Dekh*, a popular TV show on Doordarshan. That was the last time she'd claimed any kind of allegiance to him. 'Knew him', was a stretch, but by then their encounter in the lobby had been dissected and embroidered into an event that had divided her life into two halves. Before the meeting she was resigned to her fate, after the meeting there was a tiny glimmer of hope—she could have been someone else.

In the TV show, Nischol, now in his forties, had aged visibly. His hair was thinning and his gentle smile seemed like an effort. Even though she waited for his appearance on the show, she did so out of an old loyalty rather than a renewed interest. He played a forgetful middle-aged businessman in a family full of adorable misfits—while everyone around him was exaggeratedly strange, he was the vague but solitary voice of reason. Many years later, Navin Nischol was in the news again—and again he was being denounced by the media—his wife had killed herself and it was being said he'd been abusive towards her. This disturbed her deeply, but she didn't dwell on it, and put the article away without reading it. She preferred to preserve her memories in a form that gave her solace. And that was her last association with Nischol. He was no longer even a fleeting interest—life had overwhelmed her by then.

She thought about these things as she searched for Meenakshi Menon on Facebook. Perhaps she was a Meenakshi Nair now, she thought, hurriedly changing her search words. But Facebook threw up more than five hundred Meenakshi Nairs, she'd have to spend a whole day figuring out which one was her friend, if at all. She gave up soon enough, what would they have to talk about anyway?

A week or so later, a message appeared on Facebook from a Meenu S. Nair.

'Suj. I thought of u recently when our beloved hero breathed his last,' the message read.

Sujatha clicked on Meenakshi's profile and found that she was a grandmother now, and her timeline was littered with achievements at a virtual restaurant game, as well as photos with her granddaughter. Now that she'd seen her current photograph in a grey bobbed haircut, her large, dark eyes hidden behind spectacles, she barely remembered how Meenakshi had looked all those years ago.

'I thght of u 2 Meenu. How're u? It has been so long. Where r u these days?' she replied.

They kept in touch regularly after that, and Sujatha learnt that Meenakshi had two daughters, one of whom was married with a daughter of her own.

She now lived in Kochi, close to her husband's family. They exchanged phone numbers and promised to call one another.

Soon enough there was a call, where Meenakshi spoke with a measured calm; all her old breathlessness seemed to have leaked out of her with age. They spoke about their children, their husbands, and their aches and pains at great length. They recalled old classmates they still knew something about. Meenakshi had hated Canada and eventually she'd shifted back to India, choosing to live in the warm south far away from memories of sleet and snow.

'Remember when he looked at us in the lobby?' she said, when Navin Nischol finally came up in the conversation.

'At us?' said Sujatha, mildly taken aback.

'He looked at us and smiled! How could you forget, I had shouted "Navin" but he'd entered the lift by then….' Meenakshi went on.

'He looked at you?' she asked, before she could stop herself.

'Yes, you and me. Both of us, because we were staring so openly at him, we hadn't moved! And then I called out his name…but the lift doors opened. Imagine if they hadn't opened just then….'

Meenakshi laughed, completely missing her friend's agitation. She continued to patter on about that day with such ease that Sujatha realized the encounter hadn't meant as much to Meenakshi.

After the phone call, she felt irrationally angry and wished she hadn't spoken to Meenakshi at all. But a more reasonable part of her mind reminded her that nearly all memory is fiction, contorted to form a shape that seems real to some, and unrecognizable to others.

A few days later, the tomato ripened into a rich, glossy red, and others popped up alongside it, like smooth green buttons. She could hardly believe her luck. She brimmed with pride as she made breakfast for her husband and herself, taking care to flip the omelette just in time, so it would be cooked exactly right. She felt inclined to prolong the niceness of the morning and hummed while she cooked, smiling at Ajay when he joined her for breakfast.

'You saw the tomato?' he asked her. He seemed equally proud, and she felt suddenly, sharply, fond of him. She nodded, placing a piece of hot toast beside his omelette and smearing her own with thick yellow butter. As they ate, Ajay spread out the newspaper and read out loud from it, 'His last words were: turn down the AC.'

'Huh?'

'Navin Nischol's last words, since you were a fan, I thought you'd be interested to know. "Turn down the AC,"' he repeated, without looking up from the paper.

'I was better off not knowing this,' she said, immediately annoyed. She had attempted to detach herself from those memories. She hadn't answered any of Meenakshi's calls after that day.

Such mundane and disappointing last words, she thought bitterly. All she had wanted was an encouraging memory. She thought of those hot brown days in Bombay filled with hope and uncomplicated joy—she didn't want that feeling to be tainted by the ordinariness of life. She didn't wish to think of his last words. Her mind went back to that day at the Taj Mahal hotel again. She had stared unblinkingly at the actor, and he had turned back to look in her direction. Perhaps there was no way of knowing if his eyes had fallen on her alone. Because who can measure where a gaze falls, who can gauge what someone's eyes choose to see? Only when your eyes meet can you be certain that another pair of eyes have found yours. And that evening, Navin Nischol's eyes had met hers, she was sure of it.

Later that day, she plucked the tomato, and as it sat in her palm—smooth, round, and ripe—she felt reassured by its warmth.

18

RADHA, KRISHNA

NEEL PATEL

You have no idea what it was like for me the morning you left. I drove by your house as you were packing your car. I was parked on your street. Of course you didn't see me. You wore a green T-shirt and your hair, so black it shone blue, was tucked under a hat. After you hugged your parents goodbye, you followed a tree-lined path towards the highway. What a privilege it must have been to drive through their neighbourhood, to see the world through their eyes, to live a life of certainty and assurance when so few things are certain or assured.

I still remember that last night on your driveway, when you looked at me and saw nothing. Perhaps you saw right through me, into one of the houses beyond. What was it like to grow up in a house like that? Did your ego swell like a grain of rice? Did you enjoy the look of hunger in my parents' eyes? I would never know. I grew up in a small apartment above my parents' motel, with sounds of cars on the highway. I stared out my window and saw endless rows of corn. I cowered when white men shouted at my father in the lobby: *Speak English*! I danced in my bedroom to Bollywood songs, thinking of you.

If you open your high school yearbook, you will find my picture next to yours. Our first names are similar. Our last names are the same. Because of this, everyone had assumed you were my brother. I was embarrassed to tell them the truth: that I was in love with you. Of course you didn't know it at the time. What you knew instead was that I was the girl your parents forced you to say hi to at dinner parties you were reluctant to attend.

Your parents knew mine only vaguely. Your father was a doctor. My father owned a motel. Your father dressed in business suits—mine, in old T-shirts. Your mother was elegant, with jewels glistening at her throat. My mother wore the same saris for years. I saw the way your mother slit her eyes whenever I walked by. Do you know what it's like, to make a woman's face go sour? Probably you don't. Women look at you only sweetly.

We'd met in grade school, but it was at a rec centre one evening, on a cold autumn night, that I first began to notice you. I was thirteen at the time, and my breasts were budding. It was Navratri, the nine-day festival in which we danced around an altar decorated with marigold petals. That was how I had explained it to my best friend in high school, Sarah. Sarah was with me that night, in a ghagra choli. I had wanted to give her a new one but my mother had refused.

'What difference does it make?' she'd said. 'Old or new, what does Sarah care?'

You wore a baseball cap and you smelled like cologne. Your Air Jordans were unlaced, your flannel shirt untucked. Your carelessness was careful, your confidence a con. I saw right through you. Maybe you knew, because when I said hello to you, you pretended not to hear it. You strode around the room instead, looking bored. I danced with my friends and ate puris on the floor and gossiped about who had been drinking or whose breasts had been touched. You were nowhere to be found. I longed to be in your world. At school, your friends were mostly white boys and black boys who listened to Bone. Thugs-N-Harmony. I assumed you were ashamed of me. I was evidence of the world you shrugged off each morning before you entered the room.

Of course you denied all of this in your bedroom the summer you came back into my life. We were older then. You traced my eyelids with your finger, and pinched the fat on my thighs, and flicked your tongue against my neck. You said I was beautiful. What was beautiful was your reflection in my eyes. Did you think I didn't notice? The way you stood a few inches taller when showing me your parents' brick house, or their brand-new sedan, with its thick, perforated leather? You saw only my devotion to you, like Radha's devotion to Krishna, like Lakshmi's devotion to Vishnu, like my mother's devotion to my father, like the ocean's devotion to the moon. I remember my mother showing me pictures of Lord Krishna as a child, with his soft navy skin. He was surrounded by women, hundreds of them, some old enough to be his mother, all with the same doleful look in their eyes. I asked my mother what they were doing there and she said simply that they were in love. A thousand women: all vying for the attention of a man.

I swore I would never be one of those women, so I married a man who is nothing like you. His name is Jacob. He's an engineer. Brown fuzz covers his arms and his legs. His eyes, green pools the shade of summer, are flecked with gold. How can it be? That a white man could have so many colours? We'd met online. By that point, after the disaster of my first marriage, my parents were relieved; brown men had taken issue with the fact that I was divorced. White men had not. What mattered was that Jacob was successful. He was kind. According to my mother, he was like Vishnu—he restored order to my world.

Through Jacob, I was able to escape the rumours and gossip and former prison of my childhood town. Even my parents were spared, having successfully raised a daughter in a country that was not their own. The pictures I sent them—of Jacob's silver Lexus, of my brand-new Jeep, of our chocolate-coloured house in Michigan with skylights and stone floors—were proof that they had fulfilled their duty, despite what anyone else said. Jacob accepted a position as the dean of a college engineering programme. I finished my degree in pharmacy. Between the two of us, we built a life for ourselves that most people would envy. Our kids, twin girls with skin that glowed like metal and eyes so pale people wondered if they were real, were the crowning achievement of my parents' lives. When we closed on our house, they threw a party and invited some of the Indian families from our home town to see it. I hesitated at first, remembering what they had said about us, reminding her that we had never been close, but my mother insisted, and I could sense in her tone a kind of desperation. By that point, I had risen in the community's esteem. All those years my mother had pretended to be comfortable on the outskirts of the Indian community, but in that moment, I knew: she wanted a way back in. So I let her host a puja in my honour, and bury a coconut in our backyard, and invite a priest over to chant above a small flame. He blessed the property, our marriage, our lives. Jacob and I linked hands and accepted gifts and showed off the spectacular central staircase and marble master bath.

I still don't know if I love him. I see his face in the mornings and feel at ease. I hear his keys in the lock and wait for him to enter. I cook him chicken curry and watch him clean his plate. I do the things I watched my mother do, things I swore I would never do when I was sixteen. I pack lunches and wash trousers and stand on my feet for twelve hours a day, and sometimes, late at night, after scrubbing Play-Doh off the kitchen counter, I wonder if it was all worth it. The desperation I had once felt, the urgency even, is now gone. At the time, Jacob had seemed like my only option—it is clear to me, now, that he was simply a choice.

I had assumed you and I would never see each other again, and for a while, I was right. Jacob and I lived in Michigan. You had moved to California. The thread that had once bound us was severed, too frayed for repair. I had convinced myself that it was never meant to be, that we were star-crossed lovers, but when I saw you that weekend at Nishali and Mehul's wedding, in the bright lobby of a Marriott hotel, I began to wonder, for a moment, if I had been wrong.

The wedding was my parents' idea. They had wanted me to reconnect with the people from my past. I suspect the real reason was to show me off; the daughter who once had nothing, now had everything. My mother was always asking me to send her pictures of Jacob and the girls and the house and the cars, and the little things, too, like a shrimp risotto we had once ordered at a restaurant. I understood, then, that those pictures were not meant for my parents' benefit but for their friends', that my presence at Nishali's wedding, my post-marital glow, was a form of redemption.

Your parents were in Europe for the summer; your sister was saddled with kids. Because of this, it was you who came in their place. By then, the girls were in kindergarten and Jacob was golfing and no one was inspired enough to board a plane to Chicago for the wedding of a person they barely knew. So I came without them. I did not expect to see you at all, but then I remembered that Nishali—my childhood friend—was your cousin; the groom, your classmate in med school. In many ways you had more of a reason to be there than I did.

It was the night before the wedding, two hours before the sangeet, and I had just flown in. Women and children lounged on sofas in the lobby. Husbands checked into the rooms. The windows were tall and streaky. The floors, speckled tiles that squeaked loudly underfoot, were polished bright. I had picked up my room key and was waiting for my mother to drop by with some jewellery when you walked through the doors. You wore a black blazer, distressed jeans. Your hair was slicked back. A piece of luggage trailed your feet. It looked expensive. Everything about you did.

A few uncles and aunties recognized you immediately and began commenting on your weight. It was then that I noticed it. Your face was angular, your arms and legs lean; the swell of your stomach, once prominent but firm, had deflated. You laughed it off and made a joke about the pressure of living in California, and the matter was resolved. Your voice carried across the lobby and landed sharply in my chest, awakening inside of me what I'd once thought was dead. Panicked, I escaped into the elevator and closed my eyes. I had not expected to feel this way at all.

Just as I was arranging my perfumes and lipsticks and jewellery on the bathroom counter, the phone rang, and, foolishly, I hoped it was you. Perhaps you had seen me, and had asked the hotel receptionist for my room number. I remembered all those evenings when you had called to apologize and I had never answered, not because I didn't love you, but because it was obvious that you could never love me. I made my way to the telephone and glanced out the window, which overlooked the sun-drenched lobby, the tropical plants, wedding guests milling around a large fountain. I answered the phone, waiting to hear your voice again.

How stupid of me.

'Make it in okay?' Jacob said.

'Yes.'

'How is it so far?'

'It's strange.' I flicked on the TV. A newscaster's sombre face appeared, reporting a shooting. 'I don't recognize anyone yet. I haven't seen Nishali. I'm supposed to go by her room to pick up my bridesmaid outfit.'

'I'm sorry we didn't come.'

'Don't be. Now I can relax with a glass of wine.'

'Of course you can,' Jacob said, laughing. 'This is a dream come true for you.'

'How are the girls?'

'Rumi wants you to bring her a present. Simran is watching *Moana* for the third time. All in all, we're wonderful.'

'Great. I miss them—and you.'

'We miss you, too.'

I stared at the flashing alarm clock between two quilted beds, realizing it was time to get ready.

'I should go,' I said. 'This outfit is complicated, and I can barely remember how to put it on.'

'Feel free to drunk-dial me.'

I smiled as I hung up the phone, suddenly craving a drink. It had been so long since I had been in a quiet room alone. I found a bottle of white wine in the minibar and poured myself a glass. The woman was still reporting about the shooting. The voices still rose from the lobby. My suitcase was unpacked and pink and orange fabrics spilled out from it like a dragon's tongue. I closed my eyes and thought of you.

⁂

Downstairs, wedding guests sparkled in brilliant colours: crimson and lilac and silver and gold. You were nowhere to be found. I met up with a few girls from the bridal party and walked into the banquet hall. They sipped cocktails and talked about how drunk they'd been at the bachelorette party, which had taken place in Miami. I had not been there, and after a while, they grew tired of my silence, walking away from me. I ordered a drink at the bar. I stood around for a bit, smiling and waving to people from afar, when I noticed your face.

'Anything else?' the bartender asked, pouring me my wine. You wore a white kurta with gold threading and pointed elf-like shoes. I had not expected you to wear such a thing. You, who poked fun at everything Indian, who refused to watch Bollywood films, who swore you would never have an Indian wedding because they were a waste of money and time. Your hair was gelled back. You had shaved. The effect was startling: the sudden sharpness of your jaw, the hollowness of your cheeks, the slim lines of your neck, more visible now. You looked boyishly handsome, but there was wisdom in your eyes, as if you had seen things I would never know about, things I longed to understand. I had heard that you were still single. The few times my mother mentioned your name were in reference to this fact, that your parents were worried: you were thirty-five and still a bachelor. I defended you, saying it was none of their business, that marriage wasn't for everyone, that sometimes you think you know what you want and the universe has a way of telling you otherwise.

It would have been the perfect time to greet you, but my parents arrived, whisking me away towards their friends. My mother was clasping the hand of another woman, and her solicitude, the sparkle in her eyes when she introduced us, made me want to slap her.

'Anjali, look at you now,' the woman said. 'So well settled.'

Well settled. The image that came to mind was that of a very fat bird, guarding its nest.

'And the girls,' she said. 'Chal chal. Let us see. Where are the pictures?'

I pulled out my phone, scrolling through the pictures, answering her questions about their favourite colours, their favourite foods. She looked at me sharply.

'Do they love their Indian? Or do they love their burger and fries?'

'Indian, of course,' my mother said. 'Rumi adores my kichuri.'

'Kya baat!'

Had you been there, I would have rolled my eyes and told you how stupid this all was. The girls were half Indian: what did she expect? Just the other day, Rumi had declared kichuri inedible. But instead I smiled, reinforcing my mother's lie. We stood at a table and ate puffed snacks with green chutney, fat cubes of paneer. People began to dance, and through the swish of flowing fabrics—gold, pink, yellow, blue—I saw your face.

Just as I approached you, you turned around. Your back was facing me, so close that I could feel the heat from your skin. White strands threaded your lush black hair. Had they always been there? I longed to touch them, but I was too slow, and soon you were swept up into the crowd, raising your arms. I had never seen you dance before. You were always so stoic during those parties at your parents' house, as if you were waiting for all of us to leave, waiting to return to your room, waiting for the evening to be over so you could no longer pretend. Were you pretending that summer, when you told me you wished you had noticed me sooner, that you would do anything in your power to make up for lost time?

That night, I met Nishali and the other bridesmaids in the hotel lobby for drinks. She looked beautiful, with jewels crusting her wrists and her neck. We talked about dating and marriage and where we wanted to end up in ten years. Then she mentioned your name.

'He looks good—different, but good.'

'He's lost weight.'

'That's what it was. I couldn't figure it out at first.' She smiled. 'Do you still talk to him?'

'Does anyone?'

'I figured if anyone did it would be you.'

I told her the truth: that I hadn't seen or heard from you in years, and that you were living in California. She nodded, as if she had expected this.

After a while, Nishali ordered a round of shots for everyone and proposed a toast. 'Photographs are at 8 a.m.,' she said, before escaping to her room. I hung around for a bit, making small talk with the girls, showing them pictures of Rumi and Simran, answering their questions about marriage and sex, before I, too, retired to my room.

It was in the hallway of my floor, past the elevators and vending machines and a corridor stocked with an ice dispenser that hummed noisily into the night, that I saw you talking to a girl. You had changed, into a black button-down shirt over jeans. The sleeves were rolled up and the hair on your arms was thick. The girl, in a lime-green sari, was touching her hair in a way that revealed her interest in you. I burned with envy. I was reminded of high school, when girls had looked at you from afar and the gleam in their eyes, sharp as kitchen blades, had cut through my skin. But you were bored. You nodded your head, and shifted your feet, and stared at the gold dial on your watch, and laughed at her jokes in a perfunctory way. And I was relieved. Me, a woman who was married with two girls, relieved that the man I hadn't seen for years was uninterested in a girl I scarcely knew. And that's when you saw me.

'Anjali?'

It was your suggestion that we go to my room. Your room was two floors above. The girl, a young woman your mother had wanted you to meet, was the daughter of family friends. You wished her good night in a way that let her know you were not interested in her. Then you stared at me.

'I haven't seen you in ages. You look great.'

My hands shook as I slipped the key card into the door and kicked aside the towels and closed the curtains so that no one would see us, even though all you wanted to do was chat. Still, it felt illicit. You sat on one of the beds, bouncing lightly against the comforter, and I sat on the chair opposite, so there would be no confusion.

'Thanks,' I said. 'I would say the same, except there's less of you now.'

You laughed. 'Everyone keeps telling me to eat. It's called the L.A. diet: kale salads and weed.'

'You never needed a diet.'

'Everyone needs a diet.'

'God—you really are a Californian.'

Dimples formed in the hollows of your cheeks. You turned your head, feigning interest in the cardboard pyramid of TV channels on the nightstand. Your eyes flicked past the minibar, suggesting a drink.

'Help yourself.'

'Won't you join me?'

'I have to be up in five hours,' I said, glancing at the alarm clock. But you poured me a drink anyway, and I accepted it, eager to let the warm buzz embrace me again. You started unbuttoning your shirt, and my heart raced, but then you stopped at the collarbone. I could see the dark hair on your chest.

For a while it was simple. We told each other everything we had wanted to know: my marriage, your fellowship, my move to Michigan, your practice in Orange County, my husband and children and career, your bachelorhood. We had one drink and then another. At some point I floated over to the bed opposite yours, and we sat facing each other, our eyes reflecting the square light of the lamp.

'So tell me—what was so wrong with that girl in the hallway?'

'She's twenty-five.' You laughed. 'I can't date someone who's never listened to Biggie Smalls.'

'And in California? No one?'

'No one special.'

Was I special? I wanted to know. But I would never ask. I could never bring myself to hear the answer.

Instead I asked you questions about your family—your father's retirement, your sister's three kids, the lavish party your parents had thrown for their fortieth wedding anniversary. We talked about the people from our home town with whom both of us had lost touch. There were things you knew about me that my husband would never know, things I would never have to explain to you. It was easy in a way it hadn't been with anyone else.

At one point, you got up to pour yourself a drink, and instead of returning to the bed opposite mine, you sat right next to me. I could smell the cologne on your shirt. You turned to look at me and your breath was warm against my face. You said something, I can't even remember it now, but whatever it was loosened me. Did your lips purse to meet mine? Did you lean in for a kiss? I will never know. Just then, my phone rang, and it was Jacob. I had forgotten to check in.

'It might be the girls,' I said, at which you stood up and placed your hands around your neck.

'I should go.'
'Wait—stay.'
'It's late.'
'This will only take a second.'

You smiled at me and shook your head, as if you knew that it wouldn't. Then you walked out of the room. Part of me wanted to go with you, to convince you to stay, but by then I was already answering, wishing I hadn't.

The next morning, I awoke in a daze. I showered and changed into the white sari Nishali had provided each of us the night before. At breakfast, I ate gathiya with pickled chillies. I searched the room for you, but you were not there. Probably you were still sleeping. My parents introduced me to more friends and relatives, and soon the baraat began, in which we danced outside the hotel lobby. Aunties and uncles circled a horse-drawn carriage. The groom, decked in a pink turban, began to dance, flanked by groomsmen. You were not one of them. I had assumed you and Mehul were close. Obviously you were not. The drums grew louder and louder, the groomsmen jumping up and down, scraping the sky with their fingers. Women linked hands and spun in circles, their mirrored saris reflecting sequins of light. It wasn't until the procession had moved back into the lobby that I saw you, drinking a coffee in your suit.

'Save me a seat?'

I nodded, and the intimacy of your smile, the way no one seemed to notice, sent a chill down my spine. You arrived just in time, before the lights went dim and the double doors opened and the bride floated out to a gasping applause. Her chunari glittered like rubies. Her arms were shackled in gold. She looked like a bedazzled prisoner.

'Why is she walking like that?' you said, snickering. 'Does she have to take a shit?'

I laughed so loud an entire row of aunties turned to shush me. You pinched me on my arm. I flicked you on your ear. In the entire banquet facility, we were the only two people touching.

Later, when the bride and groom were preparing to walk around a fire, garlands hanging from their necks, you turned your head and asked, 'Was your wedding like this?'

I glanced at you.

'Oh, shit,' you said, realizing your mistake. 'I forgot.'

'It's okay. Jacob and I didn't have a wedding. We had a court ceremony. And don't even ask about the first one.'

We didn't talk for a while, focusing on the ceremony. At one point, you left the room altogether and returned with a glass of water. You reached into your back pocket and took out a white pill.

'What's that?' I asked.

'A party favour.'

'You really have changed.'

You shrugged. 'I have to entertain myself somehow.'

After the ceremony, we skipped lunch and went to a park. It felt daring, slipping away like that, just the two of us. The sun was high and the sky was the colour of a peacock's breast.

'I should go—Nishali will be pissed.'

'Do you even care?'

You reached for my hand and I let you hold it. I never knew a simple act could feel so tremendous, like we were moving a mountain together, striking a fire. I could tell you felt it, too. We were silent for a while, staring out at the pond and the rows of benches surrounding it and the small family of ducks with their iridescent feathers. It felt surreal being there with you, just like it had that summer.

I would have let you kiss me then, but within moments a family from the wedding came to join us.

'We've been spotted.'

'We could go to the room,' I said.

You shook your head. 'I have to meet another girl. My parents set it up. She lives thirty minutes from here.'

My heart fell, and you must have sensed this because you said, 'I guess I could cancel.'

'No, don't. We'll meet at the reception.'

'Before. I'll stop by your room.'

'Okay then.'

And for a moment I actually believed that you would.

By five thirty, you still hadn't arrived, and I got ready in my room, pinning the pleats of a black sari to my blouse. One of the bridesmaids found me and invited me to have drinks with her at the bar, so I followed her with a glass of white wine. Sitar music strummed from the speakers. Ice sculptures melted over plates. A group of men were huddled in a corner, drinking whisky and beer. I had assumed you would be with them. You were not. I stared at my phone, sending a text message to Jacob, telling him I missed him, missing you instead. Did you still have my phone number? I hadn't asked. Before long the cocktail hour ended and guests filtered into the next room, which sparkled like a crushed gem.

'Anjali,' one of the bridesmaids said, 'you're sitting with us.' I slipped into a rattan chair and stared at the backlit walls, which glowed purple and pink. The tables were covered in black lace. The glasses were fluted and crystal. My wedding was nothing like this. My wedding had only eight guests: Jacob's family and mine. I had seen the way my mother eyed Nishali at the ceremony. I had felt her hunger in the pit of my own gut.

After the speeches and dances and dinner, the reception was over. I had spent the majority of my time at the table, nursing my wine. My parents went to sleep early. The bridesmaids were drunk. According to one of them, there was an after-party in a suite stocked with pizza and booze. I declined her invitation, and she didn't push me to reconsider. You were nowhere to be found. Not among the clusters of men drinking Johnnie Walker. Not by the dessert table with its chocolate fondue. Not on the dance floor full of teenagers doing the Nae Nae. Not even outside, by the park we had visited, getting a breath of fresh air. You had not given me your room number, and so, at one thirty, after most of the guests had cleared, only a few lingering on sofas and chairs, I approached the front desk and asked if they might have it.

'His name is Ankur Patel. I haven't seen him all day. I'm a little worried.'

'Are you related?' the desk clerk, a large woman with red cheeks and snowy white hair, wanted to know.

I hesitated, remembering how in high school everyone had assumed you were my brother.

'Patel,' I said, pulling out my ID. 'See?' She laughed.

'Oh, honey. This hotel is full of Patels. You're going to have to be more specific than that.'

I smiled, stepping away.

'I wish I could help,' she called after me.

I walked past the lobby and into an open elevator. I could hear the sound of laughter above. I considered going to the party—maybe you were there—but changed my mind. My flight was before noon. I had already said goodbye to my parents—they were skipping breakfast the next morning so they could head back to the motel. Somehow, the idea of this made me sad, and I began to cry. Tears slid past my cheeks and my lips. I looked at my phone and realized that Jacob had called moments earlier, and this made me cry even harder. I pictured him in his Notre Dame T-shirt, cleaning up after the girls. They would be sound asleep in their Princess Jasmine beds. By the time I reached my hallway, I had pulled myself together, fishing out the hotel key from my purse and sliding it through the lock. The room was chilly and quiet, just as I had left it.

Only this time you were there.

'What took you so long?'

You wore the same suit you had worn that morning, but your jacket was slung over a chair, your shirt unbuttoned. The sight of you lifted me like a leaf in a breeze. You were lying on my bed, with your arms tucked behind your head as if it had been your room and not mine. I had always liked that about you, the way you could inhabit any space as if it belonged to you first.

'You missed the reception. You're a terrible wedding guest.'

'I was hoping we could skip it,' you said. 'I got back pretty late. By the time I came by the room you were already downstairs.'

'How did you even get in? I don't remember giving you a key.'

You winked at me. 'I have my ways.'

'No, really,' I said. 'This is scary. What if you had been someone else?'

'Don't worry about it.'

I searched the room for a sign of forced entry. There was nothing. I glanced back at the TV. An advertisement for cough medicine flashed across the screen.

'Now what?' I said.

It was easier this time, to have your skin against mine, your lips against mine, your fingers tracing my back, unbuttoning my blouse. You were hungry for my body, kissing and groping and sucking, and I fed you every piece. Did you remember what it was like, to have me this way? I did. I remembered the smell of your hair and the taste of your skin. I remembered the cold tickle of your fingers on my thighs. I remembered the noises you made when I did something you liked. It was a peculiar sound, so unlike your usual voice. I should have felt guilty. I should have felt ashamed. I felt everything but. I ran my fingers over you and felt the newness of your body, rigid and firm. Your waistline was narrow, your stomach defined. Your arms were like rubber, ropey and weak. After it was over, you told me your date had been a disaster.

'She was twice the size of her photograph,' you said.

I pinched you on your arm, relieved. How foolish of me.

The next morning, you woke up early and showered in my bathroom and combed your hair back in front of the mirror, enveloped in steam. You kissed me and asked if we would ever see each other again. I laughed at this and told you we would. There were other weddings, other weekends to be shared. It was just the beginning. You went quiet, and I wondered what you were thinking. I packed my suitcase while you watched me, a smile on your face. How could it be? That a smile could hide such secrets?

We went to the park one last time, and sat on a bench overlooking the pond, and you picked up a small stone and tried to skip it, missing the water. The sun was warm against my skin.

'Weddings are weird,' you said. 'All that pomp and circumstance, all that drama, and for what? Do people even remember them?'

'No,' I said, unable to hide the bitterness in my voice. 'But I'm guessing one day you'll find out.'

You didn't say anything. Then you put your hand over mine and said, very softly, 'I'm not getting married,' and I glanced at my wristwatch and realized it was time to leave.

You insisted on driving me to the airport—you had rented a car—so we slipped out of the hotel without saying goodbye to anyone. During the drive, you were silent, and I was fighting back tears. Jacob was waiting for me. But I could only think of you.

When we pulled up alongside the terminal you switched off the car.

'I'm sorry.'

'About last night?' I gathered my things. 'So you were a little late; it happens. At least we got to see each other.'

'Not that.' You shook your head. A plane descended over our heads and cast a shadow over your face. 'I'm sorry about everything else. The way I treated you, when we were young, and after—for letting you go.'

I put my hand on your arm. 'Stop.'

But you didn't. Cars rushed by and an attendant came over to tell you to move, but you only stared at him. 'To be honest—and this might sound weird—but I was a little jealous of you back then. We all were. You had this aura about you. It's like you were somewhere else. You were there, but you were somewhere else. I never had that for myself.'

I stared at you, uncomprehending. We were quiet for a while. Then you got out of the car and helped me with my luggage and when I looked into your eyes, I knew: something was wrong.

That was the last time we saw each other. I still remember the way you waited until I had walked past the sliding glass doors before getting back into your car, the heat from your embrace still warming my skin. It was impossible to talk after that. I returned to my world, and you returned to yours. Jacob picked me up with the girls, and I kissed each one of them on their heads. My life resumed its course: play dates and meetings and dinner parties with friends, day trips to a museum or a park. For months, I thought of you, our fated weekend returning to me like a dream, but then something would happen—a cut that needed tending, a fight between the kids, a large bill in the mail—and you would be plucked from my thoughts, the way a blade of grass, rooted to the earth, is plucked by a child. I didn't stop to wonder where you were, or what you were doing. I didn't do any of this until eight months later, on a cold winter morning, when I was standing alone in the kitchen and the phone suddenly rang. I had assumed it would be Jacob, calling to talk to me from work, or one of the teachers at school, calling to talk about the girls, but instead it was my mother, calling to talk about *you*.

'Something has happened.'

∽

I know what it's like: to have people say things about you that aren't true. I had heard the rumours about myself. You will never know what I heard about you. According to some people, you had developed a rare form of cancer. Others said it was something more insidious, and shameful. Still others said you were on drugs, that you had done it to yourself. You were a doctor. How could you not have known? The question I ask myself is: how could I? You said you were on a diet and I believed you. I turned my head when you popped that white pill. I laughed at you when you asked if we would see each other again. I cursed you in my head when you didn't show up to my room. I didn't think to ask what you had been doing all that time. I didn't want to know. It is clear to me, now, that you were ill.

Is that why you never married? For weeks after it happened, people would ask this same thing, as if the greatest tragedy of all was that you had left no one behind. Your parents said it was pneumonia, that you had suffered complications. But your obituary was left vague; your family was tight-lipped. There were more questions than answers, questions no one had the courage to ask.

A picture ran next to the small article about you in my parents' local newspaper; it was your high school yearbook photo. In it, you wore a gold earring in your left ear; your hair was buzzed short. How strange that you should be remembered that way. For weeks after hearing the news, I walked around like a ghost, as if I had left my own body in the way you had left yours. I couldn't sleep, or eat. I never made it to your funeral, either. Your parents didn't want anyone there. Your mother was too distraught. She called my mother one morning to apologize. She said finally she knew—she knew what it was like to have people talk about her child.

On the way to the airport that morning, I had asked you again. 'How did you get into my hotel room?' You smiled. 'I had a key.' 'Did you steal it?' 'No.' 'Did I give it to you?' 'No.' 'Then how?' You turned your head and laughed. 'I got it from the front desk.' 'But that's impossible,' I said. 'They wouldn't even give me your room number.' 'I have my ways.' 'Tell me—how?' And you did. 'I told them you were my wife.' I never told you this, but that summer, before you left, I had dreamt of marrying you. I remembered my mother showing me pictures of Lord Krishna when I was a child. I remembered the hordes of women that surrounded him. Only one of them had captured his heart, a young woman named Radha. According to my mother, they never married, but their love for each other remained, long after Krishna had died, immortalized in the small pictures that lined our apartment walls. Like you, my mother is long gone now, and the girls are in college, but the pictures remain, and sometimes, when I look at them, I can still see your face.

19

THE ANNUAL PIG PARADE OF KHARAGPORE

NICHOLAS RIXON

In the slow-moving railway town of Kharagpore—where a clipped-moustache, suit-wearing sahib of the Leftover Raj, Old Rosario, once roamed with a tiger cub on a leash and winked at ayahs when the missus wasn't looking—the most exciting event of the year took place in December.

The Annual Pig Parade, two days before Christmas, was more than just an outdoor carnival for families of Sacred Heart parish to mingle, drink ginger wine, and listen to the Earthly Cherubs sing. It was, above all else, a competition. One the Anglo-Indian pig-owners (Indians didn't own pigs back then) took very seriously. The prize was a sheet metal trophy of a pig, plated in silver, its snout in the air and a certificate bearing official seals of the Archdiocese and the Bacon & Sausage Co-operative—primary sponsor of the event.

The family that won kept the trophy for eleven months before returning it to the parish priest. The Meades won twelve years ago with their prize sow, Caroline, and when time came to return the trophy they informed the church it had gone missing.

'It's just not there,' Mrs Meade told members of her knitting circle, but the truth was out the following Sunday. The youngest of the Meade daughters blurted it out in catechism class when a nun was on the subject of Moses destroying the Golden Calf.

'Daddy hid the pig trophy in his almirah,' said little Aileen, in between sobs. 'Please don't send Daddy to hell.'

Unlike the fire-and-brimstone punishment so effortlessly meted out in the Old Testament, the Meades got off easy. The husband returned the trophy and donated a substantial sum of money towards the new convent on Second Avenue. The one good thing about being Roman Catholic was you could always be forgiven.

Basil Rosario never forgot the incident. For the last decade, it so happened the Rosario pigs always came in a close second. It wasn't because the Rosarios neglected their hogs. Basil fed them a mix of apples, walnuts, and spinach for weeks. It was just that Mr Meade was better with pigs. Every morning, as the milkman passed by on his rickety cycle, Mr Meade got out of bed, and before taking a piss, walked to the sty at the back of his house. The pigs, like children abandoned at night, cooed as they heard his footsteps squelch on the dew-soaked grass.

One Sunday, a piglet followed him to church, waddling all the way to the altar during the Second Reading. Father Vincent jumped from his high chair when he saw the piglet chewing on the lace altar cloth. Service was interrupted for half an hour as Mr Meade coaxed the chubby animal from under the altar. He was undisputedly the best pig whisperer Kharagpore had seen.

But this year Basil was determined to break Mr Meade's record.

'Come to bed, it's late,' said Phyllis.

He ignored his wife and kept pacing the bedroom, muttering. 'I'm going to win if it's the last thing I do.'

⁂

All the best posts in the Railways were held by Anglo-Indians—a hangover of the Raj. The Railways owned everything in Kharagpore, including the red-brick-green-door bungalows where all the Anglo-Indian families cocooned. Bigger the family, bigger the house.

The Meades had eight children and a fourteen-room bungalow on Fourth Avenue. Basil was a carriage inspector and the Rosarios had a two-storeyed bungalow, 229 House, not too far from the Meades. They tried, but Phyllis had her tubes tied up after the third stillborn.

Their house was on the edge of the jungle, separated by a wooden fence that had long since mingled with the branches of trees, heavy with fruit in the summer, orange and scraggly in the winter. From the higher terraces on Fourth Avenue, the trees were ripples of green all the way to the station-horizon. When April evenings stretched long, Basil would take his old double-barrelled rifle to the jungle. He'd come back with quail, partridge, and—if he were lucky—a rabbit. One day, Basil tracked a pair of black-naped hares all the way to the old banyan tree near the jungle-vein stream. This was the farthest he'd ever gone and was about to give up when he saw a tiny leg sticking out from under a cock-flower bush, shining in the shivelight.

'I found her under the leaves,' Basil said, laying her out on the table.

Phyllis stood over the filthy, naked child with spiders and leaves in her hair. The grime on her body like a second skin. 'Put up some hot water,' said Phyllis, as she carried the child to the bathroom.

Basil heard a scream and came running from the kitchen. Phyllis had the broom in her hand and the naked girl, on all fours, was barking from under the marble sink.

They named the girl Edwina.

Phyllis took it upon herself to teach this girl from under the leaves how to behave like a lady. 'Only then can we introduce her to others,' she said.

'Teach her to walk first. Can't have her on all fours like a bloody animal,' said Basil. 'We'll say she's a niece from the hills. People are different there.'

So they kept her in the room upstairs and every day Phyllis spent time trying to get her to stand up, eat with a spoon, and pick up simple words and phrases—thank you, amen, ma, and pa. Edwina picked up words and their meaning quicker than she learned to walk. She couldn't string words together perfectly, but she got her point across.

The room had a single round window facing the trees and sometimes Edwina tried to peep out, her small hands cupped around her eyes. All she could see, through the dust and grime collected on the pane, were lazy shape-shadows floating by.

The months went by in Kharagpore with the whistle of trains and Phyllis spent them trying to make Edwina walk. In two months, the girl was stooping around her room. 'You look like an old hag,' laughed Phyllis, as Edwina tried to maintain her balance and walk from one wall to the next, shoulders facing the floor. 'Stand up straight, sweetheart,' Phyllis said, with her hand on Edwina's back. 'Mama, food,' Edwina said. Phyllis hugged her close.

One evening, Basil peeped through the keyhole and saw Edwina crawling across the room like a spider. As soon as Edwina heard the key turn in the lock, she stood up straight, leaning against the far wall. 'Don't worry, I won't tell Mama,' Basil said. Edwina smiled at him, baring her gums and remaining milk teeth. The ones in front had fallen out last week. Phyllis had strung them up on a black cord and made her a necklace. After feeding Edwina and trying to teach her not to bite down on the spoon, Basil went out to his sty.

In the middle of all the muck sat Judy. 'Hello, sweetheart, look what I got you,' whispered Basil. He held out two apples and the sow got up slowly, farted, and walked towards him. She knocked the apples out of his hand and ate them from the mud.

'Such a good-looking girl you've become,' whispered Basil, scratching her behind the ears. She loved when he did that and grunted. Basil knelt down and kept stroking her belly and gave her another apple. He then filled her water trough, took a bath by the tube well, and went inside the house.

∞

Basil's father, Old Rosario, besides being the head foreman at the car shed, had also been a skilled taxidermist.

As a boy, Basil helped him stuff an eagle, deer, flying fox, a mongoose; and one of his fondest childhood memories was stuffing the tiger cub. The zoo didn't want him and, one day, as Old Rosario sat in the cane chair in the garden sipping cardamom tea, he felt a prickling sensation on the back of his hand. The cub was licking his fingers and had drawn blood.

There was only one thing to do, and it took three months from gutting to stuffing to putting the cub up in the living room, where the stench of arsenic soap and naphthalene balls hung heavy. Old Rosario hadn't managed to get the right-sized glass eyes. The cub looked wide-eyed and a little sad, at the flying fox on the opposite wall, hung upside down, claws permanently tied to an old hockey stick made to look like a branch.

The days of walking the tiger cub were over. Old Rosario died the following week in the bathroom, where he slipped and banged his head against the marble sink.

∞

The December shower that announced winter came down like bubble wrap in the afternoon, and continued through owl-time. Judy was brought into the living room, so that snakes wouldn't get to her in the sty. The house smelled of mud and rain, but not in a bad way.

'You love that pig too much,' said Phyllis, in the cane chair, going through the missal. 'Tomorrow is the feast of St John of the Cross.'

'Finally, it's time,' said Basil, on his knees, whispering to Judy as she lay on her side.

With the pig parade little more than a week away, Basil had been feeding Judy more apples and walnuts than usual. He was spending more time in the sty than in the house. The night before he had to do it, he insulated a wooden crate with jute bags and lined it with egg boards and hay.

Next morning, Judy was waiting in the garden. He didn't need to drag her to the back. She came willingly. He bound her mouth with rope, slit her neck, and held her down by her ears. By the time she kicked her trotters and wiggled her rump for the last time, Basil was covered in blood. His eyelids had flecks of blood, and his scalp, through the scanty black-turning-grey hair, was a deep red.

He gutted her and washed her out with arsenic soap. He put the skin in the wooden crate with blocks of ice and heaps of salt. In seven hours, he took the pigskin out, dried her down, and lined her stomach with wooden slats, cut to size. He had a wooden cup to put into the hollowed-out snout. Perfectly-sized wooden stilts, shaped like hooves and painted dull-black, for the short legs.

The afternoon before the parade, while everyone was in that fragile yet comfortable stage of half-sleep, Phyllis tried, and failed, to explain to Edwina what needed to be done. When the girl saw the pig, she wanted to sit on its back and take it for a ride. 'No, no,' said Basil, trying to keep his voice down. 'You have to go inside.' He held the flaps of the incision open. Edwina took off her maroon tablecloth-tunic and blinked at Phyllis who nodded. Basil tried to appear patient without looking so. Edwina laughed and went head first through Judy's neck. She turned around inside and was back to how she had grown up walking. 'All that practice to make her normal like us,' said Phyllis, looking away.

'Don't worry,' said Basil, 'it's just for a day. Few hours really.'

Judy waddled around the backyard as Phyllis and Basil sat on an upturned basket. She came to a halt, flipped on to her back, and jumped up straight again.

'Well done, Edwina,' shouted Phyllis. Basil laughed and squeezed his wife's fat wrist.

They heard the crunch of cycle wheels on the gravel road near their house. Phyllis went to see who it was, while Basil guided Judy behind a bed sheet on the clothes line. He lifted the flap of the incision and pulled

Edwina out. 'Shh,' he said, putting a finger to his lips. 'Shh,' said Edwina, mimicking the gesture and smiling her nearly toothless grin.

'Thank your mother,' said Phyllis from the front gate. Basil and Edwina came out from behind the sheet and Phyllis walked up to them with a note. 'The Meades invited us for dinner. The Bishop'll be there, too.'

'Nothing doing,' said Basil, 'we'll see them tomorrow with the trophy in our hands.'

Edwina crawled into Judy and ran from under the clothes line. Basil chased her around the living room. She jumped over the chest of drawers, grunting with happiness, knocked over the flying fox, and ran circles around Phyllis in the kitchen.

On the day of the Pig Parade, Basil and Phyllis were up earlier than usual. Edwina had spent the night in Judy, tied to a leg of the dressing table in the bedroom. Basil was whistling 'White Christmas' and making tea in the kitchen.

'Can you hear me, sweetheart?' Phyllis was on her knees whispering to Edwina. 'Hope it's not too hot in there, Ed.'

'Stop calling her that,' said Basil, bringing the kettle in. 'People'll know something's fishy. Judy's the name on the competition form and that's what you call her today.'

Phyllis looked up at her husband and saw a man determined not to fail. 'I hope nothing goes wrong,' said Phyllis, stroking Judy under the snout.

'Stop worrying, woman,' said Basil. 'We'll have her out of there in no time.' At that moment, Judy jumped over the bed and Basil clapped.

After lunch, Basil opened up Judy's neck incision and stuffed the wooden skeleton with hay and cotton.

'She'll suffocate,' said Phyllis.

'Don't be daft.' said Basil. 'It's like a bed in there.'

Phyllis had a bottle of foundation in her vanity box for special occasions. She applied the mixture to parts of Judy's skin that had begun to grey. She wrapped a pink ribbon round the pig's neck and tied it neatly in a bow to hide the incision.

'There you go, Ed,' whispered Phyllis. 'Mama'll get you out of there before you can say sausages.'

Edwina laughed and mumbled something, but the cotton and hay made it hard to hear.

Basil brought the Bible from the bedroom. 'Swear you won't tell a soul about this,' he said, staring at his wife, who put her hand on the tome and swore.

Basil looped a rope around Judy's neck and they looked a pretty sight walking down Fourth Avenue—Phyllis in her frilly dress with green bougainvilleas, Basil in his brown chequered suit, and the pig in between.

The carnival was held in the stadium opposite Sacred Heart Church. The Bishop was attending and everyone was excited to kiss his ring. A raised platform had been constructed in front of a goalpost. The Bishop sat on a high chair in the centre with Father Vincent, the parish priest, and Mr Vanjour, chairman of the Bacon & Sausage Co-operative, on either side.

The altar boy choir, lovingly nicknamed the Earthly Cherubs, began with a shrill rendition of 'Hark the Herald Angels Sing', moving on to 'Great Day in Bethlehem', and ending with a raucous, sweet-banshee-like delivery of 'Jingle Bells'. The parishioners joined in and clapped at the end of it all. The Bishop said a short prayer, threw blessings around, and finally it was time for the Pig Parade.

Five owners stood in single file with their pigs in front of them. One by one, as their names were called, they walked in a circle round the enclosed area and stopped in front of the three judges. Everyone went quiet when they saw Mr Meade and his pig, Patrick, a gleaming white balloon. He was not on a leash and followed Mr Meade to the raised platform. Mr Meade clicked his tongue and Patrick plonked back on his hind trotters.

'What a beautiful, obedient creature,' said Mr Vanjour. The Bishop and Father Vincent nodded.

Basil knelt down next to Edwina and whispered, 'You've got this, Judy. Remember, no laughing, and when you hear this sound—' he clicked his fingers, '—do that jump you showed Mama.'

Basil was the last to walk. The parishioners had lost interest by then. Everyone knew Mr Meade would take it again. The mason jars of ginger wine had been opened to breathe and people were stealing glances at the food tables—pork croquettes and plum cake.

The master of ceremonies announced their names and Basil began walking towards the podium. Halfway there, he clicked his fingers and Judy somersaulted. The parishioners distracted by the food tables missed it, but those who didn't oohed and aahed. The Bishop stood up from the comfortably cushioned chair, rubbing his eyes. Basil smiled and clicked his fingers again. Judy rolled in the grass, ran ahead, and somersaulted twice.

This time everyone in the crowd saw the pirouetting pig and broke into loud applause. Mr Vanjour's mouth hung open. The decision, wordlessly unanimous, was reached then and there, amidst all the cheering. Father Vincent handed the silver-plated pig trophy to the Bishop, and Basil, hands outstretched, climbed the steps of the podium.

Judy was left behind at the bottom, rolling in the grass. She turned to the crowd and saw Phyllis sitting pretty in her green bougainvillea dress. She began trotting towards her, but her path was blocked by a fat, bearded man holding a long rod with a noose at the end. Phyllis took one look at him and screamed.

'Run, Edwina, run!'

Judy somersaulted backwards and took off towards a gap in the crowd. Basil looked at the commotion from above and tried to stop it all before someone caught the pig.

'Mr Vanjour,' he said. 'Don't trouble your butcher. I'll deliver the pig tomorrow morning.'

Mr Vanjour put his arm around Basil. 'No trouble at all, Mr Rosario. My butcher will take care of it. I'll have your share delivered first thing tomorrow. As you know, the Bacon & Sausage Co-operative keeps half the meat and the rest goes to the family that wins. Congratulations, Basil. You've raised a truly remarkable sow.'

Down below, the butcher was having a tough time cornering Judy. She ran like no other pig before, darting between legs, around tables, and through chairs. At one point she jumped over the butcher's outstretched hairy arms, over the low stadium wall, and into the jungle.

Phyllis fell to her knees crying, 'My Edwina, my Edwina....'

'Who's Edwina?' asked Father Vincent.

'Oh nobody,' said Basil, laughing. 'I told her to take it easy with that ginger wine.'

The butcher ran after Judy into the jungle and Phyllis went staggering after them. Basil hurried over to his wife.

'It's all your fault,' screamed Phyllis. 'My daughter. My Edwina. I should never have listened to—'

'Will you shut up,' he said softly, squeezing her wrist. 'I'll find her.'

The women of the parish gathered around Phyllis as Basil and a few other men followed the butcher into the jungle. An hour went by before they came back, huffing and dirty. Mr Meade was part of the group and he recounted the chase as everyone gathered around the podium.

'It's some black magic, Father,' he said, breathing heavily. His words came in bursts. 'Judy's faster than a hyena…never seen a pig go that fast…cornered her…the old banyan tree…tell me, Your Excellency,' and he turned to the Bishop. 'Have you seen a pig climb a tree?'

'My God,' said the Bishop, settling his purple cap and crossing himself. 'Go on.'

'I could see her tail poking out…I threw a stone and—'

'You hurt my Edwina!' screamed Phyllis and charged at Mr Meade.

'Basil, please control your wife,' said Father Vincent.

Basil grabbed Phyllis round the waist and they sat down on the podium together.

'This fell out of the tree,' said Mr. Meade. He threw down Judy's skin with cotton and hay poking out. The wooden slats were broken. The neck incision was torn all the way down to the legs.

'And this too,' said Mr Meade. He took out the milk teeth necklace from his shirt pocket and held it in front of the Bishop's face.

The Bishop turned to Basil and Phyllis sitting on the podium. 'Care to explain this, Mr Rosario?'

'Witchcraft,' whispered someone from the crowd.

Basil handed the trophy to Mr Meade, picked up Judy's skin, and walked towards the stadium entrance. Phyllis ran behind him screaming, 'Did you find her? You have to go back…oh Mummy darling…my Edwina….'

He shook her off and kept walking as the parishioners stood in a semicircle, silent, and the heady aroma of ginger wine and pork croquettes hung forgotten in the dusty winter air.

∽

The truth in a rumour is like Jesus walking on water. How'd he do it? By putting one foot in front of the other, all the parishioners would say.

The upcountry tale of Judy, the somersaulting pig, has a number of adaptations depending on who you hear it from, and more importantly, what you choose to believe.

Mrs Meade told the knitting circle her husband heard a child laugh when he threw the stone at Judy's backside in the banyan tree.

'I just knew it was wrong. Devilish! No pig's supposed to jump backwards or laugh,' said Mrs Meade. 'Poor Phyllis…if she only had a child of her own…and who's this Edwina she keeps mumbling about….'

That fanned the rumour about how the Rosarios conjured up a spirit, forced it to possess Judy, making the dead pig somersault. Others say Basil sold his soul to the Devil to become a better pig whisperer than Mr Meade.

The truth, like Jesus walking on water, is not important if you already believe.

The silver-plated pig trophy found a permanent home with the Meades.

Father Vincent and the Bishop, after much deliberation, decided the Annual Pig Parade would not take place again. 'Highly misfortunate,' said the Bishop. 'They need to forget in order to forgive.'

They reckoned why worry about one family when the majority came to mass and the collection bag grew heavier. Father Vincent made a mental note to say a prayer for the Rosarios as he stared out at his parishioners crowding around the church entrance, forcing Phyllis and Basil to turn back.

That Sunday afternoon, the Earthly Cherubs cornered Phyllis on Fourth Avenue and sang:

Fat little witch,
Hump hump hump!
Let's see your pig,
Jump jump jump!

They pelted her with stones, howling and hooting with the pariah dogs, and raced away on their rickety cycles, kicking up dust and leaves.

Basil was at the car shed working overtime. As the clouds pocketed the sun and tree-shadows formed black giants looming over the Kharagpore bungalows, Phyllis went into Edwina's room and bolted the door. A lizard, on the round window, stared sideways. Phyllis cut long strips from her green bougainvillea dress, knotting them into a rope. She tied one end to the fifty-pound ceiling fan, made a noose around her neck, and kicked the cane chair from under her.

A funeral mass was denied by the Bishop, who in his letter cited St Paul, the catechism, and ready-made solace. *You have been purchased and at a price. So glorify God in your body.… We are stewards, not owners of the life of God.… Our condolences go out to you at this moment.…*

Basil and the gravedigger were the only ones at the burial.

Basil didn't go back to work in the car shed. He spent his days making long trips to the banyan tree with a tent, a bottle of toddy, and his rifle.

The ayah found him, one May afternoon, in the sty.

It was one of those summer days when the dust from the road never settled. The pariah dogs were dozing under the tamarind tree when the ayah's scream cut through the sleepy haze. They ran to the sound, past a honey vendor standing his ground on a bargain, and saw Basil Rosario lying face down in the muck.

There were three items near the body, arranged like a halo around his head. The tiger cub's glass eyes; a half-empty bottle of toddy (soaking naphthalene balls and slivers of arsenic soap); and Judy's deflated skin, pink and fresh as if she were cut only yesterday.

20

THE GIRL WHO HAUNTED DEATH

NIKITA DESHPANDE

There's only a moment's difference between ripe and rot. That's what my amma would always say. 'Fruits will blush with a succulent sweetness just before they turn over and die.'

At that time I thought it was, like everything else, a lesson on marriage.

As a child, I'd run from tree to tree in the palace gardens, plucking the figs while they were still green and hiding them under my bed. *If they stayed hidden from the heat of the sun, they would never ripen. Their time would never come.* Or so I thought, until I woke up one morning to a bloody mess of flesh and juice and the sour tang of broken dreams.

I sense that stench in the air again, thousands of years later, when he walks into the university campus where I teach. I cancel a lecture, make excuses, and take the weekend off. All day, I sit by the window in my apartment, snipping the overgrown pink bougainvillea twined with the grill. I toss the flowers, one by one, into a wide brass vessel filled with water and wait for the petals to age like prunes. When I find the courage to leave for class on Monday morning, the flowers have still not withered or sunk to the depths. It gives me a sort of hope. But when I put my books down on the class table and turn, he is there, sitting in the middle row, scribbling in the back of a notebook with a red-and-black-striped Natraj pencil.

Two young women in the front keep turning to look at him.

I ignore them and dive into teaching.

An hour later I am close to concluding, when his hand flies up in the air. I continue to speak, even though something in my stomach has caught spark and burst into bright blue flame. 'And this is the point Simone De Beauvoir is making. She says every time a woman, a female character makes a move towards self-assertion, it supposedly takes away from her femininity, her likeability…and her…seductiveness….'

I lose my train of thought as we lock eyes.

'Yes?'

He has the courtesy to look down and smile at his notebook for a moment before he says, 'This is Western thought in an Indian classroom. In our culture, the women in our stories asserted themselves all the time. Draupadi's hair left untied and dishevelled until washed in the blood of the enemy. Sita, steadfast, even in the face of fire. And who was it that haunted Death himself until he gave her husband back? Ah,' he says, his perfect bow-shaped lips curling into a smile. 'Savitri.'

The heat from my stomach jumps up to lick my face.

'Th—the women from our mythologies,' I say, stressing the last word, 'were trapped in the complexity of their own time. And were constantly punished for asserting themselves in their own ways. It's…er…an entirely different subject from what I'm discussing….'

'But ma'am,' he interrupts, waving the Natraj pencil rapidly in the air so it looks like a trident…or a pitchfork. 'They are brave women. Norm-breakers. And still seen as idols of femininity in this country.'

'If you still want to pursue this debate, you can see me after class,' I say with some force, hoping I sound brusque and dismissive. But the corners of his lips curl again, like it is some sort of an invitation. I rush out of class after the bell and sit in the staffroom among the other teachers, pretending to correct papers. No matter how gentle I am, the ticks of my red pen look like slashes.

Later, when I walk out to the terrace to get some fresh air, he is there, sitting among the potted plants. The black-and-white kitten adopted by the staff purrs in his lap. My heart jumps as he turns to look at me, stroking the kitten with absurdly long fingers.

'You don't need such an elaborate ruse to talk to me,' I say, drawing the pallu of my sari around me to shield against the strong breeze.

He beams. His teeth are mostly straight. His eyebrows thick and wormy like twin caterpillars, his dark hair, straight and windblown. He looks completely different from the last time we met, and yet, it is Death in that white T-shirt and jeans.

'I was just curious,' he says, in a deep voice that could bend the wind into submission. 'To see what perspective you would bring to a—what was it—an "Introduction to Gender Studies" class.'

I fold my arms. 'Why are you here?'

'As always, puppet. To see you.'

The wind whips around us, fiercer than usual. The sky darkens, its edges orange, as if catching fire. I don't miss the signs. There are few things Death loves more than spilling blood in the sky.

'Who is going to die?' I clench my jaw.

He rises to his feet and takes a step towards me. Then another, and another, until a hard, warm hand reaches up to touch my cheek. 'I had forgotten about your questions, Savitri.'

It's a trick. To call me by that name is to touch me in many different places at once.

I close my eyes. 'I have a different name now.'

'Hmm.... But to me you'll always be the same fifteen-year-old I found on a forest floor, weeping next to her husband's body, begging for him to be returned. How many centuries has it been? Do your beloved humans even know how to count back to that time? Hmm? Do you remember?'

Do I?

The story people tell now, they once heard from their grandparents, who heard it from theirs, who read it in a book written by a saint, who was told by five other rishis, who say they read it in an ancient text written by an elephant god.

In that story, Savitri haunted and followed Death and begged him for her dear husband's life. She impressed him with her wisdom until her beloved husband was returned to her, whole and alive.

Unfortunately, I am not that Savitri.

∽

Let me tell you a story.

Many centuries ago, I was walking through a forest with the man I had married. I was all of fifteen, no more a child, barely a woman.

But in a time when women did not choose their husbands, I had fought the rules of the world just to become his companion, his most ardent servant. That was the meaning of marriage in those days. If he wanted a drink of water, I knew to read the slightest movement in his mouth so that a jug would touch his lips before a single syllable had spilled from them. They said if I was a good wife, if I was truly devoted, I could prove all the prophecies wrong.

But he collapsed one afternoon as we picked nuts and berries in the forest. He clutched his chest, slurring words and commands. It had been a long year of prophecies and fire sacrifices. I had learned to make talismans out of salt, lemons, chillies, and mustard seeds to protect him and yet when it came down to it, my husband writhed like an insect.

Then the forest went unnaturally quiet, like it was sucking in a breath. Leaves ceased their rustling. The wind turned mute. Animal calls died in their throats. The sour smell of puckering fruit was everywhere. I thought of the figs. The gardens. Fingers of the sun reaching for them below my bed.

Heart pounding, I looked up from my husband and stared straight into the eyes of Death.

A woman.

Contrary to everything I had been taught. The opposite of all that I had read and heard in stories and scriptures, she was a woman, a god, her skin as dark as cinnamon bark, teeth artfully crooked, and eyes that looked like the very heart of dancing fire. A jewel like no other, something celestial—shone from a pin in her nose.

'Please,' I begged. 'Please don't take my husband.'

'It's too late for that now,' she said, her voice full and melodious, like the sound of a woodwind instrument. 'Go home.'

'No, please. He was the only thing that made life worth living. Please, give him back.' I started to sob.

She circled us slowly, watching my husband like he was prey. I clutched his body tightly to my own. My tears stained his cheek.

'Please, please, give him back. I love him. Please.'

This seemed to enrage and delight her all at once.

'Love...' she scoffed. 'What do you know of love, little puppet? You go where the gods send you. You pick up glass and think it's a diamond. You slice a finger and think your heart is broken. You see one face of a brilliant, many-faced thing and you think that's all you want.'

The body between us vanished. Death closed a fist. My hands clutched at air.

'I—will—serve—you,' I stammered in between sobs. 'I will go wherever you go, do whatever you want, if you give him his life back.'

She laughed and took a step away, hips swaying seductively, a hand pulling all her long, wavy hair over one shoulder. 'It doesn't work like that.'

I followed her, convinced that if I got close enough to pry open her fist, I would find my husband. But her magic was strange and intoxicating. The forest around us thickened and dissolved into whorls of colour—deep purple and the blackest black, fiery flickers of amber and midnight blue. No matter how fast I walked, it seemed like I stayed in the same place: just inside the line of her shadow. Only the stars remained unmoving above us, like a legion of distant gods, twinkling dangerously.

'If you intend to follow me,' she said, stopping after what seemed like many tedious hours, 'prepare to walk for a long, long time.'

I looked around. We were in a part of the world I had never seen before.

You have to understand. These words I use now to describe it, to remember it—I did not have this vocabulary then. I did not know, for example, that the huge grey metal monsters before me were called 'ships'. Or that the pale-skinned people going about their work, in clothes I did not recognize, were mortal, humans of another race that would descend upon my people and rule them one day.

All this I learned later, from asking.

'You underestimate me,' I said to her then, trying to ignore the new, intimidating surroundings. 'I will torment you with questions.'

She stopped in the shadow of a large vessel, turned around and laughed. Her bird-like eyes crinkled in a very human way.

'Why would I be tormented by your questions?'

'My husband....' I wiped away fresh tears at that word. 'He...he used to say I could irritate the most evolved, the best learned, the most disciplined of saints with my questions.'

Death narrowed her eyes at me. It felt like I was being watched by something larger. The universe. A dark, turbulent ocean. Some great, big beast with hooves and wings, flanks, and feathers.

'All right, puppet,' she sniggered. 'Consider it a challenge. If you manage to ask me a question that annoys me, even a little, you can have your husband back.'

My eyes must have widened in something like joy because she sneered, almost immediately. 'I should warn you. There is no question you can ask that would irritate me. No number of them.'

We walked on a while, cold to the bone, in gloomy grey weather, towards a towering bridge in the distance. Rats scurried beneath our feet. Everything reeked of waste and disease. I wondered where we were and what we were doing. She seemed to be in no hurry. 'What if you are annoyed but you pretend not to be?' I said, after a while.

'What if you…forgive me, but how can I be certain that the emotions you express to me are truly the ones you feel?'

'Very good.' She looked genuinely impressed and a little amused. 'Doubting the honesty of the gods without an ounce of fear for their wrath? What a rare thing you are! But trust me, duckling. If you ever manage to offend me, you will know.'

She was smiling but something in her tone made me shiver. I kept my questions to myself—just for the moment—so I could watch her closely, and observe how things as simple as light and air turned at her command.

It was hard to tell how long we had been walking. Hours melted into minutes, and years into centuries, into units of time that man had not mastered yet. Again and again, we tiptoed across the threshold of time and space, doing a chore here, a job there. The fist opened and closed. And when it opened again, it was always empty. No part of the world was beyond Death's reach. She ended kings and children in one strike. Sometimes, we remained unseen and I walked in her shadow, asking, asking, endlessly asking.

Sometimes, she shifted shape and took new forms—a man, a woman, something in between, neither. Perhaps, I thought at one point, she was magicking new forms for me.

I was never out of place among mourners. At first, I could only see the mothers, the wives, the daughters, and the sisters, familiar among the hurt and the grieving. What was it to me if they wrung skirts or saris, hides, or trousers? If they broke bracelets, bangles, beads, or bones? Pain was emblazoned on their skin.

Once at a river ghat, they laid a baby to rest under a rough stone. We sat on large rusting pipes. Death wore a man's form now, his bearded chin resting on his folded arms, staring into the eyes of the sun as if threatening it with his own fire.

The words staggered in my mouth but I asked the question.

'Where do people go when they die?'

He smiled. 'They go wherever they think they're going. Dying is wish-fulfilment like no other.'

'So does that mean the baby is happy?'

'I didn't say that.'

He looked into my eyes, and it struck me, for the first time, how close we were sitting. If I moved my arm, our shoulders would graze. I think he noticed it too, because a few moments later he folded his legs so that our toes touched, our knees pressed head to head. My heart jumped, like it had been jolted awake from deep sleep.

'I think he was annoyed, not because you ask too many questions, but because you ask the difficult ones.'

'Who?' I said, without thinking.

'Your husband?' Death grinned, a little surprised.

My cheeks burned. He turned his gaze back to the sun. But something between our knees buzzed with heat in spite of the cool afternoon. After the sun had plunged into the mountains, we dusted ourselves off and walked on, and the frisson that had existed minutes ago flickered and died.

In those days, when we left one place and time for another, it felt a lot like I was being blindfolded and spun in circles. I lost the ability to tell the difference between then and now and then. Like the needle in a compass, I pointed due north every time, waking in Death's shadow, under the influence of whatever magnetic pull he had. And yet a small part of me continued to quiver, long after the spinning had stopped, as though it believed my north should be something else.

'How can it be that you have the magic to travel the world,' I asked Death once, 'and we only go to the places where terrible things have happened?'

We were in a dingy tavern. A man had just collapsed, spilling a whole barrel of wine the colour of blood. The people who were trying to run for help slipped in the mess. If I didn't know the man was already dead, I might've found it funny.

Death sat before me, drinking thick, dark mead from a glass he had magicked out of nothing. 'Terrible things are happening everywhere, all the time, duckling. Humans have the great privilege to only feel grief for what happens to them.'

'I've been wishing I had that privilege for a while now. But each one gets to me worse than the first,' I sulked. 'Don't you ever want to take a break? From the constant dying and the dead?'

'If you had the power, where would you go?'

'Somewhere bright and colourful. A place that feels…alive? And at a time when nobody's sick or dying.'

He smirked as he rose from his seat and walked out the front door, his fist closed tight. I sighed and followed him out into the wet cobbled street. Little grains of sand rose out of the gaps in the cobblestones and swirled around us in a breeze that hadn't been there seconds ago. The wind picked up, eventually enveloping us to become our own private sandstorm. I grabbed the end of his kurta and followed even as the sand rained pinpricks into my cheeks. When it finally settled, I could smell roasting meats and vegetables. My toes curled into warm sand. I opened my eyes.

We were standing in an enclosure of patchwork tents. Camels, goats, and bulls ambled about, wearing strings of little bells around their necks. Sunlight danced off mirrors sewn into women's skirts. Scarlet and orange turbans coiled like snakes around men's heads.

A desert fair.

I looked over to where Death should have been and found her wearing the same skin she had worn when we first met. She was dressed in a long maroon kurta, patterned with the phases of the moon. Her dark, wavy hair hid beneath a yellow turban. The shape of her legs just showed through the thin white cloth draped around her waist. This time when she looked into my eyes, my skin rose in gooseflesh.

'Where are we?' I said, looking away.

When Death smiled, it was not soft. It was sharp and cutting. 'Somewhere bright and colourful.'

A glorious sunset seared the sky. We stopped to hear a Rabari woman sing. A scarlet ghoongat covered her face, so that only the bluish tattoos on her neck were visible; her voice was high and loud and gruff. A young man played the ravanhattha by her side, his eyes closed in devotion.

The woman's song boomed across the mela, rising higher and warmer than the new-born campfires, silencing boisterous goatherds, demanding the attention of sleepy camels and weary travellers.

Next to me, Death opened her fist in a small, graceful movement, like an infant's yawn.

Please no, not the woman, I thought. How could she silence her now, like that, mid-song?

But Death's hand waited, open, next to my own. A moment later, I understood. I opened my own fist and took her hand in mine.

'What is she singing?' I asked, leaning so that my head could rest on her shoulder.

'Her song…is a question too.' Her nose turned to bury itself in my hair. Something throbbed in a hidden part of my body.

'She says she has found every god and goddess you can name. Every kind of heaven. Every saint and sinner known.'

'So…what's the question?' I raised my head to look into her fiery eyes.

She sighed. 'Where should I go to find you, my love?'

I put my head back on her shoulder, digging into the warmth of her body.

We walked on the sands long after the fires had become puffs of ash flying on the backs of desert winds. We sat side by side with our backs against somebody's tent. I watched her skin shine in the moonlight. All this time, so many hours. She had stolen this slice of time for my joy, in a place that was alive in every grain.

I asked questions, so many of them: could gods remember being born? This job of hers—did she think it a drudgery or a privilege? Did she always work alone? What happened during wars? And famine? And didn't it confuse her to hop across time like that? Some questions she answered and some she evaded cleverly, by leaning in, half-laughing and half-sighing into my clavicle. Finally, she held a slender finger to a spot in the very middle of my bottom lip.

'No more questions,' she said, pulling away the finger and bringing her lips to mine. If you asked me what it was like to kiss Death, I would say it was like drinking moonlight while at the bottom of the deepest ocean, without ever stopping for breath. To weave your hands through her hair and hold the nape of her neck is to reach across the horizon and touch the part where the light never reaches.

At some point that night, I fell into a deep, honey-thick sleep, with her head buried in my chest. When she shook me awake, it felt like a century had passed.

The sun blazed down on the desert. A shriek seemed to be pulling apart the fabric of the sky.

'Come,' she said. 'It's time to go.'

There was no outstretched hand. Her fist was closed again.

I wiped my mouth and looked around.

The cry belonged to the Rabari singer from last night. Men and women tried to hold her back as she slapped their hands away and clung to the fallen body of the young man I had seen playing the ravanhattha last night.

Her son, perhaps?

I stared.

'Puppet. We should leave.'

I looked up at her, my eyes brimming over. She had done this to our *somewhere bright and colourful*.

I shook my head. 'No.'

She had looked surprised. Or hurt. I remember thinking it was a trick of the light. Moments later, she turned on her heel and walked away.

And I ran forward to do the only thing I knew. I pushed past the crowd and held the singer's head to my bosom and listened to her wail against my beating heart.

༄

Death and I take a bus out of the university town. It's hot and rickety, and every inch of the vehicle squeaks and creaks as we make our way down bumpy roads.

He leans his head against the bars of the window and begins to sing aloud. It's a sad song from a movie in the local tongue. I look at him in surprise. At first, his singing earns him a frown from the bus conductor and a man trying to nap behind us. But some of the women watch him with shy smiles. Some nod along to the tune.

I go against everything in my being, every lesson I've learned, and watch. I watch how his eyes remain closed when he sings. His long lashes. How his hand automatically goes to his chest, just where his heart should be, when he hits the harder notes and the truer words. When we get off and walk towards the beach, I find the courage to take his hand. He raises a bushy eyebrow at me, but I walk, pulling him into my shadow.

It has been two decades (and half a lifetime) since that desert fair. I was found, taken in, paid for, violated, then saved. I was taught language like they teach apes and babies. I was fed and re-fleshed. I built a simple life out of learning and teaching. His arrival has made ripples in that life. But I still enjoy the warmth of that hand in mine.

We buy spiced peanuts in newspaper cones. I eat hungrily. He plays football with kids in the sand. We find a small coffee shop in a narrow lane. We lean against the whitewashed brick wall. He pauses to close his eyes and inhale the smell of the coffee in his steel tumbler before drinking from it.

'Why did you choose to come here?' he asks.

'I wanted to be near the sea,' I say.

What I don't say is this: *the people here have the same dark, coconutty skin you did when we first met. They have quaint superstitions about you; they think if they sleep with their heads towards the south, you will arrive. They say tentative things like 'I'll be back' instead of final things like 'Goodbye'. They rarely wear black. They paint red-faced demons on their doors to chase you away.*

'Why did you choose to come here?' I ask him.

I want him to say it was me. I want some muscle in his human face to betray whatever affection brings him back, time and again. I want to see his hand fly to his heart like it did when he sang that song.

But there's a moment's hesitation, and it gives him away.

'Who is it? Who's going to die? Not one of my students?'

'There was a girl in your class today.... This is not some kind of personal vendetta against you, you know.'

I put my tumbler of coffee down by the shop door and tuck fifty rupees underneath. I don't wait for change.

He catches up with me in the next lane. Before he can stop it, I push him up against a wall. I can see in his eyes that he isn't surprised by the force of it, but the closeness bothers him. I lean in to let my nose graze his neck and trace the hard line of his jaw.

'Take me,' I whisper. 'Spare whoever it is and let me die.'

He pulls his head back and smirks. 'I told you ages ago, puppet. It doesn't work like that.' He brings up a fingernail to scoop away the tear streaking my face.

'You've grown so much. I thought you would see enough faces of the diamond to stop being blinded. But look at you. Still bedazzled. Still thinking your life is worth exchanging for some...human's.'

I pull away, shaking my head in disbelief. 'Why do you, of all people, look down on love?'

'Love, attachments—they're mortal weaknesses. Haven't you noticed how much humans suffer on their account? Haven't you suffered?'

It cannot be. The person standing before me can't be the same person who sang a song of separation and longing on a bus three hours ago. He cannot have known the real meaning of the Rabari woman's song in the desert.

'So you have no attachments, then?'

'None,' he says, lip curling.

My voice is a whisper but the words come out sharp as a winter wind. 'Why are you here then? Why do you return to me? Why am I, a mere mortal, allowed to see you, speak to you…touch you?'

For a second he nods lightly. And then like a slap it strikes him across the face. Fear and fury make his nostrils flare and in the flutter of a second, I realize what is about to happen. At last I have found the question that disturbs him more than the deaths of children.

The last thing I see is his fist uncurl.

And then I travel. For the longest time, the ground is torn from beneath my feet. Through dancing storms and raging sunshine, I swim backward and blackward until—

I land.

I know where I am before I can open my eyes. I smell wet leaves, the soggy bark of trees, and sweat clinging to human flesh. I feel the weight of a head in my lap, heavy like a melon.

Dying is wish-fulfilment like no other.

When I open my eyes I am there. Back on the forest floor, holding my husband's body limply to my chest. He awakens, clutching his chest, not quite like a man enjoying a song. When he looks at me, his eyes shine with something like reverence.

I sit there, numb. I am numb as he speaks to me. Numb when we return home. Numb when I gaze at my reflection in a pond and find a fifteen-year-old's face frown back at me. It's as if my compass spins endlessly now, and north is lost or torn to pieces and scattered everywhere like ash and bone.

As the days pass, our village is rife with rumour. Nobody asks what I saw or where I went. Nobody understands the price of infuriating a god. 'Savitri haunted Death until he gave back her husband,' they say. 'She must have impressed the god with her sharp mind. She must have pleased Him with her devotion.'

I am not that Savitri. No.

I am a little girl, cold in the summer sun, holding on to a basket of sickeningly sweet fruit.

21

THE TWENTY-SIXTH GIANT

PRAYAAG AKBAR

SMS (Received 4:32 A.M.):
Problem. Call when you see this.

SMS (Sent 6:41 A.M.):
What, now? I just woke up. In thirty minutes.

Outgoing Call (6:43 A.M.):
'Okay, couldn't wait. What's happened now?'
'It's bad.'
'Just say it. It's too early. Don't waste time.'
'It's Manohar. He wants some changes.'
'Changes? Changes? What kind of bloody changes?'
'The design. They need a few things changed.'
'Look, man. I'm standing in my bathroom. I went to bed something like three hours ago. I haven't had any coffee. I'm in my bathroom, and I'm staring at myself in the mirror, and I look like hell, and my razor blades are right here, and I will fricking cut myself, and then I'm going to fly to Delhi, and come cut you, and then I'll go to Manohar's bordello-looking mansion in his arse-wipe little state, and I'll show him a change or two. See how I'm not raising my voice? That's how you know I'm serious. I'm not angry at all. I'm dead fucking serious.'

'It's just a few changes, Mrig. Don't be like this. You can do it. You know you can.'

'Is he out of his mind or what? I sat in his house for three months. I showed him design after design. This Girdharilal's head, it's planted in my brain. Printed, whatever. I can't get it out.

'That's all I see. When I sleep that horrible moustache appears in my dreams. I'm not lying. I swear to god I had a dream last week where giant bronze moustaches were falling from the sky and breaking buildings and bridges and rucking up mountains and everyone was coming up to me, crying and shrieking, carrying their bleeding children, saying it's your fault, isn't it, it's your fault, isn't it? That was the worst part. They kept asking if it was my fault. They wouldn't say it. They wouldn't even come out and say it.'

'It's one of those things that can't be helped, Mrig. This is how politicians are. We knew it when we got into this mess.'

'I don't care. We have our contract. Once the basic plan was finalized, they were allowed to make three rounds of changes. That was the deal. They can't keep doing this.'

'You don't understand, Mrig. It's not some bureaucrat now. It's the CM himself. He needs the changes. They'll pull the contract in a second if we argue. They'll back out of the deal and that'll be that. We'll be left with ten per cent—for eighteen months' work. And it's not just you.

'It's all of us. Everyone in the firm, every intern, every drafter. We'll sink.'

'No, man, it's you who doesn't understand. I put everything I had into this. Every ounce of artistry and sweat and self-respect and anything else you care to name. He can't do this at the last minute. I'm done. I don't have anything left.'

'You can do it, Mrig. I know you can.'

'Need to go. I'll call you back.'

Outgoing Call (7:21 A.M.)

'Hey Mrig. Good you called. I was worried. How are you feeling? Cooled down?'

'I'm cool, man. I'm cool. Cool as I need to be. So tell me, who's going to talk to the contractor?'

'Damnit.'

'Exactly. You thought I was going to do it, didn't you? No way. No bloody way. You know what these huge Chinese contractors are like? This isn't some ordinary company either. It's owned by a guy in their Politburo. They'll have our balls for breakfast. You know what kind of breakfast they eat there? Their company started the casting last month! Last month! If I send over new designs now they will slice us and slice Manohar and slice up all of Amma India like we're stalks of goddamn celery. This is the problem, man. These politicians think they know everything. First, they insisted we work with Chinese contractors, because all the twenty-five other statues were built by Chinese construction companies, so how can our great Girdharilal's statue be built by Biharis working for Punjabis, that's what Manohar said, isn't it? I remember exactly what he said. I'm glad. I'm really bloody glad. Now the Chinese can end all of our misery. Sab ko khatam. Best way.'

'I'll talk to Manohar's people. I'll make sure you don't have to deal with the contractor. How about that? Does that work?'

Click Click Click.

'That's not even it. That's only part of the problem. It's that they're demanding changes now. After all the work we've put in. How can they do this?'

'It's because of his daughter's wedding, apparently.'

'You know how long it took to get this design right? This is the twenty-sixth giant statue in India. This isn't the first! This isn't the second! There are twenty-five of these monstrosities all over this country. Four in the ocean already, two on either coast, so we couldn't go the Liberty way. Two in the Himalayan valleys, two in the desert—you know I would've loved an Ozymandias. Four lining the course of the Ganga. Eight on the Deccan plateau. Eight! You know now planes going in and out of Hyderabad have to fly at special elevations because the statues are screwing with their radar? The twenty-sixth giant. You think I don't feel that pressure? If it was going to stand out in any way, if my work was going to be remembered for anything, this design had to be bloody perfect. It had to be absolutely everything. And that's what I did, man. That's what I goddamn did. They gave me the ugliest man in Indian history and I gave them a thing of beauty.'

'Don't cry, Mrig. Bhai. It's okay. It really is. You're right. I know you are. I know what you put into this. We did it the best way possible. We did a beautiful thing. If they can't see that, if they can't see how good it is, that's their fault.'

Click Click Click.

'But what are we going to do?'

'We're going to do it. We can't let this beat us. It's their mistake, but we can't be beaten by their mistake. We can't lose everything because they can't decide.'

'Wait a second. What was that you said earlier. The daughter's wedding. What did you say about the daughter's wedding?'

'Well—I gather—and this is just what I've been told, I don't know for sure one way or the other, I think it has something to do with Manohar's daughter's wedding.'

'I need you to explain.'

'Well, see, Manohar's younger daughter got married last night. In the morning was the shaadi and at night there was the reception.'

'So?'

'The PM was supposed to come to the wedding. At the last minute he didn't show. Apparently it was very embarrassing to Manohar. You know how he makes a big deal about the PM and him being great friends. The reception was being held in a hotel in the capital that Manohar owns. They had built a special helipad on the roof, and that hotel, apparently, it's one of those Tier-II five-stars, you know, not built like the ones in proper cities, so they had to evacuate the guests and get the roof reinforced or some such nonsense, and there was a whole production about it. The PM didn't even call to congratulate. Manohar is hopping. He has since found out that the PM went to Maharashtra for campaigning. He's taken it as a personal insult. Last night at 2 a.m. he decided to withdraw his three MPs from the coalition in the centre.'

Click Click Click.

'I don't understand. What does this have to do with the statue?'

'Manohar wants it to be taller by thirty-five metres. He's decided that's the way it's got to be.'

'Taller by thirty-five metres? Has the man lost his mind? How am I going to add thirty-five metres to our statue? Should I give him a top hat? Girdharilal goes to Ascot, is that it? Or even better, Girdharilal, Lincoln impersonator. How 'bout that?'

'Headgear isn't a bad idea, actually. Did he wear turbans? Do you know? In the photos we have of him, have you seen him in a turban? That would solve everything!'

'That would solve nothing! It would look ghastly. This isn't a sculpture from junior school art class. I can't plonk a turban on his head just because it needs to be taller. This is eighteen months of meticulous plan and design. Each fold in his dhoti is designed a certain way, keeping in mind wind and air pressure and thermal dynamics and all sorts of things you wouldn't even begin to understand. But enough of that. What I want to know is, what does our exalted PM not attending this chick's wedding have to do with the height of the statue?'

'There's a rule for these statues. I don't know if you know this, but the twenty-five statues before ours, they all followed this. If you're from the same party, or your party is coalition partners with the PM's party, you make the statue shorter than the first one, the one he made all those years ago. This is apparently a very big deal. That's why most of the statues are just that little bit shorter than 240. But there are three or four states that aren't ruled by the PM's party and its allies. Those states have built taller statues. It's their way of getting back at him.'

'Seems pretty childish.'

'You're telling me.'

'And these morons play these games with public money?'

'That is precisely what these morons do.'

'Twenty-five giant statues across the country. You know what Trevor Noah said on the *Daily Show*, right? He said it's easier now to find a 200-metre statue in India than it is to find a public bathroom. I think he's right.'

'Forget Noah. I want to know what Freud would say about all this. These old men putting up giant erections all over the country, saying mine is bigger, mine is bigger.'

Click Click Click.

'Did you hear that? What is that click click click, that incessant clicking?! Are they tapping our phones now? What the hell is that noise?'

'Don't be paranoid, brother. That's the nano-battery I gave you. Remember on your birthday? I had IT install it. That click means you have to charge it. You only have to charge your phone once a month now. That's why I got it for you, since your phone is always dying. Don't tell me once a month is too much.'

'I don't give a damn about batteries or birthdays. What are we going to do? Do I really need to come up with a new design?'

'Yeah, we'll have to send them something, I'm afraid. And we need to work fast.'

'I can think of one solution that'd fit the design. How about we give this Girdhari a halo? Like they used to do for the Buddha—the Kushan empire statues at the National Museum have them. You know what I mean, right? That plate-like halo behind Girdhari's head. Gautam Girdhari. The Unenlightened One.'

'Heh. But that's the problem, Mrig. He's not a god. I know they basically worship the guy in that state. But that's because he's the guy who gave them their identity, their caste pride, whatever you want to call it. He isn't a god. Wouldn't a halo be too much?'

'Don't talk nonsense. This is India. Here the politicians think they're gods and the god-men behave like politicians. Let's add a halo to the design. Everyone will find it perfectly natural—if they even notice.'

'Will you send some mock-ups so I can run it by them? And what if Manohar objects?'

'If Manohar objects we only have to leak it to the local press. *CM Insults Girdharilal*, headlines like that. That would wo—'

'Mrig? Hello? Hello? Mrig? Damnit.... Once a month. He only needs to charge the thing once a month.'

22

SPIDER-GIRL

PRITIKA RAO

Today, at two months shy of sixteen, Thenmozhi finally felt like a woman. She assessed herself in the tall old mirror; black and red oxidization had tainted the lower portion, giving her reflection the appearance of being swallowed by flames. The mirror used to belong to her grandmother. Old maroon bottus were stuck on the side, where the metal hooks were rusty and the mirror was losing its clarity. Like the edge of a river. Or a puddle. She tried to imagine her paati sitting here, powdering her round pitted face so that it appeared fresh and fluffy like the perfect puri.

Thenmozhi had always admired the way her paati had woken up each morning and dressed herself impeccably to go only as far as the kitchen or, at most, the front gate. Her diamond earrings would catch the light as she dusted the veranda, her moisturized hands would glisten as she sifted rice, and her lips would shimmer with the generous application of Vaseline as she narrated fascinating stories of her life and childhood. Her saris were always brilliantly coloured with patterns on the ends—peacocks, mangoes, and sometimes just geometric shapes in sparkling threads of gold. She had a rebellious attitude herself but had dedicated her life to making sure everyone around her stayed in line. What would she say about Thenmozhi today, she wondered; of the person that she was growing up to be? She had been named by her grandmother—honey: rich, pure, sweet, immortal. Was she really any of those things?

Thenmozhi appraised herself: there was a fullness in her chest, a bit of fluff over her upper lip, the discomfort of a blind pimple; just as she was gazing at her exposed neck, her mother walked through the door. An icy tremor shot through Thenmozhi's body as their eyes met in the mirror. 'What is that, Theyn?' her mother shrieked, her face coloured with concern. Her mother's fiercely oiled braid lay coiled over her shoulder like a pet snake. Thenmozhi could smell the pungent blend of coconut oil and sandalwood powder—the classic scent of Amma.

'Don't know, Amma,' she said, grimacing. Why hadn't she closed the door, she thought to herself irritably.

'Ayyo, Theyn. Does it itch?'

Thenmozhi shook her head.

'Burn?'

'Nope,' she responded, as her mother breathed down her neck, trying to get a better look.

'Let's go to the doctor. It looks really terrible.'

She called for her husband in the shrill, helpless voice that she reserved just for him.

'Yennangaaaa.' The house reverberated but there was no response.

'I can't,' Thenmozhi replied. 'I have a test today.' She saw the papers on her school desk flutter conspiratorially.

'How can you go like this?' her mother asked indignantly. She grabbed hold of the edge of her sari and tucked it resolutely into the waistband of her skirt.

'We are going to the doctor first and that is that.'

Thenmozhi sighed in defeat. Their regular trips to the hospital were a family joke, one of many. Superstitious to a fault, her mother sprinkled turmeric on everything, added too much garlic to the food, and hung far too much lemon-and-chilli at every entrance. She kept a close watch on the house help and if she spotted so much as a stray hair, they would be instructed to redo the work. If the disinfection of homes and washing of hands were a national sport, Amma would win every year. They left for the hospital immediately.

During the fifteen-minute auto ride, Amma nervously cracked her knuckles and muttered to Thenmozhi. 'I hope it's not some wretched skin disease—like eczema or psoriasis. My aunt woke up on her thirtieth birthday to a massive red scaly patch, can you imagine!'

'Let me look at it again.'

'Doesn't look like a burn, hmmm.'

Thenmozhi said nothing as her mother burbled on, just responded with a nod or shook her head, as was appropriate.

As they approached the hospital, a familiar elderly nurse saw them coming and scuttled away from the lobby. It didn't matter. Thenmozhi's mother would insist on her seeing them anyway because she had observed and approved of the way she administered injections. However, Thenmozhi suspected that what her mother really loved about Sister Nancy was the fact that she always smelled like she had doused herself in Dettol. 'She is always neatly dressed, efficient, and doesn't bother with ridiculous chit-chat' she had remarked once to Thenmozhi, adding: 'Never trust nurses who stand around and chat foolishly. This is serious work, not a schoolyard. Any number of things can go wrong. One of your father's cousins had a swollen arm for weeks because of a nurse's negligence. Terrible.' Even as a young child, Thenmozhi wondered how Amma always happened to know people with ailments very specific to whatever point she was trying to make.

'Looks like a simple rash,' Sister Nancy declared.

'But from where?' Amma barked.

'Beauty products, perhaps?'

Amma let out a barely disguised chuckle. 'This girl? She has no products. Did you try something belonging to one of your friends?' Thenmozhi shook her head.

Sister Nancy stared at Thenmozhi.

'An insect then?'

'What kind?'

'Doesn't matter, the....'

'Doesn't matter? You people have no conclusive answers these days—just conjecture....' Amma was on the verge of hyperventilating.

'Maybe spiders or ticks or bedbugs but it doesn't matter because the treatment is the same,' the nurse said, interrupting her firmly but calmly, and handing her a small tube of ointment.

'Apply this twice a day.'

Amma's eyes were sparkling with irritation but before she could say anything, Sister Nancy said, 'If you still don't see an improvement, come back to see me in five days.' She locked eyes with Thenmozhi one final time and then, abruptly and efficiently, was gone.

On the bumpy auto ride home, Amma's mind went on a journey of its own. They had no dog, so it couldn't be ticks or fleas. It couldn't have been bedbugs because Amma faithfully dusted and flipped the mattress once every few weeks. Their house was always spotless. Amma went through a checklist of possible causes. Thenmozhi stopped listening halfway through.

She knew that Amma wasn't the most reasonable person. She was once denied permission to go to a Bryan Adams concert because Amma had heard a rumour that at some concert, someone had injected an innocent concert-goer with a deadly pathogen.

'It must be the spiders.'

'Could just be the weather, Ma.'

'It is Rekha.'

'What?' Thenmozhi asked, confused.

'Rekha. I have been asking her to clean the ceilings. I am sure there are cobwebs. And it is that wretched woman's fault.'

'It may just be mosquitoes?' Thenmozhi offered.

'Mosquitoes? This is nothing like a mosquito bite. Don't be foolish. This is far more disgusting.'

The rash glared back at Amma, now an artistic blend of blue-purple and red-brown. As soon as the auto stuttered to a halt outside their home, Amma dashed into the house in a rage. A lack of clarity always drove her mad—whether it was to do with the ingredients of recipes, the whereabouts of her jewellery or gossip from the neighbours. Thenmozhi followed her sullenly to find her standing near the corner of a wall in her bedroom, staring at what appeared to be nothing on the wall.

'Rekha!' she screamed.

A few seconds later, a nervous Rekha appeared in the doorway, drying her hands on the sides of her sari.

'Yes, Amma?' she asked, innocently.

'Just look at Theyn's neck.'

Rekha hesitated, confused. 'Look at it,' she repeated, the pitch of her voice rising.

Rekha's eyes darted to the scene of the supposed crime and with a knowing sigh returned to rest on Amma's.

'Now look at these cobwebs—did I not....'

'I will clean it, Amma, I'll just get a broo—' Rekha replied, turning to walk away.

'No need to get a broom,' Amma retorted swiftly. 'Just leave.'

'Leave?' Rekha replied, hesitantly. 'But wh—'

'Out,' Amma screamed, her finger pointing to the door like an arrow on a weathervane.

'Amma, let me—'

'No. We cannot have any more mistakes in this house.'

'Amma, this is not the same as a bedsore. Paati was sic—' Thenmozhi tried to reason with her.

'Enough.' Amma thundered.

Rekha stood in the door frame watching each one of them in turn as if she were watching a tennis match.

'Rekha, please. Just take your things and go.'

'Now' she repeated, urgently.

Rekha obediently left the room. Thenmozhi felt the heat radiate from her neck and instinctively raised her hand to touch the rash. Amma walked around the room, inspecting every crevice. Rekha returned a short while later clutching a yellow cloth bag of her belongings and her blue rubber slippers.

'I will leave, Amma,' she said in a humble tone, but baring her paan-stained teeth threateningly. 'But you should know that that is not my fault. Nor is it the work of a spider.'

Amma knew this conversation was inevitable—she braced herself for a discussion about loyalty, forgiveness, the workload, vows to do better, and the pitiful condition of Rekha's family but in the two seconds that she paused to consider her counter-arguments, Rekha continued.

'That,' she said, shooting Thenmozhi a look of disdain as she spat viciously, 'is the work of a boy.'

23

TWENTY-FIRST TIFFIN

RAAM MORI

Translated from the Gujarati by Rita Kothari

'Neetu....' Mummy's shrill voice interrupted my chat. I left the drawing room and went into the kitchen.

'Mummy, please stop calling me Neetu. You know my name is Neetal. You seem to conveniently forget things. And then you make a point of repeating the same mistake. When my friend visited me recently and heard you yelling, "Neetu…Neetu…" it turned into a joke in college. People have been calling me R. K.'s mom since then.'

I stood there, seething with anger. Unruffled and calm, Mummy briskly filled up tiffin boxes.

'Who's R. K.?' she asked, as she counted the rotis.

'Oh, God. R. K. stands for Ranbir Kapoor. Neetu Kapoor's son. Now, for heaven's sake, don't tell me you don't know who he is. This is not some random boy from my college, by the way. In any case, why am I even bothering to recite an epic to an ignoramus? Listen, Mummy, it's time you shed all your orthodox nonsense. It's as stale as the leftovers in your tiffin boxes. And please get a hold on your suspicious nature. All right, tell me now, why did you need me?' I asked, twirling my dry locks with a finger.

'It's past eleven, you see, it's time to quickly send off the lunch boxes. You know I can't prepare twenty tiffin boxes by myself. Obviously, I need some help from you.' She kept working as she talked to me.

'Mummy, you managed perfectly all this while. I have only been home for the past ten days or so. How is it that you suddenly can't manage now and you feel tired? You know what, just stop all this tiffin-shiffin business. Please.'

'And tell twenty boys, "Sorry, I cannot supply you food from tomorrow"? Like that, abruptly?' She glared at me, leaving me perplexed. 'Your father has not felt the need to provide money for running this house; it's thanks to these tiffin boxes that he is able to invest and move money around in stocks and shares without worrying about household expenses. You are able to study in a fancy college because of these tiffin boxes.'

'Oh stop it, Mummy. Are you saying that Papa is running away from his responsibilities? Or that he has not bothered to care for you? He loves you very much. He gave us this house, provides food to eat, clothes to wear, and his presence makes us feel safe.'

'Even a prison does all that,' she retorted. I looked at her, wide-eyed. Was her frustration with Papa peering out of her large, shapely eyes? I couldn't read them. I have come to realize that Mummy's eyes express nothing: they are simply flat and empty. And the lines on her expressionless face don't speak to me either. They always stay the same. My mother has been like this from the beginning: unkempt, unmoved, busy, and yet, a puzzle. On the other hand, I know Papa so well that I can almost predict his next sentence.

I have seen a certain kind of routine at home ever since I was a child. Papa would be constantly occupied. What comes to mind are his phone conversations, half-smoked cigarettes, white vest, and blue lungi. He would make calculations based on the financial projections he saw on TV, and buy and sell stocks and shares throughout the day, even at mealtimes, and go to sleep a tired man at night. As for my mother, she prepared tiffin boxes for twenty people day and night. She became the pressure cooker she cooked in. Her day began and ended in the kitchen. I often feel that Mummy has tied herself to this routine. When I picture her, what comes to mind is a woman indifferent to everything, clad in a dull sari, hair coiled up in a tight, stern-looking bun on her head, locks of grey hair around her face, an expanding waistline, and always reeking of perspiration. I remember that in the early days she used to prepare lunch for five people, later it became ten, and now it's twenty. I put aside the tablet I was holding and began to pack tiffin boxes in cloth bags. When all twenty were ready, I retreated to the drawing room and resumed chatting. Mummy joined me in a few minutes. She switched on the television and began to flip through the channels.

'Mummy, don't you think you should dye your hair?' I asked, my eyes on the tablet on which I was texting my friends.

'It's fine just the way it is. In fact, it's more than fine.' As she changed channels, a Ranbir Kapoor song appeared on the screen.

'Wow! Mummy, let it be. Don't change.'

She stood up and went towards the door to look for Bhanu dada, who ferried her lunch boxes to different locations.

'Neetu, it's very exhausting now. I can't cook more than this,' she said, as she tucked her grey locks behind her ears. I threw a cursory glance at her, only to be lured back to the song on the TV. Silence hung heavy for a while. I felt that she wanted to say something to me, but was perhaps waiting for the right moment.

'Neetu, will you open the window? It's so dark in here.' I pushed down the window latch and nudged the window open to let the light in. Just then I heard the sound of the main gate being opened. I didn't bother getting up, assuming that it was Bhanu dada who had arrived to pick up the tiffin boxes. But he usually rang his bicycle bell when he arrived. In which case....

'Namaste. May I come in, ma'am?'

Wow! What a voice, exactly like Ranbir's. I put aside the tablet and peered out of the window.

A young man was standing outside our house. He seemed to be around twenty years old. Mummy looked at me and said softly, 'Neetu, you go inside....' Before I knew what was happening, the man had already entered the house. He sat down on the sofa. I kept staring at him. He was dressed in a formal body-hugging purple shirt that seemed more appropriate for a party, and black trousers. He had a pleasant and neat hairstyle and wore an elegant wristwatch. His eyes were light in colour. He had a large forehead, chiselled features, and glistening, white, symmetrical teeth—the kind you see in the commercials for toothpaste. His skin looked as though he had just come out of a spa. In short, he was a veritable five-foot-six-inch-tall package for marriage. My eyes were riveted on him.

As if he knew, he smiled at me and my mother and said, 'Hello, my name is Dhruv Majumdar. I am an engineer. I arrived yesterday in this city for six months of training in a company.'

My mother must have realized that I hadn't taken my eyes off him. I was about to say, 'Hi, I'm Neetal' but Mummy spoke up, 'Neetu, go and bring a glass of water.'

I muttered under my breath as I went into the kitchen. Mummy followed me. Before I could say anything she pounced upon me, 'At least keep a dupatta with you. We do a tiffin service from home; you never know when some boy will drop by to make a payment. Ever since you have come on vacation, they all seem to visit quite frequently.'

'Don't say anything more, Mummy. Please finish your job and go.' I was really irritated with her. All she could do was criticize me. If she wasn't yelling some four hundred times a day, she wouldn't know what else to do. While cooking, if she banged utensils or broke cups and saucers, it was a message to me to go to the kitchen. And this kitchen of hers was like a battlefield, everything was strewn all over the place.

I stood by a window looking at that fellow in the living room. My mother was sizing him up like he were a potential match on Shaadi.com; I was feeling uncomfortable. I was hardly of marriageable age, and what was my mother trying to do but....

When we returned to the living room, the young man said: 'By the way, ma'am, my room-mate uses your tiffin service. When I arrived yesterday, he was out, so I ate the meal you had prepared. I really enjoyed it. It was so tasty. And I am particularly fond of potatoes. Even the toor dal was delicious. The seasoning of the kadhi was also great. You know, I was really happy to eat such a meal. My sister-in-law used to make such food. Really wonderful.'

When I looked at Mummy's face, I was surprised to see a smile. What's more, her cheeks had turned crimson and her earlobes looked flushed! Was I imagining all this when I heard my pleased mother say, 'Thank you'? The expression on my mother's face made me feel dizzy. Of course, this guy was not merely flattering her. Her cooking had to be good, otherwise why would Bhanu dada have increased the number of deliveries from five to twenty tiffins? I immediately thought of Papa. I wondered if my father had ever said something like, 'Wah, such good food....' Or if I had seen Mummy laugh or blush before....

I was lost in my thoughts when this fellow said, 'Ma'am, if you don't mind, would you prepare lunch for me as well? It's only a matter of six months. I really like your cooking.'

'Oh, a twenty-first tiffin?' In my head I could visualize the vexations, cacophony, and stress that accompanied the preparation of twenty tiffins: utensils clashing, cups and saucers breaking, the sweat on her body, the mess in the kitchen, and everything ending with her plonking herself down the sofa in exhaustion and muttering: 'Neetu, I can't handle more…not more than twenty, this much is enough.'

I was about to decline the request at once, but before I could do that my smiling mother said, 'Not a problem. I anyway make twenty. One more it is. I will give Bhanu dada your tiffin from tonight.'

I frowned. The boy paid for a month and left. Without counting the cash, Mummy went to put it in a drawer. I stood between her and the drawer.

'Mummy, what is going on? What is this?' I asked with exasperation.

She began to dust the drawing room. 'How does it matter? One more tiffin is not going to kill me, child.'

'Oh. Now you better stop yelling for me from the kitchen. And stop breaking crockery. You are a fine one to complain to me, "Neetu, I can't manage". You have added more work for yourself now.' I knew I was overreacting. I took the keys of the scooty and left the house. When I came back home, I saw my mother smiling at me. Something nagged at me, the smile perhaps—I wasn't used to it.

From that day on, Mummy changed in small ways. Papa had no time to notice, but the changes didn't escape me. She stopped shouting altogether. She even started to hum while she was working. At every mealtime, her enthusiasm to prepare the tiffins was different now. I would pack the tiffin boxes and put them away, but the moment I reached the twenty-first tiffin, she would say, 'One minute, Neetal, don't shut that one.' I would watch in silence as she dragged a stool from the drawing room and climbed on to it. She would take out the pickle jar from the top shelf, and after filling up a small container with slivers of mango pickle, she would close the tiffin box and gaze at it with contentment. These days, potato sabzi appeared more frequently on the menu, and the other day, I saw generous amounts of it in the twenty-first tiffin. Even the rotis that went into that tiffin had more ghee on them. I found all this really childish. I watched it all and felt it was all stupid.

As soon as the month ended, Dhruv would come home to make his payment. Without planning to, I had begun to ignore him. Mummy would make special ginger tea for him, accompanied by some snacks. He would sit for an hour or so, chatting with her. From my room, I would peep out at them talking and laughing together. Their friendliness made me uncomfortable.

One day, he came up with a new thing. He said to my mother, 'Ma'am, since you cook with such commitment, why don't you start a small restaurant at home? I am sure it'll do very well.'

'I won't be able to sustain it even for six months,' my mother quipped, and the two of them laughed. It was a shock for me to see my mother making these smart comebacks.

I was beginning to feel impatient with myself as well as my father. An outsider had been able to change my mother so fundamentally, to make her laugh while we, the people who had lived with her for years, had failed to do so. On one occasion, sick and tired of Mummy and Papa's quarrels, I remember saying to her, 'Mummy what is the matter with you? You seem to pick a fight with Papa all the time.'

'Do I initiate the fights, Neetu?' she replied, with her usual flat tone and unemotional demeanour.

'It doesn't make a difference, Mummy. Why don't you just learn to let go a little? He's really perfect.'

She had put her hand on my head and said with an emptiness in her eyes, 'Beta, he's your papa, that's why he is perfect for you. He's a husband to me, and the way I look at him is bound to be different.' I remember how pale her face was then. But today, where has that pallor gone? At times, when I start thinking about Mummy and Dhruv…my thoughts hit the blades of the fan and scatter throughout the room, wounded. I don't know what I'm supposed to think any more.

The biggest shock was when my mother began to dye her hair. She looked at herself in the mirror, and asked me, 'Neetu, how do I look?' What had not been possible through all my efforts had been achieved by that fellow's visits. While it was true that all the boys Mummy cooked for came home to make payment, Dhruv stayed the longest. Mummy would seldom chat with the other boys.

Dhruv is a really special case! Now Mummy wears her hair in a loose, low bun. Her sari is draped carefully, every fold in place, held together by a safety pin. And no matter how little time she has, she makes sure to wear a matching bindi on her forehead. She would steal a moment to check her reflection on the gleaming surface of a utensil as she cooked. And gone were the sounds of vessels banging and clashing about; a mellifluous humming had taken their place. I would often scream, 'Mummy what are you doing? Where's your mind? The roti is going to burn.'

'Neetal, why are you shouting? I am paying attention....' she would reply.

'To what?' I would ask with a meaningful glance, but this would be lost on her and she would happily go back to being lost in her own world. She would drag out the stool, reach for the sweet-sour gorkeri pickle on the top shelf, and fill up the twenty-first tiffin.

I have noticed these days, that on the last Sunday of the month, namely, Dhruv Day, Mummy takes longer than usual in the shower, and lingers over her reflection in the mirror. Although she would sit on the sofa watching television, she would be waiting for the sound of the doorbell. She would run to the door the moment it rang. I was beginning to find all this quite intolerable. All these lights had begun to singe me...and that fellow constantly came up with new gimmicks:

'Ma'am, why don't you participate in MasterChef? We can put your cuisine on the international map.'

'Ma'am, you should also learn some foreign dishes, you know, progress....'

'Ma'am, do you use Tarla Dalal's cookbooks?'

Now I was the one screaming. I would knock down tiffins, break crockery, and bang utensils down but Mummy seemed oblivious to all this.

One day, Dhruv did not come on a 'Dhruv Day' but in the middle of the week. He held a present in his hand. He sat with Mummy and they sipped tea and talked.

'Ma'am, today my training is over. Six months went by so fast, eating food prepared by you. I didn't even realize how quickly time has passed.... This is a small token of my appreciation for you.' My heart began to thud vigorously. So we will not see Dhruv any more, then? Mummy unwrapped the present. It was a recipe book of cuisines from different parts of the world. Mummy thanked him. The two of them sat quietly for a while. He drank the rest of the tea and stood up to leave. I felt as though I ought to see him off to the gate, but I asked myself the very next moment why I wanted to do so considering the fact that I didn't even like him coming to the house. As he left, he turned around, smiled at me, and left, closing the gate. Numerous cups and saucers broke inside me. I felt worried about Mummy. She stood in the drawing room, unmoving, for God knows how long. I could sense a funereal silence around me. The sun had set and darkness was upon us.

At night, Mummy was filling up tiffins in the kitchen while I was folding clothes in my room. 'Neetu...where the hell are you now?' I heard Mummy shout. I rushed to the kitchen. A saucer had slipped from Mummy's hand. I noticed that Mummy's hair was tied up in a stern, tight bun. Her back was drenched with sweat and she was panting from her exertions. Loose strands of hair clung to her sweat-drenched face. I immediately filled up dal and sabzi in different tiffins. Mummy counted the rotis and began putting them in each box. When all the tiffins were filled up, Mummy went to the shelf in which the pickle jar was, dragging the stool with her. My eyes were downcast but I knew what she was doing. She brought the pickle jar down. With pursed lips, and downcast eyes, I struggled to speak, 'Mummy, you…but…he….'

My mother looked at me. Our eyes met, mother's and daughter's, and I could not bear her gaze. I looked away, out the window. Mummy also turned her gaze away. But I had noticed three lines on her flat forehead and a hazy mist clouding her eyes. Dark shadows had descended upon and between us—between mother and daughter.

24

IT ENDS WITH A KISS

RIDDHI DASTIDAR

The first time Kajri kissed a girl, she was so nervous she bit her own tongue.

When they drew apart, the girl saw the tears in her eyes and ran back through the hole in the bushes to the backyard barbecue, where the adults were nursing stale-drink breath and simmering tensions that would turn into spats once the couples got back into their cars—their children sleepy and afraid in the back seat of the vehicle.

It was a drunch. Jojo auntie liked to throw them from time to time, carefully selecting a deck of people. Some had known each other through their elite schools and colleges, played in bands with names like Flying Ducks in Tights before getting sensible-jacket jobs. Others were seeing someone in the group and brought guitars or expensive wine or owned a gallery somewhere in South Delhi.

Kajri didn't like seeing the uncles' eyes dippy from the drunch, aunties smiling wide, the adults singing off-key and laughing too-loud laughs. She'd escape to the bookshelf and read until her parents came to get her. They were always the last to leave after they'd had a one-for-the-road and put away the dishes.

Jojo auntie didn't like waking up with a hangover, so she invented Sunday drunches. She had the deepest, most soothing voice of all the aunties, was the tallest person Kajri knew and with the strongest shoulders. Kajri used to sit on them when she was a baby, directing, 'De-arr! De-arr!' while Jojo auntie was a ship and Kajri, her De-arest Pirate Pottypants.

Jojo auntie didn't have a family, so she loved her friends extra. Especially Kajri and her parents who came to every drunch. Jojo auntie called Kajri her little mint julep because she said you must always have secret names for the people you love most.

If there was anyone who would know what to do after this, it would be her. She was often kissing other aunties and she never got angry. Only once did Kajri remember her furious. Someone had said an ugly word in an ugly way. Someone who had come with someone else to the drunch. Jojo auntie paused only for a minute, and then she took a sip of her drink. Calmly, she looked at the woman who brought him and said, 'Aparna, either he needs to leave or you both do. This is my house, and this filth is not welcome here.' The man hadn't wanted to go, so Jojo auntie had taken him by the shoulder and marched him out the gate. She was very strong and had built this house herself. 'Take no shit from men, Kajri,' she said, still upset after everyone had left.

∽

The second time Kajri kissed a girl, it was six years later and she was sixteen. Jojo auntie had disappeared six months and thirteen days ago.

Nobody kissed any more. There was a sign instead, and that was just as good. You brought your four fingers to rest on your thumb, like a bird's beak. You put it on the other person's cheek and gently tapped. Once for friendship, twice for love, three times to show romance. That was a bird's beak kiss. It wasn't safe in outside spaces, and inside there were regulations.

Still the government understood that affection is important for relations and families to keep churning, so they added this to the roster of signs. They understood that people are sneaky, so they added a blinking camera in every room, in every hallway and gender-segregated bathroom. They knew that sexual frustration makes people troublesome, so there was a once-a-month sign-up sheet for married couples under the age of sixty. Over the age of sixty, ordinary people should turn their minds and bodies over to service of our great nation and God, they said.

Ever since Jojo auntie disappeared, Mumma stopped finishing her sentences. Dad said it was because since the third grade Jojo auntie had been completing Mumma's. Back when they were neighbours, and before Dad and Mumma met in college, and when Jojo auntie still had a family.

The girl Kajri kissed lived in Assurance Colony-I and was waiting to find out what the government had decided to do about college. Unlike most people, her family had actually moved to Delhi this year.

In the colonies, time went strange. It curdled. Like when you opened a milk carton and it smelt sour and came out in gloops that floated in your glass.

For Mumma especially, time had fallen sick. She was confronted with great mounds of it everywhere. A big lump in the morning when Kajri would watch her muster the will to meet tasks and people. Mumma never drank coffee before, but now she poured herself a mug every morning before disappearing down the hallway to catch a bath at 7 a.m. She didn't want to run into their neighbours in the shower stalls.

Before everything, Mumma used to spend the morning with Kajri. They'd make breakfast together and read poetry. The last such breakfast involved bread with its heart knifed out and the space filled with a runny egg and a poem about silver linings and Darwin.

Mumma still woke early. She needed to rest her head against the windowpane before smiling at people in the kitchen and wearing her sari and teaching English all day to grades eight and nine in Assurance Colony-II. The students liked Mumma. Kajri used to be jealous, but now watching Mumma go predictably to class with her crisp, pinned sari comforted her. It felt like one known thing.

Mumma had done nothing very wrong, nothing that would arouse comment outside or involve a trip to the doctor or a surprise knock on their door (polite smile, 'Just a small matter, Mrs ___. We won't take much of your time.') but she didn't want to talk any more. Back in their suite, she curled up after school and skipped lunch. She went to sleep beside the window, right on the floor.

After the first few times Dad had found her there and they had fought, he had stopped saying anything. He let her sleep there and brought dinner to the room for her and told Kajri, as if she couldn't ask any questions, 'Mumma just needs our support right now.' And so Kajri didn't ask anything. And Mumma didn't explain.

The skylight room was where she met the girl. It was on the top floor, cordoned off from a side of the dome-top terrace where the adults had their high teas and celebrations. On Diwali last month, arrangements had been made—crackers had been burst by masked men in special suits outside, and everyone had gathered under the dome to watch. From here you could see the people on top of Assurance-I as well. They waved to each other, like the old times when people still scowled at you for bursting crackers, and the street dogs ran away and hid under cars. You would sometimes find the body of a pigeon dead from shock on the road the day after Diwali. Now the birds were gone, and the people who would scowl at you had to show team spirit instead. 'I can't believe they're still doing this bullshit,' Mumma had said furiously to Dad and disappeared to their suite, leaving him to think of an excuse on her behalf.

The morning after Diwali last month, Kajri had gone up to the skylight room. The day after a celebration was usually sleepy. Parents would sleep in until 3 p.m. like all rules had been suspended and it made Kajri feel nervous. The children could get their food in the community kitchen after all. Food was always taken care of. The rules were never suspended for the staff.

That day it was 12 in the afternoon, after she had eaten a late breakfast of cold kebabs and a cold drink gone flat, pilfered from their eighth-floor refrigerator. The aluminium foil was labelled Kapoors, but the Kapoors would never know, and she didn't care. Greasy-fingered, carrying the photo album Mumma had left beside the window, she walked up and up the thirty-two flights of stairs to the skylight room.

On some floors, sounds filtered through the stairwell. Someone on the fifteenth floor was thwacking a ball down the corridor. The twenty-seventh floor was noisy with children screaming 'Taabish! Taabish! Come back, you lousy skunk!' and someone running very fast. On the thirtieth floor a couple was having sex loudly—a few relaxations were permitted after special occasions. The woman's voice moaned the way Kajri had learned to identify as 'doing it' from TV. She imagined a mangalsutra jiggling up and down. She didn't want to imagine the other thing. They would still get stern looks later on, but if they were married, childless, and had shut the door to their suite, it was no crime against the nation. *Men will toh enjoy,* Raina auntie would report giggling to Mumma, and Mumma would show her teeth later that evening over dinner time. Mumma had to come out for dinner time; she had no choice, and she had to keep smiling; she had no choice, but that was later. Right now, Kajri had reached the top and was sitting on the fortieth floor landing catching her breath. She pushed open the door to the skylight room—the only place where light pooled in from a single point above, like you were hiding in a balcony or under a tree—and froze. There was someone else in there already. It was the girl.

She was dark and long-limbed, lying on her stomach, reading something, propped up on her elbows. When she heard the door open, she rearranged her limbs like a spider and righted herself. Then she looked at Kajri through big square brown glasses. 'Who are you?' she said.

Her eyes were big, round and black, her cheekbones were apples above a pointed chin, and her small mouth was suspicious. She was wearing shorts, and long brown thighs extended out of them into knobby knees, thin calves, and feet with extremely long toes. Her head was shaved, and brown fuzz grew on it down to her neck.

'Your name?' she demanded, when Kajri stared and said nothing. Kajri's heart thudded loudly in her ears; she didn't know why, and she stuttered her name. There was something in the air immediately, and neither of them had put it there. It just was. When you know, you know, darling, Jojo auntie would have said, blowing a stream of smoke out her nose. But she wasn't here.

Instead, there was the girl, and her name was Tara and her parents worked with the government, and she wouldn't say doing what and why, but she could move more freely than most, and she hated everyone in Assurance-I as much as she hated her parents, so she was here in the skylight room in Assurance-II.

Tara should have been in college, but it was still unclear what was happening with college, so she was doing nothing these days, and suddenly she was doing nothing in Kajri's space, beside her. Tara set up shop in Kajri's imagination immediately and pushed out a bit of her lingering unease about Mumma. If it was mutual, Tara didn't show it.

The afternoon they first met, Tara asked to see the photo album in her hands, and together they pored over the photographs: baby Kajri in the grass with a floppy hat, eyes screwed up at the sun; Dad carrying Mumma with his hands around her waist, her feet kicked up a few inches above the ground, her face thrown back and hidden over his shoulder, just a wide-open laugh. A picture from drunch: Jojo auntie in most of the frame raising her glass to something, her curly hair all gathered to a side of her neck, the tip of her nose shiny with sweat, and her cheeks red from laughing. White teeth.

And then, the very last picture, the oldest, that Kajri knew would be tucked in at the end: Mumma and Jojo auntie, in school uniforms, Jojo auntie's arm slung across Mumma's lanky shoulders, and Mumma's arms clasped around her waist, pulled in close and safe. In the picture Jojo auntie has a scruffy beard, and her long, curly hair, the way Kajri had always seen it, is cut severely short. But her eyes are the same—laughing and about to say something sharp.

The first time Kajri saw the photograph, she was eight and she had started to cry. Jojo auntie didn't look like herself, she howled. Mumma had rushed to pick her up. That was before, Mumma had explained. Before we knew Jojo auntie was really a girl.

It was the only picture from that time Jojo auntie would allow to be kept. Soon after it was taken, she had told Mumma, and they had broken up after two years together. They hadn't talked for a month. Until now it was the only time in their lives they hadn't talked every day.

And now Jojo auntie was gone, and Mumma didn't seem to see much point in sticking around either. When Kajri came back from the skylight room, Dad was sitting on the floor next to Mumma. She was gathered into him like she had been gathered into Jojo auntie in the photograph.

Jojo auntie was the first person Mumma had ever kissed. 'You don't understand,' Mumma said, sniffling. 'She was my oldest, closest, best.'

'I know,' Dad said, rubbing her back. 'I know, Mithu, I know.'

'I begged her; I begged her to stay,' she wept.

'You knew she wouldn't. She wouldn't have been okay here. Maybe she's really all right; maybe there is a place.'

∽

Time got weirder. The time Kajri spent with Tara made up the whole day.

One time, Tara said, she had given a blow job to some guy she met at some party the first time she got very drunk. It was in the bathroom, and his penis was the size of her forefinger and thick and fat and smelled damp—like mushrooms, she said. She had never been able to eat mushrooms after that.

Kajri shuddered at the description. She herself had never given a blow job, and the thought of a penis—worm-like, she imagined, and boneless like one of the slugs she'd accidentally stepped on—made her squirm. Once Arjun had pulled his one out in the sixth grade. They had been best friends, and he said, 'Look.' So she looked and made a face. Then she pulled up her skirt quickly, after checking that no one was around behind the big tree during recess, and he had stuck his head down and then gone 'Ewww, it's all hairy!' And she had laughed and said, 'Yes, Mumma says you'll grow it too, soon.' And they had run off to find the others and never asked to look under each other's clothes again.

Tara laughed when she said this. Then she laughed more when Kajri said that she had never seen another vagina besides her own, and the thought of one in her mouth made her squirm too.

'Everyone feels that way at first,' Tara said, smushing Kajri's face with both her hands and shaking it violently. That was the thing about Tara— even though she was only a year older than Kajri, she acted like she knew more, and she could only show her growing affection through increasingly frequent small acts of violence.

In the second week of knowing each other she had pushed Kajri away, not very hard, when she had come to the skylight room and found Kajri combing her still-wet, waist-length hair.

Kajri liked her long hair. They only cut it twice a year at the L'Oreal Salon in the golf club. Madhuri, Mumma's favoured girl, would give her a two-hour Oxy facial, and Kajri would get a trim, forsaking four inches on the floor. Once Madhuri had called Mumma for help. She had needed an abortion, and Mumma had gone with her one afternoon. Afterwards Madhuri had come home for a week and stayed mostly in the guest room. Mumma would go in after she returned from school, coaxing Madhuri to eat or to come out into the front room and sit with them and watch some TV. She'd come out sometimes, grey-faced, without her customer-ready smile, rest her head on her fist, and watch dully.

After she left, Mumma sat Kajri down and gave her a talk about the importance of using protection, if and when she chose to do it. Kajri had run away from her, going from room to room shouting 'Ew Mumma, STOP TALKING ABOUT THIS,' and Mumma had become angry. 'This is important!' she had said. 'Stop acting stupid.' Kajri was in the tenth grade then, and she had only just furtively kissed Sanjoy D'Mello under the stairs after math tuition. They had been dating a week, and he had slipped his tongue into her mouth and run his hand down her chest, and she had pushed him away and said, 'What the fuck, D'Mello! You don't have to go for gold at once,' and run down to find Dad waiting in the car, wondering why she was always five minutes late, and Sanjoy D'Mello had told everyone at school she was 'frigid', but no one paid much attention. Kajri didn't care that much; he was hot but stupid, and she could do better. And then she hadn't felt anything for anyone, and then everything had changed, quickly. Her new life—an unchanging every day, secure under Assurance-II's massive dome with the persistent hum of the oxygen tanks.

'You're such a pretty little shit,' Tara said, after she pushed Kajri and her hair so it swished a little, filling the room with the smell of coldness and synthetic lime. But the way she had said 'shit' viciously, looking away and shaking her own head with its close-cropped hair, gave Kajri a pleasurable tingle in her stomach.

Now she was spending so much time with Tara, Mumma curling into herself bothered Kajri less. And although she wasn't exactly grateful to be trapped inside or untroubled by the knowledge that many people died in the air outside every day and were turned away by the Assurance-II security guards in full suits at the limit of their self-sufficient colony—it was pleasurable, this tuning out. She thought of Tara before she went to sleep every night. And she felt something she hadn't felt in a long time. The thrill of not-knowing. The feeling that something could happen.

Tara had nice hands. They were big, with long fingers. Kajri, who was small and soft and had been called pudgy more than once by Sonal Kapadia and Co. in class, liked to look at Tara's hands and imagine what it would feel like to have those hands hold her face, softly.

She would have asked Jojo auntie about being lesbian, but Jojo auntie wasn't here. So she imagined it. Sitting on Jojo auntie's couch, eating cheeseballs from their crinkly plastic wrapper. She would have asked, 'Do you think I'm a lesbian?' 'I don't know, my mint julep,' Jojo auntie would have said, smoking her clove cigarette. She would have smiled and tilted her head at Kajri and given her a book to take home and said not to worry too much about it. Jojo auntie would have said. 'Words are just things we use to make sense of this tangly mess of stuff.'

'Seriously, darling,' the Jojo auntie of her imagination was saying now. 'You'll figure it out.' She was squeezing Kajri's hand in hers. 'Just remember to be safe and not do anything with anyone who makes you feel bad.'

But Jojo auntie wasn't here.

If she died tomorrow, Kajri thought, she would want her ears ringing with the sound of Tara laughing. Until that Sunday she had never seen her relax. Sure, Tara was sure of herself and she made Kajri nervous. She had seen Tara smirk and smile and tease and roll her eyes and yawn and grin and scowl and grimace and sulk. But the first time Kajri saw her soften was when she made her laugh for the first time. It was like watching Tara unfurl and open into her.

There would always be a sliver of time where Tara was laughing and Kajri was there to see it.

∽

Kajri was named for a species of fish her mother craved throughout her pregnancy. Kajri maach had soft skeletons. You ate them in a single slurp. They couldn't hurt you.

The night Jojo auntie left for wherever it was that she had gone was terrible. Mumma had been screaming at her in the living room for an hour but she was unmoved. She didn't shout back. Kajri hid behind the curtain to the living room and watched.

'You can assimilate,' Mumma was shouting. 'They won't be able to tell! You're just being difficult, Jo!'

'I don't want to!' Jojo auntie shouted back, finally. 'You know I'm right, Mithu. The drones have picked up my face from the last several months. You know they have. They took Ruth away yesterday. She was getting ready to leave. Her suitcases were packed and everything. It's just a matter of time.'

'Look,' she said more quietly. 'Honestly, I just came to say goodbye to you. Because I don't know when I'll see you next.'

'Why do you always have to make life difficult for yourself?' Mumma was still screaming. Her voice was a horrible shrill sound, and now it cracked, and she was coughing from all the screaming, and Dad was passing her water.

'I can get you a job, you know,' he said flatly, going through the motions. 'That's not an issue; you know that, right? Like a management position, easy. You'd be an asset to the, to the…digital team.'

Jojo auntie said nothing, just looked at him. 'Look, it's cute that everyone's packing up for the ultimate gated colony and all, and I'm not judging you; I'm really not. You have Kajri to think about. But it's not my scene. You know it's not. I'm not going to smile at Mrs Malhotra when she stares at me too long, and I'm not going to entertain after-hours enquiries from her mister about how friendly I am. I'm not going to sign bloody petitions and donate my 1,000 rupees and wait and wait and wait while our communities beg and suffocate and die.'

'So, you're going to die on the street with them? You're not—you're not the only one you know.' Mumma was crying now. 'There are other people. Maybe in a few months once it's settled…we'll take care of you… you're not…some great saviour!'

She moaned softly, her face in her hands, 'Why are you doing this to me?' She knew she wasn't making sense any more.

Jojo auntie crouched down beside her and pulled her into a hug. 'No one needs saviours,' she said. 'These are my people.'

'Don't worry,' she said over her shoulder, as she gathered her purse and hugged Kajri, 'I don't have a death wish; we have gas masks and cylinders and supplies. I'm not stupid. There's always people fighting back.' And then she left and Mumma said, 'But why does it have to be her' to Dad, who didn't have an answer, so he handed her the tissue box and held her hand instead.

∽

'I want to kiss you,' Tara said. Because they were both girls, no one seemed to notice how much time they were spending together up in the skylight room. Even if they nestled close, it only looked like they were doing what girls do: hold hands, lie in each other's laps, run fingers through each other's hair. It's not that it wasn't allowed. It was just that everyone seemed, you know, 'normal', as Mr Santosh, the chairman of Assurance-II's board would have put it.

Tara was lying with her head in Kajri's lap when she said this. Kajri started, and then she made the bird's beak kiss. Tapped her fingers gently on Tara's face. Tara closed her hand over Kajri's and brought it to her own face. 'No,' she said looking up at her. 'I mean really kiss you.'

The red light of the camera blinked away above the door, a betrayal even in Kajri's one safe place. No one knew who was watching, but after the last six months, no one was going to risk it.

Tara took Kajri's hand now, drew it down to her neck and stopped at her clavicle. 'Don't you?' she asked.

Kajri nodded. 'Yes,' she whispered, her throat dry. 'Yes, more than anything.'

Tara sat up, her lips just inches away from Kajri's. 'I knew it,' she said, and smiled, breaking the moment. 'I fucking knew it!' She was jumping around the room.

Kajri couldn't help it; she started laughing. 'Of course,' she said. 'Wasn't it obvious?'

'It really, really was,' Tara said.

'No take-backs,' Kajri said quickly.

'What are you, seven?' Tara scoffed. Then she pulled a face. 'But we can't. Not here.'

'Not anywhere,' Kajri said.

'Well.'

Jojo auntie had told Kajri that back in her time they would kiss in public parks. When you were young and broke and didn't have a place of your own, you would take intimacy anywhere when it came to you. Of course, you still had to hide. It was dangerous to be affectionate in public.

Inside the colonies, the rooms watched you. The people watched you. You watched you.

There was only the outside.

What makes a really good kiss?

Desire.

Delay.

A really small flint of fear.

At 5 a.m. the outside was dark. Kajri felt on her arms the cold feeling of cleanness you only got from the early-morning breeze. There was absolute silence. She heard only her heartbeat thrum in her ears.

They had agreed on a spot they could both identify. By the green plastic bush, behind the lamp post whose light didn't work. Kajri pulled her mask tight, paranoid, and hurried. No guards materialized as she turned the corner. She passed the body of a small creature crumpled on the ground as she walked by as fast as she could. It could have been a cat. It could have been a baby.

Tara was waiting for her. Her frame towered over Kajri, and she took her hands and squeezed them hard, as soon as she saw her. 'Thirty seconds, K,' she said, through her mask.

They had rehearsed this in the skylight room, mimicking the motions. Undo the buckle. Hold your breath. Pull the mask down. One fluid motion; don't waste any time. As soon as you feel your shoulders and stomach start to resist, pull it back on.

Her fingers trembling, Kajri undid the buckles, her breaths already shallow. Tara looked straight into her eyes, mirroring her movements. Then she nodded and down came their masks.

Tara's mouth was hard on hers, and her fingers held Kajri's face just the way she had imagined it. Kajri held on to Tara's elbows, steadying herself. There was Tara's nose, the smooth skin of her face, her warm breath in Kajri's mouth, and the hesitant tip of her tongue on Kajri's.

It must have been more than thirty seconds because Kajri was feeling light-headed. When she opened her eyes, she was on her knees. Tara was fastening her mask for her with shaking fingers, and there were two figures approaching them from the distance, but all Kajri really noticed was the morning light spreading through the blue sky outside the dome, breaching the barrier and spilling into her.

25

GREETINGS FROM A VIOLENT HOMELAND
RITUMONJORI KALITA

I will be twelve next month, but I don't think we are ever going to celebrate my birthday again. Things have changed so much in the past few months, no one remembers my birthday. There is nobody left who cares about celebrations. Our little town is dying. It's been happening for a while now.

It began when the owls started swarming in from the eastern hills. My mother tells me an owl has twelve songs—one for each month—and then one extra hoot, niu, niu, niu. What she does not know is that the last one is the song of death. I wake up every night to its menacing screech, imagining the unimaginable all the way through to a morning that feels heavy and suspended.

My brother and I walk past the market lane with its rows of shuttered shops. A few windows are open. I signal to him to wait while I peep through one of them. Glass containers are arranged in a neat row on the shelves. There are no candies in them.

My brother waits a little way ahead of me, his hands thrust deep in his pockets, his eyes nervous and watchful. He does not like me stopping on the road—or anywhere for that matter. He wants to go straight back home and continue to plead with Mother not to send him to school any more. He sees no sense in going and I can't blame him. His buddies have stopped and I wonder if that is because of the owls.

It is a long walk home from school, but it used to be pleasant. We cross the community ground which now looks like pasture land, with knee-high weeds. I tell my brother, Dhan, not to walk among the burs because it takes too much time to pluck them from his pants later, and I have important things to do.

The community ground is mowed only before the big Bihu and Durga Puja festivals. During Bihu last year, they'd put up lots of stalls and we had very little space to walk. Dhan hopped from stall to stall, picking up so many items, they kept falling from his tiny hands. I didn't buy anything. I only wanted to watch the Bihu dancers gliding on the stage. My best friend was competing and I wanted her to win.

My parents don't allow us to participate. Only our education matters. It is the most crucial aspect of our lives, they say—the single determinant of our future. They've already decided what we will become. Now that the schools are empty most days of the month, I wonder if they think the same way.

A few goats are pulling at the overgrown grass. The cows have had their share and are chewing their cud under the bare simolu tree. Egrets hover around them, picking at ticks and flies. Once in a while the cows whip their tails and the startled egrets jump back, then resume their picking.

Dhan chases me as I circle the tree. We run till we are out of breath, then I slow down to allow him to catch up. I sing a prayer, which I'd learnt from my grandmother, to the simolu. Last year, it was in bloom and as the downy cotton floated in the air, I thought of the snow from the only English film I'd watched, where the boy kisses the girl as the flakes settle on her hair. I thought of Arnav then and felt a lump forming in my throat. I was feverish for an entire week, and when my mother asked what ailed me, I lied to her.

Lying has become easy after that first time.

⁂

I met Arnav twice and each time he treated me like a kid, handing me a Cadbury as if to soothe a distraught child. He has no idea of what I feel for him, and now that he has left, he will never know.

He has gone to a university in America, my mother says—brilliant kid that he is.

I cried several nights and ate very little, tormented by images of him surrounded by fair girls with golden hair, and eyes that were not black like mine. I imagined him swirling his tongue around difficult American words to impress them. I thought of them getting cosy and laughing at jokes I didn't understand. I was still not eating after a week, so my mother took me to the town doctor. He scanned my eyes, opened my mouth, and tugged at my tongue. Then he dismissed the symptoms as a case of appetite-loss common with kids. He said this with a roguish wink at me. I froze with shame hoping he would not name my affliction to my mother.

Arnav has been gone a year now. Does he know what is happening around here? I must write to him in the non-formal style that Miss Rosa taught us.

Dear Arnav, I hope my letter finds you in the pink of your health. Do you know after you left the town....

From the corner of my vision I see my brother raise his leg.

'Don't!' I shout at him, but he has already kicked the piece of asphalt. It lands on a tarpaulin shed. I hold my breath and wait. These sheds are everywhere in our little town: four bamboo poles with stacks of sandbags as walls, on which sits an olive-green tarpaulin roof. Behind these sandbags are uniformed men. Only the tops of their hats and the muzzles of their guns are visible. If I stretched my neck, I could see their squinted eyes scrutinizing everyone who passed.

Our little town is swarming with them, their black guns hanging from impossibly straight shoulders as they march past our homes. They have always been in our town, but never this many and never with so much purpose in their eyes. We no longer wave to them or smile as they drive by in big green trucks.

I feel their steely guns pointed at me. I imagine a bullet striking me above my collarbone in the small area of exposed flesh where my ponytail touches the back of my neck. I reach out a hand to soothe the tingle there, while holding my brother with the other hand.

Dhan's palms are cool and moist; I know he is frightened. He quickens his pace and I am afraid he will break into a run. I tell him it's all right; they didn't hear the asphalt hit the hut. I push him in front of me and clutch his shirt from behind. They will shoot him if he runs. They are shooting a lot of young boys these days. In the villages that flank our town, they make boys run in the open fields, then shoot them down as if they were balloons at a hit-the-target game in funfairs. There is a name for it which escapes me now.

The heat rises from the ground and makes blotches on my cheeks. They will darken later and won't come off even after I have scrubbed at them.

I see a green vehicle parked outside our gate. Is it about the asphalt? Did they see me peeping inside the shop? Are they coming to take my brother? I rush Dhan through the backyard gate and tiptoe to the kitchen door. My mother is there.

She must have guessed something from the way I look, for she asks: 'What have you done now?'

'Nothing,' I lie. 'Why are they here?'

Fear is clutching at my throat. I feel breathless.

'Usual talks,' my mother replies.

I want to shout at her and say that only a fool would think that. Instead, I wash myself and sit down for lunch.

Encounter! I say to myself. It is called encounter; shooting the target is called encounter. I try to follow the conversation that drifts in from the other room.

A deep male voice is grumbling: 'The schools are where they breed.... No, you can no longer trust the students....

'So what if they are only fourteen or fifteen years old? You will not believe your eyes when you see these gun-toting kids in the wild where a person with the mightiest of hearts will shit his pants.... You are gravely mistaken in believing them innocent...most of the insurgents in the area have their roots in your school. You, the headmaster, ought to be more vigilant and inform us of any suspicious activity....'

I hear my father muttering a protest but his voice is drowned by the bigger voices in the room—voices with guns. I wonder if my father is also afraid of guns.

After they leave, I stick around my mother, anticipating some elaboration on the visit. When none comes, I retire to my room.

The first time the army men came to our home, they rummaged in our kitchen, kicked our vegetable baskets, and turned our grain containers upside down. They were looking for money, or perhaps a secret letter that would lead them to the insurgents. Their heavy boots stomped the rice and the pulses scattered on the floor. They suspected that the locals sympathized with the rebels, so all our houses were ransacked, our monthly rations destroyed.

Many were taken away for interrogation; a few never came back. As they left our home, one of them tousled my hair and grinned at me.

I lie in my bed eavesdropping on my parents, and thinking of the hush that blankets our town now, and how agitated everyone became when the bodies first began appearing in the river. People were suspicious of each other and began fighting amongst themselves. Then the boys started disappearing from their homes in the night, and arguments grew muffled. Now the town communicates with signals and whispers. Sometimes I imagine the air so dense with whispers that it chokes us all.

My mother says that it has become worse since the Russian was abducted. It is the common people who suffer, she says.

The brother of Anita, our house girl, has not returned from the interrogation camp. A few men dragged him out of his hut in the dead of night—and that was more than a week ago. My father signals Anita to be quiet. There are eyes and ears everywhere, he says. I do not understand how this can be, but I will no longer take off my clothes when I bathe.

After a pause—so long that I think they have fallen asleep—my father speaks as if he were sharing a secret. His words come to me in fragments, so that it is left to me to piece them together. Two days back, Mahesh Khura, our neighbour, received an anonymous letter—possibly from the insurgents' organization. It said if he continued to collaborate with the army, he would find his sons hanging from the banyan tree in his front yard.

I cannot see my mother's reaction, but I imagine her raising a hand to her mouth. I know that she's picturing Mahesh Khura's sons hanging from the tree; and soon—in her mind—the boys will be replaced by us.

Dhan is sleeping beside me, his peace broken only in the morning when he gets up for school. I want to ask my father why he does not take us from this godforsaken town to America—like Arnav and his family.

When I sleep, I dream of the letter I want to write to Arnav but when I find the pen and paper, I no longer know what I want to write. I wake up in a sweat, the remnants of the dream still clinging to my eyes.

∽

My mother lets me sleep a little longer than usual today. School is closed for the next two days for Independence Day.

Independence Day is no longer filled with gleeful children releasing orange, green, and white balloons into the sky while a Lata Mangeshkar song plays in the background. No sweets are distributed, no songs sung. No games. There has been nothing of the sort for the past four years. We will stay indoors. It is a kind of curfew that no one dares defy, for it comes at a cost. Not even the doctors take calls on Independence Day, and the schools remain closed.

I will pass the time hoping this will not be the day I see my father for the last time. Every Independence Day, I fear for his life and wake up with the same fear.

My parents will leave their bed at dawn and my mother will light her tiny earthen lamp. She will plead to her god to keep my father safe. My father will tell her that there are others like him who go to their offices to show respect to the nation. My mother will nod and say nothing.

She knows that the ministers and government officials will leave their homes and go to the parade in official cars with their military entourages and security men. My father, the headmaster, will leave our home too; not in a car—for we have none; not in a bus—they do not operate on bandh days. He will walk five miles to the school that he has founded. He will hoist the national flag on the premises with no one in attendance. He will not blame the staff and students for not showing up. My father will sing the national anthem and thank the freedom fighters and martyrs for giving us a free country to live in.

During those hours, my mother's imagination will run riot. She will ask herself repeatedly, what could possibly happen in the five miles that he has to cover? Her mind will respond in ways that will agitate her. She will think of guns, grenades, kidnapping, the crazed river, the railway tracks, the adjacent woods.

I will watch her pace the living room, her eyes darting to and from the sad wall clock. I will watch her dash to the front yard from time to time until she finally ends up at the gate with droplets of water beading her nose and forehead.

I will look up at the August sun and think that soon it will be afternoon and father has been gone since morning. Mother will walk back slowly up the steps to the veranda, to slump on the tattered cane chair, her face empty of emotion.

I will dart towards the gate to stand on the road, shading my eyes, and squinting at the solitary figure at the far end of the dusty street. I will make myself believe that the man resembles my father, then turn back to my mother and shout, 'Father is back!'

26

GOBYAER*

SADAF WANI

While I exist as a spirit in this cold grey valley, sometimes I get tired of not being seen and perceived, not being heard, and not being able to leave my footprints on the snow as I pass by mountains, towns, and villages. However, in this valley marred by grief, complaining about these little inconveniences seems a bit absurd and, at times, quite selfish. Selfish, even for someone like me, whose entire sense of self is unresolved and perpetually in doubt. This valley that I have grown to call my home, I don't call it by its name, for it makes me uneasy. Every time I hear its name being said out loud, I fear something bad might happen. The thought of leaving this place and its disquiet crosses my mind often. In the past, I have acted upon this impulse, but every time I left, I found myself making the arduous journey back.

I leave this valley, which is my home, because I get tired of being invisible here. Sometimes, I long to participate in the events that are taking place in the streets, rivers, and markets. However, people pass through me as I reach out for them. I am ridiculed by other spirits for these frivolous desires. They mock my longing for home by saying that spirits do not have homes. I disagree. I say home is only a place, and a place is its people. So, doesn't that make these people my people, and this valley my home?

I speak about these people in the valley as 'my people' like I know them or like they know me. I speak of them as if I like them and as if they like me. In fact, I do not know them, and they do not know me. We are mutually oblivious to each other's existence for the most part. However,

---

*Heaviness or weight in Kashmiri. In the everyday vernacular, gobyaer is also used to refer to the state of being possessed by djinns or other supernatural forces.

something cuts through this relationship of oblivion and ties us to each other. There is a gobyaer on our being. It is amusing that a phenomenon as physical as weight and heaviness connects me, who is supposed to have transcended the physical realm, to these people and this place.

At first, I did not understand how a word representing something so physical could describe what I was feeling. So I started paying attention to how humans across the valley were using this word. Once I was passing through a cluster of villages by a small hill near the south of Jhelum. There, I saw that a crowd had gathered around a young boy who had fainted, just as he had reached his village, after spending a long day in the deep forest. The boy was speaking gibberish and appeared to have a concussion. It was intriguing, for I knew at first sight that it was the work of my distant cousins. The older djinns are known to take offence at humans disturbing the quiet of the deep forest. They get enraged when humans shamelessly relieve themselves under the old chinar trees that they've made their home. To teach them a lesson, and dissuade the rest of the villagers from venturing into the forest, they possess the bodies of people who've invoked their wrath. Having seen that it was just another young boy possessed by the djinns, I lost interest and started moving away from the crowd where the imam was inspecting the boy. However, as I started moving away, the imam suddenly got up, walking quickly in my direction. He stopped right before he could pass through me. It's the closest I've come to being perceived. I swear I thought he was talking to me when he said, 'Ye chu gobyaer' (It's the heaviness).

After this incident, I started getting drawn to this word, to every conversation where it was mentioned. One night I was passing by an old street towards the south of the valley, and I saw a grim-looking young man smoking cigarettes, standing outside the house of his lover from long ago. The sound of the tumbaknari, the Kashmiri drum, from the house filled up the street, where he stood for a while. There was nothing he could do and nothing he wanted to do to stop the event, but the loss he experienced throughout that night of anticipation he also called gobyaer. Similarly, towards the east of the valley, I was once roaming through an apple orchard enjoying the blossoms when I noticed an older woman in the middle of the orchard. She looked up at the May sky, overcast with dark clouds, and knew they were the clouds of misfortune and hailstones. She looked around her apple trees, knowing very well that, in a few hours, the blossoms and the promise of a good harvest would be gone. The heavy footsteps she took towards her home, as she waited for the rains to intensify, she called gobyaer, too.

However, this gobyaer prompted by personal grievances is not what connects me to these people. Since I don't have loved ones who I yearn for, or land that I cultivate, or a future to prepare for, I cannot relate to these emotions. There is an overarching feeling of impending loss and terror that goes far beyond the everyday affairs of my people, something that everyone here is always waiting for. Sometimes it is realized sooner than at other times, but each cycle of loss confirms that our fears are not unfounded. The fear grows in hearts, as does the gobyaer. I cannot tell exactly what this gobyaer does to humans, for they don't seem to hear me, so I cannot ask them anything. I am only telling you what I have overheard in open markets and closed rooms.

Having heard about it from so many people over decades, I have started seeing it as well, even though I don't experience it like humans do. I have started seeing that gobyaer has a personhood as abstract as mine. I say this because I have seen how gobyaer surrounds and seeps into people and what it does to them. When I look at my people, I see that this strange presence has engulfed their lives, the gobyaer has attached itself to their skin, sedimented in their bones, and it feeds off the hope in their hearts. It lives in their homes now, sits in their hamams, and shares their rice with them. And when they are watching TV late at night, it occupies the cosiest spot in the room, and my people pretend not to see it.

The old people in the valley seem to have found a dedicated corner in their lives for this gobyaer. They put it in the deepest pocket of their baend, which they always wear under their pherans, carrying it around with them wherever they go. The younger ones, however, are more ambitious. 'Why should we carry this burden with us all our lives? Why should we give in like you cowards did?' they ask the old ones, who do not smile, and only smoke their jijeers. Spurred on by their ambitions, some young ones travel to far-off lands, hoping they could leave this gobyaer behind. Some go to the tallest mountains, some to distant deserts, and others towards seas because it was rumoured that seawater could melt it.

One time when I ran away from the valley to travel the world and find a new home, I was surprised at how easily I could spot my people wherever I went. I had thought everybody carried this gobyaer with them until I met people who are not my people. It was then that I realized that it is something that only people of the valley have, and I also found the answer to what differentiated my people from the crowds in cities, riversides, and deserts. Naturally, I followed some of my people when I saw them outside the valley. I found some of them running through iced alleyways. Some were plodding through desert towns, and others were hiding in muddy lanes by the sea. I found a few walking briskly on the wide roads and dingy streets of big cities visiting pirs, faqirs, and shamans seeking foreign remedies for their very indigenous disease. Some of them kept running for years and years, and when they thought enough time had passed, they came back home. However, to their horror, they found this gobyaer waiting on their dastarkhwan to share their razma dal with them.

Some people who have got tired of running have now realized that the gobyaer always finds a way home. So, they have started building houses with a spare room. They make it big and cosy so that they can scream and wail in it. Men who have only one room and not enough razma dal to share cannot find a quiet place to sit with their fears. The children are always crying, and the creditors are always knocking on their doors. They deal with the gobyaer by bringing it up all the time and to everyone they can find. In the fields, in the bus, at the shop, on their verandas. They repeat the same stories every day with minor additions and deletions, of how they first encountered this feeling, how they tried to run away from it, and how there is no place like home, so they come back. 'Gari wandihai gari saasah, bari nyerihai ni zanh' (There is no place like home), they keep repeating all day. I often see women peeling vegetables on the verandas of their houses sigh in exasperation and put their hands on both their ears as they run inside. They seem to be sick of hearing the same stories every day. Women have their versions of how they encountered gobyaer and how they live with it. But the men never stop talking, and so the women always leave the room in frustration.

One of the reasons I keep coming back to this valley from faraway places is my belief that the cure of this indigenous disease cannot be found outside the valley. So, I pass through the valley looking for comfort, if not the ultimate answer. There is a small, lonesome house in an apricot orchard in the valley's northern end, where an old woman puts her granddaughter and daughter to sleep every night. In this house, there are no men, so women talk out loud without interruptions. But that's not the only reason I come back here. Every night, before putting them to sleep, the grandmother whispers a six-letter word into their ears as they fall asleep. A six-letter charm that gets you in trouble if you say it out loud in the valley, but the only known charm that puts the gobyaer to rest, at least for some time. The old woman tells them stories of the day when the charm will manifest itself, cutting through the grey cloudy sky, falling softly on the valley like morning sunlight on all its living and non-living things. It will slowly melt away what occupies the heart and weighs it down. It is said that after that day the spare rooms in the houses will be filled with the aroma of sun-dried tomatoes, the young ones will not need to run off to deserts, mountains, seas, and cities, and men will finally let the women narrate their own stories.

After the lights in the entire valley are dimmed, the last batch of soldiers and rebels have gone off to sleep, and the placards and flags have been locked in for the night, I come back to hear the same story night after night. I feel comforted watching the little girl fall asleep to this reassurance. Last night, as she fell asleep, her little fist unclenched at some point to reveal the charm she had just learned to write: Azaadi.

27

FATE

SAMHITA ARNI

We meet, as appointed, in a park in the centre of the city. You survey our meeting point with a lifted eyebrow. I see your lip curl, and from the look on your face, I know that you don't think that this dry, brown strip of land, bounded by a low gate and roads on either side, could be called a 'park'. Buildings rise, blocking out the sun. The few plants that grow are stumpy, withered things.

But it is not this that I wish you to see. Look—here, this is the spot. Right under this desiccated stump of a tree, which looks like an ogre's fist, branch-like fingers rising from the earth.

Bend down with me, here.

Kneel.

Thrust your fingers into this dark, barren earth and dig.

You ask me why we dig.

I tell you that when we dig, we will find the answer to the question you asked, a year and a day ago, as we watched the silver hood of a Mercedes, glistening with blood, crumple as it smashed into a wall. There was a body, dead in the car, and another one, sprawled on the ground, blood leaking on to the tarred road.

You had shaken your head as you snapped a picture. ('For tomorrow's newspaper,' you told the policemen who pushed you away.)

I watched you walk to the other side of the road. You bought a cigarette from the tiny kiosk on the corner of the pavement. As you lit your cigarette, you exchanged words with the kiosk owner. You both wondered at fate, at tragedy. You asked, as you watched those young, fragile bodies borne away, you asked whether a man's fate was ordained from the moment he was born, or whether it was something he made?

The kiosk owner had shaken his head. He didn't know. You didn't notice me, standing in the shadows by your shoulder, listening to you speak. Even then, I knew the answer to your question. I have dogged your steps for a year, even as you forgot the sight of those crumpled, bloody bodies, the answer on my lips. For a year and a day, I have waited to tell you.

And the time is now.

Yes, you've found it. That piece of plastic, torn, and that condom, dirty and brown after twenty-five years in the ground. It was this packet, this condom, that Ashok Lal carried in his pocket, as he drove past this park.

I see you frown. The name rings a bell. Who is Ashok Lal, you ponder, and why is he important?

Step with me into the past. The years swirl past us, and now we stand on green grass. The ogre's fist is hung with leaves. The park is green, bigger and wider. Couples stroll. The sun sets, a flare of orange in a sky that swiftly turns dark. The couples start to disappear into quiet, dark corners.

Walk with me to the edge. You see that woman? The one in the pink sari, with matching pink lipstick? Look at her closely. Memorize her face, her shape, her smile.

Careful, don't step on that bush. See, it shakes, in the twilight. There's a couple on the other side. You can hear them groan.

Aah. Here he comes. Ashok Lal, in his red Maruti 800, with a sputtering engine. He doesn't look like much, in his faded trousers and white-grey shirt. I see you start, as you stand next to me.

Yes, you've recognized him. He looks different in your time. The passage of years has fattened him, lined his face, thinned his hair—over time, this diminutive-looking young man has been transformed into the stout, fat, khadi-garbed politician, with a following of thousands. Even his name has changed—to the far more numerologically correct and astrologically favoured Kumar Ashok Lal Singh.

But right now, as he steers his Maruti 800 through the bylanes of the park, he is plain Ashok Lal, a sales manager in a tiny export office. His hard work will see him promoted. His cunning, miserly mind will help him plot his rise. Eventually, he will seduce his boss's nondescript, impressionable daughter. He will marry her and inherit his boss's small business. Under his leadership, the business will grow, lakhs will turn to crores, as he seeks shady, illegal means of making money. His belly will grow, keeping pace with his bank balance. When you finally see him, years later, he has completed his metamorphosis and turned into the politician you hate and revile, whose perfidy you seek to expose.

But now, watch him as he slows down his Maruti 800. Yes, he's looking at the women clustered on the pavement. He stops by the one in the pink sari. Her name is Rani—but that's not the name she was born with.

Ashok Lal stops his car. He gestures to Rani to get in. She shakes her head—only yesterday, her friend, Pinky, suffered a bad experience with a client in a car. Rani is wary today. Ashok Lal parks, puts on a steering lock, and rolls up his window. When he's locked the car, Rani and he walk over to the tree, the one shaped like an ogre's fist.

Yes, you lean forward, eager. You can hear them whisper, fiercely. You wonder what they talk about. Nothing much, I can tell you. Ashok is trying to beat down Rani's price.

They disappear into the shadows by the tree.

I know you want to hear, you want to see. But the air is too heavy with sound, the darkness is too thick.

No matter. I will tell you what happens. Ashok lifts Rani's pink sari. He presses her against the rough tree trunk. As his breathing quickens, he reaches for the condom in his pocket and tears open the packet. But the packet falls from Ashok's grasp. He curses. Rani curses. For a few moments they grope around on the ground, to no avail. They fail to find the packet, hidden behind a root, the same packet that you dug up.

Rani tries to move away, but Ashok has grabbed her shoulder. Rani shrugs. It's happened before. Why forgo good money, she thinks?

You can guess what happens next.

A moment later it's over. Rani holds her hands out for the money. Ashok refuses to give her the price agreed upon. They stand there, arguing, even as Ashok's sperm swims up Rani's womb.

Rani's voice rises. A moment later, Ashok is surrounded by a bevy of whores. They outnumber him. He looks around, there's not a policeman in sight. He scowls and hands over the money. He walks away, hands thrust in his pockets, muttering curses under his breath.

Rani tucks the note into her pink blouse. She straightens her sari and returns to the pavement. Ashok is only the first of three clients that night.

By the time dawn comes, she's exhausted. She's no longer in the park—that's her 'freelance' work—she's in a dilapidated house ten minutes away. By the end of the night, she's forgotten Ashok and their altercation, even though his sperm has fused with an ovum, and a fertilized embryo now drifts through her fallopian tubes towards her uterus. She has forgotten to take her 'medicine', the nasty concoction Ronny, her pimp, has given her to take immediately after unprotected sex to prevent pregnancies.

The next day, she's in bed with a cold. Ronny knows a sick whore won't have any takers. She spends the rest of the week in bed. The embryo takes hold in her uterus and, by the end of the week, a tiny heart has begun to take shape.

By the time she realizes she's pregnant, two months have gone by. It is three months more before she works up the nerve to tell Ronny. A friend suggests she tries a concoction, made for her by the neighbourhood quack, that will definitely induce a miscarriage. Rani tries it. She gets a bad stomach ache and bleeds.

But the child inside her clings to life. It's only a month later that she realizes that she hasn't miscarried. There's a bulge around her midriff. Ronny notices. He beats her that night, but not hard enough to dislodge the little life growing inside her.

See? Can you see? You can't. But I can see that heart, beating inside her, that tiny head, those veins and bones and muscles forming. I can see Rani's smile on that tiny face, I can see Ashok's clever, cunning eyes.

Ronny tells her that he will take her the following morning to Koki Bai, the woman who lives on the next street, who performs all manner of services for the residents of the brothel, services that involve, according to rumour, twisting the sharpened end of a clothes hanger into one's orifices.

Rani is terrified of this, terrified by the memory of Silky, the Nepalese girl with almond-shaped eyes, who bled for five days after the procedure was done to her, then disappeared. Ronny said she had gone home, but what Pinky and the others tell Rani is that Silky died.

Rani packs her clothes that night, and when Ronny is asleep, drunk, the other women sneak her out.

For a few months, she shelters with Auntie Lilavati, a former prostitute from Ronny's stable, who has now gone solo. Despite Lilavati's advice, Rani refuses to abort. The clothes hanger, with its twisted, pointed end, haunts her dreams. She is scared of dying, scared of pain.

Two months later, during her seventh month, her labour starts. She's taken to the hospital. Just as she's wheeled into the delivery room, a couple enters the hospital.

You stiffen beside me. You recognize the man leading the pregnant, sad-eyed woman inside the hospital. Your breathing quickens. I hear your heart beat a tattoo in your chest.

You watch him hustle her, tenderly, into a wheelchair. You watch her grunt in pain. You watch her in the delivery room, as she finally squeezes out a frail, tiny scrap of flesh. A baby, two months premature. A nurse rushes in with an incubator. You watch the baby gently lowered in. You watch as the sad woman, sweaty tendrils of damp hair plastered to her forehead, cries. She turns her head to watch as the baby is wheeled away.

Come, tear yourself away. Come with me to the ward next door where Rani is, her feet splayed, a head emerging between her thighs. A shriek and the baby slips out. It's two months early, but it's a lusty, bawling thing. Rani sinks back on to the pillows, weakly. Her eyes close, as the baby cries.

A moment later, just as the nurse exits the ward, baby in hand, Rani is dead.

It's midnight now. The nurse on duty, watching over the premature infants, is the one who assisted at Rani's labour. She frequently glances at the baby in the right crib, a weak, fragile child, the one born to the sad-eyed woman.

A few minutes past midnight, and the machines begin to beep. The nurse darts across the room, leans over the crib, the one in which the frail infant lies.

There is nothing she can do. She sighs.

It's then that she looks at the baby in the adjacent crib. Rani's baby.

She reaches towards the baby and hesitates. She bites her lip and glances at the crucifix hanging over the door. It could be a fault of the flickering tube light—but it seems, in that moment, that the body nailed to the cross, moves, the head lifts, and the eyes stare at her directly.

She jumps back, startled. She looks, a second later, at the crucifix. It is still now, a piece of dead wood. Did she imagine the movement?

Her arms extend of their own accord. It is almost as if she's in a dream. Within seconds, Rani's child has taken the place of the dead baby.

It's then that the nurse hears a gasp. Startled, she turns around and looks into the bespectacled, myopic eyes of the sad woman's husband.

The minutes tick by. Finally, the man turns to regard the squealing infant who has taken his son's place.

He nods, curt, brisk, and walks away.

The nurse exhales.

I feel you tremble beside me. You pull away. Your eyes are filled with pain, with hate. You tell me I lie, you accuse me of distorting the truth.

That's what they all say. But I look at you, and in the pain in your face, I see doubt.

Come, take my hand.

The walls shake, the lights flicker, the ground moves. The years tumble past as we travel through time. Finally, we stop. The walls have been repainted, the floor is smooth marble instead of rough concrete. It is daytime now, people scurry past. The cries of newborn infants and women in labour fill the air.

We ascend the stairs. The floor above is filled with the scent of death, filled with wasting faces, inert bodies, beeping machines, and IV drips.

You beg me to stop. You grip the bannister with one hand. You tell me that you can't continue. You try to wrench your hand from my grasp, you have begun to guess how this will end. You plead with me to desist.

I can't. You must know. I pull you to your feet, pull you past the dying. We stop in front of a door. I push it open.

Inside, your father lies on the hospital bed, thin and shrunken. His words are a whisper, his breath a rattle in his chest.

I see the tears stream down your face, hear sobs choke your throat. You stumble. I hold out my hand and you grab it. You turn your face to mine, tear-stained, stricken.

You see yourself sitting by his bedside. He beckons you to come closer. His breath is hot on your cheek, as you lean over him.

He speaks, but you can't make out the words. He moves back, stares in your face. The machines start to beep. He still stares at you. It's only when the nurse rushes in, followed by the doctor, that you realize that he has died.

But even then, as you stumble out the room, tears blinding you, you feel his eyes following you, his glance burning your back.

What was he trying to say?

This gift I give you is his answer. His shade comes to us, stepping forth from the shadows, wearing his gaunt, withered face. He raises his bony hands to touch you. He speaks now, the words have lain waiting on his tongue for years, the words that he feared to speak, the words that came too late. He tells you now that you are not the son who was born to him.

For years he believed that this knowledge would not alter your fate. He loved you. Did the truth matter? But now, in the presence of death, he realizes differently. He realizes that you cannot escape fate, that it will pursue you to your end. The fabric of his life is spread out before him, the things unknown and invisible revealed. He knows a man's life is shaped by his birth and that your fate is impossible to escape. There is a neatness, a pattern, a shape to it. By withholding the truth, he has condemned you to your fate.

Come, take my hand. Time flashes past. We return to the park, a few moments before our appointment.

Look up. The sun dazzles your eyes. But do you see those figures, meeting on the rooftop of that building? Look closely. You see yourself and you see Kumar Ashok's henchman, Chand Lal.

And there, in the distance, do you see Kumar Ashok? His bulk seems to block the sun, throwing a black, menacing shadow. His face is impassive, although sweat drips down his forehead. There is venom in the glances he darts at you, there is pure hate in the look you return.

He hates the pieces you've been writing about him. The ones that accuse him of corruption, of nepotism, of bribing the electorate. The pieces published in Indian newspapers and foreign publications. He pulled strings, he got you removed from your job. He thought that would silence you. But it hasn't.

You revile him. He has come to symbolize everything you fight against.

But it's more than that. In fighting him, you feel you are avenging the ignominious death of your father—an honest man, a small man, who lost his job as an engineer in a factory due to Kumar Ashok's wheeling and dealing. You fought for him, you used your pen and your camera to evoke his voice, to capture his despair, the despair of the individual, lost in the larger scheme of things, of a small life destroyed by the whims of conglomerates and Big Business.

And yet, you both fail to see the similarities, the clever, cunning eyes. The persistence that characterizes every endeavour. The ambitious, ruthless streak. Father and son. It's genetics that causes you to confront each other, to battle for supremacy, that has equipped you with the skills to fight each other. But you don't know that.

And it is fate that has brought you here.

Chand Lal opens a briefcase. It is filled with wads of money. He pushes it towards you.

You take it. You turn to the parapet and shake the briefcase. The wads of cash fall out. You see an urchin, far down below, jump up as he tries to catch a note as it flies past, borne by the wind.

Kumar Ashok grabs you from behind. He is furious. His veins bulge, his face is con torted in a grimace.

Your eyes are bloodshot. You're at the end of your tether. You wrestle him to the parapet.

For a moment, you are lost from sight. Next to me, you squirm, impatient, eager to discover what happens next.

You pull out a gun.

The sound of a gunshot rips through the air.

A moment later, a body falls from the rooftop, past eleven storeys, and lands, face down, in the park below, by a tree shaped like a fist.

Come, walk with me to the tree. Help me turn this body over.

We turn over the body. Blood stains your hands and mine.

You start. You scream.

It's your face, squashed and broken, staring back at you.

You hit me. You scratch at my hands with your nails. You curse me.

I'm used to this. Your hands, your curses, they have no effect on me. Everyone screams at this point. Everyone curses.

Eleven storeys above us, Chand Lal checks for a pulse on Kumar Ashok, and tries to staunch the blood flowing from the wound in his chest. Someone calls for an ambulance. It's futile, I can tell you. I have an appointment with Kumar Ashok in a few moments.

You stare at your body on the ground, and then at the tree shaped like a fist, a few steps away from us. You finger the broken brown packet in your pocket. You see the beginning and the end of your life, a few steps away from each other.

You asked, a year and a day ago, whether fate is ordained.

You have your answer.

Fate is cruel, you say. I beg to differ. I prefer to call it a sense of humour.

You ask me who I am.

You don't need to ask. You've guessed—haven't you?

28

AFTER HALF-TIME

SHAMIK GHOSH

Translated from the Bengali by Subha Prasad Sanyal

The alley was dark. The little light there was came from a hoarding round the corner. In the distance, the traffic signal glowed ominously red. The man seemed to have emerged straight out of darkness. Tall and dark. Deep blue shirt. A baseball bat clutched in his left hand. The right arm looked curled up. Maybe it was crippled. His face was hidden under his hood, but I could see his dark, flat chin and large eyes.

Lebu was my friend. We used to play cricket together. He was a great off-spinner: could even do the, what do we call it now? Right. The doosra. We used to play with a rubber ball, though.

His right arm was crippled.

He used to run up with the ball, which would be launched from his right hand as soon as his arm rose. Sometimes it'd bounce high off the asphalt, and sometimes it'd come at you dangerously low. But his bowling lacked speed. If you kept swinging hard and randomly, you could score more than a few sixes off it. A six meant hitting the lamp post in front of the Dutta residence.

Lebu's crippled right arm would tremble uncontrollably if he conceded too many runs. You could see he was getting agitated. He used to swear a lot then and there was a sort of flame in his eyes.

The first time I bumped into Lebu was when I was trying to ride a bicycle. His father sold fish in the market. I could ride, but the main road made me jittery. Used to crash into people a lot. Fell off the bike a lot, too. And, one fine day, I bumped into Lebu, literally. And promptly fell off the bike.

He helped me up.

'You're new to this, aren't you?'

'Um...I didn't hurt you, did I?'

'Don't worry, it happens. Here, I'll teach you.'

He did teach me some. But mostly, I'd sit behind him on the bike while he took me places. That's how we became friends. And then, from friends to teammates in the same cricket team.

Sometimes we'd escape to the railway tracks. We'd leave our bike leaning against the boundary wall of some nearby building and climb up on the wall. One evening, sitting next to me, he asked:

'Oi, Bablu, you called everyone for your birthday. Why didn't you call me?'

'Um, Dad gives me hell just for being friends with you. If I invite you over.... He's going to chop me into pieces.'

'Am I...bad?' He didn't sound angry or hurt. Just incredulous.

I couldn't answer him. I picked up a stone chip lying on the wall and threw it as hard as I could. A train rushed past, and the wind ruffled Lebu's longish hair. He was telling me something, but the sound of the train drowned his voice.

Lebu went to prison and I, to an Indian Institute of Technology. The story of how he ended up in jail is actually kind of funny. So, Lebu had a brother named Fotik. People called him One-eyed Fotik, though he wasn't really blind in one eye. He'd given himself the moniker. Goons, like pirates, needed a moniker like that. Children hereabouts had ambitions of becoming doctors or engineers, but Fotik wanted to be a goon.

But to be a goon you needed not just courage but also a gun or physical strength. Fotik had neither. He did know how to make nail bombs, called petos, though. Lebu was quite certain his elder brother would rapidly ascend the social ladder of the underworld. He told me one day, 'You see, like you chaps have those...what do you call it...The Joint...these chaps have bombs. First, you got to learn to make the bomb, then you got to learn how to chuck it. Then, when the elections come, you're a goon overnight.' He was speaking of the Joint Entrance Exams, the things you must pass to get into an IIT.

They lived close to the railway crossing. It wasn't exactly a slum, but the building was dilapidated. And the slums started just after you crossed their house.

Fotik had made a bomb that night. He was supposed to put it along with the rest he had made in a sack—and bury them on the edge of a marshy patch between the main railtrack and the sidetrack a few hundred metres away.

Most days, someone would accompany him, but Fotik was alone that day. There'd been some trouble with some of the boys from Atabagan. Apparently, someone had beaten someone up with a cycle chain. The elections were coming, and the party had told the goons that they were not to create trouble. The opposition could make life problematic if they were caught. Not to mention that winning here this time could mean becoming a Member of the Legislative Assembly of the state.

So, everyone else went to settle the argument, but Fotik remained with his bombs.

The area around the railtracks was deathly silent. It wasn't particularly late, though: just around 10 p.m. Fotik crossed the tracks cautiously, a crowbar in one hand, and a bag full of his bombs in the other.

Crickets chirped and a chilly wind was blowing. Fotik felt himself shudder once or twice. Three or four days ago, the body of a girl had floated to the surface in that marsh. Being submerged for days had made her skin pale...she looked almost piscine. Who knows who'd raped her. Pancha had told him he'd heard someone sobbing around here. Said the dead girl haunted the marsh, crying.

Fotik put his crowbar down, took a bidi out of his pocket and lit it. He...he could hear something. Someone was sobbing.

Damn.

No, no, no. It was nothing. No one was sobbing. It was all in his head. But wait, there was a sound by the marsh. Fotik craned his neck.

What was that floating in the water? Was it a sari! Fotik felt a chill run down his spine and goose pimples on his arms. The noise again. Like something rustling through the grass. And maybe a faint jingling of bangles.

'You son of a bitch ghost!' Fotik screamed. He bent to take a bomb from his stash and hurled it at the marsh. Maybe he'd forgotten bombs really don't do much to ghosts. They can't. But chucking a bomb does inflate your courage. The bomb arced through the air, struck the branches of a tree, and rebounded towards Fotik like a football.

I don't know if he tried to head it back, but I do know that his face was completely obliterated.

'I'll get those fuckers.' Lebu told me at the crematorium.

'Who? Your brother died because of himself.'

'Because of himself, my arse. Fuckers killed him and now they say his own bomb killed him. I'll teach those party bigwigs.'

His right arm was trembling. His eyes were bloodshot. Must've been drinking a lot. I couldn't bear to look at him and averted my eyes. I'd just got into the IIT, grown a bit of a stubble, wrote poetry when no one was looking. I was going to IIT Kharagpur in a few days. I'd already bought a textbook to prepare for the TOEFL exams. Nellie, the girl next door, smiled coyly whenever our eyes met.

I realized then that Lebu and I had grown light years apart. While I tried to console Lebu, my hand touching his crippled right arm, I made up my mind. I'd run. I wouldn't go home, I'd go straight to my uncle's.

Lebu did bomb the party office the next day. I mean, he tried to. The bomb rolled out of his hand and landed in front of the desk. Didn't bounce. Came through low, just like a slowly spinning delivery. Everyone retreated. The secretary, Bablu, drew his legs up on the chair and stared at the bomb, terrified, covering his ears with his hands.

It was going to explode any second now. Any second....

It didn't explode after all. Just lay there.

When they realized that the bomb wasn't going to detonate, they rushed at Lebu. He'd been standing there, very still, except for his right arm, which was trembling like crazy. Bablu landed the first blow: a resounding slap. Then a barrage of kicks while Lebu writhed on the ground. And then metal rods.

The police arrested Lebu that day.

I was sitting in the classroom and the Bengali teacher was gesticulating wildly. He looked at me and smiled.

'You, tell me, what's the name of Saratchandra's father?'

'Sarat's father? Uh, who was it? Bankimchandra?'

'Excellent! Very good, boy, very good. You can sit down now.'

I obeyed. It was weirdly quiet in the classroom. The students around me were wearing orange shirts and steel-coloured pants. The boy beside me was hunched over his desk, concentrating on something. His book lay open. I looked closer. He was sketching something. Someone sprawling face down. Headless. A red ball hovered over him. Who was the artist? I looked at him.

Lebu.

How'd he get here? He didn't study with us! Must've sneaked in. He'd be caned if the teacher noticed him.

'Hey! Hey! Lebu! What are you doing here? Quick, jump out of the window!' I whispered.

Lebu looked at me. 'You fouled me, didn't you?'

I couldn't breathe. What if the teacher saw him? I tried sniffling. Then I noticed the arm of the man in the sketch. His right arm. It was trembling. And the red ball was descending at great speed. I heard a whistle being blown. It was the teacher, blowing a whistle and screaming, 'Half-time! Half-time!'

Lebu slammed his notebook shut and stood up. His head retracted into his shirt and he started peeling it off his body. Others started doing the same. There was nothing beneath the clothes. Thin air. As the shirts rose, the bodies disappeared. Gradually, all the boys around me peeled their shirts off and vanished. Only our teacher and I remained in the room, clothed. He smiled at me again.

'Half-time.'

∽

I woke up, sweating like a pig. Throwing the sheet off my body, I looked at the digital alarm clock. 01:47 a.m.

Jennifer was sleeping soundly beside me. She was my colleague, and my lover, too. Jennifer was…blindingly blonde. Her ancestors were German. I gazed at her for a while. Her pale, peaceful face glowed in the blue light of the night lamp. She looked ethereal. There was a gentle smile on her face and dimples on her cheeks.

I remembered Lebu…had I really fouled him? Would it all have turned out differently if I'd held him back by force that day? No chance. He'd have ended up the same way. That's what always happens to the Lebus of the world. Or so I tried to force myself into believing.

Feeling a bit queasy, I went to the bathroom and held my head under the tap. I thought I'd throw up.

Maybe I'd just had too much to drink. Europeans can swig their drinks by the gallon. Shouldn't have tried competing. But we'd bagged a huge project, I had to celebrate! I'd been boozing mindlessly out of excitement, wondering what Thomas's reaction would be back in New York. He was my boss. Pure-bred American. Cognac. The cognac was escaping my system now. I rinsed my mouth thoroughly.

Parting the curtains, I peered outside through the window. London by night. Many of the buildings were still awake behind their windowpanes. Countless buildings of different sizes, all bunched together so close. Tall buildings, squat buildings, all of them trying to rise above one another.

As a student, when burning the midnight oil got boring, I'd escape to the terrace. The railtracks used to be shrouded in darkness; in the distance, from the slums, streaks of light would sneak out through the gaps in the roofs of asbestos sheets. Sometimes there would be flashes of light illuminating the railtracks, and distant booms.

Nail bombs. Railway-wagon thieves fighting for control of territory.

What a long way I'd come. I turned back and looked at Jennifer and felt relieved. I wanted to touch her. Make sure all of this was real.

I wanted to laugh at myself. No one had handed me a place at the IIT. I'd got it for myself.

Even the air-conditioned room felt stuffy. I wanted to be under the open sky. And suddenly, after all these years, I yearned again for my old terrace.

I put on some clothes. Let Jennifer sleep, I'd take the key to the Yale lock on the door. She didn't look like she would wake up any time soon.

The lobby downstairs was crowded. People were partying even at this hour. I crept out of the hotel.

The desolate street stretched out before me in the cold. I was reminded of the dream. Why had Lebu appeared after such a long time? Whatever. I tried to distract myself. What a huge project we'd bagged, and in Europe at that. I decided to go back home for a visit. It had been too long since I'd been where I grew up....

Lost in thought, I didn't realize when I'd entered the alleyway. It was one of those places where you were likely to get mugged. Shouldn't have risked it. The traffic signal was glowing red. The hoarding was at a distance but I could read the tagline, written in large, bold letters.

'REMEMBER.'

'Hey, mate. Give me some dough.'

Snapping out of my reverie, I saw him, as if he'd emerged out of the darkness. Tall and dark. Deep blue shirt. A baseball bat in his left hand. His right arm curled up. Maybe it was crippled. Face hidden by his cap. Dark, flat chin. Large eyes.

I couldn't see his face clearly, but I could make out its general form in the dim light. And, as I stared at him, he seemed to grow thinner and shorter. I looked at him in astonishment. He seemed to be morphing slowly into Lebu.

Lebu? How could Lebu be here?

'Hey, Paki, give me whatever you have.'

'Lebu? You're Lebu, aren't you? Don't you remember me?'

'Paki bastard....'

The main raised his bat. My skull would crack if he hit me with it. His right arm was trembling. Just like Lebu's. The light from the street light in the distance drifted towards me. I considered pushing my left leg back, to play on the back foot. What if a cricket ball came flying out of his right hand now? Would it bounce off the asphalt, or would it come at me low?

29

JOURNEY

SHANTHI K. APPANNA

Translated from the Kannada by Srinath Perur

'Madam, sorry, I cannot help you. The other occupant has arrived. You have to share this berth with him,' the TTE said and went away. The Tamil boy on the upper berth snorted: 'Madam, looks like your prayer has gone to waste....' I gave a lopsided smile; then, worried I was scowling, dissolved the smile and awaited this Bhagesh with whom I was to share the berth. The Tamil boy above and, across the aisle, Naidu, and three middle-aged sardars seemed to be awaiting him too. There was a sudden anticipation in the air, as if a ghost we had breathlessly been trying to spot was finally revealing itself. It was not as if the excitement was unearned: we had all spent some time cursing this Bhagesh. Perhaps I most of all. I would be lying if I said that I wasn't excited and warily curious at the prospect of sharing a berth with an unknown young man. But I could not possibly admit to it, and so I had spoken out more than the others.

This had happened once before. Subramani and I were newly married, living in a house with his parents, his sister, and her children. When it turned out that he and I had to share a berth to Chennai, the thought filled me with a strange thrill, a tender joy. He was at one end of the berth, I was at the other. I had covered my legs with a small shawl, and with shy smiles slowly extended a leg towards the man who was at last mine.

My excitement partly had to do with all the inconvenience and lack of privacy that came from living in a packed house. Subramani's job had him leave home at seven in the morning and return at a time of the night when only lorries remained on the roads. There was a room in which my mother-in-law slept alone, tossing and turning and farting. In the hall, my father-in-law, smoking bidis, would turn on the light at intervals to go to the bathroom. Sometimes he would wake up, say 'Listen, someone is calling.... There's a ghost in the street behind our house', go out in the middle of the night, tie an old slipper to the back door and circle the house while urinating. In the midst of all this madness, Subramani would return and throw himself down on the mattress like a sack of onions. I would have liked him to bathe before he came to bed. Not that it would have made any difference. He and I, my father-in-law, my sister-in-law and her children on the floor, we all slept in that hall. There was nothing that could happen between us. Even if I desired a little something, lying there like a lump of scorching mud, he would drift off into his own world like a raincloud out of reach.

After all of that, it was my first journey with him. I was excited. There must have been coy glances tumbling from my eyes as I stretched out my foot and tried to tickle his leg. He said, 'Ei, move your leg, I'm wearing light-coloured pants,' and stood up. I was crestfallen. I sat there gazing into the darkness beyond the window. He said, 'You should sleep now. You have an exam tomorrow.' He went and stood at the door of the compartment for a long time. The berth was swaying like a cradle. I stuck to it with legs curled up and went to sleep. In the heat of that night a thought passed through my mind: what if I had to share a berth with another man....

Anyway, over a decade had passed since then. Life, like an impassive highway, had soaked up the murmurs of the past and moved quietly on. It comes to an end one day, and until then one walks on. Who knows what surprises lie hidden at which crossroads along the way? At least, that's what I tell myself. A full ten years. A period in which there were changes, pain, a time in which matters heated up, cooled off. The sister-in-law returned to her husband's house, Subramani's parents passed away, and the house was empty. Our life had acquired stability, arrived at some sort of a juncture. I had learnt by practice to be happy for no reason in particular. I had not known earlier that it was possible to teach oneself to be happy.

'The seat isn't confirmed, it's a side berth RAC. Leave early in any case. It might help if the TTE is someone we know. See if Sebastian is on duty,' Subramani had said on the phone. Sebastian was not on duty. It looked like I would have to share the berth with this Bhagesh after all. I had made a show of wishing loudly in front of the others that he wouldn't come—but here he was, standing in front of me. I shrank into my seat so he could occupy his. He was tall, dressed in brown jeans and a blue T-shirt. He had sprayed himself with some sort of fragrance that combined favourably with the smell of his sweat. The shivering cold of an AC coach…oh God! I told my mind that it was to go to sleep quietly. If Naidu wanted he could have given up his berth for me, but it felt like the others there were not really concerned, only quietly curious about the situation.

Bhagesh didn't seem curious at all—he didn't look at me once. I pretended to be engrossed in my book while observing him from the corner of my eye. He had a bag that looked grimy. Clearly it had been wearing itself out for him for quite a while. He sat at the other end of the berth, briskly took out a bedsheet, and placed it over his legs. He drew earphones from his bag, put them on, held up his phone, and sat with his eyes stuck to the screen.

The train set off. The three sardars made their beds and lay down. After a while the Tamil boy above drew the curtain to his berth.

Here, this fellow was still sitting with his phone raised. I squirmed at the thought that he might be taking photos of me without my knowledge. I slowly raised my eyes and looked at Naidu on the next seat. He must have sensed something. He put on a show of concern and said, 'Cover yourself with a bedsheet, ma…. We're all here, don't worry. I'm feeling tired now. I think I'll go to sleep.' He brought down the berth and stretched himself out on it. I bent low into my book so my face wouldn't be visible.

'Hello, madam,' Bhagesh said. 'Why are you sitting so awkwardly? Make yourself comfortable.' He spoke Kannada well; he must be a native speaker, not Tamil or Telugu.

'What are you looking at on your mobile?' I asked.

'Why?'

It was clear that he was annoyed. But I had decided that rather than let my imagination run wild, it was best to be direct. 'No, you could lower the phone and continue looking at whatever it is you're watching. Why hold it up? How can I be sure you're not taking my photo?'

'Don't give me ideas,' he said. 'You're quite something, you know…. I hadn't thought of it, but now I'm thinking it might come in useful later.' His eyes betrayed that he was smiling under his moustache.

'What are you saying?' I asked. Even if I was angry, it had not felt unpleasant to hear him say I was quite something.

Naidu propped himself up on an elbow: 'What's going on, ma, any problem?'

'Nothing, uncle,' said Bhagesh. 'I was just asking madam to be comfortable. I told her if she wanted I could move to uncle's berth and uncle could share this berth with her.' I was taken aback by how theatrical he was being.

Naidu clearly didn't want to be stuck with any of this. 'No need for all that. I am a BP patient, don't give me unnecessary tension. I'll sleep now. Please turn off the corridor light if you don't mind. It's in my eyes,' he said and pulled the blanket over his head.

Bhagesh said with a smile, 'Okay, uncle.' He turned off the light and drew the curtain between our seats and the aisle. My heart skipped a beat. I thought it was best not to show any reaction. I closed my book and leaned back.

'Madam, turn on your bed lamp. You can continue to read,' he said. He turned off the screen of his mobile, closed his eyes, and leaned back as if lost to some song.

Had I been hasty in confronting him? This could have been a pleasant journey. I thought I should say something. 'Going to Bangalore?'

'No, Chennai. Have to attend a job interview.'

'Where?'

'TCS. Let's see how it goes....'

'Good luck. That's in Tharamani, right?'

'Yes. Do you know how I can get there? Are there buses? Or should I take an auto?'

'Plenty of buses. It's quite a distance, but our bus fares are low. Or you could take a prepaid auto, you won't have any trouble.'

'Okay.' Neither of us spoke for a while. He asked, 'Are you settled in Chennai?'

'Don't know about settled, but we live there for now. Actually, I don't think it's possible for a person to be truly settled until they die.' It occurred to me that I was saying this only to impress him, and I shook my head.

He laughed. 'That's funny,' he said, 'but you're right.'

'What music are you listening to? Can I listen, too?'

'Oh sure, it's a good song.' He pulled out the earphone plug.

Paas aayiye ki ham nahi aayenge baar baar.... The song gently filled the silence. It was in a man's voice.

'Who is singing?'

'Sanam Puri. He does old songs in a somewhat new style. I like them very much.'

'I like it too.'

He sang well. 'Lag Jaa Gale' came on, one of my favourites.

The songs floated between us. Naidu, the Tamil boy, and the others seemed to have fallen asleep. The dim light on the inside of the closed curtain; the sweet music; the pleasant sway of the running train. My heart that ran along with these things. In front of me was a young man built like a horse. Here, a woman who had swallowed the glowing ember of desire and was burning up from within. God, see to it this desire won't ripen into anything.... I looked at him cautiously. He was leaning back, his eyes closed. He looked good sitting like that.

It was still only around half past ten. There was a long way to go before morning. It would be nice to stretch my legs. Just then: a phone call from Subramani. 'Did you manage to get a berth? I tried calling Sebastian, but couldn't get through. Did you see him?'

'No. I'm sharing with some guy. It's all okay for now. I'll call tomorrow, everyone's asleep here.'

'All right. I'll come to the station in the morning. Make sure you are comfortable.'

Subramani's love is hard to explain. He's never demonstrative, but his love and affection are visible in everything he does—dusting the bedclothes before laying them out, replacing the soap in the bathroom, buying flowers for me every day on his way back from work, buying groceries and vegetables well in time so we never run out, making sure my bookshelf and dressing table are never dusty. Every morning it's his job to wake our daughter, Minni, and get her ready for school. He irons her clothes, makes sure she's done her homework, packs her lunch. To see him wiping her lunch carrier with a napkin before sending it off reminds me of my mother. Even Minni seems more fond of her father than her mother. His meticulousness, concern, calmness, the gentleness with which he spoke, these were all silent things. In a house that large, at least the clock made some sound by its ticking. Our lives went on with the same regularity but with no sound at all. He'd had a music system installed because I liked listening to old songs.

'It's music that keeps our house alive.' My thoughts found voice.

'You still need to be receptive. Look, that sardarji is asking me to reduce the volume.'

'He has a berth and he wants to sleep. It's all right.'

'Okay,' he said, reduced the volume, and looked at me.

'Even if two people think something is right, there'll always be a third who disagrees. Even when the whole world seems agreed on something, you can find a person to step up and say something contrary,' I said.

'True,' he said. 'It's not so much a question of whether something is right or wrong, maybe it's all about how people perceive things.'

'But does that mean there's nothing that can be held firmly as truth?'

'Truth is a strange thing. Look at us—if it's true that we're sitting here, isn't it also true that it can be seen in different ways by people around us?'

'What does that mean? We have no choice, so we're sitting here. What more is there to see?'

'Is there nothing more? Sometimes the real truth is never acknowledged. Instead, we go with something that only looks like it.'

'There will be misconceptions, but truth waits quietly for its turn.' My mind swirled as I spoke.

So, what was the truth in me right now? It scared me to touch it, to look it in the eye. It was true that I was sitting there with fortitude. But that wasn't the entire truth, was it? Wasn't I that very moment melting and turning into a river? When I thought that maybe there was nothing to it, I would become aware of the train of my own thought and grow alarmed. What was true here? If what one felt at any instant was to be taken as true, then the truth was something that could change with time. If it was capable of changing, then how could one call it the truth? Wasn't truth called the truth because it was absolute? Perhaps, I thought, there are no absolute truths in this world other than birth and death. I heard him snort in laughter and looked up. His eyes were closed and he seemed lost in his music. Did he laugh or not? I thought I heard him. Who knows what truth is coursing through him, I thought, and laughed.

He opened his eyes and looked at me with a faint smile, as if he had been expecting me to laugh. I imagined my secret had been discovered and grew flustered. I could not bear this investigation of truth any longer and changed the subject. 'I'm thinking of stretching out my legs. Is that okay?' I asked.

'Of course,' he said. 'But if you have to sit comfortably I too may have to stretch out my legs.' He got up and began bringing down the backs of our seats. Standing next to him I tried to read his expression but couldn't. The dim light of the bed lamp did not reveal anything in its true colours.

'Please sit down. What are you looking at? And so seriously at that? Bloody hidden truth! Why should we try to get at it, let it remain where it wants. The most dangerous search in the world is the search for truth. It doesn't matter how hard you look, whatever you find will be shown up as incomplete one day or the other. So best not to go after it. The present moment is all one can trust.'

Arrey! I was stunned. Was this man a mind reader or what? And of all the people to come to my seat—or I to theirs—it had to be this wretched fellow. It felt like some hidden truth lay behind all this, like someone was orchestrating all this without our knowledge. This scared me a little but also somehow made me feel less inhibited. Whatever has to happen will happen. All we can trust is the moment, I thought. The niggling fear inside me subsided. I extended my legs, leaned back, and made myself comfortable. My cramped joints eased themselves. I felt light. He too extended his legs. He must have felt a similar relief: he raised his arms and stretched lightly. I wondered if Naidu and the gang of three sardarjis were asleep on the other side of the curtain. They probably were, I thought. None of them had seen us sitting like this, but they couldn't have resisted imagining it, and the thought made me happy. Anyway, it was the only possibility. And so what—it's not as if sitting with legs extended has to lead to something. But was it true that there was nothing happening? My toes were touching the outside of his thighs. My legs were covered with a bedsheet, but still there was a pleasant heat. Something like heat, descending from his thigh to my big toe, passing to my toe with the ring, going through my foot, climbing up my ankle, filling my thigh, moving up to be collected, then rising higher into the body to be dissipated in stages. I remembered a story a friend had told me when we were young, thought it fit the situation perfectly, and then felt amused at how incongruous the comparison was.

A man goes to work his field early in the morning and sees there an extraordinarily beautiful woman. It's a morning after heavy rain and the mist has just cleared. The woman is an enchanting sight in a white sari the colour of the mist, her hair hanging loose. He sees her and is overcome with concern. He asks her who she is, where she is from. A misty teardrop escapes the corner of her eye. She says she's an orphan from Kerala, in need of shelter. Without hesitation he puts his cloak over the head of the misty beauty and takes her home. He lives alone at home, is still unmarried. He's thrilled: what could be more fortunate than for him to find a bride of such beauty? 'I interrupted your work this morning,' she says. 'Go finish whatever you have to do in the fields. I'll make some rotis and wait for you.' He returns home hungry, stands outside the door and calls and calls, but she doesn't emerge. He pushes open the door and enters the house to find her in the kitchen, cooking rotis. He looks at the stove. There's no firewood beneath the pan! Just her feet joined together, burning. That's when he realizes—she's no ordinary woman, but the enchantress Mohini. He runs from there in a panic. That's the story.

I finished telling it and laughed. Bhagesh did not join in. He said, 'I hope I don't look like Bhasmasura to you?'

I was startled. It might only have been a coincidence, but his question was very direct. Perhaps it came to him naturally after hearing about Mohini. Or had he seen through me and realized that his thigh touching my foot was making me burn like Mohini? But at least he was being straightforward. I was the one who had unnecessarily introduced Mohini into the conversation and tried to talk about my secret in a different light. Otherwise, what reason had I to tell this story about Mohini to a stranger at this time of night? He probably suspected this. I said nothing and just laughed again, a laugh that felt all the more pleasing for its doing me a favour and sounding natural at an awkward moment.

'Look, Bangalore has arrived. Shall I get something to drink? Do you want anything to eat?' he asked. The boiling within me subsided when he got up.

'I'd like a coffee. Otherwise I'll start to feel drowsy in some time. It's cold too.' I was really beginning to shiver at this point. Perhaps because the fire in me had gone out.

He agreed, rubbing his palms, 'Yes, it's getting cold.' It's getting cold? Did that mean he had been burning as well? His feet had been close enough to reach my waist. I drew the curtain aside and looked in the direction he had gone. Naidu was sitting up and had switched on the light. 'Are you okay, ma?' he asked, a look of concern on his face. But I was sure he was only asking as a formality. 'Yes, uncle. He seems to be a decent fellow. We've become friends now,' I said. In my attempt to be firm I wondered if I hadn't been a little harsh to Naidu. Who knew, maybe the glimmer of concern he had just shown was genuine after all. I softened my tone: 'In this situation I thought the best option was to be pleasant to him. Instead of getting all sorts of thoughts into my head and worrying, it's better to make it a safe friendship.' It felt like I was trying to justify myself to him. Whether it was necessary for him to hear this I didn't know, but maybe it was I who needed it? Was I trying to say: it's not what you're thinking, I haven't melted or burned at his touch, it's all easy and simple, no struggle here at all, I am like the calm surface of a lake. Why did I even care what they thought? 'Very good, young lady,' said the old man on the next berth. I laughed, I don't know with how much conviction. I reassured myself that I hadn't lied either—the tie of friendship could be stretched a great deal. I tried to laugh again, a little better this time. The Tamil boy from the berth above looked down into my eyes and smiled. I thought I saw some hope, some frustration hidden there. It didn't have to be about me, I'm no great beauty, but still, it must have seemed romantic to him, the idea of sharing a seat with an unknown woman and becoming friends with her. And we must admit that the dark makes certain truths visible that remain invisible in the light. Otherwise why would I, who had no real reservations about Subramani, who by almost all indications had a happy family life, orderly as an Ashoka tree growing in a neat enclosure, why would I so eagerly want to reach out for this wild creeper passing by and tie it around my neck? This thing that was troubling me—was it love? If it felt as sweet as love, then could it be false? If love was an absolute, then could it be given different forms? What is true love, where is it to be found? How do different people love differently? As time goes by, does love too lose its allure and end up as mere habit? Or perhaps, like truth, love too gives different accounts of itself the more one thinks about it, slips away like a stone covered with algae the more one tries to grasp it.

'Madam, here's your coffee.' He was an affectionate fellow after all, I thought, and in turn a fondness for him welled up within me. This made the coffee all the more pleasant.

'What brought you to Mysore?' he asked suddenly, as if to break the silence.

'My younger sister lives there. Newly married. Already, there's some trouble between her and her husband.'

'What's going on with them?' He again turned off the light and drew the curtain. They must have finished changing the engine. The train gave a small shake of the waist and picked up speed.

'The problem seems to be with my sister.... They're unable to get along. She's already thinking of divorce.'

'If she's saying this so soon after the wedding, she must have come upon some new truth.' He seemed to be smiling as he said this.

'Is this something to joke about?'

'Not like that.... But everything that strikes one need not be true. Things do change with time. Ask her to give it some time.'

'She's not the sort who listens. We spent so much on the wedding, invited the whole town. And now she wants to end it....'

'It's not like the money will come back if she stays on while being unhappy. No point worrying about the money now. The main thing is their happiness, that's all you must think about.'

I liked what he was saying. But then, we hadn't thought of happiness even when the wedding was being organized. We have linked marriages and weddings with the prestige of households, and are now trapped.

'Are you married?' I asked, changing the subject.

'Not yet. I've just broken up with someone. Let me recover. Then, I'll think of marriage.'

'Oh, so sad....'

'Nothing sad about it, it was a good thing to have happened. We lived together for three years. We used to be colleagues in Bangalore. It was all fine to begin with, but then we couldn't get along.'

'Was it something that couldn't be worked out at all?' My curiosity got the better of me.

'Something like that. We were fine for a year, then we became inseparable. Now, she says she can't enjoy sex with me.... Sorry if I'm being too direct.'

This isn't something that can't be solved. You should have talked it over, gone to a counsellor. The medical field has advanced so much.... My mind came up with the words but did not speak them. What use was love if both didn't want it? Sex should be a celebration, and that is impossible if the minds are not united first. 'I see,' I said, keeping my tone as neutral as I could.

'Yes.... What we want from life ultimately is happiness. Whatever one has or doesn't, it's best to remove oneself from a situation where one is unhappy.'

'I too believe so,' I said and laughed. But, do I really?

I was sitting with my legs folded. A cool friendship had developed between us. Even if I stretched out my legs I doubted I would feel any thrill. All that stewing from earlier seemed like a lie. 'Then?' I broke the silence. He seemed to be waiting for an opportunity. He couldn't stop talking after that. The flow of conversation went on, though it would be hard to say that we spoke of this or that in particular. I thought I would remember the night for the rest of my life. But why was my heart opening itself so easily to this stranger? Why really do we like a person? And with no good reason?

The night went by quickly. It was five in the morning, and no sign of sleep. 'My station arrives in about an hour. So it looks like no sleep for me tonight!'

'Oh, Perambur? An aunt used to live there. I visited her once…I think I'll close my eyes for a while. Or they might deduct points in the interview for my sleepy face.' He laughed, looking adorable as he did so, and I felt a rush of warmth.

'Stretch your legs out and sleep comfortably,' I said and made room. His broad chest, the hairy and somewhat rough hands resting on his chest, tousled hair and beard, taut lips, slightly curled eyebrows, and despite all that, the carefree look on his face…or perhaps it was carelessness. I liked him. Enough for a small desire to be born again. His feet touching the back of my waist brought a flame to an ember that had died out. What if I leaned forward and kissed him on the lips…I clutched the curtain and tugged it open. I shook my head. This lust was burning, intoxicating. Just two stops to Perambur. I might never see him again. And so what if I didn't. What we felt for each other so deeply at the moment might run out one day…. But who cares. I want those lips now, this moment, and there was no release without kissing them. How might he react…I had never been in such agony.

I only had one bag. I pulled it out. Everyone across the aisle was still asleep. They must be getting off at Chennai Central. Villivakkam came and went. Less than ten minutes now. I leaned over him. His lips were warm, full enough to fill my parted lips. Pressed on his chest, I felt the world had stopped.

He did not stop me. He did not seem startled either. He took me into his arms with an overpowering intensity. My mind cooperated by standing aside without thinking if what was happening was right. My body grew light, my legs flailed.

I could have asked for his number. I didn't. I could have said we should meet again, but I didn't say that either. He came behind me with my bag. He handed it over and pressed my hand. There was so much contained in that gesture. My eyes must have softened to say it was all reciprocated. Subramani was standing on the platform, the same old black shorts and light yellow T-shirt, the same calm, impassive face. I turned and waved at Bhagesh. Could Subramani have failed to notice the glow in my eyes, the red in my lips? What about the young man waving from the door of the train? Why was Subramani like this? Was it right to call his an innocent love? He lives quietly as if only the moment is true.

'Were you able to sleep?' he asked, as he picked up my bag.

'No, I'll sleep at home. Have you turned on the geyser?'

'Everything's ready. Have breakfast and sleep.'

I had just sat behind him on his bike when my sister called. 'Have you arrived? I'm furious this morning....'

'Look, don't take matters too seriously,' I told her. 'Life is to be lived as it comes. Don't go by what you're seeing now. The truth changes colours sometimes.... You know, you don't have as many problems as you think, and sometimes that is a problem in itself. Relax a bit, keep observing what is happening....'

'Thoo, put the phone down....' she said and disconnected.

I thought I heard a laugh. Could it be Subramani?

30

THE SMEAR PAPERS

SHAWN FERNANDES

You know what I've always loved? That feeling of a day winding down, when everyone knows it's time to close shop and pull down the shutters. It's like a beast settling down for the night, wheezing from exhaustion. The roar of the day slows to a gentle hum; the angry glare of a fiercely fought day gives way to softer, pregnant shadows.

Screens are switched off, drawers locked, bags packed. Everyone around me starts heading out the door, all wrinkled clothes and tired eyes. I roll back in my chair, put my feet up, and wait.

Dev shows up a few minutes past seven, hair ruffled, tie askew, and sleeves messily scrunched up. We don't really have anywhere to be, except our stifling, shared apartments. He throws himself into a chair, pops open a beer, and leans back. 'I don't know why we do it, Zed,' he sighs. 'Actually, hold on. I know why we do it—obviously. My question is, how much longer?'

To give you some context, Dev and I work for one of those mediocrity-celebrating 'media' companies. In the old days, they would report the news. These days, they sell opinions, which has been far more profitable. Not just opinions, they're now also selling the right to shape those opinions around one customer—a brand, a celebrity, a politician—and then sell the 'produced' opinion to the herd of customers we still kindly call 'readers'. So essentially, they're making money from both the source and the destination. Ah, the nobility of the free market mixed in with the reek of corruption.

Where poor saps like Dev and I figure in this sordid process is the first part. It's our job to find people looking to bend public perception their way and then negotiate how much it's likely to cost them. There's no dearth of paying customers looking for a shortcut. Why spend years building a brand when we can help them tell people what to think? A few lengthy pieces and a series of carefully planned photo ops will do the trick.

Of course, the job demands more than just logging in release orders. We've got to finesse our clients, win their favour, keep their secrets, wink and look the other way from time to time. The number of secret hotel rooms I've had to book over the years....

Anyway, back to Dev's question: 'How much longer?'

I pop my own beer, noisily gulp down half, light a smoke, and frame my answer. 'Well, that depends. If I told you I had an idea to open up a massive new revenue stream for both of us, what would you say?'

Dev snorts, 'I'd say you have one of those every week and none of them have ever made it to the next morning. Luckily, I've got fuck-all to do tonight, so let's hear it.'

'Now, consider this. People pay us a lot of money to spread their gospel to the masses. Doesn't matter what their message is, we get it out there. If you run a failing airline, but still want to bed a bevy of models, then we tell them what an inspiration you are for entrepreneurs everywhere. If you're a celeb with legal troubles, we talk about the noble causes you support. Hell, if you've married a monkey-faced millionaire for the money, we talk about your spiritual side.'

Dev is not impressed. This is all pretty obvious to him. 'Sure, we're like the PR version of the Missionaries of Charity and you're Mother Teresa. Is there more?'

'There is more, my cynical friend.' The beer's kicking in, my confidence is building, and I've got a great idea here, I know it. 'Now, imagine we're offering all of those people the opposite of our current services.'

Dev's not seeing it. 'What, you want to not spread their gospel? Do we bill them by the number of people we don't reach? Wait, hold on; we could potentially not reach every single person on earth! Fuck it, I'm handing in my resignation and booking that Gulfstream jet today.'

'Think of it this way: if our clients are willing to pay us ungodly sums of money to say good things about them, they'd probably pay us even more to keep quiet about the less savoury stuff. And you and I both know, there's a lot of information they wouldn't like to see go out into the world?'

I can see the lights slowly coming on in Dev's head. He grabs another beer and swigs deeply. 'So we're playing the WikiLeaks game?'

'Hmm.... Sure, except we get paid.'

Unlike me, Dev still possesses a 'moral compass'. How he's managed three years in this business, I have no idea. 'But isn't that blackmail?'

'You could look at it like that,' I tell him, 'or you could think of it as hitting the man where it hurts. Using their sins against them. Letting some good—as in, money for us—come out of their bad deeds.'

Dev's on his second beer now. 'But, Zed, it's not exactly *right*, is it?'

'What's right, Dev? We do the work we do and get what in return? A salary that just about keeps us fed and clothed while the company's big boys take home the real profits and most of the glory. Sure, we sell lies to the masses, but ask yourself this: if they're stupid enough to buy what we're selling, don't they deserve it? And if everyone else is raking it in, why shouldn't we?'

'Fair point,' he mumbles, 'but isn't it also illegal?'

After three beers, it's easy to sell the answer to that. 'Only if we get caught, Dev. And we aren't going to.'

Here we are, then: we've managed to talk ourselves into believing that blackmail, when carried out with the best intentions, can almost be noble.

Dev's curious about the actual logistics. 'So, how do we do this? Where do we begin? We don't start cold-calling potential customers, do we?'

'That's exactly what we do, Dev! Take the brand manager to whom we've just sold a busload of advertising. Remember when we took him out a few weeks ago and he bragged about their "high-volume, low-cost production centres"? A little prodding revealed that they illegally employed scores of underage workers to toil in dismal conditions in a little shanty in Dharavi. Once we let him know that we're looking to release that information, I'm sure his company would be happy to divert some of their advertising spends to a little PayPal account that we set up.'

'But what if he doesn't believe us?' Dev, ever the pragmatist.

'Then we throw him and his company to the wolves. We need to make an example of someone before people start taking us seriously. Of course, we've got to set up our own website. We'll need a catchy name—something like *The Dirt Times* or *Dirty Laundry*.'

'What about *The Bad Rep Digest*?'

'Sounds like a rap crew trying too hard. No, it's got to be serious; it needs to convey what we're about in cold, no-nonsense terms. I'm thinking *The Smear Papers*—it's direct, it's elegant, even a little menacing.'

Dev wipes his sweaty face; he's excited now. 'That could work! We stay anonymous and set up dummy identities to contact prospective "clients". We target one big-ticket client every month. It'll be like stealing kids' lunches at school all over again!'

It's all laughably easy. 'During the day we slog for the man, after sunset we take a chunk out of his profit margin.'

Beep-beep, beep-beep.

I pull out my phone to look at the time. 10 p.m. We've been at it for three hours. Time to wind things down. We know that this is as far as it's going to go. We do this every week, don't we? We dream up these bizarrely brilliant plans to bust out of our lives of drudgery and obscurity. Dev senses that it's time to call it a night as well. He tips the ashtray into the dustbin and starts to tie his shoelaces.

Suddenly, a light flickers on in one of the cabins down the hall. We'd figured that we were the only ones here, but as it turns out, the Head of Production has stayed back as well. He walks out of his office, towards us. Hopefully he'll have a sense of humour about all of this. He's never liked me. I'm not expecting much. He gets to our table, pulls up a chair, whips out a cheque, and places it on the table. It's a cheque for some serious money and we can't fathom why he's showing it to us.

He's smiling, which makes this even more confusing. He looks at us and says, 'You'll need to flesh out a business plan. And we'll need to figure out how to stay anonymous and on the right side of the law. For now, though, here's me telling you that I want to be your first investor.'

Dev has no words. Neither do I.

I guess we're doing this.

31

GUL

SHREYA ILA ANASUYA

for Saleem Kidwai

*A woman in the shape of a monster
a monster in the shape of a woman
the skies are full of them.*
—Adrienne Rich

The halls of this vast house are windy. There are domed lamps and carpets woven to dizzying intricacy covering every inch of the floor. Honoured guests recline on bolsters, the scent of jasmine wafting on their expensive wrists, fragrant blossoms that are theirs for the taking. But take it from this old courtesan. There are unseen women everywhere, though you will not know them even if I tell you their true names. Step into the shadows, and there they are, filling the halls.

Women who knew how to arch an eyebrow or make a bawdy remark at just the right moment, or laugh wildly, just as they pleased. Expert musicians of their time, breathtaking poets, dancers who could put any master of yours to shame. I know these women, I knew them.

Of them, only very few survived the bloody tides of the Mutiny and its aftermath. The old order, in which they had had a place, perhaps sometimes a precarious and strange one, but a place nonetheless, collapsed entirely. Begum Hazrat Mahal's unending war ended. Lucknow fell and the pale ghosts who arrived to plunder this land bit down on its jugular. All our patrons and paramours scattered; many were hanged, many more exiled. That was the moment the axis of our world shifted—and precisely because it was pivotal and bloody, it is the moment they recount the most.

Lucknow of 1858.

But what is far more brutal is the slow passing of time—what the pale ghosts started, the good people of this land made sure to finish. People of high standing, wearing crisp cotton woven by hand, lovers of music and culture all—people who couldn't move a finger without walking on the backs of those who washed their fine clothes and scrubbed their inherited mansions clean. They wrung our necks; they smiled as they did it. Over the next few decades, those of us who would not, or could not, afford to hide our origins were pushed, pushed, pushed—whirling away from the centre of the mehfil to the corners, where most of us lingered, where our daughters linger, where their daughters will linger until the last one perishes.

Some of us survived it. Some through marriage, some by hiding our true names, some by becoming safe embodiments of the very world that had been destroyed. I, Munni Begum, survived by doing all of this. This is how you still hear my voice, echoing at you from the years that stretch between us. This is the plain truth—I am among a handful who were lucky.

And then there was Gulbadan.

She arrived one morning at Zeenat Bai's establishment. I was nineteen then and had been performing for a few years. She wouldn't tell us where she came from, but that was par for the course for us. She was no girl, but time had not left its mark on her face in the way it criss-crosses most faces. It only became a kind of knowing that never left her eyes, even when her moon-face was twisted in peals of laughter.

She had exquisite, long fingers, and a perfectly straight back. She held her body with the ease and grace of a dancer. Her voice was low—honeyed when it needed to be and rumbling when the situation demanded, breaking and circling and echoing through our usual repertoire of songs that were either about love or worship, or often about both at the same time. Ghazal, thumri, qawwali—she could sing it all with ease, locking eyes with each person in the audience so that, for a moment, they felt like the only person in the world.

It was this quality that quickly made her one of the most feted tawaifs in Chowk. It was not simply that she was considered beautiful or that she could be perfectly charming; there was something else about Gul that made people of all kinds throw themselves in her path.

I saw nawabs blush when she winked at them during a performance, sigh when she seemed to consider them lovingly for a minute and then turn away, her eyes flashing like the diamond in her nose. In a matter of three months she was adding more to Zeenat Bai's coffers than could have been expected of any new entrant to the house.

There, I have told you the public version. It is no secret. Anyone who was alive then and knew her will tell you as much. That she was skilful. That she was magnetic. That she was a mistress of her arts.

But what nobody knows about her is that she was my Gul.

I was besotted with her. She could tilt her head at me and I would trace the arch of her eyebrows in my head for nights afterwards. She made me feel impossibly tender. If we were simply lounging together early in the evening, the sound of her smoke-filled voice would have me tracing circles on my thigh.

She knew it, of course, though she feigned not knowing at first. I could not have hidden it from her for all my trying. I tried hard, embarrassed at the force of my own passion, confused by the heavy presence of her in my breath, in all my days. She had reached out and taken my heart in her fist, simply, easily, just by standing before me one morning.

I suppose I should not have been surprised that she crushed it just as easily when she fled in the suffocating days following the end of the Mutiny. This is after she had lifted my chin one evening in the middle of me reciting a foolish ghazal I had written in her honour and made my heart leap to my throat when she kissed me softly. I could not believe she loved me back, and never fully trusted that she did, although she insisted as much to me in hushed whispers when we awoke entwined some mornings, or by way of thrilling notes that she passed to me even as we hurried to change our finery in the middle of crowded performances.

Her love was lush, it is true, but it was entirely on her terms.

She chose the nights I could spend in her chambers, and this I did not mind. What I did mind was the way she dismissed our relationship in front of the other girls in the house. This was by no means the first time in Zeenat Bai's house that two women had fallen in love. But because of Gul's magnetism, her popularity, the way so many of the men who came to our salons were as besotted with her as I, the household's acceptance of our relationship was hesitant. About this she did absolutely nothing; there was no sign in front of them of the ardour she displayed when we were alone together.

She remained icily silent when my eyes filled with tears if she took a lover from among our patrons. But when I tried to rebel by taking up with Samina, my age-mate and equal in the household, Gul's retaliation was swift and unforgiving. Her anger was always reserved solely for me, and only behind the closed doors of her room. There she became something else, my moon-faced Gul, when she showed her teeth to me in a way that had nothing to do with smiling. The dark spot high on one bronzed cheek, her eyes the colour of burning coal, her waist-length raven hair, her full, dark lips—all this seemed to melt away in that moment, and the enchantment of her face turned fiercer, wilder. I was in love with her; I was terrified of her. Fear and love became locked in a fierce embrace, and fed each other like air feeds fire.

But then a different, more menacing fear gripped our entire household. The pale ghosts introduced a rifle that used ammunition encased in paper greased with the fat of both cows and pigs. In order to load their rifles before firing, Indian soldiers would need to tear open the cartridges with their teeth. An entire regiment refused to do so and was punished mercilessly for disobeying. That is when, you can say, our troubles began, for many of the plans for the long months of rebellion that followed were hatched in our very salons.

Those months were subdued; the air itself felt oppressive. We had fewer performances, and when we did, the mehfils were not as joyful as they had once been. With more time on our hands, Gul and I started shopping for the household ourselves. Sometimes we took Zeenat Bai's only son, Karim, with us to help us haul our bags home. Karim's birth, unlike his sisters', had not been celebrated, nor had he been as extensively educated as them, so he earned his keep by running errands for the house and making sure our books were kept in order.

On the day before I was to turn twenty, Gul insisted she wanted to make me some kheer, and we went to buy the ingredients—thick, fresh milk, fragrant saffron, and raisins. Karim came along and the three of us were in good humour after what felt like aeons. Gul was wearing a simple embroidered kurta of white, and as usual her diamond pin flashed on her face. To this day when I think of her, it is this image of this Gul that comes to me—fresh-faced, light, laughing easily.

Perhaps this was the final moment of my innocence, the final blossoming of the years in which I had spent so much time immersed in reading and writing, understanding music and dance, learning how to converse and compose. It was a light that a darkening world cannot bear, especially on the faces of women, especially on the faces of women such as I. Perhaps someone cast an evil eye upon us. Perhaps I was too happy, despite the fact that things were crumbling around us, and I had no right to be. Perhaps I loved her too much.

For at that very next moment Gul caught the eye of a Lal Kurti. The officer stopped us with a glint in his eye, which travelled to his mouth and became a smirk as he looked long and lasciviously at Gul. My blood curdled. I wanted to tear his eyes off her and I was about to say something. She knew me so well that she sensed it and put a steadying hand on me. Karim, beside me, seemed struck silent with fear. I had never felt so humiliated.

Then he spoke, in the kind of accent we had mocked hundreds of times. 'How much for a turn with you, girl?'

I started forward, but Gul pushed me back. I whirled to look at her. In the entire year I had spent with her, I had never seen the kind of cold fury that washed over her face then.

'What did you say to me?' She spoke in a voice I did not know. It boomed with the power of a thousand more, echoes within echoes. My stomach felt cold as ice. For a few seconds, the market seemed to cease its jostling around us. Then, as suddenly as it had seemed to be sucked out of the world, the clamour came back. I saw the soldier's face tighten, but he didn't seem to be startled, like I was. 'Don't waste my time, girl. I know you are one of those nautch girls. Don't make me haul you off.'

She had arranged her face into a too-radiant smile. I knew this face well, she used it with particularly cloying patrons, who wanted to hang around too long after the mehfil was officially over. 'Come with me, sahib, my rooms are just around the corner.'

I stared at her, but they were off already. I watched them for a few seconds before I ran after them. She glanced back and shot me a look. *Stand back*, it said. *I know what I am doing.*

When she emerged from the alley she had led him into a mere handful of minutes later, it was by herself. She refused to say a word to me all the way home, while I cried silent tears of rage and confusion. The fear had returned, so intense I was virtually incapacitated, though she said nothing, and scarcely even looked at me—and it was here to stay, for the next morning she had disappeared.

We had spent the night together, but she had said she would much rather speak the next morning. I usually awoke if she did, but that night I had felt unusually laden with sleep—when we finally slept—and did not stir. When I woke up to the first rays of the sun filtering through her gauze curtains, I noticed that I was alone. The cream bed sheets—usually tied in place—were rumpled, her satin-wrapped pillow abandoned. I thought she had gone to wash her face, and stretched while I waited for her, anxious to discuss what had passed the day before.

Some strands of her impossibly thick hair lay scattered upon her lightly embroidered pillow. They made me think of our love-making the night before, how forceful we both had been, different from the languorous nights I had come to expect from our time together, nights I savoured. But the night before had left a tight knot of desire in me still, I wanted more of her—and the unanswered questions from the market only made me more restless. As the light outside intensified, I grew more and more nervous, and still she did not return.

By midday, the household began to hum with questions. By then, I had searched everywhere, every room, every balcony, every terrace. I had run out of the gates, madly, tears streaming down my face, and Zeenat Bai had to restrain me. I had punched Karim when he tried to placate me, and I had refused to stop screaming her name until they shut me up in her room. They did not do it unkindly, nor was I left alone—Samina was there with me, but nothing would console me.

I was sure she was in danger. Perhaps the soldier had returned under cover of night and taken her. Perhaps even now she lay dead in an alley somewhere. My moon-faced Gul would never have left me on purpose, I knew. She had been taken, and had I been allowed to leave the house I would have scoured the city for her, looked in every street and corner until I found her and brought her back to me.

And then, in the afternoon, just as I had fallen into an exhausted stupor, the doors of her rooms were flung open and I came face to face with three Lal Kurtis. 'Where is she? Gulbadan?'

Before they could stop me I ran out to the main halls, where more Lal Kurtis were stationed. Zeenat Bai was sitting on the floor, coolly gurgling at her hookah. The man Plowden, their captain and our sometime patron, was questioning her. Strange to see him here after so many months—he had attended many of our mujras and his wife, Lucy, had had a special fondness for Gul. She had even asked Gul for lessons. Zeenat Bai wore a tight smile on her face. 'I do not know where she is, sahib, she has abandoned the hearth that fed her for a year. She is as faithless as a wildcat.' Zeenat Bai was nothing if not astute. I knew that most of her valuables and our money had already been spirited away, just enough remained in the house that they could take. I was hopeful then, thinking she herself had stowed Gul away somewhere. But in a second, she said something that dashed my hopes. 'And I'm well rid of her, for I will have no murderer in my house.'

I shrieked then, and she started. 'Shut up, you foolish, lovesick girl. Your precious Gul seems to have killed a soldier that she was seen talking to in the market yesterday. They found him in an alley this morning, not a single mark on him, dead as a block of wood. Lord knows in what dark arts she dealt, to be able to do this.... She has left all of us here to rot, you included. Pull yourself together, or get out of my sight.'

I do not know how I spent the next weeks, months, year. At first I refused to perform, and they let me be. I kept vigil by her windows, by sunlight, moonlight, and candlelight. I scarcely ate or slept. I cried until the tears ran dry, and when I could no longer cry I read poetry she had written through swollen eyes. In my head I heard her sing, a monsoon dadra about dark clouds gathering, a woman tormented by the absence of her lover. I felt myself floating out of my body, and from my vantage point near the ceiling I saw the thing I had become: hollow-eyed, my hair unwashed and in knots, my lips dry. I had become the absence of Gul.

After a few months, Zeenat Bai herself started coming to feed me. She called the munshi to read me poetry, she dragged me to see the other girls rehearse for mehfils. Soon, she began pestering me to sing again, lamenting, screaming that all that education had been wasted on me, that I was not the first girl to be betrayed by a lover, that my name would forever be lost if I did not come to my senses.

I had begun to feel other sensations slowly, and this included a considerable degree of guilt, for I had contributed nothing to the household income for over six months. I began to sing again, though I still could not bring myself to dance. I sang with lowered eyes. But my voice, when it emerged again after a few days of careful riyaz, surprised me. I had been a competent enough singer before, my training substantial enough and my delight in poetry genuine, so that I could sing convincingly. This voice, though, was different—richer, deeper, unwavering, and immense, as though it was coming from somewhere else. Had I always had this ability and, obsessed with my love for Gul, never noticed it? Or had she, by leaving me—for I knew by then that she had deliberately left me—made me into the singer I had become? I do not know, except that now when I sang about longing I felt it in my bones, when I sang about the fecklessness of a lover I understood the words, and the bylanes and alleyways of the music itself, like I never had before. Betrayal had enriched my voice, and anger, when it gathered, fuelled my riyaz, so that I began to sing more and more, better and better, each raag I learned and each thumri I mastered an answer to Gul's desertion.

And that is the voice you now know, if you know your music. The voice that took me in the decades of my life that followed to the Delhi Durbar to sing before King George, the voice by which I made a fortune for myself, setting up my own establishment at the passing of Zeenat Bai, and eventually buying property all over the city even as many of the women I had grown up surrounded by faded into obscurity. As they retreated to the shadows, pursued by lectures on morality and demonized as being unclean, I took my spot in the light. Yet, even as I prospered, my heart crumbled.

I met and married a devastatingly beautiful businessman, Irfan Ali Khan, and became Munni Begum. His family disdained me and threatened to disown him. For a time, I was forced to give up music, but through that time he loved me truly, and could not bear to see me with my face tightened in agony as I watched others, always others, perform. Much quarreling and cajoling later, his family decided that I could sing anywhere in the country, as long as I sang nowhere I could sully their good name. And so I took off to Benaras, to Rampur, to Calcutta, with Karim acting as my manager, and a handful of young pupils in tow.

It is not that I did not love again. I was very fond of my husband, I enjoyed his gentleness, his fine mind. I liked making love to him. But I never loved him like I had loved Gul, and if our partnership lacked the inconsistency and ultimate cruelty of the one I had shared with her, it also never matched its life-giving fire. Now, what set my pulse dancing was singing, and teaching the young girls whose training I had been entrusted with. To them I was everything, they called me their mother and followed me where I went. The older ones, in some years, started accompanying me onstage.

Eventually, long after my body died, they would be celebrated, honours conferred upon them by famous men. But even as their greatness would be lauded, they would always be known as pupils of the great Munni Begum. Some would write books about their years with me, and one or two would sing forever like me, never finding that precious and irreplaceable thing—the power of their own voices. The more successful ones would train many pupils of their own, and one would start a school in my name, established in my honour. For I would become what only a handful of humans become through what they leave in their wake—immortal.

But you've read this script. Greatness, true greatness, is only conferred upon the crone. As maiden and grown woman, whispers followed me, and even as my career arced upward like a meteor, it would be years before my considerable donations to the freedom movement would even be acknowledged. I was old when they came to love me simply for my music, for by that time my origins and my story became two different things.

In one's sixth decade, it is difficult to stay angry. What fire I had in my belly I reserved for music, for the push and pull of the taan, for the trick and love affair of singing two exquisite lines of poetry in three different and expansive ways. I had outlived my husband by ten years already, and had immersed myself in caring for my pupils. Still, what artist with some ambition remaining can resist the lure of the capital? Younger women than I were thronging to Calcutta, playing parts on the stage at the big theatres—Star, Minerva, Classic. Some of them had been dancers, some could sing.

The capital called to me, the same pale ghosts who had so tormented us during the Mutiny were soliciting women of my talents to sing for a new contraption that had been created, for which a man called Gaisberg was meeting with gaanewalis both young and experienced.

It was called the gramophone player, a golden creature with a gaping flower for a head and a box at its tail. This is how you sang for it—you not only had to scream into the blasted cylinder that snatched at your voice, you had to hurry it up. A lingering thumri would not do—you had to squeeze the song, with all of its pathos and play, into less than one-third of the time you would otherwise have had with it. And, when you were done, you had to tell the machine your name, or they would not know who on earth you were.

We had taken some rooms in the Great Eastern Hotel, and it was there that Gaisberg had set up his little studio. Every day I spied the young girls going in and emerging. Gaisberg's assistant, a reedy Bengali man named Sen, had approached us—but even though we were there, Karim remained sceptical.

'I don't know, Muniya...I have heard some strange things about this machine.... Let's wait and see,' he told me.

'Like what? Don't tell me this is like that time those men came to photograph me?' I teased. All these years of working and living with me, and my poor Karim was still so naive! It went back to our upbringing—so differently were we brought up in the same house and by the same woman. My affection for him strengthened rather than waned because of this.

'Muniya, I am serious. Someone from Janki Bai's party told me that the machine...it traps bits of your soul into it every time it catches your voice. It may be best to stay away.' I began to laugh and he knew he had already lost the fight. After this, I decided to not push the gramophone issue too much with him; I knew I could make him come around in a few days. I could do what I pleased, but he was my oldest friend, and I did not like to frighten him.

The Bengalee had a review of a show in town, played by a tremendous new actress called Elokeshi. Zoha, my oldest pupil, had cajoled Karim to take us to the Star that evening to see her play Janabai.

The theatre that evening was absolutely packed. I had dressed in one of my favourite saris and put my hair up carefully into a bun, but in the quiet hush of the theatre just before the show, everyone's eyes, including my own, were turned towards the stage. I heard the soft creak of one of the doors being opened and turned around in some irritation. I should not have paid it much mind but something kept my eyes on the figure that slid quietly inside. She was simply dressed, almost nondescript, but when she passed me, I recognized her with a start, with a pain in my heart that is impossible to capture in words.

The only person I had known my entire life who could have captured it with her song was now looking directly at me, as surely as she had looked at me when I was only nineteen: Gulbadan.

And she looked exactly as she did then—how was this possible? And how was it possible that no one else noticed her, not even Karim, seated beside me? As though she was putting on a private performance meant only for me, the woman I had known as Gulbadan transformed before my very eyes. Her limbs looked somehow more supple, her hair grew longer and more lustrous, her face suddenly—terrifyingly—sharper. Her clothes changed, became a mendicant's, her forehead suddenly marked with a little ash. And, almost as though she had always been there, she was onstage, and everyone around me broke into applause.

That evening Gul—Elokeshi—gave the best performance I had seen her give. It would be a surprise if audiences forever after did not call her Jana. There was a standing ovation at the end, and she was called back onstage by the audience's cheers. She returned, bowed, disappeared.

My heart hammering, I turned to Karim, who had not recognized her at all. How could he? He had only been allowed to see her terrible beauty, the face of Elokeshi.

I did not say a word to him. I spent the night awake as I had once lain awake thinking about her after she had left decades before. But now I began to see how she could have been so clairvoyant. Her little tricks. Her great skills. Her overwhelming fame. Her ability to slip away at will. Her face, teeth bared, monstrous in anger.

She was not just a keeper of lore. She was part of its very fabric.

The next day I told Karim I had an evening appointment with Gaisberg and went back to the theatre. I watched her again. I was certain she knew I was there. And, acting upon my certainty, I went backstage. I told an attendant to let her know Muniya was here to see her. In a matter of minutes, I was inside her dressing room.

Her hair was long, loose. Her moon-face full, not a day older than she had looked when I was so much younger. Her eyebrows arched darkly on her forehead. She smiled; her face shifted, she made herself, again, the Gul of old.

'How are you, my love?' She was smiling as she once had, in the way that had wrenched my heart when I first met her...a way that she knew, I could see, still worked.

'Gul.'

'I owe you an apology, my darling, and an explanation. But I am afraid I am only able to give you one of these things. Please accept my sincerest apologies. I should not have left you like that.' She was calm, perfectly calm, calm in a way that frightened me even more.

'What I saw last night...that was you? What were you doing? What....'

'What am I? Only cloud and water, my love. I am Elokeshi on the Bengali stage. I was Mah Laqa in Hyderabad, and a long time ago, I was called Amrapali. In the coming years I will have more names and faces.

The calamities are not over for our kind, my darling one. I am so glad you made a name for yourself. It will carry you far.'

'I have so much to ask you. So much to tell. Come with me, spend some time with me.'

'I wish I could have stayed, Muniya....'

I knew then she meant to leave me again. For the first time in many years, I felt an old resentment swell up inside me.

'Why do you do this?' I asked. 'Play with a little human life?'

She turned to me then, eyes flashing. If she was capable of being hurt, I had managed to hurt her. I felt a tiny whiff of satisfaction. 'I never played with you. Never. It gets exhausting, watching people die. It is better to go when you get too close.... My love, it was good to see you again.'

With that, she opened the dressing room door, and was almost borne away by the crowd that thronged outside. It called her name, 'Elokeshi!', and wanted to swallow her up. She paused, turned. Her face was different again—tinged with softness. I saw an old fire in her eyes, older than me, older than time, a fire at which I had warmed myself in the time we had had together, and without knowing it, for years after.

We looked at one another for a long moment. Then she spoke again, this time with a new urgency. 'Listen, there is something called the gramophone now, it can copy your beautiful voice for people in another time. You must record as soon as you can.'

What was this? I could not fathom why she wanted to now focus on something so inconsequential. 'I intend to, Karim doesn't trust the machine, says he hears strange things about it.'

'What, that it captures a little bit of your soul and keeps it trapped inside it forever?' She laughed then, the same wolfish laugh that undid me as though I were still a waif of nineteen, the same fear gripping my insides as though it had never gone away. 'It's true, my love. It's all true. And that is why you must do it. Do it.' She opened the door, stepped away.

I stood there alone, blinking in the sudden light.

∞

Bombay, 1995

Amol is hooked, he can't help it. He's at Sagar Bar every night with his buddies, after a day of running around collecting for their bosses, occasionally beating up the shopkeepers and business owners who won't pay up. The work is exciting and the money is easy, and how better to spend it than see moon-faced Rosy every night?

Raju and Guru are in the mood to heckle him tonight. 'What, took your girl to Apsara Theatre again yesterday? What were you doing? Watching the picture, or something else?'

Bastards. They love their dancers too. Raju is even seeing one of the girls, Meena. Besides, Rosy doesn't let him touch her. He doesn't much care. Being with her every evening—being the man who gets to do that—this is somehow enough. He isn't used to this…this feeling. Is this what all the film songs are about?

Just look at her. The most famous dancer in the joint, men throw thousands and thousands of rupees at her in the course of one night. And why shouldn't they? Look at her whirling, her skirts aglow, the silver moons embroidered on them gleaming. She is dancing to an old ghazal, something about thousands of men driven mad by her eyes. When she dances like that, when she smiles like that and looks at him, he feels like the only man in the room.

Afterwards, he is impatient to go home. She is not one to be pushed, so he waits—what else is he going to do? He watches even as Raju and Guru leave with their girlfriends. Finally, she emerges, dressed in a simple white kurta.

'Rosy, jaan, I've got something for you. Come, let's go to your rooms, na.'

She is indulgent today. The season's first rains have begun. She had once told him the monsoon was her favourite season.

In her rooms with the gauzy curtains and the old-fashioned lamps he proudly pulls the disc out of a slim bag. It has the flat, round face of an old singer on it—it looks impossibly old, like it belongs to a different world. '*Munni Begum—Classic Hits*! See, huh?' He is delighted, nervous. He doesn't quite understand this music himself, but he knows she likes it.

The rain starts to fall gently outside, and inside they let the little needle fall on the black disc which turns and turns. The song is about dark clouds gathering, a woman looking for her lover. Rosy closes her eyes and throws her head back. He feels a rush of love overcome him. When she opens her dark eyes he thinks he can see pinpricks of tears in them. She smiles. 'It's gorgeous,' she whispers.

In the flickering light, the diamond in her nose glints, and you could be forgiven for thinking that her face changes ever so slightly.

32

MY GRANDMOTHER TALKS ABOUT SHIT

SRIVIDYA TADEPALLI

When my grandmother visits us, she stays in my room. We sleep on my tiny bed even though I am now too old to be sharing a bed with her and her snoring has got worse over the years. To sleep separately would be to admit that things have changed, and neither of us is interested in acknowledging this truth. Instead, we lie next to each other and talk until one of us falls asleep.

Over the past few years, she has become completely deaf in one ear. The joke in the family is that whenever she calls on one of us to come over to her right side, it means that she is going to be telling us something she shouldn't be telling us. I always lay on her right on my bed, and she would tell me stories about growing up in her family. Her stories have always been unnecessarily long and detailed, but old age and partial deafness have made them longer and even more detailed, and I've had to start pretending to fall asleep far too early for my own liking.

When she came to see us this time, we lay on the bed and I was just starting to fall asleep when she said, 'Do you know how much shit I've had to clean up in my lifetime?'

She sat up. I could see the time on the watch she wore on her wrist. Just an hour ago, the family had dispersed towards their respective beds after announcing that it was too late to continue any conversation. I had been reading a book when Ammamma pinched my earlobe affectionately and told me that dinner was done and it was time for our two-person slumber party.

'Do you know how much shit I've had to clean up in my lifetime?' she asked softly now, again, an hour after I heard her first snore. It didn't sound like a question this time. She was staring straight ahead so if I had chosen not to respond, she might have gone right back to sleep.

She never sits up; our conversations are never that serious. But she was sitting up this time, and she said without waiting for me to respond, 'When your Thatha and I had just got married, we lived with his parents for a while. After his mother passed away, his father became—well—difficult. He stopped remembering how to go about his day. He would wake up in the mornings and forget to put on his clothes, forget to go to the toilet, forget to eat food. When he left the house, he could never remember why he left or how to come back home. One time, he went missing for three days, and everyone, even our neighbours, went out looking for him; skipping meals and searching through the night. I couldn't eat for three days. When we finally found him, he was in our neighbour's cowshed. When he saw me, he started to sob and asked me why I had disappeared.'

'He hadn't eaten for three days?' I asked. Now I sat up too, intrigued by the image of my great-grandfather lost in a cowshed for three days. She nodded and stood up. She turned the bright tube light on and began to look through her suitcase while I shielded my eyes in pain.

'Imagine how afraid he must have been. I was the only one who took him seriously. Everyone else had already become sick of him by then. They called him attention-seeking.' She took out her bottle of lotion and started to massage her foot. 'Here, let me do it,' I said, and took her foot into my lap. 'I don't blame the others for thinking that,' she continued. 'Sometimes he deliberately gave them a hard time. When your mother started college and would bring her friends home for lunch over the weekend, he would wait until they had all started to eat before coming out naked to greet them.'

'Completely naked?' I asked, massaging her other foot now.

'Butt naked. What an awful way to see a penis for the first time.' I laughed and she blushed and hid her face, apologizing for using the word out loud. 'I was used to cleaning his susu and potty all the time. One time, I brought relatives over to see him, and he pissed and shat in the living room while they were there. I didn't want to make him feel bad, so I continued to converse with them while I cleaned it up, acting like nothing had happened. The most distinct memory I have of him is when I left Tirupathi for two days to write my exams in Chennai and came back. The whole house smelled of his shit. No one else thought to clean him regularly while I was gone, so when I saw him, lying on his bed, he had been lying in his own shit for two days, and he just smiled at me. I didn't even change my clothes then; I just started cleaning him up in the same sari I was wearing. It was difficult, but I felt so much tenderness for him that day. I still remember it.'

We got back into bed and I had just started to dream when she said, 'Last year, I was in my brother's house, and my sisters and their friends were there too. Some puja was happening, so I was sitting in Pranav's room. Have I told you he has a secret girlfriend now? All day he sleeps and all night he talks to his girlfriend. Anyway, so I was sitting in his room, and suddenly one of my sister's friends came in and we greeted each other 'Jai Jinendra' and she was very tense and said all the other bathrooms were occupied, and could she use the one in the room I was in. So I told her this was an Indian-style toilet, and that it might be difficult for her to squat. She was a large woman and fairly old also. But she was in a hurry. When she was done, she walked out normally and went and sat by my sister outside and I continued to read my book. A few hours later, Pranav came home and went to his bathroom. He had just come back from his classes—that's what he tells his father, but I know he was actually meeting his girlfriend. He and his father have been fighting about it for one year now. She's Maharashtrian, and my brother has a problem with that and I told him not to be stupid, I didn't marry a Jain boy and my life turned out better than his, but they'll never listen and Pranav doesn't make it any easier for himself either, he's so stubborn and always lying to his parents and—'

'Ammamma, he told me they broke up last month.'

'Oh. Anyway, Pranav came home and went to his bathroom, and then he ran back outside and said, "Madhu faiba, I'm going to vomit, go see the toilet." So I went in and you won't believe what I saw.'

At this point I pulled away my grandmother's blanket and covered my head with it, 'No, no, no, don't give me details, I don't want to know, please!' But my grandmother continued her story 'It was as if someone had let a demon child in there. There was shit on the walls and all over the floor, and there was some blood, but mostly just watery shit. She could have called me aside and told me that she was having trouble, and would I please not mind helping her clean it up. But she didn't even look at me again that day. By then the whole house could smell it, so I changed into my nightie and cleaned it. The poor thing must have been so uncomfortable; she didn't have a change of clothes or anything. Being old and alone is a curse, I tell you. If something like that had happened to me, your thatha would have definitely cleaned it up and then given me some medicine and a change of clothes. He was a good man. It's good he died first. Being old and alone is a curse.'

I linked arms with her. 'You cleaned it all by yourself?!'

'Who else would have done it? My brothers and sisters are all lazy, that's no secret. They're only good for pretending to be praying all the time.'

By this point, the light was on and she had already started another story. I knew I wouldn't be sleeping any time soon. I put my head in her lap and she played with my hair as she said, 'Another time, I was in your Narayanaguda nani's house, and I ended up cleaning the shit off some small boy who lived in the same apartment building. Don't laugh. It's one of my worst memories of your family. We were all talking and suddenly we heard screams from the corridor outside. Nani went to check and came back and said it was nothing. But the screaming continued, so I insisted that she tell us what was happening, and she told us casually that some child was stuck in the elevator. I asked her if she had called someone for help, and she said the security guard was there but she had asked him to wait a while before helping him come out.'

'Why wait a while?!' I asked, sitting up again.

'I don't even know if I should be telling you this story. Don't tell your mother I told you, she'll be angry with me. Apparently, that little boy used to play with the lift all the time, always going up and down for no reason. Your nani decided this would be a good time to teach him a lesson, and she left him there to scream for help for some time so he'd never play with the lift again. When she told us this, I thought I was going to cry. I'm finding it harder and harder to be around people. Your thatha always knew how to get out of such company politely, but I've never learnt to do anything other than sit and smile. Anyway, I just quietly went outside and asked the security thatha to help me bring the boy out. After we pulled him out, he just kept crying and crying. He held on to my legs tightly and refused to talk to me. He came up to my waist, that's how small he was. Why people like your nani and nana become parents, God give me the patience to understand. His parents weren't at home and he had shat his pants. So I took him downstairs and washed him under a tap. He vomited right after that, so I washed him again. And then I washed his clothes and waited with him until his parents came home half an hour later.'

'Why didn't you just take him up to the house?'

'What if she had said something terrible to him? I also just wanted an excuse to get out of that house. You'd think people become nicer as they grow older. Are you falling asleep? Don't think I've run out of stories, I meant it when I said I've cleaned a lot of shit in my lifetime.'

'I believe you,' I said and hugged her. 'But how about we continue tomorrow night? It's already three in the morning;' I pointed to her watch, 'so it's tonight, not even tomorrow night.'

'No, tomorrow night I have to tell you a very important story about your thatha and I.... Tonight, I mean.'

'You should have told me that story instead! Tell me now!'

'No. It'll have to wait.' She turned off the light, turned around, and started to snore.

33

THE ISSUE

TANUJ SOLANKI

They were both so scared of the frenetic movements of the fat lizard in their bedroom that they decided to spread a single mattress (extracted from the double bed's storage) on the living room floor. The mattress's width enforced a kind of intimacy that was different from what had been available on the wider bed, so much so that they soon got talking, for the first time, about the biggest issue in their lives at that point. She told him that she really wanted to know how he felt about her going. Knowing that was important for her. He told her that she was going and that was that. The important thing, he added, was whether she was sure she was going for the right reasons. Being practical. For example, how convinced was she that the programme would lead to bigger and better job prospects? That it would improve their finances in the medium term. She cut him short, telling him that first of all it needed to be clear that it was he who was making things difficult by not talking about the exact reasons why he was feeling what he was feeling. It was quite obvious that he wasn't feeling all right. Instead, she emphasized, what he was doing at this point was to present his insecurity as her own doubt about her future, which wasn't very helpful because, of course, she was a bit doubtful already and her decision to go was at some level a leap of faith. The living room lights were switched off and in the darkness they heard each other breathe a couple of times before he told her that 'No,' it was she who was making things difficult. Her decision to go would unsettle their current lives. He asked her if she agreed and she nodded and even in the darkness he knew that she had nodded because she was in his arms and he felt the movement on his shoulder. The most important question, he told her, was if she was convinced that unsettling their current lives was worth the trouble and that after the trouble was over their life together would be better than what they had right now. 'Ideally, it shouldn't be a leap of faith,' he said. That he used the word 'trouble' for her education, she told him, told her a lot. He tried to say something in response but she didn't let him and silenced him by saying 'One minute, one minute, one minute….' How many times, she asked him then, had he been completely convinced of the outcome of any new step that he was taking in his life? Weren't all new endeavours, she continued, leaps of faith to some degree, and if the world went by his logic, there wouldn't be anything new that anyone would ever strive for. He snorted. She told him that there was nothing worth snorting about in what they were discussing. Of course, there was nothing wrong with doing new things, he told her. But their situation was different. They had to attempt to put some reason behind it. They were married. And need he also remind her what that meant? It meant that their lives were tied. 'The expense of your education is big,' he said, 'and while you're sure that you're going to finance it on your own, and while that is something that I both admire and appreciate, there shouldn't be any doubt that if the new endeavour fails, the liability of that failure will be shared by both of us, and by our marriage. To the extent that our lives are inextricably tied together, you are also deciding for me.' At this, she lifted her head slightly and tapped his hand so that he could take it out from under her. They now lay such that they both faced the dark ceiling above where they both saw little else but a recurrent gleam on a blade of the ceiling fan as it completed each rotation, a few times per second, such that the gleaming looked to them like a flickering light, and they both thought of that flickering as the light at the end of a metaphorical tunnel; but since neither of them communicated this idea to the other, their biggest moment of connection that night, in which their inner lives had somehow led to the exact same thought, and the astounding beauty of this concordance, the stunning humanity of it, even, was lost to the universe and lost to their story as well. She asked him, in a soft voice, why he doubted her reasons. 'I wonder what reasons you think I have,' she said. 'What do you think your reasons are?' he asked. She told him that the university she had been admitted to was the best in the world to study what she wanted to study, and that she wanted to study at this stage in her life because she still had a lot to learn, and that she wanted to attend the university because it had a name and that name did, in most cases, boost the careers of those who attended it. She also made it clear that when she had asked him about his feelings a few minutes back, it was not to initiate this interrogation of her motivations but to know what emotions the knowledge of their imminent year-long separation evoked in him. 'It was an emotional question,' she said. If he had said that he was sad because he was going to miss her, it would have been enough. 'That part is true,' he said, 'it is.' But the real thing, he told her, the real thing was that in an ideal world he wouldn't want her to go or not to go because of him, but then he also understood that her decision to go had not much to do with him, and that fact hurt simply because they were married and her decision left it open for him to interpret that she was being selfish. She told him that her decision to go was, of course, her decision alone. But even in decisions that were completely hers, was it wrong to expect his support? Was it wrong to expect that he would stand by her and give her strength and even help her with the details? His support could not be made mandatory, he answered. 'You do realize that support here means nothing more than enthusiastically agreeing with your decision to go,' he said. So had he decided not to be supportive, she asked him. And were they at least agreeing to disagree, were they at least at a point where it was clear that she wanted to go and he did not want her to go? And would he mind checking what percentage of his opinion was due to his irritation at her having made an independent decision? 'Don't entangle me in the stupid patriarchy web,' he responded. 'Your independence is not in question.' Then it must be the financial strain, she told him, the strain that wasn't present but he feared would be upon him in case she didn't get a job with a salary fat enough to pay off the loan quickly. 'Yes,' he said, 'that is part of it.' And the fact that she didn't ever think of this in this light. And the fact that a job with a big salary for her would mean a job in the US. And the fact that he would have to follow her to the US. That he would have to leave his job in India. That he would have to quit his life in India. That this was not just about her doing a one-year programme at an Ivy League school but about the two of them committing to a certain kind of life for the rest of their lives, and also saying goodbye to the life that they already had, which, he felt compelled to point out, wasn't a bad life at all. 'If you haven't thought about all of this,' he said, 'then is it wrong to say that you've been a bit selfish? Or maybe selfish is too offensive a word. Let's just say you were too happy with your achievement to pause and think about what it really meant.' She told him that she had thought about it all and that she had wanted to talk about it all with him. But he never seemed in the mood, and even today it was she who had initiated the discussion. 'Your silence,' she said, 'or rather your reluctance to talk about things is itself a hurdle, do you realize that? You've drowned yourself, I think deliberately, in your phones and screens recently. When I come to you to talk about something, you prefer to stick to nods and grunts, as if words are too risky.' He told her that this silence was his submission. It was the support that she wanted. 'This is the problem, this,' she said. She told him that he was extreme, that he either had to take the high moral ground, telling her what marriage was, and what she was failing to understand of it, or he had to be the silent sufferer, mutely watching her trample over his idea of his life. For him, it was always about being victor or victim, never a partner. And when he played victim, he still expected her to comprehend his imaginary loss without even talking to him and then also to change the things that might turn that imaginary loss around. 'So you see,' she said, 'you are a victor even when you play victim.' She then told him that the final point to be made from her side was that she wouldn't go if he didn't want her to go but it would make her sad. The fan rotated as before. He rose and switched on a light. 'We aren't sleeping,' he said, 'and I prefer to see you while we talk.' Then he lay back on the mattress in his earlier position, in which he wasn't really looking at her but at the ceiling fan. He then told her that if she decided not to go because he didn't want her to and would then become sad, it would be the worst thing that she could possibly do to him. He clarified that he had never said that he did not want her to go. He had never said those words. He had reservations, and they hadn't talked about them. And, yes, it was his fault. But the situation was now at a point where he couldn't feel good with any outcome. And he certainly didn't want her to be sad because that would, in turn, make him sad and condemn them to live with the potentiality of a different life always hanging like a sword above their marriage. There would be resentment that could linger till old age. At least with her going and him following her, they would always have a life to return to if the new one failed. 'You should go,' he said, 'and we will find a way.' She didn't know what to say, and so she turned towards him, and whispered, 'I love you.' It took a quarter of a minute of inner turbulence before he decided that he did not really want to respond with a 'Me too.' She put her arm over his chest and came closer. 'I really want to do this,' she said. He didn't change his position and continued to look at the ceiling fan. 'I'm scared,' he whispered, so softly that she could not hear it. She asked him to repeat what he had said; but when he repeated those words, 'I'm scared,' a bit louder than earlier this time, they could not convey the same vulnerability that they had carried in their first utterance. Just then she shook his arm. He looked towards her and saw her pointing, with her eyes, in the other direction. He turned and saw two dark, beady eyes, close to the floor, staring right at them from a distance of a metre or so. The sight sent a chill down his spine. The eyes made a tiny movement in their direction. They jumped up from the mattress and saw the flat form to which those eyes belonged. There was a period of stillness in which none of them moved. Then, in a way he had never experienced before, something got inside him and he picked up a chappal from the floor and slapped it right on the flat thing's spine, once, twice, thrice, again and again, till he could hear her shrieks and feel her arms pulling him away and could see the bloody mess that he had made on the tiles—a body squashed and unable to move but breathing, and the tail saying no, no, no.

34

THE OCTOPUS: A FABLE

TUSHAR JAIN

Pariya Tenammi suffered from a unique problem that became the source of all his misery. It was this that rendered his life a mess, turning it into a series of unfortunate heartbreaks unfolding one after the other. For as long as anyone could remember, whenever Pariya fell in love, seconds after, he'd turn into a gigantic octopus.

He was all of eight when it first happened. One humid August evening, his new neighbour, Nomi, eagerly tagged along with her mother to be introduced to him. Pariya, shy, withdrawn, approached the playful Nomi, close to his own age, with some caution and an extended hand. An ageless offering of friendship. So, when Nomi cheekily swatted away the hand and pulled Pariya into an embarrassing embrace, he was flushed with something he'd never felt before.

In a flash, the room turned into a cauldron of screams. Shrieks bounced off the walls and seeped into the carpet, lamps, everything, ensuring no one would forget that day easily. A bawling Nomi was hurried out by her horrified mother. She was sternly told to keep her eyes averted from the nightmarish octopus.

Pariya usually remained an octopus for as long as the sheer intensity of what he'd felt lasted. Three hours later, he began to forget Nomi's face and the warmth of her fingertips embedded in his back began to fade. Gradually, he started to change back. His tentacles thinned to arms and legs and the frantic sobbing of his mother stopped. Pariya was back. Naked as the day he was born.

In those days, Mrs Tenammi was problematically superstitious. It was difficult to explain to her that things were the way they were because they simply couldn't be any other way. With a set mind and turning a deaf ear to Mr Tenammi's reasoning and well-founded scepticism, she marched to the door of every witch doctor she could find. And, inevitably, for a time, Pariya became the victim of his mother's determination. Of her resolve to find logic in a place where it didn't exist. And to cure something that couldn't be cured.

Poor Pariya was shown to countless tantriks and sadhus. He was smacked silly with brooms, rose-scented incense sticks, shimmering tail feathers of peacocks, and numberless other items drawn reverently from small, dank cupboards. To impress the paying mother, strange brown and green powders were blown into Pariya's stinging eyes, his clipped toenails were tossed into a sacred fire and spirited Sanskrit prayers were raised to the heavens. All to force out the non-existent demonic spirit of the octopus, the ashtbhuj, from the boy's body.

After six weeks of this madness, when Pariya's limbs didn't spontaneously swell into tentacles for three whole months, Mrs Tenammi considered her efforts had paid off. She would hold her triumph over her husband and bring it up frequently to settle petty disputes. At the time, she didn't know or understand that nothing had changed. But time, being kind, would allow Mrs Tenammi her complacency for another six years. Because it would be six years before Pariya found Graja, sitting in a corner of the classroom, scratching her name with the wrong end of a compass into the chipped wood of her desk.

Graja. Pariya was fourteen, chubby, and sprinkled generously with acne when he saw Graja one Friday afternoon. While he was geeky and solitary, Graja was no spring flower either. Stubborn, crazy, and with a beaky nose, which looked as if it had been mercilessly pinched out of shape, she was wild, more storm than girl. Did Pariya fall in love at first sight? Thankfully, no. It would be terrifying to imagine the enormous octopus slithering towards a cowering Graja across a chaotic, screeching classroom.

No. First came the fumblings of new friendship. A day after he noticed her, Graja, deservedly, and Pariya, mistakenly, were punished in Biology class for interrupting the flow of Mr Sen's priceless thoughts. 'The colon is an important part of the syllabus. It's worth at least four marks!' Mr Sen bellowed at Graja. To this, Graja couldn't help responding icily, 'Four marks or ten, I'm not interested in your colon.'

During lunch break, Graja walked over to Pariya to apologize for dragging him down with her. And over palms placed side by side to compare the depth of the red left behind by Mr Sen's angry ruler, a peculiar bond formed between the two. In the following week, it strengthened as Pariya began to grasp, and even find pleasing, Graja's crude humour. Graja, on the other hand, fell in love with Mrs Tenammi's cooking and the daily, almost sinful, pleasures of Pariya's lunch box.

As unlikely friendships go, it was a good one. But it didn't last longer than a month. What went wrong? What else?

It happened on a Saturday, when Graja and Pariya wandered up to the roof of the schoolhouse during lunch break to enjoy the shade and gurgling of rainclouds that seemed unaware that it was March. Sitting down on the cool floor across from him, Graja snapped open his lunch box. Peeling back the crinkling aluminium foil, she marvelled at the rich colour of the parathas and the intoxicating aroma of nimbu achaar. As they both immersed their fingers into the small plastic box, trouble busily got down to work.

The first drop of rain struck Pariya's nose in warning. Thereafter, in seconds, it grew into an onslaught. Pariya hurriedly stood up, pointlessly covering the lunch box with a hand, searching for its lid. Graja didn't move. She turned her palms to the sky instead and, catching Pariya off guard, smiled.

It was a sweet, disarming smile. It was an un-Graja-like smile. Pariya saw the smile and thought of a small boat, catching the wind in its large sails, and unexpectedly managing to pull an island after itself. That was what that smile, though slight, did for Graja. In a blink, it transformed her completely, personality and all.

What happened after that isn't all too hard to guess. Pariya was an innocent in the ways of rain. Inexperienced, he was unaware of its mischievous nature, its cunning. He had no idea how it both brought out and imbued, with the suddenness of lightning, beauty. And to see Graja like that, her dark hair thrown back, eyes squinting at the sky, and that guileless smile on her lips, Pariya didn't stand a chance.

Two minutes later, a hysterical Graja came dashing down the slippery staircase, yelling for help. There was a monster on the terrace. When the shaking superstitious guard, gripping the black thread around his neck with a fervour, opened the clunky door to the terrace, there was no monster to be found. Just a nude Pariya. With tears on his face that were indistinguishable from the rain.

The episode with Graja made obvious to the Tenammi family what the incident with Nomi hadn't. Now, that family of three knew what they were facing. This time, Mrs Tenammi didn't insist on voodoo or high-profile astrologers or black magic. All she did was hold her son as a desolate Pariya broke down in her lap. The sheer violence of that first real heartbreak spares no one. But for Pariya, somewhere, an invisible line had been drawn. A law created. My grandparents, to give them credit, never said it out loud. But when my father at fourteen wept, when the misery beat out of him in waves, he didn't just weep for the heartbreak that was burning a hole through his chest. Chubby but bright, speckled with acne but precocious, Pariya also wept for all the heartbreaks he'd never have.

After that, life went on as usual. A portentous unease descended on the Tenammi household for a while. But if Pariya was anything, he was dependable. In the years to come, he wilfully steered clear of women. What helped immensely was that puberty took its time leaving his body. It was slow and methodical in its tortures. And so, with Pariya sporting a wispy moustache, pitted cheeks that broke out in hives with cruel unpredictability, and new layers of fat on top of the old pudge, women steered clear of him too.

Years passed. Neighbours shifted in, shifted out. The long-held custom of having fresh flowers in the drawing room vase had to be discarded when the florist doubled the price of sunflowers. For a few years, seven artificial, perfumed roses were stuck down the vase's throat. Eventually, the vase was removed from the drawing room. Pariya grew to be twenty-four years old.

This is where the story gets blurry, indistinct. I have hounded my grandparents for details, repeatedly asked friends of my parents to recount important bits. But it has been of little use. Nobody knows how it happened but at twenty-four years of age, Pariya, my father, began dating an art restorer named Amyya. They dated steadily for three years before marrying in a splendid ceremony. The photographs of my parents' luxurious wedding are among my most precious possessions.

A year later, they had me, and I was all of four, when tragedy tore our small family apart. On a return flight from Anaheim, my mother suffered a fatal heart attack twelve minutes after the airplane picked its feet off the ground. My weeping father, inconsolable, trying to shake awake his dead wife, found no comfort in the uneasy-looking stewardess. As she repeated 'Sir' over and over, intoning it differently each time, my father, in his boundless grief, suffered a similar fate as my mother. While still in the air, he too was robbed of his life by an acute and terminal cardiac event.

I don't remember my parents very vividly. What I'm left with are stray voices that I often chase around in my mind. But growing up with my grandparents, I have nudged and coaxed every story and every spare memory from them. About how my father at six tried riding his first bicycle and drove it, at great, unfurling speed, straight into a distracted postman. How when he brought my mother home for the very first time, my grandparents were taken aback by her frankness and the way she addressed them by their first names. When she laughed at a witticism from my father, throwing back her head, gargling loud, raucous laughter, a silence fell on the dinner table.

There are hundreds more. But the gaps in the stories remain. I look at the pictures of my mother and am startled by her beauty. By her grace and self-possession. And when I look at my father, I'm naturally forced to wonder at the match. My father, the studious, introverted lepidopterist (I didn't understand the choice of his vocation at first, but now I do; with butterflies being strong metaphors of transformation, he picked a field full of creatures whose bodies too had secrets of their own) and my mother, the successful, gorgeous art restorer whose work took her to places like Prague and Vienna, belonged to vastly different worlds.

So, for a long time, I believed that my father did the practical thing and took the only way that truly existed for him. He played it safe and picked someone he couldn't ever possibly love. People have done much worse, gone against their very natures at times, to avoid being lonely.

This conclusion to my father's story has haunted me for a while. It upsets me to think that he not only was unfair to both himself and my mother but also, more troublingly, that he never found acceptance or happiness in any form till the very end. As much as it hurt to, I believed in this version of events unquestioningly. Until today.

I woke this morning with my mind in the grip of an image that had been shaken loose from my imagination deep down in my sleep. But what I was seeing was so rich in detail, so suffused with recognizable elements, that I instantly knew it was not something my imagination had conjured up but a misplaced piece of actual memory.

It took me some hours to dig out the remembrance, brush it clean, and be amazed at the ease with which it resolved the mystery of my parents' marriage and lives. I remember it clearly now. I recall being little. I recall getting up from a low bed and knuckling from my eyes the remains of whatever nightmare that had woken me. Then, half-naked, I sleepily tottered into the living room, ready to squeeze all my displeasure at being wakened into an awesome fit of crying. But the scene in the living room captured my attention and left me stunned. I remember gazing at them with a mixture of fear and delight for almost a minute before they noticed me there. On the couch, engulfing it, their protruding eyes fixed on the news blaring on the television, two enormous octopuses lay sprawled. Their tentacles were snugly wrapped around each other. And if my adult self truly focuses on that old image, I can see one of the two tenderly leaning its bulky head against the other's. He was happy. They both were.

Isn't life bizarre?

35

MY TIME AT BOYONIKA

UDAY KANUNGO

I'm talking of a long time ago, when I was barely past my boyhood, and the youngest employee of Alok Babu in the sari shop he owned at 72, Hatibagan market. If you make a turn at the boys' school, walk towards the statue on the square, and follow the tram tracks till they turn left into a lane, you will find yourself facing the Boyonika Sari Emporium. I remember how, in my first days, I used a dent in the brown tracks, followed by a particular pothole on the street, as a marker to stop my feet and think ahead to the day's work. Alok Babu would be sitting on his seat at the counter, checking accounts, or writing a postcard, a paan tucked into his teeth, a ribbon of smoke from the incense sticks wafting past his oiled hair to reach the garlanded portrait of his late father from whom he had inherited this business. I would greet him with a bowed head, he would nod, and I would fold my jute bag and deposit it in a distant corner. I would then go and remove my chappals and wash my feet with water drawn from a pail placed in another corner. After I'd done this, and began moving around, my footsteps, as also everyone else's, would be impossible to hear, as Tutun would by now have spread the thick rug-like mattresses on the shop floor that swallowed every sound that fell on them. Tutun started half an hour earlier than me, restocking blouses or climbing ladders to find an item stored away on the higher ledges. I would move about the shop aimlessly, eyeing the bundles of clothes stored end to end in rigid stacks and always lose count of the soft, almost imperceptible black lines on the shelves which meant, simultaneously, the beginning of one sari and the end of another.

Gradually, with the passing of days, I became familiar with the kind of clothes Alok Babu sold in Boyonika. He claimed the shop was named after a special kind of silk spun only in certain villages in lakeside forests along the coastline, but I never did find out if this was true or not. Anyway, whatever the reason for the shop's name, Alok Babu stocked saris of all kinds of cotton, a healthy range of silk, a wide variety of rather garish chiffon, a select line of Sambalpuri saris, and some thick-threaded handloom pieces. Dhiren, the man in charge of all the stock, initially moved me around the shop rather whimsically, sometimes downstairs to fetch an old, forgotten cotton garment, at other times ordering me to ransack some long-unopened, cobwebbed cabinet from whose dark depths I would have to rescue a blouse. For nearly a year this went on, a time in which I never knew what my job was, when it seemed that anything at all could be asked of me. Sometimes, just when I thought there was time to sit still, or stare at the streets outside where sounds still new to me were unfolding, Dhiren would fling a folded sari across, which I had to store in a stack according to its colour, type, and price.

For the longest time, I could not make out why Dhiren never assigned a specific task to me, but, one day, suddenly it dawned on me that there was no stack of saris that I hadn't run my hands through, no cabinet of clothes I hadn't opened, no corner of the shop I hadn't climbed up to on the ladder—with silent respect I realized that my first year of hustling here and there, as if rebounding from wall to wall, was nothing but me being slowly stirred into the air of the shop. We were quiet men and neither needed to say it to the other. We both knew that I was now a part of Boyonika.

Soon it was time for Dhiren to teach me the first things about showing a sari to a customer. On certain Mondays, when the shop would shut earlier than usual, he would call for Tutun and me, and momentarily make us the women whose gaze we had to guide, step by step, to the clothes we wanted to sell. There were some things on which we had to lose to the customer, he said—the kind of cloth, the cut, or maybe even the colour of pleats—but all around this illusion of choice, the seller must start erecting, by deft, diplomatic words and some controlled promises, the borders of his kingdom. He would pick at random one of the many saris behind the glass, their shapes stiffened by time and looking as rigid as bricks to the untrained eye. Upon the first touch of his fingers, the fabric would emit a crisp crackle, and swiftly he would fling out the piece of shabby cardboard that was the spine around which the sari had been wound many times. Keeping most of the sari still asleep in its thick folds, he would pry open a corner with a fingernail, and awaken a square slice of its print to our eyes. He would trace its intricate patterns of embroidery, running an index finger along its fringe in such a way as to focus your eyes on the subtle borders that ran thinly till the end, where they would die out in a few frail wisps of thread. Tutun and I would stand and watch raptly, our lips sealed, our eyes absorbing the turn of colours, our ears alert to his choice of words. After an hour or so of such demonstration, he would collect the different saris splayed on the tabletop into a mass, give them a slap, and announce with ironic ceremony in his voice, 'Today's training is over. To be continued.'

This was not all. Dhiren kept us close when the women waded in, parting the plastic curtains on the doorstep with their bangled arms, already eyeing the shelves. From the very first, Dhiren would have the task of gathering their gazes together and bringing them to the table. Then, feigning anger at me and Tutun, he would raise his voice to a rasp and sharply tell us to fetch this or that batch of saris. Sometimes, Tutun would join in and add orders of his own to Dhiren's original instructions—being the youngest, I had no choice but to absorb these commands as there was no one else to hand them off to. As a result, towards the end of the busiest of days, I could be seen working with downcast eyes and a sullen demeanour, as if within me lay all of Boyonika's discontent. This was the impression of me that many women must have carried away with them after their humid interludes in the summer evenings at Hatibagan market. Now that I think of it, I wonder how many slices of that thin boy with rickety legs and arms that knew no ambition still live on in some unplumbed attic of their memories, and if my bony shoulders and lanky frame are forever doomed to fringe their treasured recollections of the time when the saris they wear so fondly, own so proudly, were first unfurled before their eyes, under those dim brown bulbs on the white tabletops of Boyonika Sari Emporium.

Despite being pushed around by Dhiren and Tutun, day by day I could see how Dhiren was slowly handing me the reins of the sari department. After spotting a naive customer who would sooner or later settle on a sari, he would cajole her through a play of colours, first making her consider a few garish designs, which she would find unsuitable, and then gradually moving backwards towards the serried rows of more suitable saris—until all at once I would be the only person between her and the blinding delight of the most beguiling saris on offer.

At first, I only showed cotton. I would proceed from where Dhiren had left off, spreading out the colourful pieces, outlining the frills with my fingers before moving to more subtle designs. I would show floral prints first, then the ones with dotted artwork, followed by the filigreed embroidery that made delicate patterns, and finally saris that came embossed with abstract shapes—at this point, in my first few months on the job I would inevitably become tongue-tied and thus be completely at the mercy of the women's whims and demands. I was often unable to cope and as Boyonika was bustling enough to keep Dhiren and Tutun busy with other customers, my stumbling failures could not even be mitigated by them and I would have to endure the disheartening sight of those women slipping into their sandals while leaning on the shoe stand, and descending the steps of Boyonika, perhaps never to return. After ten at night, behind closed shutters, while we folded the unchosen saris and swept up bits and pieces of paper and other litter along with the day's dust, I would confess in a low tone the chances I had missed, bracing myself for a scolding from Dhiren. But invariably, by the time we opened our steel tiffin boxes, he wouldn't lose his temper, but only offer me some advice; we would then all have a good laugh about the day's events. After we'd eaten, I'd go home, my weary mind soothed by the thought that for all time to come I would remain the youngest employee of Boyonika, and although there were disadvantages to this, the kindness shown to me, especially by Dhiren, would always balance things out in my favour.

It never occurred to me how young Dhiren also was till one evening Tutun whispered to me that there was talk of his marriage. Alok Babu announced that very night that Boyonika would close for four days on account of Dhiren's wedding preparations, in which Tutun and I were told to lend a hand. A Calcutta wedding was too expensive for the groom and bride alike. So we went, the three of us, to the girl's place in Asansol in an all-seater inter-city foul-smelling night train. As we rattled past two small-town stations whose names I had not heard of, Dhiren told us he would be leaving Boyonika soon after the marriage. It was part of an unsaid understanding, he said. His in-laws owned two wholesale godowns in the countryside, and had promised him the job of storekeeper in one of those as dowry. It was a job that paid twice the money Boyonika did in a town in which everything cost half as much as Calcutta; indeed, Dhiren and his family had been sold on the idea of this marriage as soon as the father of the bride had made this promise. We alighted in Asansol with heavy hearts, and during the three days that Tutun and I spent there—pitching tents, lugging bags, carrying drums full of water and fruit-laden plates from everywhere to everywhere, neither of us could coax out of our hearts the cheerfulness proper to the scenes leading up to a marriage. After the wedding had taken place, on our last night in Asansol, it was very windy. Tutun and I slept under some tarpaulin tents that had already been partially taken down; I remember hearing the bride sobbing loudly. When a cleaner with a broom woke us up the next morning, we realized we had only an hour to make it to the station.

Dhiren met us briefly at the gate to the compound where a rickshaw was waiting. He had to give us a set of keys to the basement of Boyonika that he had kept close to him all this while. 'Before I forget,' he said, and kept pointing to each key while telling us what it unlocked. 'This here is for the September set of cotton ones, and this one has Ray Babu's wholesale maal, this is for that old stock of white chiffon, got it? And well, the rest you know,' he trailed off, as we climbed into the rickshaw.

'Take good care of the shop, okay, and both stay good-good!' he said, his hand neither waving nor still, but just gently rising and falling, as if blessing the air around him. I watched him till his body was borne away by the distance between us.

I returned to Boyonika as the man in charge of all saris, and found that the days did not slow down for my sake. I made many mistakes during that period of my life, not answering questions quickly enough, being inattentive, confusing clothes of one kind with another. The women kept coming and going, flinging sharp questions at my silence, a malignant twist to their faces, their words often laced with insults. Soon all of Hatibagan's shopkeepers would know me as the inept showman of saris from Boyonika whom Dhiren had foolishly trusted. But there was no one to turn to for help, nothing to be done but learn from my mistakes, figure out how to help myself. I was an orphan from a faraway village across the border, thrust into this city years ago, and for our kind only our work can save us. So I buried myself in my duties in Boyonika. In six months, I could handle all the cotton stock by myself. At the end of the year, knowing no one there, I travelled to Jorhat, through countless rain-soaked paddy fields, to collect our batch of Assamese silk saris, all on my own. By the second year, I could tell by the touch of a single thread if the stack of red and white Korial saris were from Bengal or faked elsewhere. And a few days before it would be three years since Dhiren's marriage, I managed the shop alone on the busiest Sunday in the history of Boyonika, seeing to more than a hundred women, selling a total of 122 garments, including ten Sambalpuri saris. This is all a man's life is, I thought—smile through the pain and feign greatness.

Soon, my marriage was also arranged. My father's older brother, whom I met once every two years, and on whom had fallen the responsibility of ensuring that I further the family line, came to Calcutta one day and told me over a meal that a family in a village close to where we lived, had been asking if there were any eligible young men in our house.

'So, I told them about you. "Works in Calcutta," I said. They were interested.'

One has no choice in these things. I'd known this for a long time, I'd seen under what circumstances many men and women had left their houses in white and red to think that anyone does these things willingly, so I said yes.

The bride wore red—a Banarasi brocade sari with intricate, antique designs gilded in golden thread. That was the first time I saw her, guided by a web of women towards the fire. I remember thinking that her face was only eyes, with brows dotted in white sandalwood paste; her jewellery was so big and there was so much of it that it almost eclipsed her face under the harsh, moth-crossed lights. I think we have some photographs of the event. Brides and grooms are the worst ones to ask about their own wedding, they barely know what is going on themselves, but one thing I do remember was how ruthlessly I was teased for being the groom who sold saris for a living. The slightest talk of clothes would cause gales of laughter among the group of girls escorting the bride to various ceremonial functions. 'Do you know something about henna, too?' they'd ask, flashing their palms stained with elaborate designs, 'or is it just saris you have advice for?' Or sometimes, pausing for a moment in their frolic, they'd taunt me with knowing smiles—they knew full well how discomposed I was by such teasing. 'What's this? No saris for us or the bride? Here we were thinking, "Here comes the groom, from his big shop in Calcutta," and no new clothes! Is this what life after marriage is going to be like, do tell?' Just a couple of hours before the wedding ceremony, this sort of harassment was especially excruciating; I was surrounded on all sides by these young women, who wouldn't let me go to the pandal until I gave in to their conditions. They shook out a few promises from me, one among them being that, within the first month of marriage, I'd present a brand new Boyonika sari to my wife. Although I said yes to everything they asked for, this promise did not leave my memory. Even as I returned from my marriage, watching the scenery unfold outside the windows of the night train, I was already thinking of the colours and patterns on the sari that I was going to present to my wife.

On the first Monday of married life, I took her to Boyonika. On the tram, I felt the thrill of taking someone through the things that made up my life. As we approached the spot where I usually alighted from the tram, I found it a bit difficult to divide my attention between her and watching out for the bent electric pole that was the landmark that told me my stop was approaching. Nevertheless, I managed to get us off the tram at the right stop. Alok Babu and Tutun received us at the shop. As I showed my wife around, I sang the praises of Dhiren so much that she could have been right if she thought he was a sari salesman who had passed away long ago but was so legendary that people were still talking of him, and whose spirit continued to hover among the shelves of Boyonika. Tutun showed her the spot where we sat cross-legged waiting for customers to arrive. My wife did not show any great interest in any of the things that she was being shown nor did she seem to covet any of the gorgeous saris that were stacked everywhere. Instead, she stood close to me, her eyes lowered. Only once, when I was shifting a pile of saris on a display table, did a smile momentarily appear on her face, before being quickly extinguished—it appeared that she had liked one of the saris that she had held in her hands. Noticing this, I said 'You must tell me if you like one of these pieces, hmm...maybe this one,' I said fingering a khadi sari as green as a betel leaf.

'No, no, not for me,' she said, shying away.

I whispered to her: 'Look, Alok Babu gives us some of the stock at the end of the year, some unsold saris. If you see something you like I can try to keep it for you.'

That afternoon, when we were walking back home, after hours of trying to get her to tell me what sort of sari she might fancy, she said 'You know much more about saris...but if you really want to know what

I'd like, I'd prefer something simple, anything that is not too showy. The rest is up to you.'

'And the colour?' I remembered to ask just before dropping off to sleep that night. 'Else you'll say, "don't like the colour".'

'Anything…whatever you like best,' she said. There was nothing more for a few seconds, then she said: 'White will do….'

It was indeed Alok Babu's custom, like that of most shop owners, to gift us at the end of the year a few saris that had remained unsold. Married men would take some for their wives or in-laws, but the others would spend days roaming the streets and markets of Borbazar, going from shop to shop, slashing the prices in half to get rid of the saris they carried with them like abandoned babies.

Tutun and I had never eyed any sari for ourselves the previous year, but this time around, as the end of the year approached, I would find myself, in moments when the shop wasn't busy, when I was chatting with Tutun, or folding saris to return them to the shelves, lingering over some of the pieces, hoping they would remain unsold, so I could give my wife the present I had promised her. I would remember her words and my eyes would scour the shop in search of a simple white sari.

A few days before Christmas, I finally found it. It was a jute cotton sari shipped a few days ago from Digha, whose weavers were legendary. If not for a few criss-crossing lines on its upper folds, it was spotless white. It felt at first like paper in my hands; it was stiff and crackly but was so fine it seemed it might crumble into dust at the slightest pressure. If you held the fabric up to the light for a few seconds, you could see just how fine the workmanship was. When it was fully unfurled, you could see exquisite edges bordered in blue, with a thin, dark, long indigo thread woven in many circles to create the illusion from afar of chariot wheels. Many times I turned it over and around, inside out, savouring its simple, pure beauty. I shelved it in the third row in a cabinet of cotton saris, knowing that it did not belong there either by colour or kind, but simply because it was close to me and I could constantly keep an eye on it, and hide it away, as best I could, from the prying eyes of customers.

Ten days remained till the end of the year. I would have to keep it hidden from the eyes of customers for just ten more days and it would be mine. On the ninth and eighth day before the New Year, my time at the shop was fairly eventless. Most of the day I was made to tally accounts in Alok Babu's ledger, and at other times I either chatted with Tutun or watched Azharuddin bat through two days of a test match. Till lunchtime on the seventh day so little had happened that I asked Alok Babu if I could go home to eat a quick lunch with my wife and return. Over a day-old pot of rice I talked to her about all that was happening in the shop but not my plan. She asked me to bring Tutun over for lunch on Sunday and send fried fish to Alok Babu's home. I kept nodding, her words barely registering, as I kept hoping that the next six days would be kind to me. I had begun wanting that sari so badly, I kept thinking of ways in which I could control the future so I could walk away from the shop with that prize in my hand. My thoughts began to careen about wildly. What if I opened the shop on a Sunday and made away with the sari? Even as I thought that, I shrank within myself in shame. Visions of my wife and I being paraded through the streets with all kinds of abuse being shouted at us, and visions of us begging on busy footpaths chilled me to the bone. Could I ask Alok Babu for the piece, risking a slap and maybe even a month's pay, depending on his temper? Or should I just do my job, and hope the six days would pass in the way I hoped they would so that sari I coveted would finally be mine?

The next day, a flock of ladies belonging to some big family descended on Boyonika and stood facing me, their eyes glittering with intent. They needed both cotton and silk, for they were buying a batch of saris to gift the groom's family before the marriage. Tutun and I started by offering some usual choices, we threw on the display table a few gauzy greens, reds, and yellows, knowing well that none would make a mark, but this was our usual opening salvo before steering the customers in the direction of the saris we hoped they would buy. After this I showed some khadi material, some standard tussar silks, and a few specimens of red and black Sambalpuris, hoping to end the game right then. They lingered long over the saris, went back and forth amongst themselves. Whenever I felt the threat of their gaze going towards the simple thing I valued the most, I'd fling under their eyes this or that sari, hoping that either the price or the patterns on it would grab their attention. To this end, I never spoke of jute cotton either, fearing they'd force me to show every last piece of that variety in the shop.

Who knows what god keeps watch over our days, but whoever that divinity was, he was kind to me that day. As Tutun and I continued to show saris to the rich ladies, they grew fond of a few designs, and the thought that they might pick the sari I coveted began to recede. Whenever they became unsure I tried to settle their minds by alternating between saying 'pure cotton', and 'pure silk', as the case may be. The fact that they wanted the groom's family to not think of them as misers worked in my favour—they picked showy, glittery saris afraid that they might be seen as tightwads if they presented plain, simple saris. And even though I was exhausted by the endless, heedless demands of these rich people who cared not a jot about making us cater to their every whim and fancy, that day I felt quite satisfied—I had managed to keep my treasure safe, simply by appealing to the vanity and flashiness and egos of the rich. It's a strange thing to say, but sometimes the cost of being rich ends up helping us poor.

But if there's anyone worse for us than the rich, it's the rich with taste; it's a lethal combination. After dealing with simply the rich that day, just as I was beginning to think that I could swat away anyone, a young woman came into the shop the next day.

She was dressed in a baffling mix of things—a chunni carelessly thrown over her shoulders, brown glasses paired with a nose ring, shoes that were half-sandals, half slippers—it seemed that the mismatched halves of two people were fused together in her person. Nevertheless, the overall effect was striking. Here, then, was someone who knew her own mind when it came to dressing, a person with clean, if idiosyncratic, taste. She was silent for as long as two minutes, but her eyes were darting from stack to stack, studying and rejecting saris, it seemed, simply from the look of their spines. At last, with god knows what in her mind, she approached the counter where I sat and asked: 'What do you have in cotton...something simple, not too flashy.'

Hearing these words, I silently turned back to face the same shelves that I had seen a thousand times, but never with an anxiety I was now feeling. Taking a few seconds to steel myself, I squatted down to bring out three multicoloured pieces—in red, purple and sandalwood shades—all without any designs on them. Just as I was beginning to talk about the first one, how pure its cotton was, how it had travelled through the hands of many weavers in Banaras, she stopped me with a shake of her head—

'No, no, not all this. Don't you have any light colours?'

'You mean, well, in silk we have....'

'No, no, in cotton only....'

'Let me look again, madam,' I said, and sat down cross-legged, motioning to her to sit as well. I shouted for Tutun and told him to look for the kind of thing madam wanted in the basement. We both waited in silence, nervous for me and awkward for her, till Tutun ran back up and unfolded a handful of saris on the tabletop. They were all in very mellow colours— light brown, pale peach, a soft sky blue—as they passed under her fingers one by one her face showed not a sliver of interest. As if out of mercy she pressed her palms upon the last of these saris, a piece the colour of turmeric, and said that this was, at least, 'a certain kind of sari'. God knows what she meant by that. I showed her some variations of that colour and print which held her interest for some time; all this while, I was fearing that soon she would want something simpler, even less colourful. I made an attempt, through a mention of discounts, to guide her towards silk, but the words didn't even register. Instead, she pointed to my left, where it felt I had hid my very heart. I turned and placed one finger, weak with fear, on the glass front of the display cabinet.

'This?'
'Down.'
'This?'
'No, lower.'
'This?'
'No, even further down, the grey one, with those blue-blue designs.'

I breathed in relief. My white jute sari was merely four fingers away. I took my time spreading the sari out, desperately thinking about how I might sway her attention away to some other part of the shop. There were two options before me—I could either take her so far away from that stack of saris that there was little chance of her returning, or I could convince her of the brilliance of the grey piece so she bought it right then and there. Or, perhaps I could talk up the alternatives of a few black and red Sambalpuri pieces? Her hands clutched one of the sari's corners, the opposite end of the edge I was holding, and in a few moments I had lost the cloth to her hands.

'Hmm...this is quite good, this colour is nice.' She ran her fingers over the cloth, turning its borders inside and out. 'What price?'

I named a price much lower than what the sari was actually worth, hoping it would prove to be the clincher. As the moments passed, it was hard to tell whether I was getting more nervous or angry. 'Just take it,' I was yelling with my eyes, 'what more do you want, it has a good print, it doesn't shine in the light, it is plain and simple and elegant. Just take it.'

'Well, let's see what more you have like this....move a bit to this side! I want to look at what else you have.'

'Over here, we have good....'

'Let's look at that white one....'

'Yes, this is a good piece, you'd like this....'

'No, no, not that row, over there....'

'This one, you said?'

'Arrey no baba, this, this, look where I'm pointing.'

'This?'

'The one below'

'This?'

'Lower, yes, near that....under that pink one.'

'Oh, this one?'

'Yes.'

Nowadays, I think about that moment a lot. Every now and then, on her behalf, I imagine entirely different lives for that girl, which would have led her to thoughts different from the ones she had when she made her choice. Maybe in this way I can make her not pick that piece. In another story I told myself, I had convinced her that the sari was too plain to be worthy of her, criticizing its widow-white pallor and its cheap borders in blue thread, till her tone blended with mine, saying, yes indeed, it is. Since when had the rich started to like simple things too, weren't the simple things meant for us? And of the rest, is there more to tell? My insisting on her not having the sari, her taking offence at my words, Alok Babu rushing from his chair upon hearing her raised voice, her leaving the sari and the shop in a fit of anger and bruised self-esteem, Tutun, over whom these things passed like a cyclone, standing speechless beside me, Alok Babu landing an ear-splitting slap on my face, my leaving Boyonika, my not telling my wife what the matter was until three days had passed, and her not talking with me for four days after she learned about what I had done, all these are rather long-long stories that should be cut short. Days after the incident, my mind continues to wander back to the image of that sari sleeping in a stack, and I begin to wonder what fate has befallen it—where is it now? How unaware is the woman whose body it is destined to drape of the history of hands and eyes that have caressed it?

My Time at Boyonika

Here I am on the platform with my wife, and again we wait for a train. Soon we will board the intercity to Digha, where I plan to meet someone who might need a sari salesman. Now and then I would think of writing a letter of apology to Alok Babu but one day when I mentioned this to her over lunch, my wife, her face melting in anger and tears, crying only like a woman like her could, said we would never spread our hands in supplication before that man. 'And if you do, do so alone, because I will leave everything and run away that very moment...you listening?' I didn't bring up that course of action again. I have written a letter to Dhiren, telling him everything and asking if he knows anyone who might hire someone like me. Maybe he will write back in a few days. It is tough, but I think everything will go fine, maybe I'll soon have a sari shop like Boyonika to my own name. There is something else I think about, something I know for certain. Every month, a thousand saris are shipped from Calcutta to the coast; who knows, maybe among them, hiding between the blue and green pieces, could be the sari that caused all this, and one day, no matter where I'm working, I will open a carton to find that it has returned to me.

36

SHABNAM

UROOJ

There isn't anything she misses about her husband. Not the droop of his eye as he caught sleep after asr. Not the way he slurped his chai. Not his clothes, starched so perfectly that they smelled of nothing, of no one. Clothes not lived in, not made to belong to his body. The clothes of a stranger, that perpetual stranger who did not need to raise either hand or voice to show her her place. A gesture of his newly married hand and she had been sentenced. To the smallest chamber in the house, that damp little box not fit for a small animal; three dark years spent without the mercy of sunlight or company.

Blowing out smoke, Shabnam sets the hookah down on the parapet and looks at the bazaar below. At this blue-grey hour of morning with the sun merely a hint of light on the horizon, only beggars line the lanes, sleeping in the dust. The vendors will only haul up their stalls and wares once the day begins yellowing. After zohr, boys selling flowers will appear and men with fighting birds will follow. The richer merchants and the noblemen will descend from their mansions into the market once the sky flushes pink, and the maghrib azan rings out across the courtyard. She can see it all unfolding in the emptiness below—where the jewellery stalls will go, and where the kebabs will turn on spits.

She wonders who might visit her today. Her husband's moustache floats before her, thick and contrived. A stranger's moustache. She laughs.

∽

'Sidra!'

The voice of Raziya begum, her khala, hasn't been this shrill since that incident back home. She has to stifle her sleepy laugh because she knows that her khala must be standing over her takht, right behind her, hands planted on her hips. She manages to turn gracefully in the sheets, noting Ishrat's absence from beside her, before finally coming eye to eye with her khala's stomach.

'You should've been awake at fajr, girl,' her khala speaks fast, words crammed together. Running a kotha has meant she is always in a hurry. 'If I don't see you upstairs immediately, you won't be having any lunch.'

Then she's gone, her pyjamas whipping around her ankles as she stalks off. The backs of her ankles are still brown-red from the mehndi. Celebration rarely washes off her. Sidra sits up just as her khala disappears around the doorway. It takes her a few moments to grow accustomed to the light—the sun has risen, the calls of vendors spill in from the windows. She's late. She's very, very late.

She combs her hair briskly and curses Ishrat for having left her behind. For only a moment, she feels that old fear again. The sting of a slap, the locked door. Her khala's cruel mouth, full of paan. Those days of her childhood are over though, and Sidra tightens the drawstring of her pyjamas. They aren't washed but they retain a kind of starched look, a crispness. Water travels like everything and everyone else in the kotha. Up the stairs first, then back down. Lower and lower until it reaches quarters like hers. The box of bangles sits at the foot of the shared takht, blue and shimmery. Another one of Asad's tokens. She runs out of the chamber, barefoot.

∽

Raziya begum speaks loudly to the gathered women.

Shabnam sits with the tanpura between her legs. A gift from Tariq Khan. Her fingers rest absently on the strings. Steam rises from the cup of tea placed beside her, a whiff of adrak and dalchini drifting up to her nose. Only three other women—Tashi, Nabiya, and Begum Sanjeeda—are also seated, perched atop the cushioned takht, pretty and pale among the tablas and paan daans. She finds her mind wandering again, as has become commonplace since riyaz was cut back in the last week. Her husband had never liked adrak, his leathery face twisting at its very mention.

Blankly, she spots the odd-looking, barefooted niece of Raziya begum. She's standing so close to the curtains it looks as though she might disappear into them. She only knows the woman, like all the downstairs women, through a story. A story about her regular customer; that tall, bearded man who has charmed all the women below, the man who brings her bangles every week. Stories make their way around, even if the women of the kotha don't. The upstairs and the downstairs. Like the moon and its shadow, if it had one. Shabnam lets her gaze rest on the woman for only a moment more—tehzeeb dictates that she should.

Raziya begum is talking about the Jumeraat performance. Shabnam's name has been mentioned. Tashi tips her head in her direction, proud. Some of the other women even clap. Shabnam finds herself smiling, as she has been taught to do. Begum Sanjeeda has also nodded her way. All the promise and possibility of the parikhana lie in that poised nod of Begum Sanjeeda's veiled head. She will mull over this later, as she knots Tashi's hair at night, as Nabiya laughs about one of her noblemen.

It appears as though Raziya begum's announcement for the bahaar mehfil is over. The women are moving around now, talking amongst themselves excitedly, laughing openly. Her riyaz will start soon. Shabnam lifts the tanpura from between her legs and sets it down on the cushioned takht. Nabiya is already making her way over, having lifted the thick, glossy material of her anarkali and Tashi follows in her usual elegant manner, not a hair out of place. Never has been.

Once Shabnam might have been afraid of them. That Shabnam had lived in a dark box. Now she simply stands, the folds of her pristine white anarkali falling gracefully about her. This Shabnam might live in the nawab's palace.

☙

After the communal meal of bakhar-khani and qaliya—little of which makes it to her plate, she's only ever been khala jaan's odd niece here—most of the women drift into their rooms for riyaz. Already the tabla is setting a taal for someone's feet. Sidra lifts cup after cup into the bhagona, holding it at her waist. Her khala has put her on this cleaning and washing duty again. She's also taken Ishrat into the bazaars with her.

Everything in Sidra's life—from her time to her only friend—is held at the whim of her khala, however less heavy-handed she might be now. Perhaps the short sting of a slap is better than longer humiliations.

As she makes her rounds, she becomes aware of a pair of eyes on her. She doesn't look up. Her long nose has caught someone's attention, again.

That ugly, strange feature of her father's, having passed on to her by some curse or the other.

Even as she hopes that this gaze might find more purpose for itself, she is curious. Her palms are clammy. Some childish things don't change. She takes a deep breath and forces herself to look up. There, in the distance, stands Shabnam. Dark-eyed, unveiled, draped in silvery white. Watching. Nothing on her face changes when Sidra catches her eye. Like those old statues, Ishrat had said. Unmoving. Sidra feels drab in comparison, like one of the chipping walls in the kotha, bleak and brown. Perhaps that's why Shabnam is staring.

Her khala has always talked of Shabnam in a soft voice. The one she otherwise only uses with the noblemen and British officers. She is the name by which my kotha is known, Sidra. The strength on which it runs. No other girl like her. There never has been and never will be, and I've been doing this for twenty years now. Four years working here and they've never exchanged a word, nor a look. Until now. So Sidra straightens up, even lifts her chin the way Ishrat has taught her to do. She'll speak if she has to, although her khala has always discouraged her from talking with the others.

Shabnam looks away then, as though someone might have called her name. She steps back into the doorway and is gone, the ends of her anarkali flashing as they mark her exit. Sidra worries her bottom lip a moment—another childish thing. She scoffs at herself and at Shabnam. She resumes her work then, and lifts another cup.

∞

Maghribs come and go, in secret conspiracy with restless birds.

Shabnam finds her way to the chhat each time. The weeks have crept up on her in a repeat of riyaz and entertaining, growing warmer by the day. Tariq Khan had brought some courtiers with him last night. She had sung them four ghazals until her eyes were smarting from the mashaals. They'd brought out small boxes of gemstones then and she'd lit her hookah with an eye on Tariq Khan's smile.

In the whispers of the women around her later, she had heard the name Wazeeran. A dancing and singing woman, much like her, patronized by Wajid Ali Shah. A name so carefully spoken, as if to mention it needlessly might splinter the dream. She had dreamed of the nawab's twitching toes.

She hasn't seen Raziya begum's niece as of late, not after that strange afternoon. With the mehfil fast approaching, there must be work enough for the women downstairs. Raziya begum is always taking them into the bazaars with her, to carry the fabrics and itr, to haul the flowers back to the kotha. Shabnam approaches the parapet, humming a ghazal from the night before. The niece must be down there somewhere, in the packed lanes, trailing after her khala with the other women. Something about her has piqued Shabnam's interest. Perhaps it's that one story about the bangles, the strangest one she's heard in recent months. Nabiya's always collecting these tales, offering them up at night, between laughter and sleep.

What a strange thing to know about someone, Shabnam thinks, as her gaze trails over the lanes. There is a travelling group of musicians weaving through the lanes—narrowly avoiding Mustafa bhai's kebab stall, almost colliding head-on with a trio of flower boys. The begging women appear in dusty black at the kotha's door, singing some garbled song. Young children run past. Horses whinny in the distance, perhaps some Britons are on their way over. Donkeys burdened by wares follow moustachioed men. The mosque's dome appears faint and green against the clear sky.

Ustad Rahman had told her, among so many other things—when her soft feet were still unfaithful to the tabla, when her small hands could not perform abhinaya—that this new city around her would soon become the only city to outshine the distant star of Dilli. It seems almost as if she can now see something of his words in the bazaars below her.

Something clatters behind her. She turns, having half a mind to scold whichever tea-toting child has disturbed her hour of peace, only to stop short. At the top of the stairs stands Raziya begum's niece. Her eyes rest on the cup in her hand. Her clothes, today, are almost ornate and her braid rests on her shoulder, tightly wound.

Shabnam wonders if she dances. The woman's wrists are empty and she is shorter than she looked that afternoon, much like Raziya begum. The resemblance ends there—her long nose, the pursed lips, the sharp angle of her jaw, the mole by her eye, all depart from the rounded and paan-red face of her khala. She walks over silently and stops at a polite distance, holding the cup out.

Shabnam's eyes are drawn to the small, wet circles on the side of her neck, where she must have pressed in the itr with her fingertips. The proximity and the lack of a veil suddenly make her more real than she has ever been. Suddenly, she isn't disappearing into the curtains. Suddenly, she is here.

'I've never seen you wearing the bangles.'

Her gaze snaps up to meet Shabnam's eyes. 'How do you know about that?' There is only a faint edge of panic to her voice. Not how Shabnam imagined it. Very different from her khala. Deeper, with the hint of a dialect Shabnam can't place. Not as polished as Tashi and Nabiya's ways of speaking. Her hand reaches for the cup, the bangles clinking.

'One of the girls told me.' The tips of their fingers brush. Her skin is cold. 'Word gets around in the kotha, you know, especially if the story is strange.'

Sidra steps back, committing to her silence fully. Shabnam smiles, despite herself. 'Did Raziya begum send you up? Where is that young boy—Rustom—who usually—'

'I must return. Khala will be waiting.' She fixes Shabnam with a careful look, like the kind she'd given her that strange afternoon.

She turns on her heel and vanishes down the stairs. Only when she is gone does it strike Shabnam that the woman had been wearing a pale green garment exactly the shade of peeled pistachios.

Shabnam thinks of this only because she had loved shelling them as a child, to have them appear purple-green and rough in her tiny palm, to offer them up to her elders with all the cheer she could muster. Like the many other things her marriage took from her, these nuts had been unwelcome in her husband's home. *They remind me of little worms. They give me bad dreams.* Frugal as his speech may have been, it had never made sense to her. Perhaps she'd been too young. Perhaps he'd simply been unintelligent.

Later that night, as she neatly braids Nabiya's thick hair before they put out the lamp, she asks for the niece's name. If anyone should know, it'll be Nabiya. Sidra, Nabiya says through a yawn. Shabnam secures the last of her friend's hair in a tie before sitting back on the takht. *Sidra.* It takes her a few moments to arrive at the meaning. *Of the stars.*

When Shabnam finally slips into the arms of sleep, she dreams of night skies and pale pistachios.

⁓

Sidra falls back into the rhythm of work as bahaar approaches. This earns a single word of praise even from her khala. *Good,* is all she says, and yet somehow, it's enough.

Her days begin just shy of zohr, as the sun rises in the sky, and end with Asad's warm hands holding hers until the lamp is turned out, and he is sent off, some time after midnight. The hours in between are spent purchasing fabrics, jewellery, and perfumes, as opposed to revelling in practice with the other girls. She follows her khala in and out of different shops with her arms laden with packages, first in the long line of help her khala has enlisted for this mehfil's extravagance. It is not often that they stop for even a kakori on their hurried way.

The shopping finishes before maghrib so she returns to the kotha swiftly and washes and changes into her work clothes, the ones that her khala had brought her two years ago, chiffons and satins in deep shades of purple, blue, and green; all complete with heavy zardozi work. She presents herself then to visitors of the early evening, as women like her and Ishrat have always done. As they will always do.

For only a moment, as she's pulling her hair into a braid, she wonders what Shabnam's evenings might be like. More perfumed and more pretty. Perhaps one of her friends is singing. Faintly, she recalls their fingers touching, resting against that cup. Her khala had sent her up that evening, knowingly perhaps, to another humiliation and yet—

Ishrat calls for her, sing-song and cheery, breaking her chain of thought. Sidra is grateful for the interruption. Their customers must have arrived. They're inevitably local men, traders from the market or cooks from a nobleman's home, and rarely, merchants like Asad. Four years ago, it had taken her khala and the other two baijis two long weeks to talk her into accepting male company. Now she is quick and efficient in her entertaining.

Each conversation follows the same pattern; sometimes she moves them with Ghalib mian, sometimes with Mir, and sometimes, if they press her, she sings the ghazal of some poor unknown who slipped his words into the kotha on small pieces of paper.

Assalaam-wa-alaikum—would you care for some wine?—you flatter me, hazrat—Ghalib sahib did say... now should I sing?—oh here, let me undo your—some more wine?—Walaikum assalam—yes, bring me the bela flowers next time, please—khudahaafiz, hazrat—

She happens upon Shabnam again, entirely by accident.

Her khala had set off much earlier today, leaving Sidra behind to take on the washing again. Long after she had finished, her hands were still itching from the soap. She'd been meandering around the empty kotha, barefoot.

From hard, cold floors to soft, woollen carpets. As Sidra passed through the doorway by the audience hall, she spotted Shabnam, a dark blue phantom, sitting in her usual place on the takht. Despite her better judgement, Sidra stepped quietly into the hall. Shabnam hasn't heard her come in—her eyes are fixed to the parchment resting on her leg. In her right hand, there is a bamboo reed. The ring on her index finger throws off light. A gemstone.

'Would you like to go for a walk, Sidra?' Shabnam speaks suddenly, without looking up.

She doesn't know what is more unsettling. Shabnam's perfect diction, each word drawn out like paint over a wall, or that Shabnam somehow knows her name. Sidra is in half a mind to walk back out of the hall, to return to the comfort of her takht, to never hear this voice again. Shabnam looks up abruptly, fixing Sidra to the spot with a single glance. There is something about Shabnam that demands attention. As if that were the only way with which to regard her.

'I am very hungry and the tundaywallah must be setting up for the night.' Shabnam sets the reed down on the paper carefully. 'You know I'm not allowed to step out alone....'

∞

They find a strange new closeness with each other.

Their hours run very differently and rarely converge. As Sidra runs errand after errand for her khala, and entertains her local merchants with shayari, Shabnam spends the afternoons in riyaz and sings through the evenings for groups of clean-shaven, garland-carrying noblemen.

Sidra can't place her finger on exactly when she starts to seek Shabnam out. The accidents seem to multiply, becoming intentional—sometimes she climbs up to the chhat with a cup of tea, having sent cheeky Rustom off with his friends and sometimes she just stands at the door behind which Shabnam is singing.

She trembles at that voice. Her cheeks grow wet with tears. Seldom do these accidents lead her to Shabnam, until they do.

They eat a late meal across from each other one night, when the other women have retired, when her khala is preparing a paan for herself in her quarters.

Shabnam appears more frequently around her after that, sometimes dressed in pale blue, sometimes deep green, throwing Sidra one of her unsettling glances again. Sometimes they only share a look over chai in the late evenings, and that is enough. Then something happens, something unspoken and peculiar, and Shabnam invites her for walks regularly. If her khala notices, she doesn't say anything. Ishrat only raises an eyebrow every now and then.

One rainy afternoon, they both sit side by side on Shabnam's takht and light a chillum. She tells Sidra about the parikhana, that prized and pretty home of the Nawab's dancing girls, and Sidra knows from her broad smile alone, what that place means. An odd feeling sits in her stomach long after, she avoids adrak in her chai for days after. Shabnam flits in and out.

Bahaar arrives, and the air is filled with the scent of blooming flowers and wet mud. Shabnam's performance approaches and her riyaz stretches longer into the evenings. Sidra get sharper and sharper rebukes from her khala—perhaps she has finally heard some of the stories about them, perhaps she even knows.

The two of them grow closer still until they're sharing Shabnam's takht in the early mornings, weary-limbed and spent, and she is bringing balushahis to leave by Shabnam's table, and Shabnam is pressing the faded couplets of some failing poet under Sidra's pillow, and they are sharing whichever meal they can find the time for—hot sheermaals in the bylane, and spiced roghan josh by the small mosque, packing nuktiyaan to take home for the night, and sipping shir chai at one of the stalls. They grow closer still, until there is no space between them and Shabnam is often braiding her own hair the way Sidra does, and Sidra is singing the couplets Shabnam learned first, and Sidra is hurt by the husband she never knew and Shabnam is pressing soap into her palms, hoping for calluses.

Sidra, of the stars, and Shabnam, the morning dew. Which is whom, and who is which?

∞

The mehfil unfolds like a distant dream.

When it is over, Shabnam can hardly seem to remember the face of her husband. Instead, she finds herself thinking of another face entirely. The long nose, the sharp jaw, the mole by an eye. Tariq Khan swims away. The parikhana flickers like the lamps being put out around her.

Young girls still in training, dressed in their crispest white clothes, load itr and paan daans back on to silver trays. Behind them trail younger boys—sons of some of the dancing girls—carrying used tobacco products—some of their small fingers wrapped around hookahs decorated beautifully with bidri work and ganga jamuni, while others balance fine pieces of coal on their palms.

Raziya begum is deep in conversation with Sanjeeda begum—the gold trim of her blue pyjamas glitter in the dim light. As she moves, the fabric ripples and she distractedly barks a series of rushed orders at the young children who await her commands. Shabnam watches this absently, the soles of her feet tingling. She wonders if Sidra had been in the audience, if she'd heard the singing at least. It is unlikely that Raziya begum would have left her niece without work, though.

Maybe she's with Asad. This is not usually his hour but lately, he's been stopping by whenever he likes, taking their time from them. The thought dims Shabnam more than she'd like and she lifts her bejewelled, painted hands to the bela gajra in her hair. The silver intricately placed in her maang clinks softly. Her nath feels heavy all of a sudden, the thrill of its newness lost.

She thinks back to her audience. The rapturous eyes, the slender hands joined in applause, the uniforms' buttons flashing, the embroidery striking against silk. The women in veils and heavy silver, whistling with the sarangi. Raziya begum's red teeth. So much like her missi ceremony, when her teeth had been blackened, when her first set of zardozi was handed over, when she was given her name. Shabnam. Raziya begum had clapped at that. *You will bring fame to my house, I know this. Shabnam-bibi.*

She thinks of Tariq Khan again. *You will make the Nawab very happy.* His teeth, pearly white and perfect. *You are a farishta.* The musky scent of his collar. *Just your eyes speak for the heaven from which you've been sent.*

Maybe she will bed him after all.

∞

The news finds its way down to Sidra before Shabnam does.

Shabnam will be leaving for the parikhana soon, hamshira! Khala jaan had said right from the beginning that she would, and see, she's been spoken for at court! Women laughing, chewing on their paans, lighting their hookahs. Sidra within earshot, washing another set of utensils, back stiff. *I've even heard that she finally bedded Tariq Khan! After two years worth of visits!* More laughter. *We'll never see anyone like her here again.*

Sidra finishes washing the dish stiffly. Nobody looks her way. Her stomach lurches and she leans forward to keep herself steady. This is not surprising, and yet…. She can't tell what hurts her more—that Shabnam hadn't been down to see her since the mehfil or that she would be leaving soon, seemingly without a word. Soap makes Sidra's fingers slippery so she reaches for more water. Her cheeks are warm. Another childish thing yet to change. She might cry any moment.

Never mind that her khala arranged for Asad to see her on the same night as the mehfil. Never mind that she will never know of Shabnam's mehfil performance. Never mind that Shabnam has gained dakhilat at the parikhana. What stings, as those beatings in childhood had, as the hard looks levelled at her nose, is the humiliation of it. The silence woven between them. Her khala's part in it. Shabnam's part, too.

When maghrib finally descends upon the kotha and darkness covers the establishment like an ink stain, Ishrat arrives at her door with hot sheermaals. Sidra is undoing her hair, unbraiding the memory of Shabnam's warm hands from them.

☙

Raziya begum calls visitor upon visitor for Shabnam's last days. She hardly leaves her room. It begins to remind her of the dark box she'd once left. When the last courtier departs for the palace, and she eases back on to the takht, bare and spent, she wonders if she is stepping into another box. She wonders if she should slip down the stairs and see Sidra.

In her mind's eye, the takhts are set out neatly and she knows exactly which way to turn to find her. She finds herself moving again, lifting her legs into a pair of green pyjamas. Arms slipping into the cotton. Picking up a chaddar. She knows that Raziya begum has some of the women keeping an eye on her, it seems unlikely she will be watched so late into the night.

Something tells her to make her way to the chhat instead. So she does. She follows the feeling.

Someone else is there. Standing by the parapet, back to the stairs. Looking at the sky. Shabnam also looks up. Pale grey clouds are hanging over the city. Dismal. She looks back at the figure at the end of the chhat. In the faint light, she recognizes the plait.

It's Sidra.

Her heart hammers. She thinks of their time together, from that evening when Sidra had come up with tea to this night, when they haven't spoken in weeks. She wonders if she should speak. She knows it is better not to. That it is better to turn on her heel right now and go back to her quarters. How could anything be explained now? In what words could she speak the truth?

'You know,' her voice is louder in the emptiness than she intends and Sidra flinches at the sudden sound.

She turns around but very little of her face can be seen in this darkness. Shabnam continues anyway, grateful for the shadows. 'Shabnam isn't...it isn't even my actual name. That's the name Raziya gave me when I came here.'

Sidra says nothing. Shabnam continues, 'My name is Anjum.' Her throat feels tight. Everything about this feels final. Permanent. The words tumble out of her mouth and lack all the poise she's given so much of her life to cultivating, 'Sidra, it's the name my amma gave me. You know, I've never told you about her but she could really sing. She used to sing me to... she didn't even have an ustad, you know...she just had this voice, and I...Sidra, I wanted to come and see—I wanted to meet you but I...you know, Raziya begum and I just—I have to...you need to know I...I....'

'You don't need to explain anything,' Sidra's voice cuts her off. Soft and without malice.

Shabnam's hands reach for her chaddar, needing to fiddle with something to keep that unsettled feeling at bay. She feels as though she might lose her composure any moment, might stumble forward and press her cheek into Sidra's shoulder as she'd once done so often. There is a lump in her throat. She wants so much to reach for Sidra's hand. To feel its roughness against her own. Their differences, made apparent.

Sidra walks towards her and for a moment, Shabnam thinks they might embrace. They might forgive each other. They might even speak. Sidra doesn't stop though and walks briskly right past her, her shoulder briefly brushing against Shabnam's. Parting. Permanent. The familiar scent of her itr lingers in the air around Shabnam long after Sidra has gone down the stairs, Shabnam just stands there, clutching her chaddar. Her fingers hurt from the force of her grip. The clouds drift above her, suggesting rain. Somewhere a donkey brays. Shabnam holds herself together for a moment longer. Then she cries.

Shabnam walks slower as the crowd grows. There is a moment in which the other dancing girls disappear from view, finally. She breathes easier then, letting her gaze roam unguarded from face to face. Strangers who all seem to bear a stronger and stronger resemblance to the one she has left behind. Somewhere, the long sloping nose. Elsewhere, a tightly knotted plait. There, someone's shoulders turned in like folded paper. And there, pistachio green. The old life collapsing in the new. Shabnam pauses. Yellow silk rustles at her feet. She can almost smell that itr. Sidra's name slips from her mouth. Pistachio green again. Disappearing. She starts walking again.

∽

Sidra sits on the takht with a box in her hands. The kotha is the quietest it has been in weeks. She can even hear the light breeze as it whistles through this corridor and into her room. She wonders if everyone will be dressed in yellow at the Basant mela. She wonders how she must look in her new clothes. Bela flowers in her hair—Shabnam could never dance without them. Unbidden, Sidra's hands undo the string around the box. The bangles are earthen, the same red as the monsoon mud of bazaar lanes. The thin paper in which they are wrapped is perfumed. She picks two from the box. There is an unrest in her. A voice that sounds like Shabnam's. The bangles fit her wrists perfectly. The voice quietens.

37

THE DEMON SAGE'S DAUGHTER

VARSHA DINESH

In one version of the story, nobody dies, and you get to keep the princess as your maid.

She chafes against this, longing for her silks and jewels. You scoff, tugging her after you, a tangle of jasmine wound around her arms. She's tried to break free many times, plaintively singing to the deer and the birds and the sky for help, but everything in your ashram bows to your father, even the quilt of sky above, and he is the one who bound her. And so, your princess just weeps.

But for all her faults, in that version of the story, the princess at least is a pious girl beloved of the gods. So much so that all her tears turn into sapphires and rubies, collecting in little piles by her feet. And although she protests when you sweep them into the folds of your sari, she knows that you are her mistress and she cannot stop you from doing what you want.

What you want, in that version of the story, is to take the riches from your princess's tears, buy all the weapons of Patala, and then march into Amaravati, the great celestial city, where you will kill all the gods.

Every single one of the 330 million.

And when their slithering godblood runs down the diamond facade of Mount Meru, you will bathe your hair in it, soaking in it until your scalp is drenched and your sari drips crimson, and then—only then—will your revenge be complete.

In that version of the story.

In another version of the story, which is still not the real story, you are on your knees in your ashram, trying to put your father back together. You have already tried this with frantic hands and magic, with careful hands and needles, with sticky paste from deodar trees and the decanted salts of your own tears and the drip drip of your blood churned black with incantation. Now, hours later, you are appealing to his logic: telling him how stupid you are, what an idiot-child, can't even put your father back together.

Your father is saying nothing back at all, having burst open some time ago like a ripe fruit.

In the version of the story you choose to be true, you are kneeling in your father's blood, silent. His godly killer has just fled the scene, hoisted on to a heavenly chariot, fading into a distant astral blip in seconds. In his wake, at this scene of crime, there is no revenge, no confrontation, no loud lamentation. Only silence.

Lotuses bloom vividly everywhere a piece of your father has landed. They're beneath your feet, climbing the walls. Great lotus leaves brush your face when you move, enfolding you in shadow over and over. Your princess sits slumped on the floor, blowing her nose into one.

'Did you hear it?' you ask, hushed. 'The spell. Do you know it?'

Beneath the mountain of lotus blooms, your princess is naked as the day she was born. There is no blood on her skin, clean and new, but gore drips from her hair and coats her shoulders like a grim cape.

'Answer me.'

Your princess's nod is miniscule, just a quick jerk of her head before she resumes staring pallidly at the violence.

'I'll free you.'

Your princess's eyes snap wide open.

'I'll free you from your curse, and in return, you'll tell me what you heard. Do we have a deal?'

You wonder what you will do if she says no. If she leaves you alone to deal with the shattered bone and adipose florets and stringy grey matter that is all that is left of your father. But the princess is too crafty to pass up this opportunity.

'You'll free me,' she echoes. 'No tricks.'

'None.'

'And after I'm freed?' she asks. 'What will you do?'

That is none of her business. You wring your father's blood from your hands. You crush a flower under your foot. You wait until your princess stops waiting for an answer, blood-stained face shuttering over.

When you put your arm out in partnership, your princess takes it.

There are two threads of stories here woven together into a loose braid, one bloodier than the other. Your princess is the strongest strand in the first thread. Your father is the bloodiest one in the other. Between the two, linking force, are you and Kacha.

Maybe you should have started the story with Kacha.

In a more traditional story, he is the hero after all. Kacha, in his blue silks and gold earrings. Kacha, with his silver tongue. Kacha, who even the goats liked, the traitorous bastards.

Some months ago, when his big celestial retinue arrived, all flappy-winged vimanas and heralds blowing conch shells, some of your handmaidens crowded the dance hall. They jostled each other, ankle bells tinkling, a murmuration of gentle creatures hiding vicious teeth. Each one called out a new, juicy bit of information. He wears a diamond on his chest the size of a mango! His body is strong and robust like a peach! Oh, my lady, my lady, his servants carry bowls of fruit, gold-stringed veenas, and such heavenly flowers!

You tossed your braid over your shoulder. 'If he adorns his chest with such sizeable jewels, girls, should we worry that he is lacking elsewhere?'

'He's come to study with your father, my lady,' Maniprabha said. 'What he lacks in physical prowess, he must possess in spirit.'

'Spirit,' Samyukta laughed. 'Are the gods' spirits not destroyed after centuries of losing wars against us? Are they not tired of their little sons dying like pitiful worms on the battlefields? Do they not seek peace by sending their own to study here at the ashram of the demon sage?'

'It's not peace they want,' you said. 'It's something else.'

The girls all exchanged glances at that, swooning with curiosity, but you were the mistress. You decided if you wanted to include them in your secret. You decided if you wanted to leave them hanging, spinning their theories as intricately as they worked the ashram's looms.

'The gods have sent him to sniff out a secret,' you said. 'He's a spy.'

'A spy? A secret? What secret?'

But a queen without secrets is no queen at all, and you only smiled. 'Father will need me. I must go now to welcome our new guest.'

Outside, in the seething emerald fields of your father's ashram, Kacha stood bent in half, hands clasped, all his attendants singing harmonious praises of your father's might. Your new guest's face was neither stunning nor memorable. His voice, however, boomed in messianic thunder when he spoke: 'Oh, Saint of Saints! Most Knowledgeable One in Patala! I thank you for accepting me as your most humble student.'

He kneeled, bejewelled forehead pressed to your father's feet. Flowers tumbled from the centre of his palms: jasmine and marigold, rose mallow and calotrope, oleander and parijat.

Your father cast a bemused smile on the kneeling god. Lightning flickered in his coiled beard. Raw cosmic power thrummed from him in tympanic waves, flattening the grass, buffeting the crown off Kacha's head. 'Rise, student,' he boomed, motioning you forward. You performed the welcoming rituals: washing Kacha's feet with rose water, smearing sandalwood and turmeric paste on his forehead, garlanding him with marigolds so bright the bees swarmed in droves.

'This is my daughter, Devayani,' your father said. 'It's her job to make sure that your stay with us is most pleasurable.'

Most pleasurable! Ha! You knew your father. You knew he expected you to sidle up to Kacha and seduce him, lure his secrets from his mouth, feed him lies and flirtations just like you fed milk and ghee to the snakes in the ashram's groves every morning.

Kacha was already assessing the curve of your mouth, your hip where you had shifted your sari to offer a glimpse of your skin. 'Lady Devayani,' he murmured. 'They whisper rumours in Amaravati that the demon sage's daughter is more beautiful than all of heaven's apsaras. I see now that there was no hyperbole.'

'You flatter me, my lord.'

'I look forward to studying under your father,' Kacha said. 'But I fear now, after meeting you, that I will have to work very hard indeed to stay focused.'

His shoulders blocked out the sun. The diamond on his chest, set amidst repeating lotus patterns of embroidery, made you suddenly dizzy. You stumbled, momentarily blinded, dropping your tray of rose and turmeric. He caught you neatly, long fingers folding around your wrist.

'Lady Devayani,' he said. 'I'm sure you will have much to teach me, as well.'

Your fingers rubbed unconsciously the welts his touch left on your wrists, an effect of his godblood. Each one was reddened, raised; alphabets in a harsh language carved into your skin. Your father's future murderer saw them and only smiled: a whetted thing, sharp and profane.

That was the beginning.

This is the circuitous route you take to an ending.

You and your princess leave your dead father in the ashram and descend into the realms of Patala.

This is where the demons live, in their underground cities of gold and gemstone trees. At the gates, your princess pulls weakly against her flower-chains, unwilling to go any further.

'They won't eat you,' you say. 'There are better things to eat in Patala. The exquisite glair of Naga eggs. Black-skinned fish from the river Hataki. Sweets from the tables of the demon king Bali, wrapped in sugar-soaked silver. They have no need for bland princess-flesh.'

She stares at you, aghast. You wonder how she will tell this story to the future princes lining up for her attention. You: demoness, daughter of the Dark Sage, leading her into the realms of ghosts and goblins. She: victim, hostage, held captive by a beautiful monster.

What a repugnant fable.

Your mouth turns in a curdled grimace. 'Stay with me and maybe they won't rip the meat off your bones.'

The vimana you summon to travel into the underworld is elegant, with swan wings that ruffle at every breeze and seats of blue and gold. A glittering green snake adorns its side, fat diamonds for eyes.

'O Pious Daughter!' it hisses when you board. 'How is your father?'

Your princess opens her mouth, surely to blab about how your father is currently a formless flesh-splatter, but you hum the opening words of an incantation, the syllables slippery as eels. Your princess clicks her mouth shut, pop, hands jumping in surprise to her throat. It is not until you're descending into the first level of Patala that you let her speak again.

'You're not my mistress any more,' she spits. 'Don't do that again.'

'If the demons know their sage is dead, they will march against the gods. The gods will call the sun and moon to arms, and the earth will be plunged into eons of icy nights and monstrous tides. Do you want that?'

'Don't you? It's your father who's dead—'

'Another word and I'll stitch your mouth shut. With iron.'

Your princess believes you. She looks out instead, eyes wide, at the winding streets and drinking parlours.

The first city of Patala is resplendently beautiful. The demon architect Maya's miraculous palaces glisten like beetle carapaces, all stained glass and coruscating light beams. Canopies of ivory filigree and statues of bronze adorn the wide avenues. A vista of gemstones spills slanted light across an artificial sky, illuminating the city in strange, twinkling light.

Your father always called it excess. When the demons came to him for advice, he told them not to test the gods. Build just enough marvels. Keep your palaces just a bit smaller than theirs. Do not tempt celestial wrath, and maybe the demons could keep their cities, their sorcery, their strange and darkling denizens.

'It's beautiful,' your princess says. 'I didn't think it would be beautiful.'

'Did you think it would all be vermin and filth?'

'No. I've heard the stories....'

'Women that lie with any man for a drink. Nagas that live in holes like animals. Are those the stories you've heard?'

In the gemlight, your princess looks like she wants to put her fist through your face. 'They won't come back, you know,' she says. 'Kacha's gone. Your father never loved you. So, you can snap at me all you wish, but they won't come back for you. Nobody wants you.'

But this is where she misunderstands you. This is not a story about your father, or Kacha. This is a story about you.

You are Devayani, daughter of the demon sage, mistress of his ashram now that he is gone. Your father taught you how to meditate for as long as it took to bottle thunderstorms and weaponize blood. In your grottos of horns and teeth, he instructed you on dance mantras that brought about droughts or floods. Your feet became a palimpsest of scars, layered and sliced by hours of dancing. Your very bones are carved with treatises on the importance of illusions and hypnosis, the mysteries of augury, the secretive, coded stratagems of celestial warfare.

Kacha and your father are in your past.

Your present is about you.

'Where are we going?' your princess asks.

'To the night markets. To find a locksmith who knows sorcery. Your shackles are demon-made and answer only to the one who put them on you.'

'But your father is dead.'

'Someone there will know how to free you.'

'And after that?'

You turn your head away, pressing your lips together, pretending to feast your eyes on the sights. It doesn't take your princess too long to stop asking.

In any version of your universe, this is heaven's most coveted secret, your father's greatest legacy: he can raise the dead.

After the day's battle climaxed, when the battlefields smoked and dozed uneasy at night, your father would walk through mounds of corpses and broken chariots, chanting the incantations. As he walked, demonic corpse-soldiers rose in his wake, shambling after him into the ashram.

You and your handmaidens would sit at the looms, weaving the soldiers' new skins. The dead could not live in the skin they'd died in; their souls hung out of it, untucked, and they flopped about like fish. When the new skins were finished, you and your father stitched them on to the demons, dusted off their thick clubs, and sent them back to war.

The gods and demons have been at war for centuries. The gods were forever dying, being sucked into the karmic pipeline, cycling through reincarnation like leaves buffeting helplessly in a gale. The demons died and simply came back, as if dying was nothing but a mild inconvenience.

It ruffled some big heavenly feathers. Bruised some tall celestial egos.

You and your father were prepared for spies. Many from heaven's ranks had come here before, pretending to seek tutelage, burrowing instead for information on the resurrection spell. But none were as subtle and determined as Kacha.

He was a good student. He studied deep into the night, poring over palm-leaf texts while your father meditated. He took diligent notes and debated for hours with your father on complex cosmic paradoxes. When he was not taking lessons, Kacha whittled wood into fantastic creatures that followed you around. There was a parrot with a green glass eye, and a rabbit so small it would fit in the cup of your palm. A monkey swung from the folds of your sari, bringing you flowers and oddly patterned stones.

Or he would write you: Today I watched you dance. I have seen celestial apsaras dance in Indra's palace above Mount Meru. They are not as skilled as you are, Devayani. Or: I wish these treatises on conjuring spirits and calculating cumulative karmic scores were as arresting as your singing, Devayani.

You pretended to be charmed, blushing whenever he sent you a new message. His overtures of love cloyed in your mouth like oversweet rose jam.

At Kacha's request, you took him on tours of the ashram. You showed him the looms and the dance hall. You let him row the two of you out to the middle of the lotus pond, far enough in dawn's fog that there was nothing in either direction but mist-shrouded blooms.

'This is where apsaras are born,' he told you, plucking a plush pink blossom. 'In the hearts of flowers, soft as morning dew. Have you seen an apsara?'

You shook your head.

'I'll show you one day,' he said. 'Oh, Devayani, don't you chafe at being locked up here in your ashram? Such a clever girl should see the world. I could take you.'

Kacha came to see you after his lessons, coaxing you to feed the deer with him or augur the shapes of clouds in the sky. He tucked flowers behind your ear and told you stories of Amaravati, his home in the skies. He made you a model of it with clay and silk and precious things, laying out wide boulevards and golden gates, sparkling indoor waterways, food halls where celestial cooks prepared the loveliest of dishes for the gods' banquets.

'What does an ascetic's daughter know of sweets?' he lamented. 'When I take you to Amaravati, I will bring you to the halls and let you have your pick of the sweets. Sugar wafers drizzled with honey so light it melts on your tongue. Milk and khoya confections with surprise berry hearts. Frosted, sugar-soaked cucumber garnished with candied petals.'

A coy grin parted your lips. 'You seem to have a sweet tongue, my lord.'

Tangerine flowers rinsed through the trees like flotsam. Butterflies spun in spiralling drifts. Kacha's smile sharpened. 'Would you like a taste, my lady?'

His touch made you burn and bubble, a beautiful firework held too close to skin. Pain bloomed, white and scalding, and you cried out again and again. Still he, feigning oblivion, pressed his mouth to yours, seeking the heat of your tongue.

He did not taste sweet. He tasted like iron, and salt, and the acid tang of godblood. You clenched your fists tight enough to carve bloody moons into your palms but did not pull away.

This was what your father expected from you, after all.

That you would dance close enough to serpents that they showed you their venom. That you would sit through the heat of a hundred scorpion stings. That you would bathe in godblood, if required, let it slough your skin off, if only it meant you could catch your father his godly spy.

'Oh, Devayani, my love,' Kacha cried, when you parted at last. 'I fear our happiness will be short-lived. The demons suspect me of being a spy. I fear they are plotting to harm me. I am terrified that if I die, our love will break your heart. How could I bear leaving you? How could my soul rest, knowing you will be in pain?'

And here, well-rehearsed, you assured Kacha with syrup-thick words that he need not fear. You would speak to your father on his behalf. You were the demon sage's daughter after all. You promised: your love would always protect him.

The very next day, you found Kacha dead for the first time.

∾

The night markets occupy the riverside of the third level of Patala.

The river here runs aureate, casting a glow over the ghosts and goblins that call the city its home. Boats full of men row across it, blowing long plumes of fire. When the fire fans the surface of the water, it spits and hisses, turning into ropes of gleaming gold which adorn the chests of the vendors at the market.

The market is a dizzying tangle of wares, sourced from all seven of Patala's realms. Foggy glass tanks, teeming with bathypelagic creatures from the primordial ocean of the lowest level. Spines of gods, crackling with power, battle-won and encased in silver by Maya's craftsmen. Fangs of panthers and elephant hair, sold by all manner of strange netherworld folk: mottled-blue vetalas, living upside-down in trees; grey-skinned pisachas, feeding on corpse-flesh; dark-eyed rakshasas, shifting shape into whoever you desire the most.

You once purchased your dancing bells from here, from a pisacha woman whose breath was thick with death and sorcery. It is to her you go now, tugging your princess behind you.

She blanches at the sight of the shop. 'This doesn't look like the house of a locksmith.'

Rows of skulls line the shelves, and bones hang from the rafters, tinkling grotesquely. Vertiginous drifts of corpse-ash execute strange calligraphy in the still air. The pisacha woman shuffles to you, bells decorating the hollows of her desiccated ribcage, jangling with each step she takes.

'Pious Daughter,' she rasps, her flickering tongue dusty grey. 'You smell of death and blood. What can I do for you?'

Your princess quivers. 'No tricks,' she whispers. 'You promised.'

Your promises are not worth much. Still: 'My father made these bonds,' you tell the pisacha. 'Can you break them?'

'Upala can do all sorcery,' the pisacha says, glassy eyes focused intently on your princess. 'Snip, snip with the magic knife. Cuts through even Indra's armour.'

While Upala goes to get her magic knife, your princess gives you a suspicious look. 'If it's that easy, why couldn't you just do it yourself?'

'I have other business here.'

When Upala comes back, you ask the price of her magic knife. Your princess's brows furrow. A piece of bone from your father is still stuck in her hastily washed hair. You think of saying something but then turn away, deciding to let her have the pleasure of discovering this ghoulish accessory all to herself.

∞

In some versions of your story, which you do not want to be the story, you are nothing but the querulous daughter of a powerful man, spending your days conversing with twee forest creatures. You learn dance and music, but never the spells and incantations that make them your weapons. Your father never thinks to teach you because what use is teaching a daughter?

In those versions, you are simply a distraction in the tales of conflicts between powerful men. A girl living in the margins of her own story.

Those versions of you are not ambitious. Those versions of you do not go exploring Patala, or demand things from your father. Things like: tell me how to brew elixirs, or teach me how to enter another's consciousness, or give me the secret of resurrection.

In every version of you that exists, your father chastises you for demanding the resurrection spell.

He banishes you from his hut when you persist, corralling you to your dance hall for weeks. In your rage, you break every pane of glass adorning the latticed walls. You kick at pots of saffron and turmeric and indigo. You dance in the mess, painting the hall vivid in your anger, casting spells to turn all your handmaidens into brightly dyed rabbits.

Your father lets you.

'The only obstacle to the victory of the gods is the resurrection spell,' he tells you while you sulk on the floor, boneless. 'It's a secret I must guard closely.'

'I'm your daughter,' you spit. 'Why can't you teach me everything?'

Your father's eyes flash, miniature suns. 'You act like a spoiled child, Devayani,' he says, dispassionate. 'What if I teach you the resurrection spell today and you, fickle as you are, teach it to any simple paramour the gods might send to trick you? What if I teach you my greatest secret and you use it on birds to look mighty in front of your handmaidens?'

In every version of your story, you try to show him that you are more than that. That you have bled and scarred yourself to be worthy of him. You siphon secrets. You feed men sweet poison. You press shlokas into silk and bone and metal, turning them into potent weapons. You are a blade: a bejewelled one, but a blade, nevertheless. You can be equals.

Your father only laughs. Your role is set, he says. You are the demon sage's daughter, using your beauty and middling magic to set snares for his enemies.

But you want to be more than that.

You want to be his heir.

When he hears this, your father laughs so long and so loud that all hell and heaven reverberates with the sound. So long and loud that the blades of grass seem to shake with it, trees all joining in, your handmaidens hiding their faces with rabbit paws while they try not to gloat at your shame.

(Nobody's laughing in the end, when Kacha rips your father apart. But that part comes later.)

This is the story of how you find your princess: after your father laughs at you, you leave the dance hall a mess of pigments and tears. Your sari is dirty from days of tantrums. Your handmaidens are still rabbits, so you go alone to the river, where you stare in loathing at your reflection for what feels like eons.

When you enter the water, the river swirls about you in icy, varicoloured eddies. Red for ambition. Blue for humiliation.

You stay for hours, sobbing, breathing a fortitude prayer.

At dusk, you are disturbed by a fit of laughter.

'Do you think she thinks she can wash away the embarrassment?' a voice whispers. Your spiritual cognition identifies the speakers: the king's daughter and her favoured handmaiden. 'Look,' the princess continues, and you know she's pressing her feet against your discarded sari. 'She's the daughter of the demon sage, yet all she wears are rags.'

'She's a demoness,' her handmaiden says. 'This is what they know, princess.

Corpse-ash and charnel house raiment. Filthy things that smell like death.'

'Neither a dutiful daughter nor a talented sage. No wonder her father has been so displeased.'

It is frivolously cruel. You think of cursing the princess, something inventive and alienating: all her lovers will turn into frogs, or everything she touches will turn to slimy snails.

The princess is beautiful, after all. Delicate face and dark gaze rimmed with rings of kohl. Her fingers are red from the dye of the henna plant, elegant when she reaches down to pick up your sari.

'Come and get it, hut dweller,' she laughs. 'Come out of the water.'

It is silly, childish cruelty. But you are a child yourself, hurting because of a father you can never please. And so it is that you clothe yourself in the foam of the river, skimming the crests of small waves to weave yourself a sari. So it is that you rush out of the water, sputtering in your anger. So it is that you fall right into their trap: a muddy hole in the ground.

They must have dug it hours ago.

You twist your ankles, scrape your elbows, lose your illusory river-garb. Naked, wet mud slicks and slithers over you, weighing you down with its stickiness. Something else is in there, foul-smelling, squishing underfoot as you try to stand. You cry out when you see it: fish guts, at least a day old, likely gathered from the palace kitchens. The smell sears your nostrils. You retch, and your tormentors' faces glisten with mirth far above you, bright from the sun.

'There, there,' your princess says, satisfied. 'Isn't that hole much more befitting for a demoness?'

You ready yourself to curse her, but she surprises you once again. Something small falls on to your lap from the surface. You scramble for it, panic squeezing your throat, and lift up a rabbit.

Its hue is unnaturally pink. Its neck is broken.

The next one is grey, still warm and twitching. As you hold it—her, her, one of your girls, which one?—your spine turns to ice. Your tongue goes slack in your mouth. The horror of it mutes you, blinds you, stoppers your blood in your veins.

'Can't bring them back to life?' the princess asks. 'Maybe your father will show them mercy?'

Later, burying the small bodies of your handmaidens, you will wonder if the princess had known. If she had understood the weight of her cruelty.

If she had even had reason, save that she was a princess of something, and you were the disagreeable daughter of the demon sage.

You will never ask her this. Not when you are finally rescued, and your father—apoplectic at the loss of perfectly good servants—curses your princess to be your handmaiden. Not when you set her to impossible tasks, picking up stray leaves in the garden with her teeth, or polishing the dance hall floor with arms bound behind her back. Not even after your father is dead, and his blood is all over her, and you barter with her for her freedom.

Your princess killed six of your handmaidens that day. You do not know how to weigh cruelties on a grand karmic scale, but you think the balance is still tipped in your favour.

You make one more stop before you leave the night markets.

Your princess, newly freed, continues to trail after you, terrified of goblins and ghosts. Her fingers are laced tightly in yours, the scent of her fear sharp and distinctly peppery.

'What will you do?' she keeps asking. Devayani, whose father is dead. Devayani, whose Kacha has fled. What will you do now?

'You're free,' you snap, hiding Upala's knife in the folds of your sari. 'What will you do?'

'If I go back to my father, he'll just make me marry a prince.'

'How terrible for you.'

'I don't want to marry a prince,' she sneers. 'I want to learn the things you know. I always have.'

You give her your most contemptuous look. 'Is that why you murdered my handmaidens? Because you were jealous?'

Your princess's face briefly crumples. 'I didn't know,' she says. 'They were rabbits, how was I supposed to know?'

'As character traits go, a rabbit-killer isn't much better.'

'I was angry. All this knowledge you have, all this potential, and you waste it all on Kacha—'

'You said it yourself. He's not coming back.'

'True,' your princess says, restlessly. 'So, what now?'

You settle your face into its grimmest expression. 'The demon sage is dead,' you drone, bored. 'Killed by his own treacherous student. It's time for retribution.'

You swivel right, dipping into the dim liquor shop of a Naga distiller.

Gold scales dapple his hood, and a ruby glistens atop it. He is surprised to see you, enquiring in his sibilant tongue as to your father's whereabouts. You wait until after you have made your purchases to tell him: 'He's dead.'

The Naga's hood rises in shock. His lidless eyes travel over you, trying to discern if you are joking. His coils shift closer.

'He's dead,' you repeat. 'Tell everyone in Patala. Their demon sage is dead. Killed by the traitorous gods!'

And then you leave, turning around and racing down the market, feet slipping against mottled glass and gleaming stone. Your princess trails behind you, hand in yours, gasping.

'This is why you came!' she pants. 'This is what you wanted. For them to know, to panic. This is what you wanted, isn't it?'

You hide your smile. As your vimana rises, you can hear the whispers begin, rising to screams by the time you are in the sky.

In the version of the story you tell the demons later, you will give inventory of all the different ways Kacha died in his pursuit of the spell.

The first time you let him go cold, godblood congealing against singed grass, while you tried to understand. He was sprawled just outside the dance hall, a great swathe of his flesh ripped out, ribs cracked open, his insides glinting like a ruby geode. The expression on his face was that of a man trying awfully hard to look dignified while something tore him open like an orange being peeled.

You stood staring, mind racing, silent in the afternoon's blood-rich breeze. The proximity of his body to your favourite haunt meant that he had expected you to find him. But why? Simply because he guessed your love for him would propel you to accelerate his resurrection?

You paced for a bit, shooing away the flies and the birds. It was only after you held his heart in your fist that you made your decision.

You tore at your hair and burned your fingers taking his heart to your father, screaming, wailing, begging until your father cried out that you had become exactly what he predicted: a weak-hearted, foolish girl, giving her heart away to sweet-talking paramours.

'I love Kacha,' you wept, disconsolate. 'He is no spy, Father, only my beloved. And now the demons have killed him for no crime but his love for me!'

You were adept at acting. Your father had demanded you be. Now you were putting on a show, playing a part, and he stormed and blustered at you, betrayed.

'You will not take me as your heir,' you spat, your throat raw, eyes stinging. 'At least give me my lover.'

'Be quiet!' roared your father. His lightning whip cracked across your shoulder: searing, splintering your collarbone. 'I will raise him from the dead because he is my student. Only because of that. End this stupidity, Devayani. He does not love you.'

While your father resurrected Kacha, stitching him into a skin you had woven so lovingly, you hid behind a wall, craning to listen. But your father did not need words for the spell any more, only the power of his mind. And so thwarted, you ignored Kacha for two days, sulking in your hut while your shoulder healed.

A little before the second time, Kacha lamented repeatedly that he was afraid the demons would kill him again. You wept into his chest. He sighed: 'Oh, Devayani, why does fate test our love so?'

The two of you were lying in a boat, buoyed gently by the waves of the lotus pond. You pretended not to notice a lowly demigod creeping towards you. Sunlight glimmered on the assassin's golden crown, throwing shards of brightness in your eye. Kacha motioned with his fingers, as if telling him to hurry up.

You ignored them, playing the part of an idiot, sighing, and pressing your lips to Kacha's neck. When the hitman struck, arterial godblood splashed all over you. It slithered down your throat, liquefying your lungs. You spat out a glob of blood contemplatively, and then collapsed against Kacha. When you woke next, both you and he had new skins, and neither of you were any closer to figuring out the spell.

The third and final time, you followed a secretive Kacha into the forest without his knowledge. There he met with his co-conspirators, other demigods, all dressed unobtrusively in the fashions of demon folk. 'The gods are growing tired of waiting,' they said. 'How long until you have the spell?'

For all his dying, Kacha had managed to glean only a few words of the incantation. He caught them each time his soul was yanked from the astral plane, an echo of a whisper that was not enough. The gods needed all of it, the whole spell, and they needed it fast.

It was time to do something drastic.

This time, you watched as the gods cut Kacha's throat on his instructions and burned his body. You watched them mix his ashes into a chalice of your father's favourite wine. It flummoxed you, this new trick. How was this different from the other times?

But then, as you paced your dance hall and your princess swept the floor, realization crept up on you. 'Come with me,' you said, tugging at her chains. 'I need you.'

You took her to a glade, far from the ashram. She huffed and spat on the floor, demanding to know what you were going to do. Throw her in a hole of fish guts? Ask her to pluck fruits with her teeth?

'You'll see in a moment,' you promised. Then you bit your lip against the unpleasantness, took out a knife, and got to work.

Later, when your father requested his favourite wine, it was you who took it to him.

You, dutiful daughter of sweet comportment, had poured him just the quantity he liked. He, pleased with you for once, downed the first cup in a single swallow.

'I am tired of fighting you, Devayani,' he said, a deep sigh fluttering his beard. 'Must we bicker with each other because of an outsider?'

You kneeled, folding your hands in your lap. 'Forgive me, Father, but Kacha is not an outsider to me any more. He has promised to marry me and take me to Amaravati.'

Your father's face twisted in ugly displeasure, but he hid it under a smile. You poured him more of the wine. He swilled it and said: 'If you want him so much, perhaps I can consult the celestial astrologers. But if you intend to marry, Kacha must leave the ashram this instant. It is not appropriate, the two of you living in such close proximity.'

You nodded, contrite. You had seen this coming. 'You will not regret this, Father,' you trilled, hands clasped to your chest. 'Kacha is wonderful.'

'If you believe in his intentions, I believe you,' your father said, sly. He drained the last of the wine. 'Where is Kacha? I have not seen him today. We must find him, instruct him to leave.'

'I've seen neither Kacha nor the princess all day,' you lied, wringing the hem of your sari to appear concerned. 'But there were some strangers in the forest today. And a strange smell of fire in the afternoon.'

A flickering in the air, like ghosts convening.

Your father's expression began to change. A storm descended upon his face, dark and tempestuous, and he snatched the wine glass off the floor.

He peered into it, swirling it this way and that, face twisting in a horrific grimace when he spotted the flecks of ash.

'What is it?' you asked. 'What is it, Father?'

'Daughter,' he said, eyes wide and thunderstruck. 'I have been tricked.'

Varying expressions of disgust crossed your father's face. Someone, he raged, had tricked him. Mixing Kacha's ashes into the wine! Knowingly feeding him his own student! What wicked treachery! If the gods came to know, they would destroy the cities of Patala. They would plunge both sides into a catastrophic war. And how was your father to explain, great sage that he was, that he had not been cognizant of Kacha swimming around in his wine?

You wailed, crumpled on the floor, 'Oh, Father! Father, what will we do?'

'There is no other way,' your father said, through violent retching. 'I must resurrect him.'

'But he's within you! If you resurrect Kacha now, it will kill you! Won't you be ripped open? Torn apart?'

A long, querulous moan escaped your father. He clutched his stomach. 'Go, make us both new skins,' he said. 'I have no choice. I will need to teach the resurrection spell to the part of Kacha within me. Once I resurrect him, he can tear himself out of me, you can stitch him up, and he will revive me. Kacha knows the situation. He wouldn't want to start another war.'

'Or,' you ventured, quietly, 'you can teach it to me. And I can revive you, Father, after you resurrect Kacha.'

The simpler solution. The safest, most obvious one. But even then, your father's gaze for you was stinging. 'You don't have Kacha's aptitude for spell and sorcery,' he scoffed. 'You concern yourself with middling spells and think too highly of your own talents. Your place is at the looms, and later at your husband's side. Understood?'

Your face stiffens into a rictus. 'Yes, Father.'

'Go now. No time to waste.'

You worked the warp and the weft at the looms, possessed by a strange calm. The weave slithered and moved, enlivened by the sorcery of its production, quickly taking shape under your skilled hands. Just as they were done, two skins perfectly woven, you heard your father scream: a wretched sound. It went on—bones cracking like fireworks, spine splitting with a wet crunch—for a long while. Only when it stopped did you move, skins thrown over your shoulder, bare feet crushing the grass beneath your feet as you ran.

The scene in the hut was a nightmare. On the floor lay Kacha: bloody, stirring, watching you with empty eyes. He strained weakly in your direction. You threw the new skin atop him, careless. He keened, tugging uselessly at it, fingers grazing your thigh. You simply stepped past him, towards where your father's blood splattered the hut floor, crying out: 'Princess!'

A loop of jasmine, pristine, unspooled from the rapidly blooming lotus-field of your father's ribcage. You took it in your hands and pulled. It took you a few tries before you could see her, head and neck crowning, blind terror in her face as you yanked her free of your father's torso.

You had made two skins, just like your father instructed.

One for Kacha. One for your princess, whom you had murdered earlier in the glade, mixing her remains with that of Kacha's in the wine.

As you slipped the skin over her, stitching her up tight, you could hear Kacha slithering about. He shuffled and croaked, half-alive, struggling to slip into the skin. His technique was poor, having never practised it himself. Did he wonder why you were not weeping at his side? What was he thinking, in his untucked mind, that his eyes were starting to cloud with terror?

You began to scream. Loud, deliberate, rending your throat. The scream ripped itself out of you even as you worked fastidiously at fixing up your princess.

Help, he's killed my father!

Help, the gods have murdered him!

Kacha belly-flopped, new skin fluttering like that of a half-sloughed snake. Footsteps sounded, running into the hut. You smelled godblood and stayed kneeling, clutching your head in despair, pretending to splutter and choke on your own grief.

Just a poor, helpless woman, bereft of both father and lover.

Behind you, there was gasping and grunting as Kacha's people carried him away. In front of you, your princess panted and mewled, stretching out her new skin, gaping at you with the sick terror of something faced with both its destroyer and creator.

You could hear the gods' chariot outside, wheels aflame, taking to the sky with Kacha still flailing uselessly at the back. When Kacha was nothing but a spark in the sky, you straightened up, taking in the scene.

Your father dead. Kacha indisposed. Your princess the sole, accidental keeper of the resurrection spell's secret.

There was silence now, hazy and friable, broken only by your princess's fitful crying. Into that stillness you spoke, hoarse and hushed, the question that would both begin and end your story: 'Did you hear it? The spell. Do you know it?'

And in your princess's affirmation, her awed terror, her perfect new skin and the bloody crown of her head, you glimpsed a strange new future: dark, malleable, free for you to shape.

An hour after you return from Patala, you have at last finished collecting your father's skin, piled neatly what is left of his ribs and hips, and placed fragments of his spine in wraps of golden silk.

Your ashram is starting to fill with scores of demons. There are kings and queens, pisachas and vetalas, rakshasas and Nagas. There are demonic maidens so fragile they waver in the wind. Their loud lamenting rises like song, thrilling your blood, raising the hair on your skin.

You do not know where your princess is. Her absence makes you strangely lonely, but you have let her go. She kept her bargain by teaching you the resurrection spell and deserves her freedom. This is all she owes you, after you cut her throat to outsmart Kacha. Now, the two of you are even.

Briefly, you wonder what your father will think. That in the end it was not Kacha who betrayed him, but you. You wonder if he will be disappointed. But: oh Father, what did you expect? He had never seen you for what you really are: a weapon, gluttonous for power.

You will suck the marrow of it, for as long as you please, and the sweetness of it will linger on your tongue far longer than any memory of love.

Upala's knife cuts easily through bone. You put away the last sliver of your father's skull, collecting all the remains in a wide-rimmed container. The lotus blooms have all withered away. Outside, the demons wait: for explanation, lamentation, confrontation. You can taste their hunger for vengeance and blood in the very air.

You have rehearsed the version of the story you will tell them. The one where you screamed, and wept, and fantasized revenge on Amaravati. The one where you promise you will help them annihilate the gods—all 330 million of them—and bathe in their blood at the top of Mount Meru.

There is no version of the story branching from here where the demons do not follow you to the ends of the universe. You are the holder of the resurrection spell, the avenger of your father, the saviour of demonkind.

You are no longer the demon sage's daughter. You are the demon sage herself.

But before you speak to them, you will pour them all liquor. A sip to remember your father, to honour and celebrate his great life.

In each glass, you will place a tiny piece of him, obscuring the taste with the strength of freshly purchased Naga wine. No piece of him will go to waste. You will make sure of it.

In this way, distributed bit by bit amongst the demonic army, you will scatter your father's remains, that he may never be brought back whole.

One last safeguard to make sure that this is the deterministic version of your story: the final draft, the inevitable conclusion.

You drink your cup of wine, forcing it all down in one gulp.

Then you go out to start your war.

38

CRIPPLED WORLD

VEMPALLE SHAREEF

Translated from the Telugu by N. S. Murty and R. S. Krishna Moorthy

Saying the dua, and rubbing my face with cupped hands, was my daily ritual when I got up in the morning. But today I could not feel my right hand. When I looked for it, I found it severed from my body and lying cold and lifeless in one corner of the bed. I could not make out how this had happened. There wasn't a trace of blood around. It was as cleanly sawn off from my person as a neem branch sundered from a tree with a sharp saw.

'Oh no! My hand has been cut off,' I shrieked in fright.

My wife hurried into the bedroom. 'Oh, my! Was it because of this that you were making such a racket? I was frightened to death thinking it was about something else. Good riddance! Keep it safely in the almirah. We'll go to the doctor when we are able to find the time and get it reattached. Why are you so scared for every small, silly thing?' She left as quickly as she had arrived.

Only then did I notice something about her appearance that made me even more scared than before. Her left hand was missing. She was a southpaw. Whether to serve food, pick up a glass of water, scribble something in a notebook, dust a room, or even beat our seven-year-old child, Chandu, she would use only her left hand. And now, that all-important hand was missing. Forget about my severed hand, how and when had she lost hers? I wanted to call her back to ask her, but refrained from doing so. I knew she would snap at me again, and I would get no worthwhile explanation for her missing hand.

So, I said my prayers with the left hand, rubbed my face with it, and got up. I placed my severed right hand carefully next to my wife's left hand in the almirah.

Finishing my ablutions quickly with my left hand, I got dressed, ate my breakfast and, with the lunch box dangling from the stump of my right arm, I hurried to where my scooter was parked so I could head off to work. On the way, I saw the owner of the house that we were renting approaching me. To my surprise, both his hands were missing.

I cursed to myself, 'There is something terribly wrong with the world today!'

I wanted to ask the man about his two missing hands but didn't know what to say if he asked about my missing right hand in turn. So I said nothing, and simply gestured that I was going to the office and started the scooter. To my astonishment, I discovered that I was able to drive the scooter with a single hand. It wasn't because of any great skill on my part, it appeared that the scooter itself was designed to be driven single-handed. In fact, all the people on the road were driving single-handed. Some of them drove right-handed, others drove left-handed—that was the only difference.

How did the world get crippled overnight?

There was a famous hospital on the way to the office. People were lined up before it holding their amputated hands. Ignoring a *No Parking* sign I parked my vehicle and asked bystanders nearby what the queue was for? Their answer blew me away. Apparently, the people who were queuing up had lost their hands almost a year back. When they had applied to have them reattached, the waiting period was so long that it was only today that they had received the appointment they had sought for the requisite surgical procedure.

My goodness! At this rate, I would have to wait a year for my turn! What's the alternative? So many crippled people in this country! I was under the impression that this had begun only last night. If everyone was to wait a year for treatment, they might as well get used to living with just one hand. In fact, they would probably find it difficult to adapt to living with two hands once the missing hand was reattached. 'No, that shouldn't happen to me,' I thought. I must apply and get an appointment to get my hand reattached as soon as possible.

Leaving the scooter in the *No Parking* zone, I hurried towards the application counter. The queue there was even longer than the pilgrims' queue in front of the Tirupati temple. At least there, it was rumoured that the temple authorities were making arrangements for more areas to queue in, but here there seemed to be no such plan. It might take a week before my turn came. I saw that some people were attending to their personal hygiene while waiting in line. Others were besieged by hawkers and other vendors who were harassing people to buy something; if they didn't oblige, the aggressive hawkers would swear at them. Sometimes, they would even thrust goods into the hands of the unwilling buyers and forcibly try to take money out of their pockets. If they continued to resist, they were being pulled out of the queue to be shouted at and humiliated in front of everyone else.

I was only missing one hand. If I were to stand in this queue, I was not sure how many other limbs I would lose. I was already late to the office. It would require enormous stamina, pockets full of cash, and a week's leave to fight one's way through this queue. I left for the office.

The security guard greeted me with his lone hand. Greeting him in return I took the lift and reached my office floor. Everybody was effortlessly working at their computers with one hand.

'Can I do it as expertly as they?' I wondered.

Keeping my lunch box aside, I eased into my chair and switched on the computer. Hurrah! I did not feel any handicap working with just one hand. My left hand was able to negotiate the keyboard and mouse simultaneously. Everything seemed fine. The only thing I regretted was that nobody seemed to notice that I had lost a hand. That really hurt me.

I said to the colleague next to me: 'Till yesterday, every one of us had two hands. What happened to one of them all of a sudden?'

He laughed rather laconically.

'You are an inattentive fool! It's been a long time since all of us lost one of our hands. It was only because you continued to have two hands that you didn't notice that our hands were missing.'

He was right. That was the way of the world. Only when we miss something do we notice it in others. All these years I had taken little notice of him because he was a colleague, and it was only when there was a crisis that he had caught my attention. What a startling insight he had presented to me! Even as I was mulling this over, I felt proud that I had been able to hang on to both my hands for so long!

Suddenly, remembering the leave I had to take to submit the application at the hospital, I entered the office of my boss. He was operating his computer with his feet. I did not notice when he had lost them, but both his hands were missing!

For a second, I felt it was not proper for me to ask for leave. But then, realizing I had no other choice, I said: 'Sir! I need leave for a week. I need to submit my application at the hospital to get my hand reattached.'

He looked at me as though I were an idiot. Then he said: 'If I'd been able to find the time, I would have had my hands reattached long ago. I simply couldn't get away to submit my application. If every one of you goes on leave to get your hands reattached, I will have to shut down my business. Tell me, how is that bloody hand going to serve you? Get lost and get on with your work!'

That's what corporate culture is all about. Nobody cares about their fellows, nobody is considerate, all that matters is the work. Employees need to go about their routines as though there is nothing is wrong, even as their limbs fall off one after another. Because I lost my hand, I had begun noticing that people were missing their hands. If I were to lose my head, perhaps, I would see how many people around me were headless.

I sank into my seat after that dressing-down from my boss. When I looked at my watch, it was already one o'clock. My stomach was growling. A crazy thought passed through my mind...if only hunger were also short a hand and a leg then this need to appease it would be reduced by half. I walked across to the canteen, found an empty table, and settled down to eat my lunch. However, before I could open my lunch box, Sarayu, my HR friend, came running over to me with a box of sweets. Announcing 'good news', and without waiting for my response, she pushed a laddu into my mouth. I began munching on it, while enquiring with a raised eyebrow what the good news was.

'Yesterday, my baby, my darling, the apple of my eye...forgave me whole-heartedly,' she declared happily.

'Forgave you? Come on, how can you be so sure?'

She paid no attention to my cynical response. She deposited the box of sweets on a nearby table and hummed happily as she waved both her hands at me. I examined them keenly to see if they had been reattached. But, no, they were perfectly natural...like the plumes of a royal swan. They were a treat to watch. She excused herself to offer sweets to somebody else. Suddenly it struck me why I had lost my hand the previous night. Unable to overcome my grief, I broke down and sobbed, 'Chandu, my darling! Can you please forgive me for raising my hand against you?'

39

SUNDAY, BLOODY SUNDAY

VINEETHA MOKKIL

In the Bakshi household, it's a family tradition to drink together on Sunday evenings. When we were kids, Nikhil and I used to sit at the table, orange juice in hand, watching Ma and Papa clink their glasses. We had a guessing game going.

Guess what whisky tastes like?

★Cow piss ★Honey ★Cough medicine.

Wine?

★Grape juice ★Goat's blood ★Gutter water.

Vodka?

★Acid ★Oil ★Lemon juice.

Whatever my pick, Nikhil would sound disappointed. 'Wrong!' he'd say, putting on a grown-up voice. 'You're such a baby, Tara.'

Ma and Papa have kept up the Sunday tradition all these years. No matter where Papa was posted—desert, mountain, glitzy metropolis, or godforsaken outback—they would clink their glasses as the sun set on the week. Bahadur would bring out the bottles and glasses promptly at six. Whisky and soda, gin and tonic, wine, vodka, ice cubes—check, check, check. Bahadur ran our household like a well-oiled machine. Papa's major domo, Ma's man Friday, our devoted housekeeper-cum-handyman-cum-cook.

The Sunday in question, Bahadur served us our drinks in the living room. The light outside was fading. A chill crept into the air like a ghost. Ma wrapped a shawl around her shoulders. The burnt orange fabric was the same shade as the autumn leaves fluttering over our driveway.

Papa swigged his whisky. 'Cheers, guys,' he grinned, raising his glass.

Nikhil proposed a toast. He was in a great mood. His internet start-up had caught some big-shot investor's fancy. There was no way but up for his business from here.

Everybody looked nice and relaxed. Even Rudy, our cat, forever the haughty overlord, purred like a well-fed baby from under the table. This was it. The perfect moment, the perfect season to break the news. I took a deep breath, dived in. I'd rehearsed my lines a million times.

'I'm seeing someone. From work.'

Ma's face lit up like a Christmas tree. Papa's grin grew wider.

'Dating a fellow officer?' Nikhil teased me. 'Don't you guys have a country to run?'

I ignored his snark. Ignored the panic bubbling up inside me.

'We met at the Academy in our training days. At Mussoorie.'

'Aww...how romantic!' Ma sighed.

'We're from the same batch....'

'The Indian Administrative Service—A Love Story,' Nikhil joked without smiling

'So, what's his name?' Papa's baritone filled the air. 'When do we meet him?'

'Invite him for lunch or dinner,' Ma smiled, making mental notes about the menu. 'Weekend, weekday, any time.'

'What's the problem?' Nikhil asked, mistaking my panic for reluctance. 'Is he a vampire? A vegan?'

'Faizal's not a fussy eater. Feed him anything, no complaints.'

'Faizal?' Papa's smile vanished.

'Faizal Mohammed.'

Ma stiffened and folded her arms across her chest as if she needed protection from me.

'He's from Kashmir,' I said. 'His parents live there. No siblings. Poor thing's an only child.'

Nobody said anything. Nobody moved. My parents and my chatty brother turned to stone.

'He's a really nice guy,' I mumbled, hating myself for sounding defensive. Faizal was the gentlest man alive. He could calm down an angry mob, keep his cool even when he was faulted for no fault of his own. He loved to quote Shakespeare and Faiz and Neruda and Dickinson. Recite verse after verse from memory.

Nikhil snapped out of his trance. 'So, you're dating him. It's not like you're getting married or anything.'

'We are,' I kept my voice steady. 'We want to....'

Rudy crawled out from under the table and climbed up into my lap. Rudy, my friend. Ally in all battles, bloody or not.

'You want to marry a Kashmiri!' Papa gagged on his whisky as if it were hemlock.

'Please don't make it sound like a crime.'

Ma wept quietly. Nikhil leaned sideways and put his arm around her shoulders. I felt alone even though there were four of us in the room.

Rudy burrowed deeper into my lap, determined to stick by my side.

'We're not in a hurry,' I said. 'Meet Faizal when you feel like it. No rush.'

Papa scraped back his chair and stood up. He was a tall man. Six-foot-one. A fighter pilot who had trouble fitting into airline seats. A fighter pilot trained to see the world in black and white.

'You're making a terrible mistake.' His tone as grim as a judge's at a hanging.

'Faizal's not a jihadi,' I snapped at him. 'He's an IAS officer like me. He has a good heart. And a very sharp brain.'

Ma sobbed. She didn't bother to wipe away her tears.

'Is it because he's a Muslim?' I asked. 'All Muslims are terrorists?'

'I know Kashmir,' Papa gave me a pitying look. 'I know how Kashmiris operate.'

'That's so unfair!'

'Indians who hate India. Indians who bad-mouth the country every chance they get. You can't trust these people.'

'Faizal's not like that!'

'Dig deep and you'll see.'

Nikhil stared at me from across the table as if I were a nine-headed monster. Ma wept.

'Meet him before you make up your mind. Give him a chance, please.' My request hung between us—a rickety bridge no one would cross. I waited for a kind word, a whiff of compromise. In the end, I gathered Rudy in my arms and walked out. The house was very quiet, very still. My footsteps rang out like gunshots in the night when I went up the stairs.

There is a before and after in every life. That Sunday cleaved mine in two. Life before and life afterwards—two mismatched halves that would never form a whole. Conversations became a tightrope walk. At mealtimes, the air was taut with tension. Anything I said was open to misinterpretation. A word, a joke, even the simplest gesture could set off an explosion. Rattled, I retreated into silence.

In the mornings, I skipped breakfast and left for work early. Faizal was my oasis of calm. He spotted silver linings in the dark. His infinite, almost annoyingly saintly capacity for keeping the faith was stronger than my doubts. He swore the cold war at home would end soon. We started spending more time together after work. Coffee in our favourite cafe, walks in Lodi Garden, the lush green refuge in the heart of Delhi's urban sprawl. The garden brought out the poet in Faizal—he burst into song in the bamboo groves, recited love poems before the Lodi emperors' magnificent tombs, kissed me in the rose garden, serenaded me under the sprawling oaks.

Time slowed down when I was with him. The sun shone bright, the sky blazed blue. But evening always deepened into night, and night brought me no comfort. At home, a strained silence reigned. Dinner was the worst. Ma picked at her food distractedly. Papa chewed on his rotis with barely contained rage. Nikhil plodded on like a mourner at a funeral.

Bahadur hovered around the dining table, fussing over us, worrying that the whole family was coming down with something serious. Rudy sat at my feet, gazing at me with adoring eyes. I smuggled some fried fish to him. He arched his back, rubbed up against my legs, and expressed his eternal gratitude. He was easy to please.

Sleep was a major casualty of our cold war. I tried everything—drinking herbal teas at bedtime, listening to soothing soundtracks (the song of the sea, the whisper of the wind), even counting sheep, clichéd as it is. Nothing helped. I was up all night, tossing and turning, stumbling out of my room like a sleepwalker at first light.

One night, tired of sparring with insomnia, I decided to go for a walk. A full moon hung in the sky. Stars blinked. Rudy came running to me, sensing my plan to step out. Wherever I was headed, he would follow. I slid back the bolt on my door. I jiggled the handle. Once, twice, thrice. The door wouldn't budge. Rudy butted his head against the door, sniffed at it, ran around the room in circles. He was as frustrated as me.

We gave up on our walk. All night, the door stayed shut. When sunlight started to trickle in through the curtains, I heard a soft click—the sound of a key turning—someone tiptoeing around, the sound of my door being unlocked. I froze. For the first time in my life, I was petrified by fear in my own house.

When I went down for breakfast with Rudy at my heels, Nikhil was huddled on the couch, his nose buried in the newspaper. Ma and Papa were out on the lawn, striking yoga poses, basking in the honeyed morning light. Bahadur brought me a cup of tea and asked if I'd slept well.

'I'm under house arrest,' I said. 'How can I sleep well?'

Bahadur made a quick exit. If a fight was brewing, he wasn't going to get caught in the cross hairs. Taking sides was a dangerous business, and Bahadur was a careful man.

'Why lock me up?' I raised my voice. 'Was that your idea?'

Nikhil looked up at me from his newspaper. His chin was covered in stubble. Dark circles shadowed his eyes. 'Don't yell at me, Tara,' he said. 'I have a headache.'

'What's next? Armed guards? Cops chasing after me on the street?'

'Stop it,' he said, massaging his temples. 'Your door's jammed, we'll get it fixed. End of story.'

I didn't have the stomach for a fight, so I backed off. Nikhil went back to reading the paper, and I headed to work. All day, a niggling feeling—fear, worry, a whiff of sadness—trailed after me like a shadow. Faizal's jokes didn't make me laugh. The future was a maze. Navigating it, even with Faizal by my side, looked like a hopeless business.

Weeks of strained silence at home, weeks of tightrope walking, and then the wind changed direction without warning. When I walked into the house on a Friday evening, Ma and Papa were grinning like children. They were dressed in their best, and Bahadur had cooked up a feast. Nikhil was home too. Talk and laughter and friendly banter drifted in the air.

Relieved, I sat down to dinner. Ma served me an extra helping of kheer. She'd made the dessert, my favourite, herself. We ate in peace. Chatted like we used to. Papa laughed at his own jokes. Nikhil and I pulled his leg. For an hour I convinced myself that peace had returned. For an hour I tricked myself into believing we had gone back to being the way we were before I took Faizal's name on a Sunday evening and the walls closed in on us.

When Bahadur came in to clear the table, Papa and Nikhil made a strategic exit from the room.

'Stay,' Ma smiled at me from across the table. 'Let's talk.'

Lulled by the feast and glasses of red wine, I leaned back in my chair. Ma spoke softly, strung her words together with care. The Kohlis—General

Kohli and his wife, golfer and philanthropist, Sunita Kohli—had come by the house that evening. Their son, Vikas, was a heart surgeon who was famous for saving lives in San Francisco. A fine young man with an excellent pedigree. A green card holder. A respected member of the Asian–American community.

'A perfect match,' Ma smiled. 'You two would make a great couple.'

And then it dawned on me that nothing had changed. We were still stranded on opposite shores. The evening had been an illusion, a conjurer's trick to reel me in. A prelude for this proposal. A means to an end.

'He's not Faizal,' I explained. 'And Faizal's the only man I want to be with.'

Ma kept at it. A stream of advice, followed by angry tears and a bitter speech forged from disappointment. Papa was counting on me to make the right choice. Nikhil expected better from me. How could I be so stubborn? How could I humiliate my family this way?

I didn't tell Faizal about the heart surgeon. The Kohlis and their son had nothing to do with us. They were not part of our story. I didn't tell Faizal about my locked door either. His peace of mind was not mine to wreck.

We spent lunch hour together at the office, took off for our walks in the evenings, caught a movie or a concert on the weekends, went book shopping at Midland, a landmark etched as clearly as the Qutub Minar on the mental map of the city's booklovers. The store had an impressive collection. The owner, soft-spoken and balding, would dig up any book you demanded like a magician onstage. He chatted with all his customers. He knew the regulars by name.

A bookstore is the last place you expect to see spies at work. A strip joint or a pub with poor lighting, no surprises there. But Nikhil picked Midland to spy on Faizal and me. There he was, my lanky brother, dressed in a white shirt and jeans, peering at us from behind a stack of books, his gaze following us like a laser beam. A minute later he was gone. Poof! A puff of smoke. A lightning flash. A pain in the neck. I would've laughed it off if I didn't know for sure that my brother never walked into bookstores, never read for pleasure even if a book jumped into his arms and begged to be read.

I was tempted to confront him. Order him to back off. But things were so tense at home, the peace—or what passed for it—so fragile, I chose not to make it worse by questioning him. I kept an eye out for him wherever we went. He could be trailing after us on the streets, driving at a discreet distance, mapping the routes we took. He could be hiding behind a bush or a giant banyan in the garden, making notes about our evening stroll. The vigil was exhausting. I couldn't let my guard down even for a minute.

There was good news on the night-time lockdown though. Nervously, I tried my bedroom door every night. Miraculously, it swung open, letting me breathe easy. Ma and Papa kept conversations with me to a minimum. There were no heart-to-hearts, but the angry tears and accusations slowly dried up. Nikhil started to thaw, too. Sometimes he shared a story about his day with me at the dinner table. Sometimes he cracked me up with a joke.

'Told you things would work out,' Faizal said. 'Give it time, my love. Just give it time.'

My heart stopped fluttering like a panicky bird. The days stopped weighing down on my head. The nights stayed the same, though. In spite of my pleas, sleep refused to return.

One night, I was hunched over my desk, checking a file I'd brought home from work. A knock on the door made me jump. Rudy rushed to the door before I got there.

'Hey! It's me,' Nikhil's voice, a whisper, a reassurance.

I let him in. Rudy settled down at the foot of my bed, at ease.

'Ma sent this up,' Nikhil handed me a glass. 'Warm milk with saffron.'

'Thanks!'

'Guaranteed to put you to sleep.'

'We'll see,' I said, desperate to trust Ma's remedy.

Nikhil didn't stick around to chat. Long day at work, he was dying to go to bed. We said goodnight and I shut my door. Rudy purred softly from his perch.

I stayed up for another hour—checked my file, waded through a swamp of officialese and made sense of it. The night was quiet. No roar of traffic, no blaring horns or alarms. The silence was a balm. An invitation to drift off to sleep if ever there was one. I put away my papers and switched off my reading lamp. Rudy leaped into my lap, made me lose my balance, and sent the glass of milk crashing to the floor. Before I could say a word, he crouched down and lapped up the milk, his pink tongue darting in quick bursts till the floor was wiped clean.

'Rudy,' I bent down to pat his fluffy head. 'Silly boy, Rudy.'

He purred and purred, and rolled over on his back. Milk was bliss. He was a good boy, easy to please.

I left him there, on the floor, and headed to the bathroom. Sleep or no sleep, a warm bath always made me feel better. Minutes later, when I came back into the room, Rudy was curled up on the floor at the exact spot where I had left him. But he wasn't moving. Or purring. Or giving me goofy looks. His eyes were shut tight. I knelt down and scooped him up in my arms. He was so cold and stiff, so quiet.

'Rudy,' I called out to him, loud enough to wake my family, loud enough to wake the whole town.

I cradled Rudy in my arms, rocking him gently like a newborn babe. I slid the bolt back on my door. Yanked the handle. Yanked it hard.

The door wouldn't open. The door wouldn't budge.

40

THE CROSSING

VRINDA BALIGA

What does it look like, this border on the open seas? You imagine a vast wire fence, bristling with barbs, anchored magically atop the waves, rising and falling with the heaving waters. You have been seeing variants of this image for many nights now. In your nightmares, it lies in wait like a mythical beast of yore for you to draw near so it can rip you apart with its clawed tentacles.

There are fifty of you in the cargo hold of the rickety old boat, crammed into a place that would have been snug for even a quarter that number. The waves are high and choppy. Babies and young children wail their despair, but the adults among you, equally helpless, have, by now, learned to ignore their cries. When someone throws up, no apologies are made to those the vomit spews on. The time for such niceties is past, and personal boundaries have long evaporated in the heat of the crammed quarters. Indeed, it is difficult to know which of the numb limbs you are tangled in are your own.

Parcels, the handlers call you. Like anonymous packages wrapped in brown paper, each indistinguishable from the next, with neither name nor address stamped on to set you apart. Sometimes, they just refer to you as cargo, eliminating even the individuality implied by the plural.

'It won't be long now,' mutters a youth with the eyes of an old man. This is his third attempt to get across. Twice, he has been turned back.

'They try to turn you back before you cross over,' he says. 'Before you become their headache.'

He dispenses nuggets like this with the authority of a veteran. One of the boats that attempted the crossing the previous week never made it, neither this way nor that, he tells you. There were too many aboard, and the whole shebang capsized. He looks critically around as though contemplating which of you can be jettisoned if need be. You don't know his name. You haven't asked. Names have long ceased to matter—they are use-and-throw articles, of no value, easily discarded.

Your own name, the real one that belonged to the person you once were, has faded far into the recesses of your memory. Your family, too, is a mere blur of unfired neurons by now. Like an old poster, it has been plastered over with the new, changing faces you encounter every day. You can no longer picture the woman who had clung to your arm a lifetime ago, shouting, 'No, he's too young. He can't go alone. I won't let him!'

There was a time, not so long ago—no, aeons ago—when with all the optimism and folly of youth, you had thought of this as an adventure. A brave, pioneering escapade, full of dangers and obstacles you would smite with your wit and strength and courage. A hero's journey.

You had all gone together to the agent—your father, mother, younger brother, and you—your meagre possessions packed and ready. But the agent had counted the notes your father placed in his hand and shaken his head.

'This will cover the cost of just one,' he had said.

'But you told me....'

'That was eight months ago, brother,' the agent said bluntly. 'The rules of this game keep changing depending on the situation on the ground. I told you so, didn't I?'

It had taken eight months to come up with the money.

'Smuggler,' your grandfather had muttered when your father had first told him about the agent and brought up the need to sell off a substantial portion of family land to pay for the trip. 'Trafficker,' he had hissed.

'Agent,' your father had insisted.

But your grandfather had turned away, shaking his head.

He's just bitter; he's too old to come. You immediately felt ashamed of the unworthy thought. But not too ashamed.

Had it all been for nothing then, the sale of land, the acrimony at home? But no, the agent had a suggestion.

'Send your eldest one,' he said, looking you over. 'He seems a strong lad. He'll find work easily enough. He'll be able to send for the rest of you in a couple of years.'

Your father stared at the notes in confusion. If you took the money back home, it would become the seeds that would lie unproductively in the belly of your rocky, barren land, waiting for the rains that would not come, it would become the tiles for your leaking roof, the part payment to the moneylender—some of the hundred things that needed to be bought or fixed or done just to keep going. It would be back to square one. Hell, you had never left that square all your lives. But here, in the agent's hands, perhaps....

'No, he's too young,' your mother protested, clinging to your arm. 'He can't go alone. I won't let him!'

'He's old enough,' your father declared.

There was no time for elaborate goodbyes. 'It won't be long,' you told yourself in the back of the agent's truck as you gazed at your family, growing ever smaller, already receding into your past. Your father looked determined, your mother was in tears. Your younger brother stood sullenly by their side, bitter at having been deprived of the journey you had both anticipated together.

'Don't worry, sister, I'll take good care of him,' the agent had promised your mother as he pocketed the money.

Two days later, you crossed a barbed fence in the dead of night and then the agent was gone, replaced by a different one, who knew nothing of you or of the promise.

Still, those first couple of weeks hadn't been so bad. You were among people more or less like yourself, who spoke the same language, had the same mannerisms. Spirits reasonably high.

'It won't be long,' you told each other and believed it.

Stories were exchanged amongst you, of friends and relatives and acquaintances who had gone before. The sister of an acquaintance in the neighbouring village whose family now had a house in a dreamy, leafy suburb. The distant cousin of a distant cousin who ran a successful business and sent money home every month. The village carpenter who had left, confident of making a fortune with his superior woodworking skills. And in the evenings, around motley campfires, there was always a game of cards to be enjoyed. And there was always someone among you who could catch a tune and sing some wrenchingly familiar song, conjuring up, for a few tantalizing moments, home in the back of a truck trundling down a dusty path.

But as the journey dragged on and on, the lilt eventually faded from your songs, and the vigour from your eyes.

The handlers changed every few days, but they could all as well have been the same person for all the difference it made. They were all invariably gruff and harsh, a far cry from the agents who had been so full of rosy pictures and promises. They barked orders: 'Sit there.' 'Come here.' 'Don't do that!' 'Shut up!' You had to shell out money for every small luxury—a blanket, a smoke, some medicine. And if you asked questions, they were likely to be answered with a fist or a boot.

'It won't be long now,' you muttered, more out of practice than conviction.

Darker stories began to be narrated—the niece who was lost en route, the infant who had never made it…and why had nobody ever heard from that village carpenter, anyway? Was he dead, or pretending to be dead so he would not have to send money back home?

You would never do that, you promised yourself. You were determined to work hard, earn heaps of money, and be reunited with your family. But, with every passing day, it became increasingly difficult to hold on to such intangibles as promises and determination.

There were days when you would have given anything just to return home.

Once, when you were huddled over a campfire, you spotted a map one of the handlers had carelessly left about. With your heart in your throat, you picked it up and slipped it under your clothing. For an entire hour you carried it close to your chest, right next to your wildly beating heart, till you got a moment to yourself. You opened the map out surreptitiously, one eye looking over your shoulder, and smoothed your hand over its crumpled body. The whole world lay in front of you. But where were you? You could have been anywhere on its flat surface—you hadn't the slightest clue where you could plant your finger to begin tracing the way back home.

The map merely showed you how lost you truly were. In the end, you put it back before it was even missed.

And always, a new border loomed on the horizon. One more hurdle to be crossed. Yet another test of your collective will.

Some of you fell behind, out of sickness or the inability to pay your way further. Others, equally bedraggled and glassy-eyed, took their place—more parcels from different countries, speaking other languages and dialects, all travelling on an invisible, underground conveyor belt, from destinations barcoded in the lines of their faces.

Even the amorphous identity of homogeneity melted away, and eventually the only lingua franca was the language of desperation, which, with a few minor hiccups and pidgin welds, you all understood.

There were new passes, identity cards, documents with your photos pasted over unknown names that were now your own. You were told who you were, where you were born and when. What you did for a living. Who your family was. What your dreams and aspirations were. The entire story of your life was dictated to you, and you were made to recite it again and again till you got it right. Your identity was hammered out on a forger's anvil and handed to you. But it was an evasive shapeshifter. It waited just long enough for you to allow yourself to occupy it before changing once again. One day you were a plumber, the next a student. A fieldworker on some days, a factory worker on others. You were altered from week to week, from place to place, from circumstance to circumstance, till you could hardly recognize yourself any more.

There was only one constant—borders, fences, walls—no matter which way you turned or how far you went.

Sometimes, you were let through unmolested, with payment or favour discreetly changing hands. When there were no 'friends' about, you had to take detours—long deviations over mountains and across rivers. The rivers claimed some of you, the mountains more.

You remember the tattooed face of a middle-aged woman whose name you don't know. She had walked in silence for days in the bitter cold, hugging a bawling infant to her chest. Then, one day, she just sat down and refused to get up. You—all of you—left her there and moved on. There was no other option.

She had been with a family group—a man, an elderly woman, and two young children.

'She was a cousin, a distant cousin,' the man said, resorting to the past tense already. 'We should have never brought her along, but she had nowhere else to go.' He seemed unable to stop talking. 'What should I do? Stay with her and let my own children die? We should have never brought her. But the agent said it would be easy….' And all the time, hot tears melted the frost on his cheeks in little rivulets of grief.

The woman didn't once call after you, beg you to stay. She sat there on the rock, still as a statue, nursing the infant at her breast.

And that night when after a long time you thought of your mother, it was that woman you saw in your mind instead. That was when you realized you couldn't remember your mother's face any more.

Perhaps it was then that some part of you gave up, when the individual 'you' stopped its flailing struggle to break through to the surface every now and then and allowed itself to be subsumed by the collective 'you'.

So, here you are, this is what it has all come down to—this rickety boat and this tangle of limbs. If the boat goes down, who will the waters have swallowed? Will it only be a number, a collective statistic that floats face down on the surface of the ocean? Will your souls be as inextricably tangled in death as your bodies now are?

It won't be long, you repeat to yourself...yourselves. But, already, an eternity has passed.

What lies beyond this mythical border on the sea? What if the place you have run to is as bad as the place you ran from? What if, in its own different ways, it is even worse? What if you have been running around in circles all this while? You find you can't summon the energy to care either way.

ACKNOWLEDGEMENTS

This book has been a collaborative effort in many ways so I'd like to thank my wife, Rachna Singh, and all my editorial colleagues at Aleph—Aienla Ozukum, Pujitha Krishnan, Saba Nehal, Kanika Praharaj, and Karishma Koshal—who helped me put it together. As always, Bena Sareen designed a cover that was superlative and Rajkumari John and P. K. Sharma ensured its production values were superb. Vasundhara Raj Baigra and her team marketed the book brilliantly and A. K. Singh and his team ensured it was available everywhere. My thanks to them all. However, the teamwork that helped shape the book notwithstanding, I am solely responsible for any omissions or quirks in the selection as also any other flaws the book might have.

Grateful acknowledgment is made to the following copyright holders for permission to reprint copyrighted material in this volume. While every effort has been made to locate and contact copyright holders and obtain permission, this has not always been possible; any inadvertent omissions brought to our notice will be remedied in future editions.

∞

'The Alligator of Aligarh' by A. M. Gautam was first published in the *Bombay Review* (May 2020). Reprinted by permission of the author.

'Making' by Aishwarya Subramanian was first published in *Breaking the Bow*, edited by Anil Menon and Vandana Singh (Zubaan, 2014). Reprinted by permission of the author.

'The Devouring Sea' by Amal, translated by A. J. Thomas, is used by permission of the author and translator.

'The Current Climate' was first published in *adda* [October 2021] by the Commonwealth Foundation. Reprinted by permission of the author.

'The Power to Forgive' by Avinuo Kire was first published in *The Power to Forgive,* copyright © Avinuo Kire (Zubaan, 2015). Reprinted by permission of Zubaan.

Acknowledgements

'A Story That Lived' by bhavani was first published in *Papercuts* (Volume 18, Summer 2017) by the Desi Writer's Lounge. Reprinted by permission of the author.

'Eggs Keep Falling from the Fourth Floor' by Bhavika Govil was shortlisted for the 2021 Queen Mary Wasafiri New Writing Prize and first published on wasafiri.org. Reprinted by permission of the author.

'Air' was originally published in *After Hours*, volume 5 of the *Helter Skelter Anthology of New Writing*. Reprinted by permission of the author.

'The Teeth on the Bus Go Round and Round' was first published in *adda* [January 2021] by the Commonwealth Foundation. Reprinted by permission of the author.

'The Adivasi Will Not Dance' by Hansda Sowvendra Shekhar was first published in the anthology *The Adivasi Will Not Dance* (Speaking Tiger Books, 2017). Reprinted by permission of Speaking Tiger Books.

'Swimmer Among the Stars' by Kanishk Tharoor was first published in *Swimmer Among the Stars*, copyright © Kanishk Tharoor (Aleph Book Company, 2016). Reprinted by permission of the author and publisher.

'Public Record' by Karan Madhok was first published in the Winter 2022 edition of *Epiphany Magazine*. Used by permission of the author.

'The Great Indian Tee and Snakes' by Kritika Pandey was first published in *Granta* in partnership with *Commonwealth Writers* on 23 June 2020. Reprinted by permission of the author.

'The Account Officer's Wife' by Lakshmikanth K. Ayyagari was first published in *Out of Print* (September 2021). Reprinted by permission of the author.

'Lorry Raja' by Madhuri Vijay was first published in *Narrative Magazine* (Winter 2012). Reprinted by permission of the author.

'How to Host Your Europeans' by Meena Kandasamy was written when she was Writer-in-Residence at the Redbridge library. It was first published in the *City of Stories* anthology published by Spread the Word in association with the London network of libraries in 2018 and is reprinted by permission of the author.

'Mrs Nischol' by Meera Ganapathi was first published by *Firstpost* (July 2021). Reprinted by permission of the author.

'radha, krishna' by Neel Patel was first published in *If You See Me, Don't Say Hi*, copyright © Neel Patel 2018 (Penguin Random House India, 2018). Reprinted by permission of Penguin Random House India.

'The Annual Pig Parade of Kharagpore' by Nicholas Rixon was first published in *Catapult* (January 2019). Reprinted by permission of the author.

'The Girl Who Haunted Death' by Nikita Deshpande was first published in *Magical Women,* edited by Sukanya Venkatraghavan (Hachette India, 2019). Reprinted by permission of the author.

'The Twenty-sixth Giant' by Prayaag Akbar was first published in *Mint* (December 2018). Reprinted by permission of the author.

'Spider-Girl' by Pritika Rao was first published in the *Bangalore Review* (February 2022). Reprinted by permission of the author.

'Twenty-first Tiffin' by Raam Mori, translated by Rita Kothari was first published in *The Greatest Gujarati Stories Ever Told* edited by Rita Kothari (Aleph Book Company, 2022). Reprinted by permission of the author and translator.

'It Ends with a Kiss' by Riddhi Dastidar was first published in *adda* [October 2021] by the Commonwealth Foundation. Reprinted by permission of the author.

'Greetings from a Violent Homeland' by Ritumonjori Kalita was first published in *adda* [March 2017] by the Commonwealth Foundation. Reprinted by permission of the author.

'Gobyaer' by Sadaf Wani was first published in *Himal Southasian* (July 2021). Reprinted by permission of the author.

'Fate' by Samhita Arni was first published in *Out of Print* (September 2021). Reprinted by permission of the author.

'After Half-Time' by Shamik Ghosh, translated by Subha Prasad Sanyal, was first published in *Granta* (September 2018). Reprinted by permission of the author and translator.

'Journey' by Shanthi K. Appanna, translated by Srinath Perur, was first published in *Indian Quarterly* (January–March 2018). Reprinted by permission of the author and translator.

'The Smear Papers' by Shawn Fernandes was originally published in *After Hours,* volume 5 of the *Helter Skelter Anthology of New Writing*. Reprinted by permission of the author.

'Gul' by Shreya Ila Anasuya was first published in *Magical Women*, edited by Sukanya Venkatraghavan (Hachette India, 2019). Reprinted by permission of the author.

'My Grandmother Talks About Shit' by Srividya Tadepalli was originally published in *After Hours*, volume 5 of the *Helter Skelter Anthology of New Writing*. Reprinted by permission of the author.

'The Issue' by Tanuj Solanki was first published in *Out of Print* (June 2017). Reprinted by permission of the author.

'The Octopus: A Fable' by Tushar Jain was first published in the *Bombay Review* (July–August 2017). Reprinted by permission of the author.

'My Time at Boyonika' by Uday Kanungo was first published in the *Bombay Review* (June 2020). Reprinted by permission of the author.

'Shabnam' by Urooj is used by permission of the author.

'The Demon Sage's Daughter' by Varsha Dinesh was first published in *Strange Horizons* (February 2021). Reprinted by permission of the author.

'Crippled World' by Vempalle Shareef, translated by N. S. Murty and late R. S. Krishna Moorthy, was first published as 'Arm Stump' in *Indian Literature* (Volume 59, Number 5) by the Sahitya Akademi in September/October 2015. Reprinted by permission of the author and translators.

'Sunday, Bloody Sunday' by Vineetha Mokkil was first published in *The Punch Magazine Anthology of New Writing*, edited by Shireen Quadri (Niyogi Books, 2021). Reprinted by permission of Niyogi Books.

'The Crossing' by Vrinda Baliga was first published in *The Punch Magazine Anthology of New Writing*, edited by Shireen Quadri (Niyogi Books, 2021). Reprinted by permission of Niyogi Books.

NOTES ON THE CONTRIBUTORS

A. J. Thomas is a poet, writer, and translator from Kerala. He was the editor of the Sahitya Akademi's journal, *Indian Literature*, until 2010. His translation of M. Mukundan's novel, *Kesavan's Lamentations*, won the Vodafone Crossword Book Award in 2007. He was also honoured with the Katha Award for his translation of *Salaam America* by Paul Zacharia.

A. M. Gautam is an internationally published author whose work explores and examines India's sociopolitical curiosities through the lenses of speculative fiction and magical realism. A short story by him was included in the *Best Asian Fiction Anthology* by Kitaab, Singapore, in 2018, and most recently his work has appeared in the April 2022 issue of the literary journal *Orca*.

Aishwarya Subramanian is an assistant professor of English at O. P. Jindal Global University. She has previously worked as an editor, book reviewer, and columnist. She holds a PhD in English literature from the University of Newcastle. She's also a reviews editor at *Strange Horizons*, an award-winning magazine of speculative fiction.

Amal is a Malayalam novelist, short story writer, graphic novelist, illustrator, and cartoonist from Kerala. He is a graduate in painting from Raja Ravi Varma College of Fine Arts and a post graduate in Art History from Visva-Bharati Santiniketan, Kolkata. His first novel, *Kalhanan*, was shortlisted for the Kerala Sahitya Akademi Award and later won the Sidhardha Award and K. Sarasvathi Amma Award. His second novel, *Vyasanasamuchayam*, won the 2018 Kendra Sahitya Akademi Yuva Puraskar and Basheer Yuva Prathibha Award. He has received several other awards including the Kerala Sahitya Akademi Geetha Hiranyan Endowment for best short story collection in 2019. He lives between Thiruvananthapuram and Tokyo.

Aravind Jayan is a writer from Thiruvananthapuram. He's the winner of the 2017 Toto Award for Creative Writing (English) and was shortlisted for the Commonwealth Short Story Prize in 2021. His first novel, *Teen Couple Have Fun Outdoors*, was published in July 2022.

Avinuo Kire is a writer and teacher. She is the author of *The Power to Forgive and Other Stories*, *The Last Light of Glory Days and Other Stories*, *Where the Cobbled Path Leads*, and a collection of poetry, *Where Wildflowers Grow*, and has co-authored an anthology of oral narratives entitled *Naga Heritage Centre, People Stories: Volume One*. Avinuo lives in Kohima where she teaches English at Kohima College.

bhavani is an independent writer. Her short fiction 'A Fragrance that Could Have Been' was the winner of the 2016 *Out of Print-DNA* Contest. Her fiction and non-fiction has been published in *Papercuts*, *Spark Magazine*, *DNA*, *Mint*, and *National Geographic Traveller*, among others. A student of yoga and animal telepathic communication, she is plant-powered, earth-inspired, and lives with her husband, rescue dog, and five-year-old daughter in Mumbai.

Bhavika Govil was born in New Delhi yet dreams of the sea. She is the winner of the 2021 Pontas & JJ Bola Emerging Writers Prize for her debut novel in progress. Her short fiction won the Bound Short Story Prize, was shortlisted for the Queen Mary Wasafiri New Writing Prize, longlisted for the Toto Award for Creative Writing (English), and was a notable contender for the Bristol Short Story Prize. She has performed at the Edinburgh International Book Festival, Paisley Book Festival, and Push the Boat Out Festival. She has a Master's in creative writing from the University of Edinburgh. You can read her work at bhavikagovil.com.

Dilsher Dhillon is a writer, actor, and one half of a screenwriting partnership with his twin brother, Mansher. A major theme he explores in his work is the notion of trying to live a meaningful life in an inherently meaningless and indifferent world. He previously daylighted as a consultant and financial journalist before taking the plunge into full-time creative work. He divides his time between New Delhi and Mumbai.

Dinesh Devarajan is a product manager with a major IT services firm. His story 'The Teeth on the Bus Go Round and Round' was shortlisted for the 2020 Commonwealth Short Story prize. The story 'Dead Heat' won the *Sunday Herald* short story competition, 2015. His short stories have been published in the *Times of India*'s Write India, Season 1, and the short story collections *Two is Company* and *City of Gods*. He was part of Season 5 of Anita's Attic, a creative writing mentorship programme curated by the writer Anita Nair. He is working on his first novel.

Hansda Sowvendra Shekhar is a doctor from Jharkhand. He received the Sahitya Akademi Yuva Puraskar in 2015. His critically acclaimed books include *The Mysterious Ailment of Rupi Baskey* (shortlisted for the Hindu Prize and Crossword Award), *My Father's Garden* (shortlisted for the JCB Prize), and *The Adivasi Will Not Dance* (shortlisted for the Hindu Prize). Sowvendra translates writings from Santhali, Hindi, and Bengali into English.

Kanishk Tharoor is a writer based in New York City. His journalism, criticism, and short stories have appeared in international and Indian publications; his short fiction was nominated for a National Magazine Award. He studied at Yale, Columbia, and at New York University, where he had a fellowship in the creative writing programme.

Karan Madhok is a writer and a graduate of the MFA programme from the American University in Washington DC. He won American University's 2018 Myra Sklarew Award for the best MFA thesis (prose) for a section of his forthcoming novel, *A Beautiful Decay*, entitled 'Vishnu was shot in America!'

Kritika Pandey is a Pushcart-nominated writer from Jharkhand and a graduate of the MFA for Poets and Writers, University of Massachusetts, Amherst. She is the recipient of a 2021 residency grant at the Helene Wurlitzer Foundation of New Mexico and a 2020 grant from the Elizabeth George Foundation. She is the overall winner of the 2020 Commonwealth Short Story Prize, having been shortlisted for the prize in 2018 as well as 2016. Her works have appeared in *Granta*, *Kenyon Review*, *The Common*, *Bombay Literary Magazine*, *Raleigh Review*, and *UCity Review*, among others, and have been translated into Malayalam, Italian, Bengali, Marathi, and

Pashto. She is the winner of the 2020 James W. Foley Memorial Award, the 2018 Harvey Swados Fiction Prize, the 2018 Cara Parravani Memorial Award in Fiction, and a 2014 Charles Wallace India Trust Scholarship for Creative Writing at the University of Edinburgh. She is a 2014 Young India Fellow and holds a bachelor's degree in Electronics and Communications Engineering from BIT, Mesra.

Lakshmikanth K. Ayyagari is from Visakhapatnam but now lives in Rajahmundry, a city on the banks of the river Godavari. His day job involves data, predictions, s-shaped curves, and loan defaults. On most nights, he finds warmth and comfort in literature.

Madhuri Vijay was born and raised in Bengaluru. Her debut novel, *The Far Field*, received several honours, including the JCB Prize for Literature, the Tata Literature Live! First Book Award, and the Crossword Book Award. Her short stories have appeared in the *New Yorker*, *Best American Short Stories*, *Best American Non-Required Reading*, and *Narrative Magazine*.

Meena Kandasamy is an anti-caste activist, poet, novelist, and translator. Her writing aims to deconstruct trauma and violence while spotlighting the militant resistance against caste, gender, and ethnic oppressions. She explores these themes in her poetry and prose, most notably in her books of poems such as *Touch* and *Ms. Militancy*, as well as her three novels, *The Gypsy Goddess*, *When I Hit You*, and *Exquisite Cadavers*. Her latest work is a collection of essays, *The Orders Were to Rape You: Tamil Tigresses in the Eelam Struggle*. Her novels have been shortlisted for the Women's Prize for Fiction, the International Dylan Thomas Prize, the Jhalak Prize, and the Hindu Prize.

Meera Ganapathi is the founder of the digital publication, *The Soup*, and the author of children's books including *Paati vs UNCLE*, published by Puffin India. Her essays on art and culture have appeared in various Indian and international publications. She currently lives between Mumbai and Goa.

N. S. Murty has an M.Sc. in Applied Mathematics and an M.A. in English Literature from Andhra University, Waltair. Murty was also a graduate student of English Literature at the University of Houston, Texas, in Spring 2011. He has published two collections of his poetry, *Incidental Muses* and *PenChants*;

two collections of Telugu poems translated into English, *The Wakes on the Horizon* and *The Voices of the Surf*; a collection of the 100 best poems from world literature rendered into Telugu with a brief introduction for each poem, *Kavitvamto Edadugulu*; and a collection of best short stories from world literature rendered into Telugu, *Katha Lekhini*.

Neel Patel is a first-generation Indian American writer from Champaign, Illinois. His novel, *Tell Me How to Be,* is forthcoming. His work has appeared in the *Paris Review, Elle India, American Literary Review,* and *Hyphen Magazine,* among others. He lives in Los Angeles.

Nicholas Rixon is an Anglo-Indian writer and editor based in New Delhi. His fiction has appeared in the *Indian Quarterly, Catapult,* and *The Statesman,* among others. Originally from Kolkata, he is working on a novella about the Anglo-Indian community. His published short stories and essays can be found at nicholasrixon.com.

Nikita Deshpande is the author of the novel *It Must've Been Something He Wrote.* Her short stories have appeared in the anthologies *Magical Women* and *Grandpa Tales.* Her poem was included in the anthology *The World That Belongs to Us.* Her writing has been published in the *Rumpus, Grazia, Scroll, Buzzfeed,* and *Firstpost,* among others. She was awarded a Vermont Studio Center fellowship to work on her fiction. Nikita enjoys romance novels, stone fruit, and homemade filter kaapi.

Prayaag Akbar is a novelist and journalist who has worked at *Outlook* magazine and *Scroll*. His novel, *Leila,* won the Crossword Jury Prize and the Tata Literature Live! First Book Award. It was also adapted into a series by Netflix. His writing has appeared in *Caravan, Aeon,* and the *Indian Express*. He currently teaches literature at Krea University in Sri City.

Pritika Rao is an economist and writer from Bengaluru. She has a master's degree in economics from the University of Warwick and has worked in the areas of analytics, behavioural economics, and healthcare. She is the editor of *Rewrite Mag*—a repository of rejected writing. In 2018, she won second prize in the *Sunday Herald* short story competition. Her work has also appeared in the *Times of India, Bangalore Review, Soup Magazine, The*

Swaddle, and *Alipore Post*, among others. Her work has been shortlisted for the 2022 Commonwealth Short Story Prize.

R. S. Krishna Moorthy was born and brought up in Vizianagaram. Krishna Moorthy was friends with the famous Telugu short story writers Bhamidipati Rama Gopalam (Bharago) and Avasarala Ramakrishna Rao. Starting his career as stenographer in Bhilai Steel Plant, he retired as OSD in Ferro Scrap Nigam Ltd. His short story collection, *Chayachitralu*, bagged the Jyeshtha Literary Trust Prize in 1997. He also won the Katha–British Council South Asian Translation Award 2000 for his translation of Allam Seshagiri Rao's story 'Mrigatrishna'.

Raam Mori was one of the youngest recipients of the Sahitya Akademi Award in 2017. His short story collections in Gujarati, *Mahotu*, *Coffee Stories*, and *Confession Box* have received great acclaim in Gujarat. He also writes columns, plays, and scripts for television and films.

Riddhi Dastidar is a Delhi-based writer and reporter working on disability justice, gender, human rights, and culture. Their work has won a 2020 TFA Award for Creative Writing, 2021 SCARF Media for Mental Health Award for reportage, and been shortlisted for the 2021 Commonwealth Short Story Prize, and 2021 Wasafiri New Writing Prize. They are writing their first book of fiction under the mentorship of novelist Deepa Anappara, as a 2022 South Asia Speaks Fellow. Find their work at riddhidastidar.com or follow @gaachburi on social media.

Rita Kothari is the Vani Foundation Distinguished Translator and has translated widely from Gujarati and Sindhi. A multilingual scholar, Kothari speaks and writes on language politics, translation theory, Partition, and border studies. She is the author of *Translating India*, *The Burden of Refuge*, and the translator and editor of *The Greatest Gujarati Stories Ever Told*. She teaches at Ashoka University, Sonepat.

Ritumonjori Kalita was born and brought up in Assam. 'Greetings from a Violent Homeland' is her first work of fiction published in an international journal. Until recently, she taught English in a school in Pune. Currently, she lives in Gothenburg.

Sadaf Wani is a Kashmiri writer and researcher. Her work has been published in *Himal Southasian*, *Scroll*, *Wande Magazine*, and *Inverse Journal* among others.

Samhita Arni wrote *Mahabharata: A Child's View* at the age of eleven. She is author of the graphic novel *Sita's Ramayana* (which appeared on the *New York Times* bestseller list), *The Missing Queen* and, most recently, *The Prince*.

Shamik Ghosh has published a number of short story collections in Bengali. He was awarded the Sahitya Akademi Yuva Puraskar in 2017 for his collection *Elvis O Amolasundari*. He lives in Kolkata.

Shanthi K. Appanna has published two short story collections in Kannada—*Manasu Abhisarike* and *Ondu Bagilu Mathu Mooru Chillare Varshagalu*. She won the Kendra Sahitya Akademi Award and the Sahitya Akademi Yuva Puraskar for her first book. She lives in Chennai.

Shawn Fernandes is fascinated by stories that feature an upending of the status quo, stories that dig deep into the crevices and minutiae of our daily lives. In addition to fiction, he has also written on music and culture. He is currently working on his first collection of short stories as well as his debut EP. Shawn lives and works in Mumbai.

Shreya Ila Anasuya is a writer from Kolkata. Shreya's fiction has appeared in *Strange Horizons* and the *Magazine of Fantasy & Science Fiction*, among others, and has been recognized by the Toto Award for Creative Writing in English, the Otherwise Fellowship, and the Sangam House Residency. Her story 'Gul' was originally published in the anthology *Magical Women* (ed. Sukanya Venkatraghavan) and was adapted into a stage show.

Srinath Perur is the author of *If It's Monday It Must Be Madurai*. He has translated Vivek Shanbhag's novel, *Ghachar Ghochar*, and Girish Karnad's memoir, *This Life at Play*, from Kannada. His work has appeared in *India Today*, *Fountain Ink*, *Indian Quarterly*, *Guardian Cities*, *Caravan*, *Hakai*, *Mosaic*, and *n+1*. He lives in Bengaluru.

Srividya is a queer educator and writer. She lives in Chennai with her partner and two cats, and dreams of having seventeen one day (cats not partners).

Subha Prasad Sanyal is the winner of the Harvill Secker Young Translator's Prize, 2018. His translation of a collection of Nabarun Bhattacharya's short fiction, *Hawa Hawa and Other Stories*, is forthcoming. He is currently pursuing a master's in English from Jadavpur University.

Tanuj Solanki is the author of three books of fiction. His debut novel, *Neon Noon*, was shortlisted for the Tata Literature Live! First Book Award, 2016. His second book, the short story collection entitled *Diwali in Muzaffarnagar*, won the Sahitya Akademi Yuva Puraskar, 2019. His novel, *The Machine is Learning*, was longlisted for the JCB Prize for Literature, 2020 and was listed by *The Hindu* as among the ten best fiction books of 2020. Tanuj is the founding editor of the *Bombay Literary Magazine*. He lives in Gurugram and travels frequently to Mumbai.

Tushar Jain is an Indian poet and writer. He is the winner of the Srinivas Rayaprol Poetry Prize, the RaedLeaf India Poetry Award, the Poetry with Prakriti Prize, the DWL Short Story Prize, the Toto Award for Creative Writing, and has been nominated twice for the Pushcart Prize. His first play, *Reading Kafka in Verona*, was longlisted for the Hindu Metroplus Playwright Award. His work has appeared in various literary magazines and journals such as *Aaduna*, *Papercuts*, the *Madras Mag*, *Vayavya*, and others. His debut collection of poetry, *Shakespeare in the Parka*, was published in 2018.

Uday Kanungo works as a Writing Tutor at the Centre for Writing and Communication, Ashoka University. His fiction has featured in *Indian Quarterly* and the *Bombay Review*, and he was the winner of the Toto Award for Creative Writing in English in 2022. He has also written reviews and essays for publications such as *Newslaundry*, *The Hindu*, the *Assam Tribune*, and others, and he translates fiction from Odia and Hindi into English.

Urooj is a twenty-four-year-old queer poet and visual artist based in Delhi. Their work was longlisted for the Toto Award for Creative Writing (English). They're currently working with a production house on an upcoming docuseries. They also make zines, take photos, and hoard books. They hope they'll keep their houseplants alive this year.

Varsha Dinesh is a writer and marketing professional from myth-haunted Kerala. She is a member of the Clarion West Workshop class of 2022. Her work has previously appeared in *Strange Horizons* and *Podcastle*. She is an avid enthusiast of folklore, theatre, and pop music. She is currently working on her first novel.

Vempalle Shareef won the Sahitya Akademi's Yuva Puraskar in 2011. Born in Vempalle in Kadapa district, his story collections include *Katha Minar* and *Topi Jabbar*, and a collection of children's stories, *Thiyyani Chaduvu*. A TV journalist, he began his literary career by writing children's stories. His stories have appeared in many anthologies; some have been translated into English and Maithili. His story 'Jumma' received a special mention in the nationwide competition held by *Muse India* for regional stories. His awards include the Chaso Award, Karnataka Sahitya Parishad Award, and the Andhra Pradesh Ugadi Puraskaram.

Vineetha Mokkil lives in New Delhi. She is the author of the short story collection, *A Happy Place and Other Stories*. Her stories have appeared in *Santa Fe Writers Project Journal*, *Why We Don't Talk*, *Quarterly Literary Review, Singapore*, *Asian Cha*, *Bombay Review*, and *Gravel Magazine*, among others. In 2018, she won the New Asian Writing Short Story Competition and was on the shortlist for the Desi Writers Lounge Short Story Contest. She received an honourable mention in the Anton Chekhov Prize for Very Short Fiction 2020.

Vrinda Baliga is a writer and editor based in Hyderabad. She won the 2017 Katha Fiction Contest and was also honoured by the FON South Asia Short Story Competition 2016, and New Asian Writing Short Story Competition 2016. She received a Sangam House Fellowship in 2014. She is the author of the short story collections *Name, Place, Animal, Thing*, *Arrivals and Departures*, and *Mixtape*. Her work has been published in the *Asia Literary Review, Himal Southasian, Indian Quarterly, Muse India, Reading Hour, Out of Print*, and others.